RUNNING GIRL

ALSO BY SIMON MASON

RUNNING GIRL

WITHDRAWN

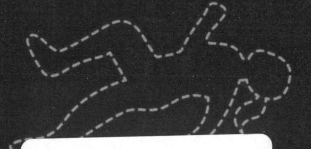

SIMON MASON

dfb
David Fickling Books

SCHOLASTIC INC. / NEW YORK

First published in the United Kingdom in 2014 by David Fickling Books, 31 Beaumont Street, Oxford OX1 2NP.

www.davidficklingbooks.com

Library of Congress Cataloging-in-Publication Number: 2016005739

ISBN 978-1-338-03642-8

10 9 8 7 6 5 4 3 2 1   16 17 18 19 20

Printed in the U.S.A. 23
First edition, September 2016
Book design by Ellen Duda

For Gwilym and Eleri

1

Dirty weather blew into the city. It crashed against the towering glass office blocks in the west and pelted the spires, domes, and grand facades of the historic center. It spread north across hospitals and schools, and south across clubs and casinos. Darkening and accelerating, it raced east across the sewage works, the industrial park, and the car plant. And at last it fell on the Five Mile estate, blackening cracked asphalt, flooding blocked drains, and beating against the windows of Flat 12 Eastwick Gardens, where sixteen-year-old Garvie Smith lay on his bed, hands behind his head, staring up at the ceiling.

He was a slender boy with a beautiful face, wearing slouch skinny jeans, a plain hoodie, and muddy high-tops. He had been lying there, in exactly the same position, for two hours. Staring.

His mother appeared in the doorway. She was a solid lady from Barbados with a broad face and clipped black hair misting over with gray. In her hand was an official-looking letter, which she folded away in her coat pocket as she glared at her son. She opened her mouth. Sixteen years of being a single parent had not only thickened and toughened her, but given her voice startling power.

"Garvie!"

He showed no sign of having heard.

"*Garvie!*"

"I'm busy," he said at last, to the ceiling.

"Don't mess with me, Garvie. Why aren't you studying?"

"I am studying."

There was a pause while his mother turned her attention to his room and its contents; not just the tumult of dirty laundry, piles of equipment, and overflow of general rubbish, but also—and in particular—the little table reserved for studying, unused for months and heaped with everything but books.

"Studying what exactly?"

There was an even longer pause while Garvie thought about this. "Complex numbers," he said at last.

His mother began to take deep breaths. He could hear her.

Without taking his eyes off the ceiling, he said, "Say my study guide is unit a—"

"Garvie!" Her voice was a low growl.

"And my studying is unit bi—"

"Garvie, I'm warning you!"

"Then my *studying* is the complex number $a+bi$, where i has the property $i^2=1$." He paused. "It's what they call an unresolvable equation."

"Garvie!"

He was silent.

"Are you smoking that stuff again?"

He didn't reply and didn't change his position, and his mother stared intently at his impassive face. He could hear her staring.

She was about to tell him he was a complete mystery to her.

"You're a complete mystery to me," she said.

She was going to say she didn't know who he was anymore.

"Garvie Smith?" she said. "I don't know who you are."

He heard her draw an especially deep breath. She was about to run through her usual list. It was a long list and needed a lot of breath.

With a minimum of elaboration and maximum force, she listed several relevant things. That Garvie's room was a box filled with junk. That proper studying is done sitting at a table with books and a computer (switched on). That Garvie Smith was the laziest boy in Five Mile, the laziest boy she'd ever heard of anywhere, perhaps the laziest boy in all history—not to mention rude and inconsiderate and *difficult*. That he was getting himself into worse and worse trouble every which way—and don't think she didn't know all about it. And that his exams, less than two months away, were absolutely his last chance to redeem himself.

He didn't respond.

"I'm warning you, Garvie," she said. "You shift yourself. Shift yourself right now. Get off your bed, get your books out of your bag, and turn on your computer."

She was on her way out to the hospital, where, as deputy nurse manager in the surgery unit, she often worked irregular hours. The letter which she had come in to discuss was now forgotten. She glared fiercely at her son one last time before withdrawing. "When I get

3

back," she said, "I want to see this room completely tidy and a neat pile of work all done. I mean it, Garvie. You don't go out, understand? You're grounded till that studying's done."

Snorting, she left him, and a moment later there was the bang of the flat door slamming shut behind her.

Her son the mystery carried on staring at the ceiling. There were a couple of things his mother had forgotten to say and he said them to himself now. That he was a boy whose alleged "genius" level of IQ had never helped him achieve a single A in any subject in five years of secondary schooling. ("Not one, Garvie!") That he was a boy from a good home who was getting into trouble—and not just for missing schoolwork or an untidy bedroom or general laziness, but for truancy, drinking, and ("Don't you deny it, Garvie!") for smoking *that stuff.*

He carried on staring at the ceiling. The rain carried on beating against the window.

What *was* genius? Watching difficult numbers fall into place? Remembering what other people didn't or seeing what they missed? Yeah, well. What did numbers *do*? What happened that was worth remembering? What did he see that made him doubt for a second that life in general wasn't some slow-motion, meaningless, crappy, *boring* little ball of cheap carpet fluff?

Therefore he carried on staring at the ceiling, fully clothed, muddy high-tops on, his face completely still. An unusual face with his jet-black hair, coppery complexion, bright blue eyes; a double take sort of face, the result of his mixed-race ancestry. But a face completely blank with boredom.

An hour passed. Rain crackled against the window; cars hissed by on the highway. Another hour passed.

Then something else hit the window.

With a yawn, Garvie pulled himself off the bed and went over to look out. Standing hunched on the patch of grass below, a sharp-faced boy with thin wrists raised a hand. Felix. Felix the Cat. He was one of Garvie's friends that his mother classed as "trouble."

"Is your mum in?"

"No."

"Coming out for a smoke?"

"All right."

Garvie put on his old flaky-leather jacket and went out of the flat and down the stairs. It was nearly dark outside. The rain had temporarily stopped and the wet front of Eastwick Gardens shone black and yellow under the lamplight. Behind the block of flats was the highway, quieter now, and the looming black silhouette of the car plant, and behind that farm fields and scrubland. The other way was the estate—a maze of roads and streets, of pebble-dash connected houses and maisonettes, garages and corner shops, wire fences, grass strips and cracked curbs, all ordinary, familiar, and dull.

A cab came past and honked its horn, and Garvie lifted a hand to the driver, Abdul, a friend of his mother. Then he joined Felix and they set off down the road together, jackets zipped up against the damp evening chill, ambling along the line of parked vans, past the electrical suppliers and betting shop, toward Old Ditch Road, where the kiddies' playground was.

Felix glanced about him continually as he walked, as if on the lookout for unexpected opportunities. He had a long white face flecked with pimples, and big black eyes. He was light on his feet, like a dancer. Garvie kept pace with him, head down, strolling along with his usual loose stride.

After a while he said, "Another Friday night in paradise."

Felix looked sideways at him, snuffed, and wiped his sharp nose. Then they went on in silence until they reached the playground.

There were a few others there already, hunched on the too-small swings and tiny merry-go-round. Ordinary boys with hoodies and wet hair and a dislike of being bored. They slapped hands and looked about them and settled back down.

"What's the plan?" Garvie said.

There was a general shrug.

Smudge suggested going down the pub. "Or what about that new bar in town? Rat Cellar, innit?" Felix knew the bouncer there, but not in a good way. Dani mentioned the casino, Imperium. But they'd have to collect a few fake members' cards and get togged up, and the whole thing seemed like too much of an effort. Anyway, none of them had any money. In the end they sat there in silence.

"All right," Garvie said. "What've you got?"

They pooled tobacco and papers. Tiger had a half pint bottle of Glen's cheapest, two-thirds empty, Dani had a couple of cans of Red Stripe, and Smudge had a bag of sherbet lemons. They passed everything around. Felix had been to see Alex earlier and he rolled a small one and sent that round too.

They had some jokes. Tiger and Dani played chicken with an old sheath knife Tiger had found at the back of Jamal's, and Smudge fell off his swing and gave himself a nosebleed. Garvie sat apart, gazing in silence over the nearby rooftops toward the distant lights of the tower blocks downtown, blurry in the murky phosphorescence that lay above the city. He'd grown up here, had known it all his life, and knew beyond all reasonable doubt that it was an utter bore. Town was a bore, with its shops and stores, City Hall, and pedestrian precincts. The old quarter of cafés and restaurants was a bore. The new business district was a bore. The malls and superstores that sprawled along the highway were bores. And the Five Mile estate was the biggest bore of all. Sighing, he began to roll a big one.

"Hey, Sherlock," Smudge said. "Got a mystery for you. Off one of them puzzle sites."

Garvie looked across to where Smudge sat grinning. Nature had not been kind to Smudge. He had the face of a middle-aged butcher and the expressions of a ten-year-old child. He sat squashed into a seat on the merry-go-round, his pale, round face glistening with rain-wet, his little mud-colored eyes gazing at Garvie eagerly. Garvie shook his head. He took out cigarette papers, selected four, and began to stick them together.

"Busy," he said at last.

"It's a good one. Serious."

"What's the point, Smudge? The motive's always the same."

"Like what?"

"Sex or money."

"Two things I don't have a problem with, personally. Come on. Bet you a big one you can't solve it."

The boy rubbed the bristles of his big cropped head with sudden concentration, sighed with satisfaction, and resumed grinning. Garvie ignored him. He sprinkled in the stuff and licked the edges of the vast patchwork of papers.

Smudge began anyway.

"On the first of June, Lola Soul Diva's found facedown on the floor of her luxury apartment. She's been stabbed from behind." He paused and thought for a moment. "Right in the spleen," he said with satisfaction.

Garvie rolled, pinching at the sides.

Smudge went on. "There's no sign of a struggle except the index finger of her left hand, busted where she fell forward. No bruising anywhere else, clothes not ripped, glasses still on her nose not smashed, watch still on her wrist—her *right* wrist—not smashed."

He grinned slyly. "Good, innit?"

"No," Garvie said with a sigh. "It's crap. Like life itself, my friend." With his teeth he twisted loose bits off the ends of the monstrous breezer, examined it for a moment, and casually tossed it up into the corner of his mouth.

Smudge went on: "In her right hand she's holding a pen. Lying next to her is her private diary. On the page for that day she'd written *Told Big Up I don't love him no more.* At the top of the page, next to the date, she's written in this shaky writing *6ZB.* Got it? *6ZB.* Next to her diary is a ripped-up photograph of her husband."

He grinned again. "Good, innit?"

"No," Garvie said. "It's a bore. Sex or money. Sex *and* money." He flicked a match alight with his thumbnail and ignited the breezer.

Smudge continued doggedly. "Three men admit to visiting her that day. Her husband, who's this pro poker player with a bad limp called Dandy Randy Wilder. Her manager, Jude Fitch Abercrombie, a hard suit with his left arm in a sling. And her boyfriend, this half-blind wild man called Big Up Mother. All of them give the police good explanations for their visits."

He wiggled his eyebrows. "It's brilliant, this, innit?"

"Utter twaddle," Garvie said, taking a long drag on the breezer and turning his eyes upward.

"All right then, Sherlock. Work it out. Who did it?"

Garvie exhaled and passed the breezer to Felix. "No one did it," he said.

"Come on, champ, you can do better than that."

Garvie sat silently in a cloud of smoke, gazing across the darkened field beyond the playground.

"You got to think of what she wrote," Smudge said. "Especially"—he paused dramatically—"*6ZB.*"

"Nonsense."

"And while you're at it," Smudge went on, "give some thought to that undamaged watch. On her *right* wrist."

The breezer went round and came back to Garvie, and he took a long drag, and then another.

"You know," Smudge said, "I'm actually gutted. Thought you were good at this sort of thing. You smoke too much of that stuff, probably. Softens the brain. Do you want me to tell you what happened?"

"No one did it."

Smudge tutted. "All right. If you can't guess I'll have to tell you. Her manager did it."

Garvie blew out smoke. "No, he didn't."

"Did, actually, Sherlock. Shall I tell you how I know?"

Sitting there in his cloud of smoke, Garvie said in a bored voice, "She's wearing a watch on her right wrist, so she's probably left-handed. But she wrote 6ZB with her right hand because of her broken finger so her writing was shaky. So it's not 6ZB at all. It's 628. And if you match those numbers to the months of the year in her diary—June, February, August—and look at the initial letters, you get JFA: Jude Fitch Abercrombie. Her manager."

"Oh." Smudge looked puzzled. "There you are, then. The manager did it."

"The manager didn't do it because the murderer stabbed her from behind through the spleen."

"So?"

"The spleen's on the left, Smudge. Only a left-handed person would do that. And the manager had his left arm in a sling."

10

Smudge opened his mouth and shut it again, and his whole face sagged a little. "Shit," he said at last. "I must have told it wrong."

Garvie leaned over and patted him on the arm. "Don't worry about it, Smudgy. Life's like that."

They sat on the merry-go-round, knees tucked up to their chests, hoods pulled over the heads. The breezer went round three times more, shrinking to a speck of fire and vanishing at last after stinging everyone's lips. Glen's cheapest had gone a long time earlier. They finished the Red Stripe, and Smudge ate the last of the sherbet lemons, and they even ran out of cigarettes. The rain came on again, gently at first, and at last the conversation died. In the wet of the darkness they sat there listening to the noises of rain and the occasional passing car.

"Oh God," Garvie said. "If something doesn't happen soon I think I'm going to lose control."

Smudge looked interested. "What do you mean by 'soon'?"

"Now, or in the next few minutes."

And at that moment a siren went off next to them, so brutal and sudden it threw them into the air like rag dolls. Mouths open, hearts pounding, they just had time to see two police cars scream to a halt at the park gates—lights buzzing, doors flying open, policemen leaping into the road—before scattering randomly across the muddy grass toward the darkness.

2

The police were also at "Honeymead," one of the new houses on Fox Walk, down off Bulwarks Lane, a quarter of a mile away. At the end of the cul-de-sac a squad car was parked across the road, doors open, light still flashing, no one in it. Everything was quiet. There was a hush, as if all the neighbors watching from behind their curtains were holding their breath. From inside the house a woman suddenly cried out once, high and shrill. Then there was silence again.

In the little conservatory at the back of the house, Inspector Singh of the City Squad looked out the window into the darkened garden as he waited for Mr. Dow to calm his wife, who had collapsed onto the sofa. It was a small garden, like those of all the houses in the cul-de-sac; tidy too, with a narrow strip of patio, a neat square of lawn, and three sides of flower beds packed with shrubs. An ornamental bird-bath gave it a touch of light fantasy. The house was the same, he'd noticed: very small, very neat, with unexpected fancy details here and there, like the elaborate door chimes and bamboo-cane furniture.

Inspector Singh was a man who noticed things. He had a silent face and still, watchful eyes. The reticence of his features—narrow mouth, refined nose, regular jaw—might have made him seem anonymous, but his machinelike alertness was conspicuous to everyone he met. Conspicuous too was his uniform—not a requirement for inspectors but something he personally insisted on.

He turned back to Mr. and Mrs. Dow, who sat together, quietly now, on the bamboo-cane sofa. Mrs. Dow gave him an angry look, her face wet and twisted. Singh had seen the expression before on the faces of other mothers. She was frightened, and under her fear was resentment and shame. He glanced across at the constable, Jones, who was staring at his boots.

"Mrs. Dow," he said carefully. "By far the likeliest scenario is that your daughter's perfectly safe. For reasons of her own she may have decided to go somewhere and she'll contact you when she wants to."

Even as he said it he didn't believe it. Mr. Dow looked at him with disgust. "Until then," Singh went on in the same careful way, "we'll do all we can to try and locate her. We're checking the hospitals. An alert's gone out to the community officers. In the meantime it would be helpful to know a little more about what happened."

Mr. and Mrs. Dow each gave a small, reluctant nod.

He said, "Let's start with the basic facts."

There weren't many. Chloe Dow, aged fifteen, had gone jogging and hadn't come back.

"What time did she leave the house?"

About seven o'clock, they thought. Neither Mr. nor Mrs. Dow had actually seen her go. She'd left a note on the living-room table, which they found when they came in from late-night shopping: *Gone for a run. Back 7:30 p.m.* Usually she ran for about half an hour.

Singh made careful notes in his book. "And where did she go? Do you know?"

Mrs. Dow shook her head. It could have been any one of her usual routes. Down Pollard Way and back through East Field. Along the bypass to the merry-go-round and back. Up Old Ditch Road, out beyond the highway on the track that goes through Froggett Woods to Battery Hill. Or somewhere else. She'd left no clue. Just: *Gone for a run.*

"And when she didn't return, what did you do?" he asked.

The Dows looked at each other. Nothing, at first. They were angry with her. There had been arguments recently. They plated her dinner and put it in the fridge and tried to watch television. Around nine o'clock they couldn't stand it anymore and began to phone round Chloe's friends, asking if they'd seen her. After that, Mr. Dow went out in his van and drove along Chloe's usual jogging routes looking for her while Mrs. Dow stood at the kitchen window staring at nothing. When he got home she phoned the police.

"And here you are," she said bitterly.

Singh paused. He said, very carefully, "Is there any reason you know of why she might have decided not to come home this evening?"

Mrs. Dow made an angry snorting noise. "Why do you keep saying that? She hasn't run away!" Her lip trembled and her face began to crumple. "Something's happened to her," she shouted through her sobs.

* * *

Standing again at the conservatory window, Singh checked his phone. The station had forwarded a couple of texts from community officers. A late-night jogger had been stopped on Pollard Way. Some kids loitering in Old Ditch Road playground had been questioned. He deleted the messages and checked his watch: 11:30 p.m. Lost in thought, he stared out into the dark and rainy garden. At this time of night, as the weather worsened, there was little chance of a community officer spotting anything. Besides, he already had a bad feeling about Chloe Dow. As Mr. and Mrs. Dow knew, girls who go jogging don't usually decide to run away from home at the same time.

As he stood there thinking, something in the garden distracted him, and he screwed up his eyes and peered out through the wet window. But it was nothing; only shadows of the shrubs stirring under the rain. Then a call came through from the duty officer asking for an update, and Singh turned and walked back through the conservatory, talking. He hadn't gotten as far as the dining room when there was a loud crash behind him from outside.

Spinning round, he looked back through the conservatory window and caught a glimpse of fencing buckling in the shadows of the shrubbery and the sudden outline of someone leaping.

"What the . . . !"

Mr. Dow was on his feet, staring. Jones was already running toward the front door, like a dog suddenly let off the leash.

Singh put his hand on Mr. Dow's arm. "What's behind the garden?"

The man pointed. "Roadworks depot that way. And the Marsh Fields over there."

Singh called after Jones, already out the door, "Take the depot!" Then he was running too.

He ran into the rain and slithered across the illuminated grass at the side of the house, glimpsing the rainy outline of Jones, ahead of him, already climbing the fence.

"Left!" Singh shouted at him. He wasn't sure if Jones knew his left from his right. "Toward the depot!" he added.

Jones vaulted over and disappeared, and Singh heard his footsteps thumping in the gravel path beyond. A few seconds later he scrambled over himself, losing his grip on the wet boards and falling heavily to the ground on the other side. Up again, he ran panting under the shelter of trees along the back fences of Honeymead and the other houses, scanning the undergrowth for signs of disturbance. But it was too dark; he couldn't even make out the broken fencing. Stopping to listen, he heard only his own ragged breathing. And then, very faintly, something else, up ahead. Footsteps. Someone running. He wiped the rain from his eyes and ran on again, faster now, on his toes, with maximum efficiency, down the path to where it bent toward Bulwarks Lane. He sprinted through a wicket gate onto the rough ground of the Marsh Fields, and came to a stop on the grassy humps of the empty common, looking around for a movement in the shadows. But there was nothing. Everything was suddenly still and quiet, except for vague rain noises in the leaves of the trees all around and his own panting. Out of the darkness rain fell on him whitely. He was too late. Whoever had been in the Dows' garden had disappeared.

Silently he turned and retraced his steps to the house.

Jones was there already, with nothing to report. He looked at him oddly and smirked. "Sorry, sir. It's slipped."

Singh stared him down. "Get some light and check the garden," he said. "Take a look at the broken fencing." After Jones had gone, he adjusted his turban—ill-fitting bulletproof police-issue—and wiped his face dry before returning to the conservatory, where the Dows were waiting, Mr. Dow bitter, Mrs. Dow terrified.

"Why was there someone hiding in your back garden?" Singh asked. He didn't mean to sound accusing; it was just his manner.

"How should I bloody know?" Mr. Dow said.

Mrs. Dow began to wail. "It's something to do with Chloe," she said. "I know it is! Why is she doing this to me?" And she collapsed against her husband, weeping again.

Now it was half past midnight. Singh refused to be tired. Sitting stiffly upright at the table with Mr. and Mrs. Dow, he began once again to ask questions about Chloe. "What I need," he said, "is a more detailed ID. A recent photograph, if you have one. A short description. What she was wearing. The teams will need it for first thing tomorrow."

"*Tomorrow?*" Mrs. Dow's face crumpled. "Aren't you going to do something *now?*"

There was a moment when he thought he was going to lose his cool. But Inspector Raminder Singh never lost his cool. It was his trademark; one of the reasons why he was both so respected and disliked by his colleagues.

Mr. Dow came back into the room with a photograph and handed it to Singh. As soon as he saw it he had the bad feeling again.

"I see," he said. He hesitated. "It would also help us," he said carefully, "if you could tell me more about your daughter. What sort of girl is she?"

To his surprise, Mrs. Dow did not burst into tears. She stared at him with loathing.

3

The new day dawned, still raining. All morning drizzle fell in a steady flicker from the heavy sky, hampering the police search as it fanned out through wet neighborhoods into the waste ground and industrial parks at the eastern edge of the city. The car plant streamed, the highway was a cloud of spray, and black puddles bulged in the gutters of the streets like oil from a spill. At Flat 12 Eastwick Gardens the windows steamed up in the kitchen, where Garvie Smith and his mother sat arguing about the night before. Mrs. Smith had an inkling that her son had been out seeing his unsavory friends, and Garvie was emphatically denying it.

"I can't help it if you have a suspicious mind," he said.

"I have no such mind. I'm asking—"

"What sort of mind do you think you have?"

"Don't try to distract me. I want to know—"

"Uncle Len thinks it's a suspicious mind."

"Uncle Len—" She stopped herself. "This has nothing to do with Uncle Len. Or my mind. I'm asking you. Did you go out last night? I know for a fact you didn't do any studying."

She glared at him sitting at the table with his chin on his hands, looking difficult. It was not easy to argue with Garvie. He was unpredictable.

"Well?" she said.

Before he could answer—if he was going to answer—the doorbell rang. Giving him a look that clearly suggested he should stay where he was, Mrs. Smith left the kitchen, and at once Garvie got up and began to drift in that apparently idle way she hated toward his room. He hadn't quite reached it when he heard her return.

"Garvie?"

He stopped when he saw the look of concern on her face.

"There's someone here who wants to ask you some questions."

A policeman in a turban stepped forward. He looked small standing next to Mrs. Smith, almost dainty. There was nothing you could call an expression on his quiet face. But he looked at Garvie steadily, sizing him up.

"What about?" Garvie said.

"About last night." The policeman's voice was quiet too, and careful, giving nothing away.

"Yeah? What about last night?"

Garvie's mother frowned at him. Still standing, the policeman took out a notebook and leafed through it. Looking up, he said, "At eleven o'clock you were with a group of boys in the Old Ditch Road play area."

("That's interesting," Garvie's mother said.)

"Says who?" Garvie said (avoiding looking at his mother).

The policeman looked at him silently for about a minute. Something new registered on his quiet face: a dislike of Garvie. No stranger to this expression in the faces of officials he encountered, Garvie looked back until, finally, the man lowered his face to his notebook again and read out half a dozen names, including Ryan "Smudge" Howell, Ben "Tiger" McIntyre, and Liam "Felix" Fricker.

"So?" Garvie said. "It's not illegal."

The inspector's eyes hardened. After a moment he said, in a voice of barely restrained contempt, "Do you want to have a conversation with me about what's illegal?"

Garvie's mother opened her mouth. "Well, Inspector, I hardly think—"

He said, "We can do one of two things, Mrs. Smith. I can conduct this interview with your son here, in my own way. Or we can all go down to the station."

Garvie's mother's eyes narrowed, but she gave a brief nod.

"Sit down," the inspector said to Garvie.

Garvie sat in a slouch at the table, hands thrust deep in his jeans pockets, while the inspector continued to stare at him. Garvie knew what the man was doing. He was trying to intimidate him. Some policemen shouted and threatened. Some just stared. Singh was a starer.

Garvie stared back, coolly.

"Perhaps, Inspector, you could explain what this is about," Garvie's mother said.

"A girl has gone missing."

"Missing?"

"She left her house yesterday evening and didn't return. There's been no sign of her since."

"What girl?"

"Her name is Chloe Dow."

Mrs. Smith put her hand up to her mouth. "Chloe, Garvie!"

A flicker of something crossed Garvie's face; then it was gone. He turned to his mother and frowned at her.

"You know her?" the inspector said in his quiet, cold voice. It was a question, but it sounded like a statement.

They were both looking at Garvie now, his mother's face worried and cross, the inspector's face hard and accusing.

"I know *of* her," Garvie said at last. "She goes to my school. She's in my year. I see her, I talk to her. I don't *know* her."

There was a silence.

"Define 'know,' " Garvie said.

Singh said nothing, just stared. It was easy to see what sort of a man he was. Uptight. Ambitious. The smudge on his turban suggested long hours, dedication. An exam passer, Garvie thought. A disciplinarian. A man disliked by his colleagues.

His mother didn't like him, either; he could tell that. Garvie settled himself back in his chair and waited.

The inspector said, "You're *acquainted* with her, then. And what sort of girl is she, in your opinion?"

"Not the sort who disappears."

"What do you mean?"

"You must have seen a photograph of her."

Raising an eyebrow slightly, Singh said nothing.

"Anyway," Garvie added, "what's all this got to do with me?"

After explaining that Chloe had gone jogging and that Old Ditch Road was on one of the routes she might have taken, the inspector embarked on a lengthy series of questions about the night before. What time exactly had Garvie gone to Old Ditch Road? What route had he taken? What had he seen? Where had he run to when the police arrived? Mostly Garvie answered "Can't remember," or simply shrugged. Once or twice he ignored the question.

Gradually, as the interview went on, Inspector Singh's quiet, careful voice became less quiet and careful.

"Perhaps you can explain what you were doing at Old Ditch Road last night," he said.

"Perhaps you can explain the link between what I was doing and what's happened to Chloe," Garvie replied.

"Garvie," his mother said, but mildly, "try to answer the inspector's questions."

"What's the point? They're the wrong questions." He sat up and leaned forward, and looked directly at Singh. "How do you know she went jogging at all?"

"We know."

"How?"

"She left a note."

"How do you know she didn't just leave it to throw people like you off the scent?"

Singh said nothing. But his face tightened.

Garvie went on. "How do you know *she* left it? How do you know she left when you think she did? How do you know she didn't leave the note then change her mind?"

Singh remained impassive, but a muscle jumped in his left cheek.

"*They're* the right sort of questions," Garvie said. "Seems to me."

After a moment's cold silence the inspector began to talk—perhaps a little faster than before—about the nature of police work, which was no doubt obscure to members of the general public—but Garvie immediately interrupted him with a casual wave of his hand. "Listen, man. I know all this already. My uncle works with the police. Forensics." He looked at Singh and, pointedly, at the insignia on his sleeves. "High up," he added.

Singh suddenly stood, and Garvie allowed himself a little smile. His mother gave him a quick, fierce look and he knew what was coming to him later. But it had been worth it.

Mrs. Smith got to her feet. "I'm sorry we can't be of more help, Inspector," she said.

For a moment the man stood there, perfectly still; then, without changing his expression, he thanked Garvie's mother for the opportunity of asking her son his questions.

"By the way," he added (his voice now as calm and quiet as at the beginning), "two grams of cannabis were taken off Liam Fricker at Old Ditch Road last night." Turning back to Garvie, he fixed him with that deliberate stare. "You told me what you were doing wasn't illegal. It was. It's my job to ensure you don't break the law. It's your mother's to explain why smoking weed is bad for you and I'll leave her to do that now."

Then he turned and walked away, and Mrs. Smith went after him to the door.

Garvie stayed where he was, staring at the kitchen table. He didn't like the way the conversation had ended. He'd been outplayed by Inspector Smudgy-Turban Singh. Hearing the front door close and his mother's footsteps coming back slowly and heavily across the living room, he braced himself.

There was a long silence. When he finally lifted his eyes she wasn't even looking at him. She was fiddling with the radio, a distracted look on her face. Quietly he got to his feet and began to drift toward his room in that apparently idle way that she—

He was halted by the local news coming on suddenly. Police were looking for fifteen-year-old Chloe Dow, a popular student at the Marsh Academy and a promising athlete, who had disappeared the night before.

His mother stood there listening, her hand up to her mouth, and despite himself, Garvie listened too.

Search teams were combing the east of the city and outlying land, the radio reporter said, hindered by the persistent rain. There were, as yet, no leads. Chloe had left her house at about seven p.m. to go jogging and hadn't returned. No one had seen her; no one knew where she had gone. She'd just disappeared. Detective Inspector Singh of City Squad said they urgently needed to hear from members of the public who might have any information.

"Pompous little man," his mother said. "But oh, Garvie." She let out a sigh. "*Chloe.*"

Turning to him, she gave her son a long quiet look.

"What?" he said at last.

Gently she said, "You didn't tell the inspector you used to be her boyfriend."

Garvie looked away toward the window. There was an expression on his face his mother hadn't seen for a long time and it took her a moment to recognize it. It wasn't the usual expression of blank boredom that she knew so well, but a hard, puzzled look—as if, for the first time in years, something had actually gotten under his skin and made him think.

He said something under his breath. It sounded like "Sex or money," but that didn't make sense.

"Garvie?" she said.

But he was lost in thought.

4

What sort of girl was Chloe Dow? Not the sort of girl who disappears without a trace.

Five feet six in her stockinged feet. Shoulder-length blonde hair, very straight and fine. Violet eyes. Beauty spot on the side of her pert little nose. Famous frontal development. She was far and away the most noticeable girl at the Academy. People noticed what she wore. She took care they did; at school she only needed to hitch up her regulation knee-length pleated skirt half an inch to turn everyone's head, including the teachers'. Outside school everything she put on made the maximum impact, as if her body instinctively knew how to make it all match and hang and fit together. People noticed the way she stood too, like an artist's model striking a pose. They noticed how she moved, weighty and floating, supple and taut, as if she walked everywhere in a sort of hush—the tense hush of boys watching her; the hush of mesmerized imaginations as they saw her crossing her legs in the dining hall, or stretching in provocative silhouette against the classroom window, or appearing round the corner of C Block and walking in that way of hers across the yard to the hall. She was an athlete and kept herself trim and firm. At lunchtimes and after school boys found themselves loitering by the track, where they might notice her glide round the corner of the bend toward them, all silk and shifting weight and blonde hair flying.

Garvie knew all this. He had briefly gone out with Chloe a year earlier. But that was something he didn't want to remember, with that famous memory of his; not something he found easy to remember, least of all now.

He frowned. City Squad's chief constable had come on the radio, appealing like Inspector Singh for anyone who might have seen Chloe on Friday evening to come forward, and despite himself Garvie thought of her again.

Chloe Dow had gone jogging and hadn't come back. It was shocking. But it wasn't interesting. No. The interesting thing was that no one had seen her. The most noticeable girl in the whole of Five Mile had gone running, and no one had noticed.

"Garvie?"

He turned to his mother at last and said angrily, "How many times do I have to tell you? I was *not* her boyfriend. I went out with her, like, *twice*. There's a *difference*."

His mother watched him go, not idly but quickly, into his room, and after a moment she turned again to the steamed-up kitchen window, peering through it at the rainy sky beyond.

"Please God they find her," she said again to herself. "Please God they find her soon."

5

But it was another two days before the police found Chloe Dow. On Monday morning, as dawn was breaking, frogmen from the search and rescue team pulled her from Pike Pond, a small patch of brown water in farmland out by Froggett Woods.

By ten o'clock the mobile units were in place and the scene-of-crime staff had sealed the area and erected a temporary morgue. A little way off, calm as ever but perhaps paler than usual after three largely sleepless nights, Inspector Singh stood waiting for the forensic pathologist to come and approve the removal of the body. He had been there since before six, examining the area, breaking off only to perform his morning prayers as the sun came up. Even now, as he waited, he continued methodically to make notes on what he saw.

Pike Pond lay at the edge of the trees in a dip of waste ground littered with rusty agricultural machinery and tufted with marsh grass, boggy in places after the rain. Beyond, half hidden behind a tumbledown wall, were the abandoned buildings of an old farm rotting quietly in a concrete courtyard of weeds and rubbish. From this courtyard a rutted track ran out, circled in front of the pond, and headed away across the fields to skirt the southern edge of Froggett

Woods toward the highway. Singh followed it with his eyes to the point where it disappeared. His best guess was that at about 7:15 p.m. on Friday, Chloe Dow had come running down this track. According to her parents it was one of her favorite routes. Generally she would run as far as the pond, turn onto the footpath at the edge of a field of rapeseed, and circle back toward the sports club playing fields, Bulwarks Lane, and home. Only, that Friday she didn't make it home.

Singh went down to the pond and walked round it once more, staring at the ground. Three days of heavy rain had obliterated whatever clues there might have been. The turf was still wet, springy and clean.

He looked up when he heard his name called and returned to the track to greet the pathologist.

Len Johnson, uncle to Garvie Smith, was a burly man, liked as much for his genial nature as for the forensics expertise he had amassed over twenty years of service at the hospital. To young officers, even those as stiff and uncompromising as Raminder Singh, he was an avuncular figure, friendly and encouraging.

"Raminder."

"Leonard."

They shook hands and walked together to the tent where the body was.

"You leading on this?" Len Johnson asked.

"Yes."

"Your first?"

"Yes."

"Good for you. I'm glad. Nasty one to start with, though. Major news item. You must be about the youngest DI ever to take on something as big as this here."

Singh's face went blank. The pathologist had touched him on a sensitive spot. "My age is irrelevant," he said.

"It wasn't a comment on your lack of experience, Raminder. I was just—"

"If you don't mind," Singh said, "we should get started. We mustn't lose any more time."

They went into the tent and the pathologist made a quick initial survey, Singh watching impassively as the big man's hands moved lightly over Chloe Dow's body. He leaned forward to peer at her clouded eyes, the tips of her white fingers. He touched her neck, very lightly, where the skin was discolored.

"Strangled?" Singh asked after a while.

"Probably. But you know how it is. Always more complicated than you think. We'll run the tests and get something more accurate back from the lab later. For now, all we can do is move her to the morgue." He looked at Singh. "And get formal identification. Was she living with her parents?"

"Mother and stepfather."

"The hardest bit." He put his hand on Singh's shoulder. "Good luck."

Singh gave a little nod. They went out of the tent and walked back round the edge of the pond.

Singh took out his notebook. "How long do you think she's been dead?" he asked. "Best guess."

"Very hard to say before the tests. The water complicates everything."

"Naturally. But in your experience?"

They stopped, and Len Johnson knitted his brows. "When did she go missing?"

"Seven o'clock Friday evening."

"I'd be surprised if she wasn't killed almost immediately. Within an hour or two, say. The rigor has more or less disappeared. In water that temperature I think we're looking at fifty-five, sixty hours minimum."

Singh looked at his watch and wrote in his notebook.

"But don't quote me yet," Len Johnson said. "Wait for the results from the lab."

Singh said, "The chief is keen to make progress."

"Of course he is. But there's keen and there's stupid. Sometimes it's hard to tell them apart. Especially with our chief constable. Don't quote me on that, either."

They shook hands again, and Singh watched him go back to his car to pick up his kit; then he turned and went his own way up the track again, looking around.

News travels fast on the ground. By the middle of the afternoon people had started to arrive at Pike Pond to see if the rumors were true. Some were locals, elderly residents of the big houses on the other side of Froggett Woods; others were ghouls who had been following the investigation on the local news or drifters with nothing better to do on an overcast afternoon. Schoolkids were among them, including Garvie Smith and his friends. Slipping out just before last lesson, they cycled up Bulwarks Lane and across the playing fields, left their bikes at the edge of a field of rapeseed, and walked through marsh grass toward the pond. Inspector Singh and Leonard Johnson (and the mortal remains of Chloe Dow) were long gone by then; a few white-boiler-suited scene-of-crime officers remained, conducting their searches in and around the pond, and a couple of ordinary constables manned the police tape. Garvie and his friends made their way to a hillocky spot in the waste ground where they had a good view.

"Can't believe it," Smudge said quietly, looking down at the scene in despair. "We missed the body." He looked devastated, and a little bewildered, as if he'd just discovered he'd lost his lunch money.

Felix raised an eyebrow. "You think they'd've let us take a peek at it?"

Garvie stood to one side, not saying anything, while Smudge and Felix looked around.

Smudge had a thought and brightened. "What do you think? I reckon he was hiding in that ruin over there. And when he sees her coming down that path he sneaks out and grabs her."

"Who?"

"The mad rapist, whoever he is. Hiding over there in the rubbish, waiting for her."

33

Felix considered this, stroking his sharp face with his thin fingers. "Unless it's a spur-of-the-moment thing. Say he's up to no good, doing a deal or something, and she appears, accidentally, and takes him by surprise, and all of a sudden he's trying to stop her screaming and he's ripping her clothes off and . . ." He trailed away.

Smudge looked over to Garvie. "Hey, Puzzle Boy! What's your angle?"

Garvie ignored him.

Smudge and Felix began to talk about Alex, a friend of theirs. Alex had gone out with Chloe for a long time, longer than anyone else they knew, and when she split up with him a few months earlier he'd fallen apart. He'd more or less left home, acquired various bad habits, and now spent all his time hiding in a squat in Limekilns, where no one visited him except some drifting strangers, a few buyers, and Garvie Smith. He was never seen in school, where everyone knew he was still obsessed with Chloe Dow.

"What's he going to do when he hears about this?" Felix said, and Smudge shook his head sadly.

Less than half an hour later they found out. A battered Ford Focus with no side mirrors came lurching down the farm track. Before it reached the rise above the pond the passenger door jerked open, and a boy wearing a red-and-yellow varsity jacket fell out and scrambled to his feet. He was big and black and he was crying. It was Alex. He stood there for a second with his hands in his wet hair, and screamed. Still screaming, he ran down the slope toward the water. The two constables only just managed to reach him as he went through the tape. He flattened one of them and they began to fight.

"He's not happy," Smudge said.

Felix said, "Not sane, either."

They ran across the waste ground toward the spot where their friend was struggling. He was shouting abuse—most of it at the policemen, but some of it apparently at the dead girl. For a boy usually so gentle and passive he was in a horrible state of rampage. They heard him shout, "You stupid bitch, what did you do it for?" then he took a hit and was on the ground with his face squashed into the turf, not saying anything anymore. Before Smudge and Felix could get to him, he'd been subdued, and one of the policemen came under the cordon and forced them back. There was nothing for them to do then but give the copper a bit of abuse and retreat up the rise to watch Alex being led to a squad car and driven away.

"His head's not right," Felix said. "What does he think, she did herself in?"

"Going to get himself done in if he's not careful," Smudge said.

After the excitement was over people began to leave, drifting away in twos and threes. By six o'clock most had gone.

Smudge said he was off. Felix too.

"You coming, Garv?"

They looked at him and at one another. For hours Garvie had said nothing, standing apart and looking around vacantly. Finally now he spoke:

"What was she doing here?"

Felix and Smudge exchanged glances.

"She was jogging, Garv. Everyone knows that."

"Why here?"

"Because it's one of her jogging routes. They explained it on the news."

"Really?"

"Yeah."

"You think they *explain* things on the news?"

Felix and Smudge were silent.

After a moment Garvie said, "Did you like her?"

"Chloe?"

They shook their heads.

"I'd have given her one," Smudge added helpfully. "But I didn't like her. No one *liked* her, Garv. You know that. I mean, no disrespect, but you know that better than most." He hitched up his trousers, scratched, and tried to look sympathetic.

They stood there without further comment, gazing at the pond.

Felix said, "Are you coming, then?"

Garvie shook his head. "Think I'll wait a bit longer."

"What do you mean, 'a bit longer'?"

He glanced at his watch. "Another thirty-eight and a half minutes."

They gave him another look, and Felix shrugged his thin shoulders. Then they got on their bikes, and Garvie watched them as they cycled off down the track where the Ford Focus and the police car had gone, where Chloe used to run.

Beautiful but dislikable Chloe. Smudge was right: No one had liked her. And she hadn't liked anyone else. She was hard, pushy. It was the second most noticeable thing about her. Garvie had never known anyone so ambitious. She was going to be famous; nothing was going to stop her. She was staking everything on a chance at the big time. It was the risk-taking, gambling streak in her. Modeling was the obvious route. Her looks would get her so far, and for the rest she'd use her contacts and trust to luck. She' was always trying to meet people who mattered. Networking. Even in year nine she was writing to the men and women whose names she found in magazines devoted to fashion and movies. The rich, the glamorous, the powerful. Recently she'd started trying to crash the parties these people went to. She'd turn up at hotels, clubs, casinos, looking extraordinary, smiling sweetly at the doorman. Sometimes—so she said—he let her in. As a result, according to her, she'd done a few shoots already. A couple of months short of her sixteenth birthday she had just been beginning the great adventure of her fame.

As Garvie considered these things he walked to and fro across the soft, wet ground. Once he stopped and crouched down to examine something: a narrow flattened indent in the grass where something heavy had been lying. A piece of old machinery perhaps. A metal bar of some sort. He wondered why it had been moved, what it had been used for. Then he resumed walking, until finally, looking again at his watch, he saw that it was the time he'd been waiting for: 6:45 p.m.

He looked up at the sky.

At just this time three days earlier, as she changed into her kit, Chloe had looked out her bedroom window, deciding where to run. He was seeing now what she'd seen then. He squinted, then frowned. The still-light late-afternoon sky was tinged with the faint shadow of pre-sunset twilight. In the next quarter of an hour or so, daylight would start to fade.

And now he made himself remember something he didn't want to: his final date with Chloe a year earlier. It came back to him, the way his memories always did, with the clarity of the immediate present. He saw in his mind the café in Five Mile Center with its shiny pine tables and matching chairs; he smelled the scent of pastries and coffee, heard the echoey noise of Saturday-morning shoppers. He saw Chloe sitting opposite him, wearing a blue halter-neck top and gray jeggings, typically simple but classy, and a pair of silver earrings he'd never seen her wear before, shaped like crescent moons. She was talking, as usual. He could hear her. She was telling him about a deal she'd gotten online for some new running kit. Her voice sounded funny; she was talking too fast. He could see her face, her violet eyes glancing here and there, her lips parting and closing as she spoke. She was telling him she was going to wear the kit at lunchtime when she went for a run, up through Froggett Woods to Battery Hill and out to Pike Pond. She was telling him something about Pike Pond. Then she was getting out a tissue and dabbing at her eyes. And then there was that moment, never to be forgotten but hardly to be remembered, when she looked at him straight for the first time all morning with her wet eyes shining, and said, "That it, then? Good-bye?" And, when he didn't say anything to that: "Good-bye, then, Garvie Smith. You can never say I didn't want it to work."

He frowned. He'd remembered enough. More than enough.

He looked at the waste ground, the pond, the ruined farm. There was no one else around now except for a constable down by the water staring at his boots. Picking his way through weeds and garbage, Garvie went across to the farm. He'd never been here before, didn't even know its name until he found a rusted sign lying in the grass: FOUR WINDS FARM. A farm no more. He stepped through the broken wall into the courtyard and looked around, fixing everything in his memory: the old mattresses piled up on the porch, the smashed windows, the elder bushes rising in spikes out of the half-collapsed roof. In the courtyard the concrete was blackened here and there where people had lit fires, and under a corrugated shelter at the side was a burned-out car, skeletal and orange with rust.

A lost place. A place for lost people.

What had Chloe told him that morning in the café, about Pike Pond?

"It spooks me. I don't go up there late. Not even in the afternoon if it's getting a bit shadowy."

At 6:45 on an April evening there might have been daylight still, but Chloe would never have chosen to run to Pike Pond. Not at that time. Not willingly.

He frowned again.

So what was she doing here?

Finally it was time for him to leave. The sun set, blood-orange red leaking along the horizon toward the car plant. Sitting on his bike at the edge of the field of rapeseed, Garvie looked back one last time, watching the shadows gather rapidly over it all. It was a bad place to die. Chloe had been right: It was spooky. The woods were nightmare-gloomy, the farm was a corpse, and Pike Pond was cold and black, like a pool in a fairy tale going all the way down to hell.

The last thing he saw before turning to cycle home was the silhouetted shape of the constable standing by his squad car parked on the farm track, still staring at his boots.

Next morning Chloe Dow was everywhere, as if she'd been absorbed into the very fabric of the city. She was on the news ticker running round the side of Tropp Tower, on the giant electronic billboard in Market Square, on newspaper headlines and television and computer screens throughout the city. In both public and private media one image dominated all others: the snapshot (given to Singh by the Dows on Friday night) of a crazily good-looking Chloe in matching running tank top and shorts innocently squinting through sunlight at the camera. Dubbed "Beauty" in the tabloid press (victim, inevitably, of "the Beast"), she was discussed in a thousand conversations across the city, in council chambers and cafés, law courts and Laundromats, offices and rooms, not least in the shops and streets of Five Mile, crowded suddenly with huge numbers of police and journalists, all obsessively focused on the same thing.

In death, beautiful Chloe Dow was as famous as she had dreamed of being when alive.

The City Squad issued statements several times an hour. They were aghast, like everyone else. But they were confident of bringing the perpetrator to justice. The chief constable, a narrow-faced, dead-eyed man with cropped hair, was confident. The city mayor was confident. Detective Inspector Raminder Singh, newly announced as the leader of the investigation and appearing on screen in a freshly laundered turban, was confident. The police had expertise, method. They were rigorous, careful, painstaking, dedicated, energetic. They would get their man. This was their promise to the people of the city.

Garvie Smith, on the other hand, had no method. He was no expert in any conventional sense of the word. Not even his mother—*especially* not his mother—would claim he was painstaking or energetic. He made no promises. But at eight o'clock on Tuesday evening, in a house not four miles from the City Squad headquarters, he was pestering his uncle for information.

He was at Uncle Len's to babysit his three-year-old cousin, Bojo, while his mother went out with her brother and Aunt Maxie. First they were all having a drink. And he was pestering.

"Garvie!" his mother said for the third time. "Will you leave it alone? All that's confidential."

"So?"

Though he didn't often exert himself, when he did he went at things his own way, with a looseness, a lazy swing, a laid-back persistence that was appealing to his friends if not to his mother.

"Sorry, Uncle Len. She didn't mean to interrupt you. You were just telling us about the autopsy."

Aunt Maxie laughed.

His mother frowned. "I don't know what's got into him. He'd be better off devoting his famous mental ability to his math study. Which I hope he's remembered to bring with him. After a certain incident at Old Ditch Road playground, he's grounded till further notice."

Garvie Smith gave her a look, serious for a second, then turned back to his uncle and grinned one of his grins. His uncle sighed. He knew what his sister was going through with her son, but he was a tolerant man and he'd always liked his nephew. Garvie had the cheeky attitude and looks that uncles find hard to resist. There was that grin for a start. That black hair and those blue eyes—extremely attractive also (so his uncle had heard) to the girls of the neighborhood. In fact, there was something generally pleasant about Garvie Smith, famous slacker of the Marsh Academy; his uncle could see that, even if his mother couldn't. It was just a shame he was so bone idle.

His uncle sighed again. "I know everyone's talking about it. I've seen the coverage. That poor girl's picture's everywhere. But your mother's right. It's confidential. Anyway, I couldn't give you anything even if I wanted to. This isn't TV, Garvie. We haven't had a chance to do the work yet."

"You've done the autopsy. You told us."

"Preliminary autopsy. As for the rest, it's still in the lab. Will be for several days yet."

"There," his mother said. "You have your answer."

"Okay, then. Just quickly remind us what the preliminary autopsy covers."

"Garvie!"

He caught the tone of her voice and at last fell silent. For half an hour no more was said about the matter. But when Uncle Len went into the kitchen to get some more drinks he found Garvie at his shoulder, grinning that grin of his.

"Oh no, Garvie."

"Cause, mechanism, and manner of death. That's what the preliminary autopsy covers, right?"

Despite himself, Len Johnson smiled. "Your memory's still functioning. But seriously—you're not going to get anything else out of me. Get down that bottle of ginger ale. Since you're here you can make your mother a drink."

Garvie slowly mixed apricot fizz in a jug. As he mixed he began to talk to himself, quietly at first.

"Cause of death? Must be strangulation. The guy on the radio said she'd been strangled."

His uncle ignored him.

Garvie took a glass out of a cupboard, apparently still deep in thought, murmuring to himself, "*Mechanism* of death?" He hesitated. "Suffocation? Doesn't sound quite right. Stifling? No. Choking? Course not. There must be some other word."

"Asphyxia's the correct term for—" Uncle Len bit his lip. "That's it, Garvie. I just told you. You're not getting anything else out of me."

Garvie grinned. "No need. Manner of death's easy. Homicide, right? Unless she strangled herself."

His uncle sighed. "Seriously, Garvie, I literally can't give you any more information. I know you're curious. And I'm assuming it's because you knew the girl."

He peered at Garvie. "In fact, didn't you used to go out with her?"

Garvie made his face blank.

"I remember her. Nice girl."

Garvie's blank face stayed blank.

Uncle Len changed the subject. "Anyway, Garvie, apart from the fact that I have actually taken a professional oath, I simply don't have the information to give you."

"You've examined the body, haven't you?"

"Very briefly. I've made no report yet. I'm awaiting the results of the tests."

"There must be photographs."

"Not for you to see. Anyway, they're still being worked on. Not a single photograph of Chloe Dow has been released to the police."

"But you can—"

"I can't!" Len Johnson finally raised his voice. "Stop it now, Garvie! I'm telling you, I don't have anything definite. We're still guessing. Listen to me. This is the truth. The only concrete information we've sent through, apart from the brief diagnosis you've already worked out, is the preliminary description of what she was wearing. And like the rest of the population, you already know that from the news, and it's very boring. She was out running and she was wearing her running kit. That's it. That's all. No juicy details, no gory descriptions. Now take that drink to your mother—and think of something else to talk about for twenty minutes before we head off."

Garvie didn't move. He stood there scrutinizing his uncle in silence.

"What is it now, Garvie?"

"How old are you, Uncle Len?"

Taken by surprise, his uncle hesitated.

Garvie said, "That inspector, that Singh guy, he thought you were coming up to retirement."

Uncle Len made a small puffy noise of indignation.

"I told him you're a lot younger than you look."

"I'm not sure that's much of a compliment."

"It wasn't meant to be a compliment."

"No, well. I'll be fifty in August. Born in Barbados, as you know. On Grand Kadooment Day, if you know what that is."

"I can find out," Garvie said, and went with the drinks into the living room, leaving his uncle, who was preparing to explain all about Grand Kadooment Day, standing bewildered in the kitchen.

After they had gone, Garvie Smith sat alone in his uncle's front room, thinking. He thought about complex numbers. They were interesting, the way they didn't add up. Like a very noticeable girl going missing without anyone noticing. Like her body turning up in a place at a time when she would never have willingly gone there. He thought too about the dead body itself: a simple nought, a brute fact, a thing on an autopsy gurney. Perhaps even that wasn't as simple as it sounded.

Time passed slowly in Uncle Len's house now that Garvie was on his own. He ate all the snacks that Aunt Maxie had left for him, and settled Bojo when he woke up, and watched the usual crap on TV. He even thought about getting out his math homework until he realized he had forgotten to bring it. But he couldn't stop thinking about Chloe Dow's dead body, about autopsy reports and confidential preliminary reports. Photographs. He was pretty sure Uncle Len hadn't been telling him the truth. After all, he had examined the body. Photographs had definitely been taken. Information existed, even if it wasn't officially "available."

At ten o'clock the television news came on, and inevitably the main story, much extended, was the Dow investigation. Garvie watched an awkward interview with Detective Inspector Singh, who appealed again for witnesses to come forward, and footage of Mr. and Mrs. Dow disappearing through a media scrum into the police station. There was an emotional interview with Chloe's "best friend," Jessica Walker—a slim, dark-haired girl whose pretty face was blurred with leaky mascara—sobbing her way through the questions, repeating over and over that Chloe was the best, the kindest, the most beautiful friend she could have had, and blurting out at the end that she would love her forever. Garvie snorted; he knew what sort of friend Jessica had been. More interesting to him were the factual reports. The cause and mechanism of death were announced as strangulation and asphyxia, the estimated time of death between four and nine on the Friday evening, but more probably between seven p.m. and eight p.m. Prolonged immersion in the water made it difficult to be more exact, a spokesman said, a fact which might have been deliberately exploited by the murderer. Chloe's body, fully dressed, had been weighed down by an iron bar, though the source of the bar remained unknown. Her cell phone, found submerged in the pond near her body, was being examined; inevitably data on it had been destroyed.

The now-familiar photograph of Chloe appeared several times during the program, as if to corroborate not only her beauty, which was plain to see, but her kindness, her popularity, and her heartbreaking girlish charm. Every time it appeared Garvie flinched a little. He knew the photograph. He remembered taking it.

He shut off his memory. When the news ended he turned off the television too and lay on the sofa in silence, staring up at the ceiling. He was not the worst boy in the world. But he couldn't stop thinking about those autopsy reports, photographs, Chloe's body on a slab. After five minutes he got up off the sofa and made his way upstairs.

7

Uncle Len's study was a small room created out of a partitioned spare bedroom, next to the room where Bojo slept. Garvie opened the door and peered in. In the shadows he could see a desk with a computer on it under the window, a gray filing cabinet, and several shelves filled with medical and legal books. Flipping on the light, he slipped inside and shut the door behind him.

There was a smell in the room. It was his uncle's smell: peppermints and licorice.

He started with the easy things. The filing cabinet was a disappointment: everything in it looked old, and the headings on the file dividers—*Committee Meeting Minutes, Budget Reports, Annual Reviews*—suggested general business rather than specific cases. He turned to the desk drawers. Two were empty, the third filled with back issues of an old magazine called *Calypso Magic!* That left only the computer.

He turned it on, and for a moment sat staring at the password field. Then he went into the bottom drawer of the desk again and got out one of his uncle's old magazines and browsed through it until he found what he was looking for: a piece on Grand Kadooment Day, the calypso carnival celebrating the end of the traditional sugar crop in Barbados. Every year—he read—the carnival took place on the first Monday in August. In the year the magazine was published—2007— the date had been the sixth. What Garvie wanted to know was: What had it been in 1962?

He looked up at the ceiling for a moment, and slowly blinked. In 2006 the first Monday would have been the seventh. In 2005 the first. In 2004 the second. So: a recurrent series of seven integers beginning with six and ending with five in a sequence forty-six integers long. Nice. Add an extra day for each of the eleven leap years. Divide by the number of series: eight times with one left over, the first number in the next series, which is . . . six.

Uncle Len was born on the sixth of August.

That was the easy part. For the next ten minutes, in mounting frustration, he plugged into the password field every possible variation of the words "Maxie," "Bojo," "Leonard," and "Barbados," together with 06, and got nowhere. He was just about to give up in disgust when he realized what he was missing. He was overlooking what Smudge liked to call the "bleeding obvious." He typed in *Calypso06* and unlocked the machine.

The last item in his uncle's sent box was headed *Dow: Preliminary Autopsy Findings*. It had an attachment. For a few seconds Garvie sat very still, listening for any noise from downstairs. Briefly he wondered what he was going to see. Her body on the autopsy table? That body with its pale and flawless skin? Was he going to see those arms again, that throat, the almond-shaped navel? He took a deep breath and opened it quickly, and frowned.

It was a short plain document, completely unillustrated, less than two pages long, and he saw at once that it was exactly what his uncle had described. Headed simply *Clothing*, it contained eight paragraphs of text tediously itemizing facts such as size, material, and color, and two virtually unintelligible comments added in the margin (*Check microbial damage* and *Non-component debris?*). It was very dull. There were no photographs of the clothing, no photograph of Chloe, no description of her injuries, no account of discovering the body— nothing Garvie had hoped to find. Pushing his chair away from the desk, he went to stand at the window, staring out at the empty street below in disappointment.

After a while a thought came to him. Not a thought; a feeling. Not really a feeling but a sort of mental itch. He tried to catch the tail of it, couldn't, and frowned.

He glanced back at the computer screen. The itch itched and wouldn't go away. At last he returned to the desk, scrolled back to the beginning of the document, and read it again. Nothing could be more tedious. But something, somewhere, was wrong. That was what his itch told him.

He began to go through the report a third time, slowly. It was like reading a foreign language.

Item: Ladies running tank top. Color heliotrope. Size small (6). Helly Hansen "W Pace Supportive Singlet"; synthetic fiber. Fading to labels. No visible damage.

Item: Ladies running shorts. Color heliotrope. Size small (6). Helly Hansen "W Pace Lightweight Shorts"; synthetic fiber. Fading to labels. No visible damage.

Item: Ladies sneaker sock. Color white. Size 5.5–7.0. Rohner "Ergonomic Sneaker Socks"; synthetic fiber. Wear to toe and heel. Oil stain on heel.

Item: Ladies sneaker sock. Color white. Size 5.5–7.0. Rohner "Ergonomic Sneaker Socks"; synthetic fiber. Wear to toe and heel.

Item: "Shock Absorber Max" Sports Bra. Color white. Size 34D. "Coolmax" synthetic fabric.

Item: Pair of "Icebreaker" Boy Shorts. Color white. Size small. 100% pure merino.

Item: Ladies running shoe, left foot. Color lime green with orange pattern and laces. Size 6. Asics "Lady GEL-Torana 4 Trail Running Shoes"; synthetic materials. New. No visible damage.

Item: Ladies running shoe, right foot. Color lime green with orange pattern and laces. Size 6. Asics "Lady GEL-Torana 4 Trail Running Shoes"; synthetic materials. New. No visible damage.

An hour later Garvie was still at the desk. It was late now but he had lost all sense of time. He continued to read the same sentences over and over, and the itch prickled furiously. Somewhere, threaded through the document like an almost-invisible crack in a glass, was a flaw—something that didn't make sense. He hadn't found it yet. But he was going to.

He was going to use all his famous mental ability to find it.

Location: notoriously claustrophobic basement interview room, a windowless bunker.

Aspect of interviewer: cold and expressionless.

Aspect of interviewees: n/a.

DI SINGH: Are you okay now? Can we continue? So, you worked all day at the Marsh Academy, where you are . . . [*Sound of rustling paper*]

EILEEN DOW: Health visitor.

DI SINGH: Health visitor. And then you went down to Five Mile Center, to meet your husband. And you arrived there at about six?

EILEEN DOW: Yes.

DI SINGH: What time did your husband get there?

EILEEN DOW: Same time. Mick'd been working at a property in Dandelion Hill.

DI SINGH: And you stayed at the Center till what time?

EILEEN DOW: Seven. I think.

DI SINGH: Then you drove home. In Mick's van?

EILEEN DOW: Yes.

DI SINGH: And Chloe wasn't in when you got there?

EILEEN DOW: No. I told you. She'd gone already. There was just that note.

DI SINGH: On the living-room table?

EILEEN DOW: Yes. [*Sound of crying*]

DI SINGH: I'm sorry to have to ask you these questions. [*Silence*] Can we continue?

EILEEN DOW: Yes.

DI SINGH: Did you notice anything unusual in the house when you got there?

EILEEN DOW: Like what?

DI SINGH: Anything out of the ordinary. Signs of a disturbance. Things out of place. Things missing.

EILEEN DOW: No. Nothing like that. Mick keeps the house spotless.

DI SINGH: I see. Then you've told me [*sound of pages being turned*] what happened after that. You had dinner, you plated Chloe's dinner and put it in the fridge. At nine you rang Chloe's friends. I have a list of them [*sound of pages being rustled*]. A little after nine Mick went out in his van, looking for Chloe. When he got back, at half past ten, you called the emergency services. All that's correct? Good. Now, Mrs. Dow, I'd like to ask you just a few questions about Chloe. I'm sorry to have to do this. But it will help us to know more about her. Can I proceed?

EILEEN DOW: I suppose so.

DI SINGH: Was she happy?

EILEEN DOW [*silence*]: I don't know why you ask me that.

DI SINGH: You mentioned [*sound of pages being turned*] you'd been having arguments.

EILEEN DOW: *I* wasn't happy. Chloe was all right. They love it at that age. The arguments.

DI SINGH: Did you argue a lot?

EILEEN DOW: Yes. No more than usual. She could try my patience.

DI SINGH: What were the arguments about?

EILEEN DOW: Nothing much. The usual. Staying out late. Not telling us where she was.

DI SINGH: Boys?

EILEEN DOW: She didn't have any trouble with boys, no. Girls, yes. Boys, no.

DI SINGH: She had arguments with her girlfriends?

EILEEN DOW: You know what girls are like. [*Silence*] Perhaps you don't. Bitches. Bitchy to Chloe, anyway.

DI SINGH: In what way?

EILEEN DOW: Gossip. Lies. All the backbiting that goes on. She had stuff stolen, I know that. From her locker at school.

DI SINGH: Who were these girls?

EILEEN DOW: Ask her teacher. They know. I tried not to get involved. Jessica Walker was the worst. Two-faced little cow.

DI SINGH [*sound of writing*]: I see. To come back to boys for a second: Did she have a boyfriend?

EILEEN DOW: No. She used to. Alex something. It wasn't serious, not for her. She had other boyfriends, before that. She was always popular, with boys. I don't remember them. Garvie Smith I remember. He's nice, Garvie. A real charmer.

DI SINGH: That's . . . interesting. [*Sound of writing*] But Alex . . . Had he been bothering Chloe?

EILEEN DOW: No. I don't think so. A bit, maybe. He was upset. I suppose they argued. I don't know. I didn't involve myself.

DI SINGH: Did Chloe argue with her stepfather?

EILEEN DOW: . . . Not really.

DI SINGH: No?

EILEEN DOW: Well, yes. But . . .

DI SINGH: They *did* argue?

EILEEN DOW: No, but . . . They never really . . .

DI SINGH: Did they or didn't they argue?

EILEEN DOW [*angrily*]: It hardly matters now, does it? It doesn't make any bloody difference now, does it? [*Sound of sobbing*]

DI SINGH: I don't want to upset you, but it will help if—

EILEEN DOW: She was jealous. If you must know.

DI SINGH: Jealous?

EILEEN DOW: Jealous of me. Ever since Mick and I married. I suppose she thought I didn't give her as much attention. Or something. Actually, she was jealous of me being happy. That's the truth.

DI SINGH: Was Mr. Dow aware of this? Did it upset him?

EILEEN DOW: He doesn't get upset. He's very fair. He was always the peacemaker when . . . [*Sound of sobbing*] I just keep asking myself why. You know. *Why?* [*Sound of nose-blowing*] What have I done to deserve this? I know you're not going to give me any answers. I know that. There aren't any bloody answers. You don't even—

Singh leaned forward abruptly and turned off the tape recorder with a click, and sat upright in his chair, in the sudden silence of the bare room. The interview studio was oppressive, a small white box harshly lit with electric light. It didn't bother Singh. He'd been there since concluding the interviews two hours earlier. He sat gazing expressionlessly at the wall.

After a while he opened his notebook and wrote:

Father, motorcycle accident, 2002. Mrs. D, medication? Stress-related, check records. Remarriage "saved her." Arguments with C?

He sat motionless for a while longer. Then he wrote:

Manual. Big picture made up of little details.

Again he reflected. Finally, he wrote:

They are five. Kaam. Krodh. Lobh. Moh. Ahankar. And he carefully underlined *Ahankar*—egotism—the last and most prevalent of the five evils of the Sikh faith.

Pausing only to glance at his watch, he removed the tape from the old-fashioned police-issue recorder, and replaced it with another. He pressed Fast Forward, and listened, and pressed Fast Forward again.

For much of the interview Michael Dow had simply corroborated the events of Friday. Most of the day he had been working at a renovated council property on The Oval at Dandelion Hill. The carpenter and electrician who had been with him left at four o'clock, and he stayed on till five forty-five to finish a stretch of painting before driving to the Center to meet his wife, as she had said. But his most interesting comments had come near the end of the interview.

Singh found the right place and pressed Play.

DI SINGH: Finally I'd like to ask you some general questions about Chloe, if I may.

[*Silence*]

DI SINGH: Is that all right?

MICHAEL DOW: It'll have to be, won't it?

DI SINGH: How would you describe your relationship with Chloe?

MICHAEL DOW [*silence*]: Not great.

DI SINGH: Not great how?

MICHAEL DOW: It was hard for her, me moving in. Hard for me too. But she didn't like it. Too used to having her own way. [*Silence*] She didn't like me.

DI SINGH: Did you like her?

MICHAEL DOW: I thought she'd been spoiled. I told her so. She didn't like that, either.

DI SINGH: Did you argue?

MICHAEL DOW: No. She wanted to argue with her mum. I only got involved calming things down.

DI SINGH: You must have found it difficult.

MICHAEL DOW: Not as difficult as this. [*Silence*] She was only a kid.

DI SINGH: Yes. [*Silence*] I realize you're angry, that's only natural.

MICHAEL DOW: A bloody *kid*!

DI SINGH [*pause*]: I understand Chloe had problems with girlfriends.

MICHAEL DOW: No.

DI SINGH: Oh. Mrs. Dow thought there had been instances of abuse, theft.

MICHAEL DOW: Nothing much.

DI SINGH: I see. What about boys, then? Did she have trouble with boys?

MICHAEL DOW: Yes.

DI SINGH: What sort of trouble?

MICHAEL DOW: A girl like that. What sort of trouble do you think she had?

DI SINGH: Harassment? Sexual harassment?

MICHAEL DOW: Half the bloody school were harassing her.

DI SINGH: Who?

MICHAEL DOW: Ask at the school.

DI SINGH: Alex Robinson? Was he harassing her?

MICHAEL DOW: Yes.

DI SINGH: What was he doing?

MICHAEL DOW: What wasn't he doing? After she dumped him he went psycho. Phone calls, texts . . . he used to follow her around in the street till he started spending all his time getting whacked at that squat in Limekilns.

DI SINGH: Did you ever see him in your garden?

MICHAEL DOW: No. He used to keep clear of the house.

DI SINGH: Any other relationships? Current boyfriend?

[*Silence*]

DI SINGH: Was there someone?

MICHAEL DOW: I don't know for sure.

DI SINGH But you suspect something?

MICHAEL DOW: She was behaving odd. These last few weeks. She wasn't usually secretive but I think she was keeping something hidden. Like on Thursday night. You know, the night before she was—

DI SINGH: What happened on Thursday night, Mr. Dow?

MICHAEL DOW: She came in late, about one, and I could hear her crying in her room. That wasn't like her at all.

DI SINGH: Do you know what had upset her?

MICHAEL DOW: No.

DI SINGH: Did you ask her?

MICHAEL DOW: She wouldn't let me in her room. She told me to eff off.

DI SINGH: I see.

MICHAEL DOW: That wasn't like her, either, to be fair.

DI SINGH [*sound of writing*]: Do you know anything else about Thursday night?

MICHAEL DOW: No.

DI SINGH: Where she'd been? Who she'd been with?

MICHAEL DOW: No.

DI SINGH: You didn't see anyone pick her up? Drop her back home?

MICHAEL DOW [*silence*]: No, but . . . I don't know about this, but . . . When she came in I was still awake, and I got up and looked out of the bedroom window, and there was this car in the street. I might be wrong but it looked like it was just pulling away.

DI SINGH: What sort of car?

MICHAEL DOW: A Porsche. That's why I noticed it.

DI SINGH: Are you sure?

MICHAEL DOW: Looked like it to me. And I thought to myself: What's that doing in our street?

DI SINGH: What color?

MICHAEL DOW: Black, I think. Can't be sure. Something dark.

DI SINGH: You didn't see the driver.

MICHAEL DOW: No. But I'm guessing it wasn't a schoolkid.

DI SINGH: Someone older. You think Chloe was involved with an older man?

MICHAEL DOW: I don't know. I can't even be sure it was pulling away. Might just have been passing.

DI SINGH: Had you ever seen the car before? Or since?

MICHAEL DOW: No, never.

DI SINGH: Did you talk to Chloe about it?

MICHAEL DOW: How could I? I didn't have the chance. I didn't even bloody see her again. [*Silence*] Jesus. As I said, she was only a kid. She didn't think of the risks. They never do.

DI SINGH: Thank you, Mr. Dow. You've been very helpful. I don't have any more questions.

[*Silence; noise of chairs scraping on the floor*]

DI SINGH: Actually, there's one more thing. I see you've had an accident of some sort.

MICHAEL DOW: I fell off a ladder at work. [*Sound of paper rustling*]

DI SINGH: What's this?

MICHAEL DOW: Contacts for the carpenter and electrician I was working with. I wrote them down for you. You need to check everything out, don't you?

DI SINGH: Yes. Thank you. Mr. Dow?

[*Silence*]

DI SINGH: I know how hard this is for you. I said the same thing to your wife. I want to say how much I commiserate with you. Your stepdaughter had the whole of her life before her. I assure you we won't rest till we bring her killer to justice.

MICHAEL DOW: [*Sound of angry snort*]

This time Singh left the tape running; it fizzed emptily in the quietness of the room. He picked up his pen and wrote a single word: *Porsche.*

Then he got stiffly to his feet and walked away from the desk into the corner of the room, where he stood facing the wall as if in sudden despair. It was a strange, inexplicable thing to do. Then, after a moment, in a harsh mutter, he began to perform the rehras. It was a little after midnight.

"She had her whole life before her," Mr. Winthrop, the principal, said.

Leading a special lunchtime assembly devoted to Chloe Dow, he stood on the stage of Main Hall, flanked by the head of year and Chloe's homeroom teacher, addressing year eleven, and year eleven sat in silence, listening.

Mr. Winthrop was not by nature an emotional man, but as he spoke of Chloe's talents and achievements, and of the contribution she had made to school life over the last five years, he twice came close to breaking down. His voice was both wavering and uptight. After he had finished speaking, Miss Bell, Chloe's English teacher, read a poem, and she too showed signs of distress. Finally Miss Perkins, the head of year, a woman who usually never gave the slightest hint of emotion, made several announcements of a purely practical nature, and these too were delivered in a strange tone, hushed and angry.

Year eleven was reminded that Chloe's death, nearly a week earlier, was different. Not an ordinary tragedy. Not an illness or an accident. Murder.

They were reminded too that the police were on site conducting interviews with both staff and pupils. Interviewees would be notified.

Other pupils should not offer statements unless they had something of vital importance to say. Conversations with the media were strongly discouraged.

Chloe's funeral would be by invitation only. The privacy of her family was to be respected at all times. Cards of condolence should be sent through the postal system, not pushed through the letter box. Unannounced visits to the Dows' home were absolutely forbidden.

This atmosphere of almost religious strangeness persisted, and year eleven remained subdued until at last the special assembly ended and they left the hall; it was only then, as they went out of the building into the brisk April light, slowly fanning out in twos and threes along the concrete paths to their next lessons, that normality returned and people began to talk as usual.

"She was still a cow," Smudge said. "I mean, it's crap getting done in, but still. Chloe Dow, 'extinguished hope of the future.' What's that about?"

Felix said, "What do you want them to say? 'Chloe Dow got throttled but let's face it no one liked her'?"

"But they were really choking up. Even Queen Bitch, and she hated Chloe's guts."

Jessica Walker came past. "Hi, Garvie."

"Hey, Jess."

They all stopped to watch Jessica Walker slink across the yard toward Upper School and round the corner of C Block.

As she disappeared two policemen came round the corner the other way, heading toward the office.

"Here already," Smudge said as they watched them. "They don't usually move so quick. When my brother got that stuff nicked out of his van they were four months just logging his statement."

Felix shrugged. "Yeah, well. This is a national murder inquiry, Smudge. And it turned out your brother had nicked that stuff in the first place."

"That's not the point."

"What's the point, Smudge?"

"Point is, Dow's still getting people to jump for her even though she's dead. Typical bloody Dow. When I'm interviewed I might just tell them what people really thought about her."

"No one's going to interview you, Smudge—you don't know anything."

"Don't know anything about Chloe Dow?"

"Don't know anything about anything."

After a brief but passionate assertion of his all-round knowledge, Smudge shambled off to science (though it wasn't where he was meant to be), and Felix and Garvie sauntered on, across Bottom Pitch and up the grassy slope to Top Pitch. It was quiet up there. Beyond the touchlines the hawthorn trees were full of early blossoms, thick and white as cheese, and when they got to the top they could see all the way across the city, vast and gray and ugly.

They lit up.

"Smudge is right," Felix said. "No one liked her."

"Alex liked her."

Felix exhaled smoke, squinted. "I know it's not like she was *always* horrible, but even when she was being nice there was something not-nice about her. Like last week. It was MacAttack's birthday, right, and she brought in these chocolate brownies she'd made, and when he was doing the roll call she goes up and does this presentation to him as if it's on behalf of the whole class—she even kissed him on the cheek—and somehow it was all about her, not about him at all."

"Pushy," Garvie said. It was one of Chloe's nicknames.

"The brass girl."

They sat looking across the city.

Garvie looked at his watch and said, "Where should you be?"

"Geog."

"Are you going?"

"Haven't decided yet."

"I really think we should go and see Mrs. Dow."

Felix looked at him. "What, now?"

"I think so."

"Okay."

They flicked away their butts and set off down the slope.

Felix said, "What are we going to see her for?"

"To pay our respects, of course, Felix."

"Are you sure? She's a bit insane, Garv. Specially now."

"Don't worry. We'll catch a ride in Abdul's limo and I'll tell you what to do on the way."

Felix looked at him sideways. "You all right about all this, Garv? I know you and Chloe—"

"Forget it." Garvie's face was a blank. "It's a puzzle, Felix. A problem. Something to be solved, that's all."

"Yeah, yeah, I know. Sex or money, right? Though I guess it's pretty obvious in this case."

Garvie said nothing more, and together they walked down from Top Pitch, back through the main school, out of the front gate and, without a backward glance, headed for the taxi stand at the shops.

Abdul was from Morocco. He had cropped black hair, a narrow, stubbly face, and the gentlest smile in Five Mile. When he arrived in the country he'd spent his first three months in the hospital with a kidney infection, and Garvie's mother had befriended him; she'd even helped him sort out some of his paperwork for immigration. Ever since, he'd been a grateful friend of the family.

Garvie tapped the window. "Hey, Abdul."

Abdul's whole face beamed. "My Garvie man, how is, how is?"

He came out of his cab grinning, shook Garvie's hand, kissed him on both cheeks, and finally pressed his fingertips to his heart in a gesture both tender and daft.

"How is?" he said.

"Is good, thanks. Any chance of a lift up to Fox Walk?"

"For you, Garvie man, is *plaisir.*" Abdul glanced at Felix. "You bad man," he said sternly. "But Garvie friend. Is welcome."

"Cheers," Felix said. "I promise not to nick your backseat."

They drove up Town Road past the DIY superstores and electronics warehouses.

Abdul kept glancing nervously at Garvie in his rearview mirror. "Fox Walk," he said at last. "Is home Miss Dow." He touched his forehead with his fingertips. "Miss Dow decease."

"That's it," Garvie said.

"We're going to pay our respects," Felix added helpfully.

Abdul's reflection scowled at him.

They drove onto Pollard Way past the business park.

"Miss Dow nice nice girl," Abdul said.

"Yeah, well. Nice-looking, anyway."

Abdul nodded.

"Did you know her, Abdul?"

"No no. Never." He shook his head violently. "People say bad bad things."

"What bad things?"

"They say black man do this. Police come ask question."

"Have they asked you?"

"They come soon," he said. "Quick quick."

"Don't hold your breath. They've got about a thousand kids to get through first at the Academy."

They turned onto Bulwarks Lane and pulled up by the corner of Fox Walk. Abdul refused payment. His jitters had gotten worse and he seemed anxious to be away.

"Don't panic, man," Garvie said. "Her killer's going to get caught soon."

Abdul nodded. "Police catch him."

"Doubtful. But there are others on his trail."

Garvie patted him on the shoulder. "You've got nothing to be worried about," he said. And Abdul managed to look even more fearful.

10

Two miles away, in an ugly building located at the edge of the business district, Detective Inspector Singh stood in front of the large operational chart fixed on the wall and addressed his team leaders. They were two days into the investigation and this was the third time he had addressed them. In his careful, cold way, he was stressing the importance of the case, the urgent need for a speedy resolution. There was tremendous public pressure to solve it. There was unremitting media interest in it. There was the close, personal attention of the chief constable. Need he say more? There was silence in the room. He would say more, anyway. They had a duty, a moral imperative, to bring the perpetrator to justice. This was the murder of a fifteen-year-old girl that they were investigating. Moreover, he had given the chief constable his personal guarantee that the operation would fulfill all criteria for success.

He fixed them with a quiet stare, and a little frisson of discomfort went round the office.

"And I'm expecting that you will give me the same guarantees," he said.

Seated beyond his desk, his four colleagues looked back at him. Detective Sergeant Bob Dowell was a City man, tough and apt to be cynical; he had a big, bald head and a pug's nose and a habit of clearing his throat before being abusive. From time to time there were rumors he was struggling with gambling debts, but no one denied his determination or resourcefulness. Detective Sergeant Darren Collier was a friend of his, a small man—smaller than Singh—but already running to fat. He was dependable; some thought him sly. Inspector Lawrence Shan had been flown in from the InterCity Division, a sharp-faced officer with homicide expertise, recommended by the superintendent. Detective Sergeant Mal Nolan was the only woman on the team. She was shrewd and forthright and gave no quarter in arguments. Singh was aware of being the youngest in the room by at least ten years, and by far the least popular.

"You'll get used to me," Singh said quietly, "just as I'll get used to you. We work the same way. Methodical. Rigorous. We go the extra mile. We follow our instincts. And because of these things, and because right is on our side, we will succeed, and we will succeed fast. Now let's get to work."

He drew their attention to the updates in their dossiers, then to the operational chart behind him. "Thursday evening and Friday afternoon," he said. "Blanks. We know she was out on Thursday. But where? Who was she with? Something happened to upset her but we don't know what. Friday afternoon we know even less. Absence records from the Academy show she missed all her lessons. It seems she was at home prior to leaving for her run at seven, but there's at least six hours unaccounted for."

He turned back to them. "That's a lot of questions. Where are we with the answers?"

Bob Dowell and Darren Collier's teams had been conducting the door-to-door investigation along the routes to Pike Pond. The working assumption was that Chloe had left her home at around seven p.m. to run up to Pike Pond while there was still light. There were as yet no reliable sightings, which was unusual but not, as Collier commented, unprecedented, given the weather conditions and time of evening. Lawrence Shan's team had begun to interview Chloe's teachers and school friends, but it was too soon to come to any conclusions. Mal Nolan's team was trawling police records for local criminals, sex offenders, vagrants, and anyone else out of the ordinary likely to have been in the Four Winds area. She had also been conducting interviews with the residents at Froggett Woods, as yet without result. The calls record for Chloe's phone, expected from the service provider, had been held up by "unresolved technical issues."

Dowell spat into a handkerchief and grimaced. "It's all slow work," he said.

Singh nodded. "Too slow. I want your ideas."

The big man pursed his lips. "Most perps are known to their victims. The key suspect here is Dow."

Singh gave him a flat look. "The reports are in the dossier."

"I haven't had time—"

"We have to make time. I interviewed Mr. Dow last night. You'll find the transcript in section one. Also the transcripts of my interviews this morning with the electrician and carpenter who were working with Dow. They were with him till about four in the afternoon. They confirm that he fell off his ladder, which accounts for the injuries to his face. Also that after they left him he carried on working: The paint job was all finished when they arrived first thing on Monday morning."

Collier said, "All right. But they didn't actually witness him finishing it on Friday afternoon."

"No, but a neighbor confirms he was there. It's the fourth transcript in the dossier: the interview with Mr. Snedding. Snedding could hear him at work all afternoon. Dow had the radio on. He didn't pack up till about five forty-five; Snedding watched him get into his van and drive off in the direction of the Center. He met his wife there at six. It all fits." He paused. "What doesn't fit is the Porsche Dow saw on Thursday night."

There was some skepticism, led by Dowell. "Not a lot to go on, is it? No proven connection with Chloe. Dow didn't see her get out of it. He'd never seen it before. He wasn't sure what color it was, or even if it was a Porsche. Probably he was half asleep."

Collier agreed. Nolan pointed out how time-consuming it would be to follow it up with any degree of thoroughness.

Singh leafed through the dossier. "We're starting to learn something about Chloe Dow at the Academy. She liked to go out, apparently. To a club, to a bar. It could be she was meeting an older crowd."

Nolan said, "She liked to give the *impression* she was going to clubs. Girls that age, girls of a certain sort, they talk themselves up."

"You don't think she was actually going out?"

"Too soon to tell."

Singh thought about this. "A black Porsche," he said. "It's a cliché. Tinted windows, spoiler, side skirts, techno wheels."

Collier said, "Pimpmobile."

Singh returned to the dossier. "This boy, Alex Robinson. We took him in after that rumpus at Pike Pond."

"Yes?"

"Picked up twice in the last six months for selling weed."

"He's nothing. He certainly doesn't drive a Porsche."

"Most perps are known to their victims. You said it. They went out, she dumped him, he went off the deep end. He's a big lad with anger-management issues. He smokes too much dope."

"Okay."

"I want to know who his friends are. Who does he run with? Is there anyone he knows driving a Porsche?"

There was a silence in the room. Singh looked straight at Collier.

After a moment Collier said, "All right, I'll put some people on the Porsche."

"Good."

They got to their feet, but Singh was still staring at Collier.

"One more thing."

He waited until they had all sat down again. "I'm still waiting for the report on the Dows' garden."

Collier flushed. "I didn't think—"

"I told you," Singh said. "When I was at the Dows' there was an intruder. In the garden."

"I just thought . . . Probably it was just a local kid. A neighbor."

Dowell cleared his throat. "Park a squad car on the front lawn; it does wonders for the local youth's sense of curiosity, I find."

Shan laughed. Even Mal Nolan smiled.

Singh waited until there was silence. Then he waited longer, looking at Collier.

"I'm sorry," Collier said. "I didn't think you were serious."

Singh said quietly, "I'm always serious. Next time put one of your men on it." Ignoring them, he returned to the dossier, leaving them to make their exit. For an hour afterward he worked on; then he put on his coat and went out to his assistant in her pod outside his office.

She passed him a dozen messages, all from journalists. "Some of them have called several times," she said.

Singh nodded and put the note in his pocket. "I'm going out," he said. "I'll be at the Dows'. In the garden," he added.

11

All the houses in Fox Walk had vinyl doors and windows with the new fittings. Felix examined them critically as he and Garvie waited on the doorstep of Honeymead. They'd knocked twice already but there was no answer, so they stood there waiting, looking smart. They'd straightened their hair and tucked in their shirts and checked the undersides of their shoes for dog shit. Garvie was holding a bouquet of chrysanthemums and a condolence card from Jamal's.

But no one was home.

"Tell me again why we're paying our respects when school said absolutely no unannounced visits?"

"We're not paying our respects, Felix."

"Oh." Felix looked interested. "What are we doing here, then?"

"We're gaining entry."

"Why didn't you say? If you want to gain entry, it's no problem. All these houses have those new vinyl doors and windows. All you have to do is—"

"Not my style, Felix. I prefer to knock."

Felix looked at his watch. "It's two o'clock. The middle of the day, Garv. No one's in."

"I disagree."

"Then why's no one answering the door?"

"You overestimate Mrs. Dow's powers of locomotion. We must wait."

As they waited, Felix passed the time by helpfully outlining the very quick and completely effective way of opening the modern vinyl door. Felix the Cat. As in "cat burglar."

"Shh, Felix. Here she comes."

There was a shadow in the frosted glass of the front door. It wavered, there was the knuckle-cracking noise of locks being released, and then the door swung slowly open to reveal Mrs. Dow in her dressing gown, hair awry, face vacant and bewildered.

"Dear Mrs. Dow," Garvie said, stepping forward with the flowers and an angelic expression. "We're sorry to disturb you. But we wanted to say that we're thinking of you at this very difficult time." And he bowed his head.

They sat on the bamboo-cane sofa in the conservatory drinking iced tea while Mrs. Dow said how touched she was that Garvie had thought of her. She was glad to see him again. His flowers were in a vase on the table and she peered at them vaguely and attempted a smile. She apologized for her appearance. She hadn't been sleeping well, she said, and the doctor had prescribed some pills.

"Mick will be sorry to have missed you. He's still at work."

Garvie said he was sorry to have missed Mr. Dow too. He even looked sorry.

"I'm so happy you came," Mrs. Dow said with a sadly quavering smile. "I know how fond of her you were, Garvie. I was so sad when Chloe decided to—"

"Yeah, I know."

Felix gave him a look, which he avoided.

"What I mean is," he said, "I know how much I'm going to miss her. She was"—he looked at Mrs. Dow with his clear blue eyes—"remarkable. All credit to you," he added softly.

Finding no words, Mrs. Dow smiled and nodded, blinking back tears.

He went on: "We ought to leave you in peace. But can I ask you a favor before we go?"

She nodded again.

"Thing is, Chloe and I were doing some math together last Friday morning, and I lent her a calculator. But it's really my mum's and she uses it at work so I just wondered if there was any chance of picking it up. It would get me out of a bit of trouble, to be honest."

Mrs. Dow got to her feet, swaying slightly, and led the boys upstairs.

"The police said they were going to seal her room, whatever that means, but they haven't yet."

Felix tutted politely. "Police!" he murmured.

As they went along the landing Garvie complimented Mrs. Dow on the tidiness of her house, and she smiled. "Mick does it. He can't bear mess. You won't believe this," she said, "but I'm really very messy."

Garvie said he didn't believe it for a moment but unfortunately Mrs. Dow was determined to be believed, and though they were only a few paces from Chloe's room she at once stopped and began to talk in a rambling, emotional way about herself and her husband, apparently the tidiest man in the country. "He has a system for everything," she told them—for laundry and housework, and even for those "awkward little things" like paying the bills. "Would you believe it, he keeps receipts of everything he buys!"

"I can hardly believe it at all," Garvie said. "This is Chloe's room, isn't it? Shall I just . . . ?"

But Mrs. Dow had forgotten all about Garvie's mother's calculator.

"He looks after me," she said, with a hint of tears at the corner of her smile. "He'll see me through, I know he will."

Behind her back Felix rolled his eyes at Garvie. And at that moment the telephone rang.

"If that's Mick now," Garvie said, "don't worry about us. We can just grab the calculator and be on our way."

The phone rang on and Mrs. Dow hesitated only long enough to give Garvie an appreciative squeeze of the hand before going downstairs to answer it.

Chloe's room was very feminine. There was a fluffy rug on the carpet, a dozen lace-fringed pillows on her bed, and a lightshade made of pink beads. The top of her chest of drawers was crowded with cosmetics, cans of hairspray, bottles of perfume, hair ties, and costume jewelry. On the windowsill was a long line of photographs of Chloe at different ages in matching purple frames. On her bed twelve teddy bears were ranged in size. And it was all reflected in the full-length mirrors on the front of the long built-in wardrobe opposite.

"I don't like this room," Felix said. "What am I doing here?"

"Keep your ears open. If you hear Mrs. Dow coming back up, get out there and distract her."

"Why? What are you going to be doing?"

"Looking for clues."

"What sort of clues?"

Garvie didn't answer. He stepped over to the wardrobe and slid open one of the doors. Inside were Chloe's clothes—hundreds of them, immaculately stored: neat shelves of woolens and accessories, boxes of shoes and racks of tops, skirts, dresses, and trousers, everything color-coded and in order.

"Good luck with that," Felix said. "I'll look for clues over here."

For a while he leafed through the magazines on Chloe's desk, then inspected the jar of colored pens. Next to the jar was a small packet of photographs of Chloe wearing a blue dress and white jacket, taken recently. Pinned to the cork bulletin board were a variety of cards, lists and invitations, which he read carefully twice. "Lots of clues here," he said over his shoulder. "And here." He began to fish around in Chloe's wastepaper basket. "Look at this, Garv. Bolloms the dry cleaner. And look at *these* . . ."

Turning round with a plastic bag in one hand and a torn pair of fishnet tights in the other, he suddenly flinched and dropped them both.

He stared. "What the fuck are you doing?" he whispered.

Garvie was standing in front of the wardrobe mirror wearing one of Chloe's miniskirts with a halter-neck top. The skirt was red, the top a pale cream.

"Do these go together?" he asked. "Be honest."

Felix swallowed. He watched as Garvie changed out of the skirt and halter-neck top, and put on a pair of blue-mottled harem pants and a turquoise tank top.

"How about these? Come on, Felix, help me out."

"Yeah. Very nice, Garv. But—"

"What shoes should I wear with them?" Garvie took out a pair of gladiator sandals. "What about these?" He swapped them for a pair of navy tennis shoes. "Or these?"

Felix said, in a low, troubled voice, "You're a very unusual boy, you know that, Garv."

"Just tell me if they match."

"Oh yeah, they match. They match your blue eyes, you freak."

Felix watched aghast while Garvie tried on more clothes. He held them up against himself, arranging them in different combinations, squinting at his reflection in the mirror. Wet-look gray jeggings and a wide-neck T-shirt in pink and a short white jacket smelling very crisp and clean. Sleeveless orange bodycon dress with zebra-pattern flip-flops. Skinny black jeans and a blue shirt with pale gray snow boots.

Black jersey skirt with red clogs. Gray denim skirt over sheer black tights with snake-print kitten-heel slingbacks.

Felix looked queasy. "Tell me you're not thinking of nicking them. I couldn't bear to see you in this sort of getup at the Old Ditch Road playground."

Before Garvie could answer there was a noise downstairs. A voice. "Boys?"

Garvie put back the last of the clothes and slid shut the wardrobe door.

"We have a problem, Felix."

"The problem's all yours, Garv."

"Everything matches."

Felix frowned. "Course it matches. This is Chloe. So what?"

Garvie sighed. "So when she went running on Friday evening she was wearing someone else's shoes."

"*What?*"

"You know what heliotrope is?"

"Yeah." Felix hesitated. "Sort of machine, innit?"

"It's a color, Felix. Pinky-purple. Very chic. Chloe was wearing heliotrope shirt and shorts—and orange and lime-green shoes. Orange and lime green, Felix!"

"So?"

"Look at her wardrobe, man. Everything's beautiful. Say what you like about her, she had taste. Lime-green and orange shoes? They're ugly. And they don't go with anything. Definitely not with pinky-purple."

Felix understood. "But if they weren't hers," he said slowly, "why was she wearing them?"

"That's the question."

As they looked at each other in silence they heard Mrs. Dow coming up the stairs.

"Boys? Are you there?"

Garvie patted Felix on the shoulder. Then, taking a calculator out of his pocket, he went out into the hall with the good news that he had found exactly what he'd been looking for.

12

Standing on the tiny square of lawn in the Dows' garden, Detective Inspector Singh was struck again by its neatness. The trimmed grass. The immaculate flower beds. The newly creosoted fence. The birdbath. Only the broken fencing spoiled the air of complete control. He allowed himself a slight frown. The area hadn't been sealed off, as instructed. Before beginning his examination, he glanced back toward the house and saw Mrs. Dow looking down at him from an upstairs window. She disliked him, he knew. But he nodded politely, and her face withdrew sharply.

A thought of that boy Smith came into his mind, and his face tightened. He made a mental note to tell Lawrence Shan not to bother interviewing him at school. He would deal with Smith himself, if need be.

He returned his attention to the garden. A quick initial survey showed only the obvious. A few messy footprints in the soil behind the shrubs. The broken fencing. Someone had crouched there hidden for a while, then had suddenly fled, risking being caught, clambering over the fence and bringing it crashing down in the process. Why?

Inspector Singh did not deal in the obvious. He dealt in detail. Stepping carefully around the flowers and shrubs, he began to examine the area. He worked methodically from left to right, slowly turning over leaves, twigs, and the top layer of soil using a palette knife adapted for the purpose. For some time he examined the footprints by the collapsed fence, too blurred to be used for identification but suggestive at least of someone fully grown, solid even, and the fence itself, the cracked panel hanging crookedly like a bird's broken wing, and posts splintered to the bare pale wood where someone—someone heavy and energetic but probably not so athletic—had scrambled over. He remembered the crash that night, and the toppling outline of a figure obscured by darkness and rain. But there was nothing here to help him now. After half an hour he had found nothing of interest and he walked back onto the grass, frustrated, and stood there thinking.

According to Sikh religious texts the truth is eternal and present everywhere. He thought of this. He also thought of the police manual. If you can't find what you're looking for there are two likely reasons: You're looking in the wrong way or you're looking in the wrong place.

He went across the lawn, through the shrubbery, climbed over the broken panel of fencing and out of the garden into the lane beyond. There he resumed his search. Slowly, patiently, he examined the strip of scrub on both sides of the path and the path itself. Slowly and patiently he moved crab-wise backward and forward, delving with his specially adapted palette knife.

He found absolutely nothing.

Finally it was time to go. He had to talk to Mrs. Dow on his way out, to check if the bedroom upstairs had been sealed, but first, to stretch his legs, he walked down the path along the house-backs and through the wicket gate onto the Marsh Fields, where he had run last Friday night. In daylight it looked smaller, the grass scruffier, the trees spindlier. The air tasted of cold water. He sucked in a lungful and turned to go. And stopped suddenly.

Bending down, he picked up a small scrap of something nestling in the shaggy grass. It was a piece of wood—a clean splinter two inches long the orange color of new creosote. Stuck to it by a thread was something else, brightly colored in red and yellow. A button.

He brought the button up to his eye. The words FAMOUS STARS were embossed around its edge. It was a button off a Famous Stars and Straps varsity jacket.

He stood there on the spongy grass of the Marsh Fields, completely unmoving, staring at the button. He had seen someone in a red-and-yellow varsity jacket in the last few days. Who? Someone wearing a varsity jacket, scowling at him, he remembered that much. But who? Methodically he racked his brain.

And he remembered. Taking out his notebook, he wrote down a name and closed it again and turned, all in the same quiet, efficient way, and went back to Fox Walk.

13

Garvie and Felix split up when they got to Pollard Way, and Garvie went on alone up Bulwarks Lane. It was now three thirty and he had half an hour to kill before going home if he didn't want his mother asking awkward questions. The out-of-town traffic was heavy, vans and trucks nudging slowly toward the highway, and he fell in beside them, walking in a ripple through their fumes, frowning to himself.

Chloe Dow was the most straightforward girl he'd ever known, a girl who hid nothing. Everything about her had been on display—not just her looks but the ambitions she never stopped talking about, the fantasies she'd spun, the gossip she'd peddled. She was stunning—and ordinary. Not the sort of girl to do something strange like go for a run in someone else's ugly shoes.

Not the sort of girl to have secrets. Until now.

Frowning, he went past the betting shop, past Burger King, past the long flaking front of the old Whiteways Insurance offices, and had just reached the shops when a car came to a halt at the curb next to him and a familiar voice said, "Get in."

He bent down and peered through the wound-down window.

The policeman with the turban looked back at him. "Get in the car," he said.

Garvie peered closer. "Is it tidy? My mother's very particular about that sort of thing."

The inspector did not reply. He pushed open the door, and after a moment Garvie got in.

It was very tidy.

"I've just been speaking to Mrs. Dow," Singh said, "and she told me you visited her house this afternoon."

His voice was deadpan and his eyes were deadpan too; there was nothing in his expression to show he was angry. But Garvie could tell he was.

"Yeah. I'm a personal friend."

"And that while you were there you went into Chloe Dow's bedroom, despite the fact that the bedroom is a crime scene, off-limits to the public. As you must know from your very high-up uncle."

"But I thought crime scenes were immediately sealed by the very efficient police to prevent people going in them."

Singh's mouth tightened. "It's being sealed now."

"Oh well, better late than never. Thanks for letting me know."

He opened the door.

"Get back in the car," Singh said.

Garvie hesitated, then closed the door again.

For a few moments Singh looked at him unblinkingly. "Do you own a varsity jacket?" he asked.

Despite himself, Garvie was taken by surprise. But he recovered. "Don't you have to have a warrant to ask me that sort of question?"

"Do you or don't you?" Singh said.

"No. As it happens. Why? Do you think I should get one? Would it improve my image?"

When Singh spoke again his voice was, if anything, even quieter than before. "Ever since this investigation began you've been interfering with official police business."

"No, I haven't. I'm—"

"I know what you are."

Garvie raised his eyebrows.

"There's a system for dealing with people like you. If you continue to interfere you'll receive a statutory reprimand, copied to your mother and principal. If you don't stop after that, a curfew order. After that, tagging. After that, a residency requirement in a correctional facility."

"That's a lot of paperwork."

"You're not listening to me."

"You're not listening to *me*, man! I'm not interfering, I'm helping. I'm helping you work it out."

Singh stared at him with a different sort of expression, Garvie couldn't tell if it was astonishment or disgust.

"You're trying to work out who killed Chloe Dow?"

Garvie shook his head in exasperation. "No! I'm trying to work out who stole her running shoes."

For a moment there was a flash of something else in Singh's face, quickly replaced by a new sort of coldness.

"Get out," he said, and his voice was not as quiet as before. "Out!"

Singh pulled away into the traffic, and Garvie stood on the sidewalk, thoughtfully watching him go.

Before he could move on, a voice came up the street. A soft voice. "Been a bad boy, Garvie Smith?"

It was Jessica Walker. Approaching with a slow wiggle, she draped herself round a nearby parking sign and gave him a look.

She was a slender girl, very pretty, with a narrow white throat and big black eyes. Her hair was black too, and Garvie noticed that though she'd been in school earlier she'd already changed out of her school shoes into a pair of strappy wedge sandals, also black.

"They going to put you away, Garv?"

"Yeah."

She hung off the parking sign, looking after Singh's car as it disappeared past the Driftway. "But he's gone. And you're still at large."

"Yeah. He couldn't handle me by himself. He's gone to get reinforcements."

Jessica looked at Garvie with her big eyes. "Not really, Garv?"

"No, not really, Jess."

She laughed, and her nose crinkled. "You're funny." She came off the parking sign and stood next to him. "Got any cigs?"

"Yeah."

"Got one for me?"

They sat side by side on a bench next to Jamal's with a view of the bins outside the burger joint, and Jessica crossed her legs and blew smoke against the side of Garvie's face. Her legs, he noticed, were very pale and smooth, with a waxy sheen on them, like fruit.

"This is nice, Garv."

"Isn't it? Listen, Jess, I want to ask you something."

"Something nice?"

"Not really."

She stopped smiling.

"What sort of stuff did you use to nick off Chloe?"

She jerked her head back indignantly. "I didn't nick anything off Chloe!"

"No? No money?"

"Never any money."

Garvie considered his cigarette for a moment. "Did she ever ask *you* for money?"

"What? Like money for the shop?"

Garvie said nothing. He smoked.

"You mean proper money? No. Never. Why would she?"

She scrutinized Garvie, and her features gradually softened. When she spoke again, her voice was sympathetic.

"Garv? I know you're upset. You can't hide it from me. I know what she did to you, and I know it doesn't make it any easier, and I know—"

"You didn't like her, did you?" Garvie said.

She jerked her head again. "What do you mean? She was my friend."

"What about all those things you used to say about her behind her back?"

"What things?"

"You know. How she was shagging MacAttack, how she drove Alex to drugs, all that sort of stuff."

"I never. It was other people saying them. I only might have repeated them. Anyway, some of them were true."

"Like what?"

"Like about Alex," she said, and shut her mouth abruptly.

There was a silence. Garvie nodded. He knew as well as anyone what Jessica thought about Alex: Six months earlier he'd dumped her for Chloe, and Jessica hadn't known who to hate more. Poor Jessica Walker, unlucky in love.

"Jess?" he said, more softly.

"What?"

"When did you last see Chloe?"

Something went across Jessica's face, a little flurry of emotion, and she began to chew the inside of her cheek.

"Can't remember, actually."

"But she was your friend. Your best friend. You saw her all the time, didn't you?"

"Yeah, well. Course." She folded her arms. "Must have been at school that day. Friday. Friday morning. At school."

"Right."

While she glowered, Garvie sat quietly smoking, until at last she glanced at him and managed to smile again, and when she finally spoke, it was in her usual sexy wheedle.

"Garv? Why do we have to talk about other people all the time, Garv?"

"You want to talk about something else?"

She nodded and he sat back.

"All right." For a moment he continued to smoke thoughtfully, then he said, "How about complex numbers?"

She looked at him doubtfully. "Can't we just talk about me?"

Snuffing out his cigarette, he took a scrap of paper and a pencil out of his jacket pocket. "A complex number, Jess, is made up of a real number and a number in an imaginary dimension. Call it z. There's a formula, right: $z=a+bi$. i means b's in an imaginary dimension. Right?" He drew quickly.

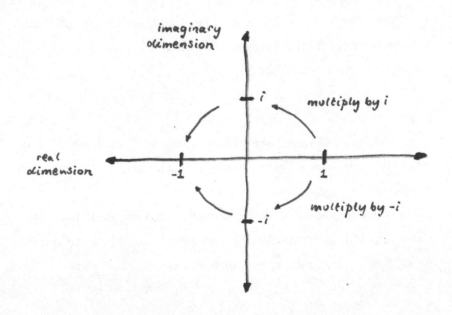

Jessica squinted at it. "Looks like math," she said with distaste.

"i^2 is always -1. You'd think that was impossible, right?"

"I would, yeah. Like, totally."

"Well, it isn't. In an imaginary dimension the impossible's possible. See? That's where i is, up there, and $-i$, down there. On an *imaginary* axis. Now, you don't compute i numbers, you rotate them, by ninety degrees, into that imaginary dimension. $1 \times i$ moves you up there, where i is. Multiply i by itself to get its square, and you rotate another ninety degrees, and end up there, at -1. Same thing for $-i$, by a different route. Elementary. Yeah?"

"Yeah, yeah, course." Jessica attempted a smile and produced a slight twitch. "But what's that got to do with *me*?"

Garvie looked at her thoughtfully. "I don't know yet."

He drew another diagram.

"Here's a complex number: $z = a + bi$. See? That point there. Point of a triangle. A cinch to work out. Let's say $a = 4$ and $b = 6$. $z = \sqrt{4^2 + 6^2}$. $z = 7.211$."

She scowled.

"All right. Here's another complex number. Call it 'What Jess did.'"

"Why?"

"'Cause Jess is complex. $a =$ something real, something solid—I don't know, let's say . . . 'Chloe's running shoes.'"

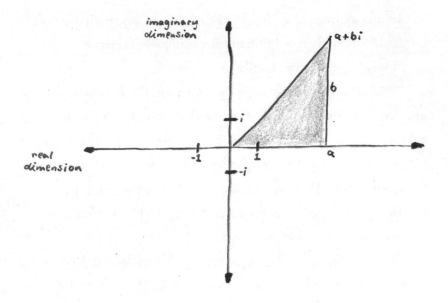

Scowling, Jessica turned away and began flicking ash all over her skirt.

"*bi* is trickier," he said. Pausing, he looked at her. "Hmm. I'm going to call it 'Bad feeling.'"

"What d'you mean, 'Bad feeling'?"

"Bad feeling between Jess and Chloe. And all we have to do now is work out the result."

There was a silence. After a moment he said quietly, "See what I'm getting at?"

Jessica finished her cigarette in one long furious drag and obliterated the butt on the bench armrest. "There are times, Garvie Smith, when I'm not so keen on you."

He nodded sympathetically and patted her knee, and she said in a soft wail, "Garv, I don't get it. Why do you have to keep bringing other people and strange numbers and stuff into it? Can't we just talk about *me*?"

She slid round on the bench and curled up her legs and put her feet in his lap and wriggled her toes.

He sighed. "All right."

There was a long silence.

"Well, go on, then," she said.

"What nice big feet you've got, Jess."

For a moment she looked at him, horrified, her eyes big with shock. Then she recovered herself and was properly cross. Kicking her legs free, she jumped off the bench and stood facing him, little fists clenched.

"Temper," Garvie said mildly.

She said, "You know what's wrong with you, Garvie Smith? You just don't care about anybody but yourself!"

In a fury, she turned from him and wiggled away as fast as she could round the corner of Jamal's.

Garvie sat there a moment longer, thinking. He thought about Chloe's feminine room and the horrible sunset up at Pike Pond and Jessica's feet. Jessica's feet, particularly. But most of all he thought about the way she'd looked at him, not in anger, but in horrified surprise.

With a sigh he got up and walked back into the street. There was a news bulletin outside Jamal's which said NO CLUES YET IN "BEAUTY"

MURDER, and he glanced at it without expression and headed for home.

"You really don't care about anyone but yourself, do you?" his mother said from the doorway, where she had materialized with her usual sudden solidity.

Interrupted in his thoughts, Garvie kept his eyes on the ceiling and sighed very gently through his nose.

"Two hours ago he phoned," she said, "to ask where you were."

"Who did?"

"Mr. Trindle."

"Who's he?"

"Your geography teacher."

"Really?"

His mother glared at him. "So what's the answer?"

"Answer to what?"

"Where were you? Obviously not in your geography lesson."

For a moment he considered telling her he'd taken flowers round to Mrs. Dow's, but before he could open his mouth his mother said, "This isn't anything to do with the investigation about Chloe, is it? You're not getting mixed up in that, are you?"

He registered the dangerous note in her voice. "Course not," he said.

"Well, then?"

"I didn't go anywhere. I was just told Trundle had canceled his lesson."

"Trindle."

"Whoever."

His mother began to do the breathing thing, and, lying there, he braced himself for the usual argument, the storm of outrage at the untidiness of his room, the verbal assault on his unauthorized absences from school, the outcry against his general lack of effort. He sensed it coming. But it did not come. Cautiously, he glanced at her. Although her face was the familiar bunched mask of disapproval, she was holding something unfamiliar in her hand. A letter. A letter in an official-looking, somehow foreign envelope. While he was still considering this, she suddenly sat down heavily on the end of his bed and he blinked in surprise.

"What're you doing?"

"You better listen to me for once," she said. "I've something to tell you."

"Can't it wait?" He paused. "I was trying to study."

Without warning she told him anyway, and he sat up and stared at her.

"What?"

She told him again. The director of human resources at the Queen Elizabeth Hospital in Bridgetown, Barbados, had written to her inviting her to apply for the position of Senior Nurse, Surgery.

"But it's in Barbados."

"It is."

"And you've got a job here," he said. "Why would you want to go there?"

She told him. Money was tight here. The flat was expensive here. In Barbados the living was a lot cheaper and, as it happened, the house in Bridgetown where her elderly mother used to live was still standing empty, just waiting for someone to move in. There was family there too—Garvie's other uncles and aunts, and more cousins than she could remember.

She hesitated. "And I think you'd be happier in Barbados," she said.

"No," Garvie said.

"All right," she said. "I think it would be good for you living in Barbados."

"No," he said again.

"It's not for you to say yes or no. It's my decision."

"I won't go."

"What will you do?"

"I'll crash with friends."

His mother sighed. "I'm serious, Garvie. I'm done watching you do nothing. I'm not going to stay here and watch you get into trouble."

"I'm not getting into trouble."

"I want you to stop before it gets serious."

"I told you, I'm not getting into trouble."

There was silence while he suppressed a memory of what Inspector Singh had just said to him.

She got to her feet. "I have another week or so before I give them an answer." With a slow, fierce eye she looked around the room. "If you want me to turn the job down you better start showing me why living here is so much better for you. You've got exams next month."

After she'd gone, Garvie sat alone, looking around—as she had done—at the hideous mess of dirty laundry and rubbish. Somewhere in all that was his schoolbag. Perhaps.

He got up wearily, but in the kitchen his mother put on the radio and he stopped to listen. A voice came to him, flat and crackly but still recognizable: Detective Inspector Singh making a statement.

There had been a new development, he was saying. The police had shifted their focus to the Market Square precinct in the center of the city. He appealed to anyone who thought they might have seen Chloe there between the hours of six and midnight on Thursday to come forward to assist them. But he would not give a reason for this shift in focus, nor would he answer questions about CCTV pictures of the area or explain what Chloe might have been doing.

"Is there anyone specifically helping you with your inquiries?"

"The investigation is making progress," he said shortly. "I have no further statement to make."

"Are there any suspects at all, in fact?" the reporter asked.

But Singh declined to comment.

Garvie lay down quietly on his bed again, and stared at the ceiling. Market Square: a small crooked block of cobbled streets long since redundant as an artisan center, revived now as a picturesque collection of cafés, bars, restaurants, and high-end clubs, all discreet awnings, clever floor lights, and menus in French, and strikingly more in period now than it had been a few hundred years earlier. The natural habitat of the old and rich.

Garvie gazed impassively at the ceiling.

Chloe had liked to talk about Market Square as if she knew it intimately. But her personal inclination was for the bigger, more popular venues in The Wicker—the natural habitat of the young and famous. She wouldn't have shied away from Market Square, but it wouldn't have been her choice.

Garvie's eyes narrowed slightly.

It would have been someone else's choice.

14

As the days passed there was no subsiding of media interest in the "Beauty and the Beast" murder, rather the reverse, and on the day of Chloe's funeral it boiled up to a new intensity. The news channels were jammed with Chloe: her youth, her charm, her dreams, her hopes, her mystery, her murder, and, like a piercing memory never to be forgotten, her picture: that snapshot, that face of heartbreaking innocence and beauty. At the Marsh Academy the camera-toting press besieged the gates in ranks of eight and nine, kept at bay only by the diminutive Miss Perkins, in whom they recognized, uncomfortably, a determination more extreme than their own.

On Top Pitch, at lunchtime, Garvie Smith sprawled on the grass, exhausted. He'd been to three lessons *one after the other*, and was seriously beginning to doubt if he could keep up this level of attendance any longer. With Smudge he shared a calming Benson & Hedges as they listened to Felix report on the funeral, which he'd witnessed earlier in the morning during period one.

It had been a private family affair at Five Mile Methodist Church. But by chance Felix had been on the roof of the newsagent's opposite at the time.

"Nothing private about it," he said. "Massive crowd. Super-massive. All these reporters and photographers. Cameramen, TV crews. About a thousand coppers in the line, looked like. But the weird thing was how everyone was really, really quiet. Eerie quiet. Like it was a . . . a . . ."

"A funeral," Garvie said.

"Well. Yeah."

"What were you doing on the roof?" Smudge asked.

Felix looked vague. "Just looking for something."

Smudge said, "I reckon this is the biggest thing that's ever happened in Five Mile. Can't turn on the TV without seeing her face. And think how many coppers we've had here." He paused and looked at Garvie. "Have you been interviewed yet?"

"No."

"Really? Everybody else has. Even me."

"I'm not cooperating."

"You told them that?"

"Not exactly. They told me."

It was strange, the way the police had ignored Garvie. As Smudge said, they'd interviewed everyone else, not just Chloe's friends but almost all of year eleven, and teachers too, even the janitor and the school nurse. Every day kids were called out of their lessons to go to Tech 2, the "interview room," and sit at the end of a row of tables borrowed from the dining room for what was always called a "little chat about Chloe." It was meant to be confidential. But information given in the strictest privacy in Tech 2 circulated freely in the rest of the school, and at any given time the kids knew significantly more than the police did. It was no surprise to them that Chloe had been the victim of rumor and petty thefts, and that Jessica Walker was behind a lot of it. Or that Chloe was herself the source of other rumors involving luxury cars, millionaire admirers, modeling contracts, and besotted teachers. They were familiar with the notion that she had not just one but several stalkers. They even had a shrewd idea what sort of testimony was being given by the teachers; in fact, they could have informed the police themselves that Mr. MacArthur often gave Chloe a lift home after her training sessions at the track.

But some interesting information came the other way. Conducting his own interviews over cigs up on Top Pitch or in the alleyway by Marsh Fields, Garvie had learned about police interest in three key issues: a black Porsche, the fact that something had upset Chloe on Thursday night, and her unexplained absence from school on Friday afternoon. He'd also learned that the police had been disappointed not to find Alex at the Academy; they were keen to interview him again.

"All that about the Porsche is bollocks though, Garv."

"Is it, Smudge?"

"You know what she was like. 'It's so comfy riding in a Porsche, Smudge. It's so quiet, Smudgy. Everything matches, Smudgster.' Just Chloe-speak, Garv. Like a fantasy."

Garvie thought for a moment. "What about Thursday night? Anyone know where she was?"

Smudge shook his head. "The one question of theirs I couldn't answer, to be fair. Word is she was down Market Square, at some bar. The Black Cat. I don't know."

"Felix?"

"Apparently she said she was going to Jess's, but she never."

"And Friday afternoon?"

Smudge shrugged. "Taking it easy, probably. Friday afternoons I like to go home for a nap. You know, before going out. I need my beauty sleep."

Felix said, "You need more than a nap, my friend. You need to sleep for a thousand years."

"What's your theory, Garv? Know what I reckon?"

"What do you reckon, Smudge?"

"I reckon a vagrant done it. One of them drifters sleeping rough at Four Winds."

"Very likely."

"Yeah, but this is the best bit. Not any old vagrant. Her dad. Her real dad."

"Her real dad's been dead ten years, Smudge."

"Yeah, but come back. From the dead."

Felix chipped in. "Yeah. 'Cause he's been in hiding."

"That's it. In Bolivia, or Kathmandu, or maybe down the Town Road, you know, above a shop."

" 'Cause he's a drugs baron."

"And a zombie. And he's come back to . . . claim his daughter."

"And he shows her the tattoo on his wrist, to prove it to her."

"Yeah, yeah. Tattoo of a llama, like they have in . . . wherever he's been."

"Yeah. But she fights back."

"So he kills her."

"Kills her dead."

"I reckon that's how it happened." Smudge coughed modestly. "What do you think, Garv?"

Garvie took his time finishing his Benson & Hedges, and flicked the butt into the long grass, and said, "MacAttack is a teacher."

There was a long pause while Smudge and Felix looked at each other.

"So?"

"So he doesn't drive a Porsche."

"Yeah, but all that about a Porsche is—"

"Let's pretend for a second it's just as likely as the llama-tattooed zombie real-dad theory."

"I think you're pushing it, but all right."

"MacAttack doesn't drive a Porsche, so where would Chloe go to find one? Where would she go to meet some rich young tosser with a Porsche?"

"Actually, that's pretty simple," Smudge said. "That's easy, that one. Imperium, innit? Down the casino. Plenty of rich idiots in their shiny Porsches down there."

Garvie smiled. "Smudge, my friend. You're a genius. In disguise."

Smudge went pink and spent a long time examining his feet, and when he lifted his head, saying, "Yeah, but what do you think about the—" Garvie was already halfway down the slope toward C Block.

15

At first Abdul didn't recognize him. He was out of his cab, opening the back door and letting him in with all his usual little clicks and murmurings of politeness when he suddenly stopped.

"My Garvie! Is you?"

"The same."

"My Garvie man, what have they do to you?"

They had put him in a single-cuff Jil Sander shirt, vaguely purple, a black dandy jacket by Acne, some Ralph Lauren stretch chinos, also black, and a pair of black brogues. They had hung fake-gold bling from his wrists and neck, and had gelled his hair into shapes unsuspected in the natural world. And they had wrapped around his face a pair of nearly genuine Ray-Bans, acquired—no one knew how— by Felix.

"It's what they call dress code," Garvie said.

Abdul made high-pitched clucking noises of disapproval. "Is foolishness."

"Is Imperium's. Same sort of thing, really. Can you drop me off by the bowling alley next door?"

"*Oui, bien sûr.* We go quick quick so you lose all you money."

They drove down Bulwarks Lane onto Pollard Way and onto the Town Road out of Five Mile toward the city center. The night was lit up with the yellow fizz of streetlamps and the white glare of shop windows and the pulsing red points of the cars' rear lights.

"I trust the police are leaving you alone, Abdul."

At once the little man began to gesticulate anxiously. No, they weren't. They'd questioned him a second time. Did he know Chloe Dow? Had he ever given her a ride in his cab?

"They ask you yet about a black Porsche?"

"*Oui*, they ask." Abdul looked at him in the rearview mirror. "You know black Porsche?"

"Yeah, course. Do you?"

Abdul nodded confidently. "*Oui oui*. I see black Porsche."

Garvie frowned. "Really? Where?"

"Here, there. Big man drive. Big big like this." He puffed out his cheeks.

"There must be dozens of black Porsches in the city, Abdul."

Abdul shrugged. "Big big man," he repeated. "I see him here, see him there. I tell police. They write down their little book. Nothing happen. I know." He tapped the side of his head significantly.

"Who is he, this big man?"

Abdul shrugged again. "He big play . . . big play . . ." He sought for the right word and failed to find it.

"Playboy?"

"*Oui*, Garvie man! *C'est ça*. Big play *boy*." He rubbed his fingers together. "He big big money."

"Well, that figures. He drives a Porsche."

They came at last to The Wicker. Once full of warehouses and workshops, the road had been reclaimed from old industry for entertainment, and now it was a strip of bars and drinking clubs, fast-food outlets, bowling alleys, lap-dancing bars, comedy clubs, movie theaters, and casinos. Everywhere was the colored wash of lights, the muffled thump of music, and the faint, harsh odor of fried food, booze, and aftershave. At nine thirty it was just beginning to get busy.

Abdul let him out at the bowling alley and tutted at him.

"I know, Abdul. Is foolishness."

The man nodded. "Lucky for you I know not tell your mother."

The night was mild and damp. A group of men came past wearing costumes, and Garvie stood in front of the bowling alley looking across at Imperium Restaurant and Casino at the end of the block, a low sleek building of stone and smoked glass fronted with fake Roman columns and a row of miniature potted orange trees, all trimmed into perfect spheres. Soft blue light illuminated it all. The chunky doormen were ostentatiously dressed in dinner jackets and black bow ties. A brilliantly lit giant billboard above them showed a young woman dressed almost entirely in tassels, clapping her hands next to a slogan that read ALL YOU GOT TO DO TO WIN IS PLAY! Garvie turned away, crossed the forecourt of the bowling alley, and slipped down the side of the brick wall separating the properties until he was lost in the shadows. A few moments later he was in Imperium's rear parking lot, an irregular patch of broken concrete in no way compatible with the elegant front.

A two-minute search turned up nothing like a Porsche, black or otherwise. He strolled away into the shadows on the far side of the parking lot, where he lit up and lounged thoughtfully against a less-than-sparkling Renault Clio, waiting. In a little while a couple of cars pulled in, and as the people made their way round to the front, Garvie joined them, and together they went past the doormen—who gave Felix's older brother's membership card no more than a cursory glance—and into the casino.

The carpets were plush, the fittings posh. Garvie went down a hallway lined with slot machines to a sunken circular lobby done out like a miniature amphitheater, where a woman dressed in a short white toga standing behind a fish tank in the form of a Roman urn gave him the eye. Smiling affably, he went on through the cocktail bar, past the restaurant, into the gaming rooms, taking it all in. It was ancient Rome, Hollywood style, a stage set of excessive effects made semi-tasteful by low lighting. The Imperium theme was everywhere: classical statues in ivy-hung alcoves, patches of mosaic on the floor, frescoes, vaguely erotic, on the walls, and the soft sound of lyre music piping from hidden speakers. The Imperium logo, a gold wreath on a gold urn, blazed from the purple baize surfaces of the gaming tables and stood in small gold sculptures above the roulette wheels. It even featured in the plastic name tags pinned to the togas of the waitresses who circulated with trays of drinks: Agrippina, Sabina, Flavia, Livia, and other famous women of ancient Rome.

It was crowded. From every corner of the place came the standard low-grade hubbub of people enjoying losing money, a soft chatter and occasional laughter titivated by the rattle of roulette balls, cards slapped on tables, and the chunter of coins out of one-armed bandits.

Garvie stood in the bar looking around. About four hundred cut-glass bottles of liquor gave back a soft, comforting gleam. Had Chloe come here? She'd talked about Imperium, but then she'd talked about all the clubs and bars in the city. He thought again of that streak in her character, the love of risks. It was a good place to take a risk, to stake it all, to hope for a lucky break. To win. That was her style.

Taking a glass of complimentary sparkling wine from a passing "Agrippina," Garvie set off round the gaming areas, weaving through groups of gamblers and spectators. He sauntered into the baccarat and poker rooms, where a few older men sat silent and intent on the cards that the toga'd croupier flipped from the baize with a thin wooden spatula, and sauntered round the roulette and blackjack tables, crowded with people determined to have fun, and past the noisy slot machines glowing against the dark walls, and sauntered on further to the cocktail bar, where the crowd was thickest, people sitting with drinks and canapés while the white-toga'd waitresses went among them with trays of finger foods and drinks.

For some time he stood by the roulette table, watching. He hadn't seen roulette played before. It was interesting, mathematically. Thirty-eight numbered pockets on a shiny wooden wheel: eighteen red ones, eighteen black, and two—marked 0 and 00—green. The wheel spun in one way in a red-and-black blur, and the white ball ran in the other.

Like a little runner racing round a track, it ran until exhausted, falling at last, bouncing and clacking, into one of the pockets.

The house paid out thirty-five to one on a bet placed on any number. It didn't pay out anything on 0 or 00. Garvie thought about this.

A probability of $1/38$ of winning your bet, a probability of $37/38$ of the bank winning.

$$-1 \times 37/38 + 35 \times 1/38 - 0.0526.$$

In other words, the bank always had a 5.26 percent better chance of winning than the player. Put another way, over the long term the player *always loses*.

Garvie thought again of Chloe and how, if she came here, she came here to win.

There was a commotion suddenly at the other end of the lounge. One of the waitresses had spilled a drink on the shoes of a man who sounded as if he'd been losing at the tables.

She apologized in vain. A man appeared—a bald giant in a black-and-gold striped shirt stretched tight over his watermelon belly. He started smooth-talking the man with the slightly damp shoes and clicking his fingers at the barman and shouting at the waitress. Garvie couldn't hear what he was saying, but he saw how he jabbed his fat finger into her face. It was several minutes before she managed to totter away with her tray, and by then Garvie had seen enough to fear the worst. Grabbing a tumbler of water from the bar, he went out of the lounge the other way fast, and caught up with her as she was trying to negotiate a Staff Only door in a quiet corner among the slot machines.

As he watched, she hesitated, took a step backward, a step forward, wavered, and started to slowly spin.

"Hey," Garvie said, and caught hold of the tray as she went down in a heap, a slow flurry of white toga and dark-brown hair and a soft muffled thump on the nice casino carpet.

He stood there balancing the wildly tilting tray in one hand, and she lay in a faint at his feet, her legs tucked up neatly together, her arms almost lazily spread out at her sides, and her hair fallen back from her face.

The tray balanced itself at last and he glanced down. And stood there staring, the tray forgotten in his hand.

She was beautiful. She was so beautiful he seemed to feel his skin dilate as he looked at her. Her face was very pale, her mouth soft and red, her nose small and precise. Her eyes fluttered open and he saw that they were gray.

"Here's something your mother obviously never told you," he said. "Never faint with a full tray of champagne flutes in your hand."

She sat with her back against the wall while she sipped the water he'd brought. For a minute she was silent, then she gave herself a little shake and said, "I'm okay now," and she sounded it too. Her voice was light and musical. When she looked at him her gaze was clear and amused. "So you can stop looking so pleased with yourself."

Garvie just stared. Her gray eyes were so cool and humorous and large they seemed to pull him in.

"You can stop staring too. Haven't you ever seen a girl dressed up like a harlot from the first century AD?"

At last he found his voice, or bits of it. "I'm Garvie," he said. "Garvie Smith."

"Hypatia. As you can see. Thanks for catching the booze, Garvie. Spillages come out of our wages. Call them wages."

"Hypatia? Nice. What's your real name?"

She smiled, and her mouth curved up toward two neat dimples. "Real names not allowed. They—"

"Come out of your wages, I bet."

"Call them wages."

They stood together by the slot machines looking beyond the roulette wheel and blackjack tables to the coffee lounge, where Bald Giant was now berating the barman.

Garvie nodded. "I don't want to know *his* real name."

"Scumbag," she said. "Though he has others."

"And who is he?"

"He owns the place." She hesitated.

"And?"

She looked at him curiously.

"You can trust me. Hypatia."

She nodded. "He's a complete bastard. Actually, I don't think I'm giving away confidential information."

They watched him back the barman up against the racks of bottles. He flashed gold when he moved. He lifted a fat finger and prodded the barman in the chest, hard.

"He's a big man," Garvie said thoughtfully. "A big, big man. Do you happen to know what sort of car he drives?"

Again she looked at him curiously. "I don't know anything about cars and I don't want to. But it's low and sleek and black and expensive."

Garvie nodded. "It would be," he murmured.

Together they watched the big man as he left the bar. There was a smaller man with him now, in tow, who paused and looked over at where they stood, and scowled.

"Got to go, Garvie Smith. Nice talking to you. But here's a little tip. Finish that bubbly and leave before they check your member's card and find out you're only seventeen or whatever."

"Sixteen," Garvie said. "But thanks. Whatever your name is."

He watched her disappear through Staff Only. A flip of white tunic, a brief brown swirl of hair, and she was gone. Sighing, he turned and made his way through the bar and past the coffee lounge toward the lobby. The small man was scowling at him again, but Garvie ignored him, sauntering on slowly, acknowledging the receptionist behind her fish tank, who smiled at him once more as he passed, sauntering up the circular steps through the glass doors, opened for him by a man in a bulging dinner jacket, and out onto the small frontal plaza, where he encountered Detective Inspector Singh just coming in.

"Good luck at the tables," Garvie said and, putting a finger up to one of his quiffs, carried on into the street and down The Wicker in the direction of home, leaving Singh standing there in a state of silent fury.

16

He stood in front of them, his back to the operational chart, even more uptight than usual. It was the ninth day of the murder investigation and their nineteenth briefing.

He said, very quietly, "I've just come from seeing the chief."

He paused, looking at them.

"The chief has asked me to remind you of something."

He cleared his throat softly, and the muscles in his neck stood out briefly.

"He's asked me to remind you that Chloe Dow was blonde."

They shifted uneasily on their seats, embarrassed, but Singh took no notice. Very carefully, as if they didn't understand, he explained what the chief had meant. That Chloe Dow's picture was going to be in the news everywhere, all the time, nonstop, until the case was closed. This was important—he explained—because it meant that public interest was going to remain at fever pitch. And this was important because it meant that politicians, justices, the heads of criminal investigation, and the self-appointed guardians of a thousand pressure groups would continue to call the chief constable every hour of every day to ask how Singh and his team were progressing with the case.

"And you know why that's important," he said.

There was a grudging silence in the office.

"So let's get to work."

Before he asked them for their reports he briefed them on his interview the previous evening with Nicholas Winder, owner of the Imperium Casino and Restaurant, a typed report of which was already in their dossiers. As they knew, Winder drove a black Porsche. As the report stated, he also had an alibi for the Friday night.

"I hope you've found time to read the transcript. Winder was in the South of France. His Porsche was locked away in his underground garage. Winder lives alone, and only he has the keys to either the car or the garage. It's a nonstarter."

"Pity," Nolan said. "I've personally worked on three cases against him, none of which came to anything. He's a scumbag and ought to be in jail for a hundred other things."

Dowell grunted. "Time to shift resources away from the Porsche. It was a flaky lead to begin with."

Singh made no reply. He asked Collier to begin the briefing with his report on Market Square on Thursday night.

"Big fat zero so far," Collier said. "Nothing showing up on CCTV. No sightings in any of the bars. We're still shaking down the cabbies. But it's not looking good. I think maybe the kids are wrong about this."

Singh frowned. "Lawrence?"

"What the kids are telling us is that Chloe talked a lot about going out to the Market Square clubs. Two places in particular: Chi-Chi and the Black Cat. Half the kids believed her, half didn't. It's hard to tell what the truth is."

Singh flicked through his dossier thoughtfully. "She wasn't quite the girl the media have been showing."

"No. Not so innocent. Pushier. Lots of boasting about modeling contracts, celebrity parties, rich boyfriends, fast cars, that sort of thing. The Market Square clubs and bars are part of that."

Singh turned to Mal Nolan. "Mal?"

"None of this nightlife is corroborated at home. But then, Mrs. Dow seems to have known very little about what her daughter did. Certainly, Chloe could make herself look older if she wanted to. I don't think she'd have had any problem getting into places. I think probably some of what she said was true."

Singh gave no reaction. After a while he turned back to Shan. "Anything else to report from school? What about this teacher? MacArthur."

"A case of guilty conscience." Shan opened his file. "Seems he often gave Chloe a lift home after school. Very often. She used to train on the track and he'd wait for her and run her back in his car. He denies meeting her at other times, but he's defensive. Married, of course. Three kids. Doesn't look as if he's slept since she was killed."

"Anyone else?"

"No other teachers. But the janitor there's a strange man."

"Strange?"

"Nothing I can put my finger on. It's just he gives me the creeps."

"In what way?"

"He's odd. Sort of bottled up. Might just be the nervous type. But he looks like a man who could really lose it. He has an alibi for Friday, so maybe I'm making too much of it."

They waited for Singh to respond, but again he was silent. A tight, distracted look came across his face.

"You haven't talked to the boy Garvie Smith, have you?"

"No. You asked us not to."

He nodded. "I've dealt with him already. He's not helpful. He's"— he searched for the right word and failed to find it—"unhelpful." His mouth twitched. "Let's move on. What's the news from Froggett Woods?"

Mal Nolan said, "Spotty. It's hard to track down all the residents. Quite a few are away traveling on business, some are on holiday. We'll get hold of them all eventually. But in any case most of the houses are round the other side of the woods; it's not likely they'd have heard much going on at Pike Pond."

For a few long moments Singh was silent.

"Pike Pond," he said at last. "Something about it bothers me."

Dowell shrugged. "It was one of her usual routes. She went there a lot, so her mother says."

"It's . . ." Singh paused. "Spooky." He corrected himself. "A fifteen-year-old girl might find it spooky."

"Her favorite route," Collier said. "Besides, it was still broad daylight when she went."

Singh looked at him, thinking. "But the woods. Those ruined buildings." At last he bent his head to the dossier again. "No sightings of vehicles along the road there on Friday."

"No."

"A few references to vagrants. Who are they, Mal?"

She put down two photographs. "Steven Wallis. Known as the Waterman. In and out of Hope House. Sleeps rough sometimes up at Four Winds Farm. And Lloyd Johnson. Twenty-eight. Cautioned for aggravation a few years back."

"Aggravation?"

"Harassing a girl. Claimed she led him on."

"No one else?"

"One more. Not really a vagrant." She put down a third photograph.

Singh nodded. "Alex Robinson."

"Chloe's ex. Six months ago he was picked up at Four Winds selling cannabis to another schoolkid. We've talked to him once already, as you know, after the rumpus he caused at Pike Pond. 'Uncooperative' is how I'd describe him."

"He'll cooperate with me," Singh said. "I've got something else I want to talk to him about." He shut his dossier and sat thinking, and they waited for his summing up.

"Lawrence, bring in MacArthur and shake him down. Bring in the janitor too. I want you to trust your instincts. Mal, locate those two vagrants. Darren, I want all the angles explored at Market Square before we move on." He paused and looked at Bob Dowell. "Bob, I want you to stick with the Porsche inquiries."

In the silence Dowell cleared his throat and the others looked around the room.

"There isn't a kid at the school believes in this Porsche," Dowell said in a low voice.

"Perhaps they're wrong. Just as they might be wrong about Market Square."

"And we've covered all black Porsches in the city already. All of them."

"Then widen the search."

"We don't have the manpower to widen the search."

"Then pull people off the door-to-doors." Singh fixed him with a stare. "I want us to follow our instincts. And this is *my* instinct."

There was silence.

"Any more questions?"

Dowell began to gather his things together.

"Before you go," Singh said. "The calls record. Lawrence?"

Shan winced. "There's still some sort of technical problem, according to the supplier. We've sent down some guys to speed them up."

"I don't think that's effective. You'll need to go down yourself."

Shan nodded.

"Final thing. Why hasn't Alex Robinson been interviewed at the Academy?"

"He's stopped attending."

"Where is he?"

"Some squat out in Limekilns."

"Get me the address. Right. That's all."

It was eleven o'clock. When the others were gone, Singh got up and went into the corner of his office and stood facing the wall. For a moment he was irresolute. His face was pale, the skin around the eyes dark. He began to recite his prayers but, glancing at his watch, broke off and left the office without looking back.

17

Rain came on again as the cab emerged from the underpass. It was a little after half past one; double chemistry was just beginning back at school.

On the other side of the highway traffic was light, no more than a few security vans and council trucks driving between jobs. The sidewalks were quiet too. The only kids Garvie saw were some lads from Sandhills smoking in silence outside a newsagent's. While the cab waited at lights, one of them caught sight of Garvie and gave a brief salute, and Garvie wound down the window and put out a hand as they pulled away. Though it wasn't his neighborhood, he had friends all over the city.

Abdul gave him another nervous look in the rearview mirror, and Garvie said, "What is it, man? You've been twitching ever since we set off."

Abdul attempted one of his famous smiles and his face got stuck halfway. "Miss Dow," he began, and bit his lip.

"What about Miss Dow?"

"Police come visit yesterday."

"Again? That's the third time, Abdul."

"Ask this, ask that. Ask everything, Garvie man. *Très* hard people."

"*Très* dim people. What did they ask you about?"

"Ask all about Thursday." He shot Garvie another anxious glance. "I say, is Friday when Miss Dow decease. *Friday.* I don't work Friday. They say no no, Thursday. Always Thursday. Ask me—who you drive, who you see." He licked his lips. "Where you papers."

"You've got your papers, Abdul."

Abdul looked petrified.

"Do you want my mum to come over and give you a hand? She'll talk to the police for you. They won't know what hit them."

Abdul reached back between the seats and squeezed Garvie's hand.

Garvie said, "It's okay, man. It's safe. You don't need to worry."

Abdul's smile worked properly again.

In the drizzle they drove down Strawberry Way, past the community center, through the Strawberry Hill estate with its garages and tower block, out toward Limekilns.

"Anyway," Garvie said. "Tell me what you told the police about Thursday."

Abdul told him, with his hand against his heart most of the time. He hadn't picked up Chloe on Thursday evening. He hadn't seen Chloe. He hadn't been near Fox Walk. He hadn't seen or picked up Chloe's mother or stepfather. He hadn't even thought about Chloe. He swore it.

"Let's forget Chloe a minute." Garvie thought. "Did you pick up *any* female passengers that night?"

Only one. Abdul picked her up about six from the shops near the Academy and took her down to Market Square in the city center, where most of the bars and clubs were.

"What was she like?"

She wasn't like Chloe.

"It's all right, man. You can forget about Chloe. I'm just interested."

The woman was much older than Chloe for a start, maybe twenty, maybe twenty-five—it was hard to tell with some women. She had a lot of very black hair. And a lot of makeup. Abdul tutted to himself. She was a strange woman.

"How strange?"

She wasn't sure where she wanted to be dropped in Market Square. She made Abdul drive round the one-way system three times while she peered out the window. Then there was the funny business with the tip.

"What business?"

The woman seemed to have no idea how much to give. As if she'd never been in a cab before. She took money out of her purse, put it back, got angry with herself, and in the end gave Abdul a twenty, more than the cost of the ride itself. He'd given it back to her, and she'd gotten flustered and bolted and left him with nothing.

"*Très perturbée*, Garvie man." Abdul laughed and waggled his finger at his head. "Eh? Crazy like cat."

Garvie said nothing for a while.

"Abdul?"

"*Oui?*"

"What was she wearing, this crazy woman?"

Abdul considered this. A blue dress, he thought. And a white jacket. She was dressed up to go out, even though she didn't seem to know where she was going.

"And where did you pick her up?"

"By shop."

"Which shop?"

"Aphrodite shop. You know?"

"Aphrodite's beauty salon?"

Abdul nodded.

"Is that where she'd been?"

Abdul hadn't considered this before but now he saw that Garvie was right. She had so much hair and so much makeup, she must have been in Aphrodite's, getting ready to go out.

They drove on a little way in silence after that. They were in Limekilns now. Here the houses were all prefabs, with wood-paneled fronts and lean-to porches with corrugated plastic roofs. The roads were patched with iron plates. There were no shops. It was a poor area. Garvie wound down the window and leaned out, and even the air tasted poor.

Abdul let him out at a deserted street corner. He was looking anxious again. "This bad bad place, Garvie man."

"It's okay, Abdul. I have a friend lives here. Listen, Abdul."

"Yes?"

"About that woman. Did you tell the police about her?"

He shook his head.

"Maybe you should. Just to be helpful. They might even be grateful."

Abdul looked doubtful, but Garvie didn't say anything else, and in the end he drove off.

Garvie turned off the street and walked down a dirt path across waste ground heaped with rubbish and brambles, under an old railway bridge and along a ditch until he came at last to an abandoned-looking maisonette with boarded-up windows.

Parked outside was a squad car.

At that moment the front door of the maisonette opened and a policeman came out, looking thoughtful. A policeman in a turban. For a second he stood on the doorstep, musing. Then he looked up and his expression changed at once.

"Detective Inspector," Garvie said politely. "Our paths cross again."

Singh removed all traces of surprise from his face and came down the path. "I warned you about interfering with police business," he said.

"I'm not interfering with anything," Garvie said.

"Then why are you here?"

"I just stopped by to score some drugs."

Singh stared at him.

"But," Garvie added considerately, "I promise not to make the transaction until you're far away."

For a moment Garvie thought Singh was going to lose his cool; but the man just blinked and, stepping backward, took a notebook out of his pocket.

At that moment his phone rang. Frowning, he turned away to answer it. Garvie heard him say, "Yes. What do you mean, another technical hitch? Never mind, it doesn't matter. I'm coming now. Yes, now."

He gave Garvie a long bitter look as he went past him and got into his car.

Garvie waved good-bye as he drove off, but the inspector did not return the gesture.

Inside, the squat was semi-derelict: bare boards and crumbling plaster covered in graffiti. There was a smell of old smoke. Downstairs in the front room a couple of kids stopped playing cards when they saw him.

"Got anything for us, Smith?" one said in a whining voice.

"Not today."

The kid spat on the floor and they went back to their game, and Garvie went past them up the splintered stairs to where Alex was camping. Once a back bedroom, it was now a wreck. The sagging ceiling had split open and someone had tried to rip out the washbasin. Alex was lying in a sleeping bag on a mattress in the corner rolling a breezer. He was wearing his varsity jacket, and Garvie looked at it a moment before going over. He crouched down next to him and they touched knuckles.

"Back again?"

"Can't keep away, man. Such a lovely place."

Propped up on one elbow, Alex went on rolling. He was big and powerful for his age: six five at least, and broad. Good-looking too, in a screwed-up-eyed, street sort of way. Until recently he'd been the Marsh Academy's premier athlete, star of the soccer team and all-round action man. But though he looked tough, he was usually gentle, soft even. When Chloe dumped him he'd fallen apart. Since her death he seemed to have lost the will to live. Like the squat itself, he was in a state of terminal disrepair, his former laid-back manner a distressing sham.

"Don't think it's much good for your health, to be honest," Garvie said.

Alex shrugged.

"Or your nerves. Those kids downstairs get nastier and younger every time I come here."

Alex said, "I got protection."

"Protection! You sound like a TV gangster. Don't you miss your mum and sister? Or your home comforts? I still remember your mum's stews."

Alex scowled. "I'm no pussy."

Garvie looked around. "What would your mum say about this place, big man?"

"I can look after myself."

"What would Chloe say?"

Alex shut his mouth and gave Garvie a fierce look, which Garvie ignored.

"What would she say, Alex?"

There was a long silence in the squalid room.

"Leave it, Garv," Alex said in a low thick voice of gravel and chalk. "She ain't around to criticize no more."

Reaching into his sleeping bag, he took out a small packet and tossed it toward Garvie.

Garvie shook his head.

"What you doing here, then?"

"Interfering with police business."

Alex rolled his eyes. "I done my bit. Okay? Got punched on, spent a night in the cells. Your man in the turban's just been here again."

"I know, I just met him. Looking surprised."

"Surprised?"

"Surprised he didn't find a Porsche parked outside, I think."

Alex sneered. "All that about a Porsche. Is nonsense, Garv. You know that. She didn't ride in no Porsche."

"Still. Everybody knows dealers drive those things. Singh probably thought you had three or four."

"Not even funny, Garv."

"Blinkie drives one."

Alex's glance flicked at Garvie and swerved away again. "Who?"

"That gangster you run with. Dude with the eye patch."

"I don't run with Blinkie."

"But he has a Porsche, right?"

"Maybe. How would I know?"

"And it's black. Right?"

"I don't run with Blinkie. I never been in his Porsche."

"All right, Alex. Stay calm, mate. I'm just trying to get inside Plod's head."

Alex grimaced and rubbed his hand across the top of his head. "I can't take much more, Garv."

Garvie nodded. "I know. What did you tell him, by the way? The plod."

"Nothing."

"Good. Just a few questions, then. Won't take long."

Alex finished rolling his breezer, lit up, and lay back down, scowling up at the ceiling.

"I'll be gentle with you," Garvie said.

18

Location: slum dwelling; upstairs room; decor distressed; smell of wet chalk and piss.

Aspect of interviewer: casual; cute; dressed in black, rumpled Marsh Academy school uniform.

Aspect of interviewee: tense; shiny-faced; dressed in white tank top and trackies.

DI GARVIE SMITH: So. You were harassing her.

ALEX ROBINSON: [*obscene phrase*]

DI GARVIE SMITH: Calling her, texting her, following her.

ALEX ROBINSON: You know it. [*Smokes, passes breezer*] Everybody knows it. So what?

DI GARVIE SMITH: So what happened?

ALEX ROBINSON: Nothing happened. She didn't want nothing to do with me. No calls. No texts. She'd walk away from me in the street even.

DI GARVIE SMITH [*smokes*]: You used to watch her at the track, right? After school.

ALEX ROBINSON: After school, lunchtime. She used to get the Scot to come shoo me. Like some little dog. You seen it, Garv.

DI GARVIE SMITH: I remember. [*Passes breezer*] So was it you stole her running shoes?

ALEX ROBINSON [*snorts*]: That's weird.

DI GARVIE SMITH: Weird?

ALEX ROBINSON: Your man in the turban asked that too.

DI GARVIE SMITH [*laughs*]: Singh's learning. *Did* you steal them, Alex?

ALEX ROBINSON: Never took nothing of hers. Wish I had, almost. Something to keep. [*Smokes*] If you want to know about Chloe's stuff being stole, ask Jess. [*Passes breezer*]

DI GARVIE SMITH: I already did. This is good, by the way. [*Lengthy silence*]

ALEX ROBINSON: That it, then? Detective Smith.

DI GARVIE SMITH: Not quite. Done any deals up at Pike Pond recently?

ALEX ROBINSON: No, man.

DI GARVIE SMITH: Sure?

ALEX ROBINSON: I ain't used that place for . . . I don't know. Weeks. I told all this already to the copper.

DI GARVIE SMITH: So when did you last see Chloe? Was it on the Friday? Friday afternoon?

ALEX ROBINSON: No way on Friday.

DI GARVIE SMITH: Thought you kept tabs on her every day. Isn't that what stalkers do?

ALEX ROBINSON: Thursday I saw her. After school. She was on the track. Didn't speak to her. Didn't even get near her. Usual story. Pretended I wasn't there.

DI GARVIE SMITH: Here. [*Passes breezer*]

ALEX ROBINSON [*smokes*]: You done now?

DI GARVIE SMITH: Nearly. Last thing. Just tell me what you told Singh just now.

ALEX ROBINSON: I didn't tell him nothing. [*Passes breezer*]

DI GARVIE SMITH: Yeah, you did. Something secret. Something you're not telling me. He told me on his way out.

ALEX ROBINSON: He *told* you?

DI GARVIE SMITH: The expression on his face told me. Just before he looked surprised he looked thoughtful. Like someone who's just found something out.

ALEX ROBINSON: Garvie, man, you're a freak. All right. It's not such a big deal. I was in Chloe's garden on Friday.

DI GARVIE SMITH: You said you didn't see her on Friday. So it must have been Friday night, later on.

ALEX ROBINSON: Yeah. Late. No, I didn't see her.

DI GARVIE SMITH [*smokes*]: What were you doing? [*Passes breezer*]

ALEX ROBINSON: Nothing. Just watching the house. Thought she might show up. [*Smokes*] Wasn't the first time I'd been there at night, to be honest. It used to help, to see her sometimes, you know, up in her bedroom window. Not that night. Not any night now. [*Silence*] Anyway, when Plod turned up I went over the fence.

DI GARVIE SMITH: And he saw you.

ALEX ROBINSON [*shaking his head*]: No way. Too dark for that. I was just unlucky.

DI GARVIE SMITH: Unlucky how?

ALEX ROBINSON [*lifts up the sleeve of his jacket*]: See where the button's gone? It got ripped off on the fence going over. He found it. [*Passes breezer*]

DI GARVIE SMITH: What a clever plod that Singh is. [*Smoking*] That's good, Alex. But you're still not telling me the truth, are you?

ALEX ROBINSON: What's not the truth?

DI GARVIE SMITH: You weren't in the garden to catch a sight of *her*, were you?

[*Silence*]

DI GARVIE SMITH: You wanted to see her new boyfriend, didn't you?

ALEX ROBINSON: Jesus, Garv. Your man told you that too?

DI GARVIE SMITH: You told me.

ALEX ROBINSON: What? When?

DI GARVIE SMITH: Don't you remember what you shouted at Pike Pond? "What did you do it for, you stupid bitch?" Felix said you must have thought she'd killed herself, but that didn't make any sense. I wondered what she could have done to make you so mad. And I thought maybe seeing someone new.

ALEX ROBINSON: All right, then. You worked it out right.

DI GARVIE SMITH: How long had you been looking for him?

ALEX ROBINSON: Few weeks.

DI GARVIE SMITH: And who was he?

ALEX ROBINSON: I don't know. I never found out. She hid him.

DI GARVIE SMITH [*passes breezer*]: But you had some idea of the sort of person he might be.

ALEX ROBINSON: Yeah. Bastard sort.

DI GARVIE SMITH: Obviously someone she didn't want people to know about.

ALEX ROBINSON: Right. She was hiding him away.

DI GARVIE SMITH: Someone older? Maybe someone she met clubbing. Some married guy.

ALEX ROBINSON: I don't know, Garv.

DI GARVIE SMITH: Someone a little bit dangerous maybe. Someone with a bit of money. And a Porsche.

ALEX ROBINSON: That's bollocks about the Porsche. I never saw no Porsche. You know what she was like, Garv. Just dreaming. She was definitely seeing someone, though, I could tell. I could tell something else too. She wasn't happy. [*Smokes*] You're right: It was making me mad.

DI GARVIE SMITH: But you don't have any idea who it might have been?

ALEX ROBINSON: No.

DI GARVIE SMITH: But you were looking for him?

ALEX ROBINSON: That's right. And would've found him, in the end.

DI GARVIE SMITH: And what would you have done to him when you found him?

ALEX ROBINSON: [*smokes in silence*]

DI GARVIE SMITH: Right. And what would you have done to Chloe?

[*Silence*]

DI GARVIE SMITH: Alex? Alex, mate. You didn't do anything stupid, did you?

ALEX ROBINSON [*smokes*]: Listen to me now. I know what you thought of her, you and Smudge and Felix and everybody. You didn't have a clue, none of you. Didn't have the first idea who she was. No one knew her, except me. It's true. I was the only one. Not her mam, not the Scot, not the bastard sort. Not even you, Garv, and you shared time with her. Only me. So how could I hurt her? Never would have happened. Never, never. No matter what she did to me. People say otherwise, they're going to learn—

DI GARVIE SMITH: Calm, man. Calm. I understand. Still, we have a small problem.

ALEX ROBINSON: What small problem now?

DI GARVIE SMITH: You're right, I've been coming here too often. That button on your sleeve?

ALEX ROBINSON: What about the button?

DI GARVIE SMITH: It's been missing over a month. The button Singh showed you is from someone else's jacket.

ALEX ROBINSON: *What?*

DI GARVIE SMITH: That's right.

ALEX ROBINSON [*silence*]: But that means . . .

DI GARVIE SMITH: You weren't the only one hiding in Chloe's garden.

[*Silence*]

Garvie got to his feet, nodded, and went over to the door. Alex lay in his sleeping bag, staring in confusion at the remains of the breezer between his fingers.

Garvie stopped in the doorway. "Oh. Nearly forgot. Couple of things. Did she ever ask you for money? Probably not, seeing as you weren't speaking. But did she?"

"Money? No. Even if she was talking to me, why would she ask me for money? I ain't got no money."

"Good point. All right, something else. About Thursday after school. After training at the track."

"Yeah?"

"She went home?"

"I think."

"MacAttack give her a lift?"

"Not that night." Alex frowned. "He was there, though. Pretending like he'd just run into her accidental-like, as usual. Looked as if she was going to ride with him but they just talked, then she walked off."

"You didn't follow her?"

"I knew she wasn't happy with me. I wasn't going to make things worse."

"I see. Did she have her kit bag with her?"

Alex slowly shook his head. "No. Nothing."

Garvie nodded. "Good. Now we know where her running shoes were that night."

He loitered in the doorway a moment longer, thinking. He said, "And what was she wearing?"

Alex looked blank.

"Come on, Alex. Think. It's funny, but the key to all this always comes back to the same thing. What. Was Chloe. Wearing."

After a long time Alex said, "Now you say it, I remember. She didn't have on her uniform no more. Some sort of dress."

"Color?"

"Blue. And a white jacket."

Garvie nodded, fell silent. He stood in the doorway without moving.

"You all right, Garv?"

He looked up. "Alex?"

"What?"

"You're not going to do anything stupid now, are you?"

He shook his head. "No, man."

"We're going to find out who killed Chloe."

"Okay."

"Will you do something for me?"

"What?"

"I might need you to come into school for half an hour or so tomorrow."

"Why?"

"Never mind that now. I'll give you a call and let you know. But you'll come?"

"If you need me, I'll be there."

Before he left Garvie looked back at his friend in the sleeping bag. "Hey. It'll be over soon. And when it's over, you'll be able to leave this place and go home. Think of that. Think of your mum's stew."

Alex didn't say anything. Turning heavily in his bag, he faced the rotting wall.

19

One of the problems with Marsh Academy was the way it looked. It looked like a cross between a prison and a rehab center: three securitized blocks of bile-colored brick and smeary glass set randomly along a sprawl of asphalt yard marked out in colored paint for younger kids' games. It was inconvenient too. On the one hand, everywhere was a surprisingly long way from everywhere else. Getting from one lesson to the next frequently involved a lengthy trek along scuffed corridors, up and down dimly lit stairs and in and out of desolate, echoing halls. On the other hand, some places were far too close to one another. The year eleven lockers, for instance, were in the corridor right outside Tech 2, where the police interviews were still taking place, with people going in and out all the time. Worse, Tech 1, Garvie's homeroom, was just round the corner. Worse than both these things, at the end of the lockers was the door to C Block 8, where, in period three, Garvie Smith was meant to be having further math.

But it couldn't be helped.

Chloe Dow's locker was third in from the end on the top row. Like the others, it was fifty centimeters or so tall and thirty wide, and it opened and shut like the lockers at swimming pools, with a key on an orange plastic fob. Even when it was locked, it wouldn't be hard to break in with a bit of force, but—as Garvie had discovered—there was no sign of any force on the door of Chloe's locker: no scraping, no scratches, no buckling. The metal door was straight and clean.

Garvie stood there for a moment considering this. Then he retreated from the lockers—taking care to slip quickly past the door of C Block 8—and went back down the stairs.

He found the janitor in his room. He was a young man with strong, stooped shoulders and a watchful, sullen attitude. His name was Naylor and he was known to be an oddball. Although he was often seen stomping around the school with his toolbox or wheelbarrow, fixing things or sweeping up, he rarely spoke and never made eye contact. He was considered good-looking, however. Silent and rough round the edges. Girls noticed him.

He didn't seem to understand what Garvie wanted. This was because Garvie was being deliberately obscure. Five minutes later, sullenly grumbling, he accompanied Garvie across the yard to C Block, up the stairs and along the corridor to the lockers outside Tech 2.

"I don't know what you're after," he said again. "You need to see a teacher. I'm busy. I got no time for this. *Bloody* kids," he muttered under his breath.

"Won't take long," Garvie replied. He went up to Chloe's locker and tried to open it with his key. "See? My key's not working. And I really need to get my stuff."

Naylor said scornfully, "That ain't even your—" and stopped, as if astonished at himself.

Garvie looked at him curiously. "Not my what? Not my locker?"

Naylor didn't reply. When Garvie met his eyes he immediately looked away and began to chew his lip. "I ain't got time for this," he said again. He gave a nervous twitch.

"Oh wait," Garvie said. "You're right. It's that girl's. The one who got . . . Funny how you knew it was hers."

Clenching his fists, Naylor began to take deep, scratchy breaths.

"Why don't you open it anyway?" Garvie said.

Naylor became oddly still. He lifted his head and looked at Garvie, his face rigid, his eyes cold, as if calculating how to deal with him.

Garvie took no notice. "I mean, with your pass key," he went on. He paused. "No need to break in and risk leaving telltale scratches, is there?" he added quietly.

A look of fury flashed across Naylor's face. Glancing quickly down the empty corridor, he took a step forward and pushed his face into Garvie's.

Backed up against the lockers, Garvie raised his eyebrows.

"Why can't you bastards ever leave me alone?" the man hissed.

Then a voice came from behind them, a voice with just the right amount of threat in it.

"Hey, you."

Alex Robinson was striding down the corridor. Naylor turned and, after a moment's hesitation and a last, twisted look at Garvie, flung himself away and went off in the other direction with that peculiar stomping walk of his.

"Sorry I'm late, man," Alex said. "So long since I been here, couldn't remember where the lockers were."

"Perfect timing. Just thought I'd like you here in case he kicked off."

"Is that what he was doing?"

Garvie considered this. "Don't know. Probably he's harmless. But odd. Very odd."

Together they watched Naylor disappear.

"What was he doing here, anyway?"

"Trying not to tell me what I already knew."

"What was that?"

But before Garvie could reply there was a sudden clipping footstep in the corridor behind them, and a familiar sarcastic voice said, "Well, well. Two birds with one stone."

They turned.

Miss Perkins—Queen Bitch and Garvie's math teacher—stood in the doorway of C Block 8 fixing them with one of her celebrated stares.

"Alex Robinson, report to the head. Garvie Smith, welcome back to planet Earth. I've just been talking to your mother on the phone."

20

It was the end of another seven-hour morning. Singh sat in his office with Shan and Nolan, discussing the new development. A cab driver had come forward to tell them about a young woman he'd picked up on Thursday evening.

"He wouldn't swear to it. In fact, at first he insisted it wasn't Chloe. I'm not even sure why he came in—he's a confused sort of guy. Foreign gent. The woman he picked up didn't sound a bit like Chloe to begin with. She had black hair for a start. But when I showed him Chloe's photograph he started to change his mind. The thing is, the woman was that heavily made up it was hard to recognize her at first. False eyelashes, hair extensions, the works. And guess where he picked her up?"

"Where?"

"Aphrodite's beauty salon."

"Aphrodite's? That's near the Academy, isn't it?"

"Just round the corner. He picked her up at six."

"She could have gone there straight from the school track."

"Making herself look different," Nolan said. "Black wig. Lots of makeup. Making herself look older."

Shan nodded. "That's it. The cabbie said she did look older than Chloe—at least twenty, he thought. But she acted young. When he dropped her off she had no idea how much to tip him. She gave him way too much. He gave it back, he said."

"I bet he did," Mal Nolan said. "They're like saints, those cabbies." There was a silence.

"Anyway," Shan said. "The beautician at Aphrodite's confirmed it. It's solid. It was definitely Chloe."

There was a pause. Singh said quietly, almost to himself, "She was just a kid. That's what her stepfather said. He was right. She dressed herself up to look older, she pretended she was sophisticated, but she didn't even know how to tip a cab driver." He sat in silence for a moment. "What did she get herself into?" he murmured.

He looked up at Shan. "But the obvious immediate question is, where did the cabbie take her?"

"You can guess it. Market Square."

They sat in silence for a moment absorbing this information.

"We need an artist's impression, Lawrence."

"Already onto it. Should be ready in a couple of hours."

"Mal, I want you to go down to the Dows' and see if you can find the blue dress and white jacket. We were right to be looking at Market Square. But we were looking for the wrong person. I'll get on to Darren. He needs to rerun the CCTV, re-interview the Market Square crowd. We're not looking for a blonde schoolgirl, we're looking for an older black-haired woman in a blue dress and white jacket." He reflected. "She might have met someone in a place there—or she might have been picked up and driven somewhere else." He paused. "In a black Porsche, perhaps."

He looked up, and Nolan met his eyes and shook her head. "Still no sightings at Pike Pond and we've interviewed nearly everyone now. There's just a couple of guys left, both abroad and not returning our calls—one in the Australian outback; one, I think, in Botswana. Anyway, so far the only vehicle seen up there Friday night was a van. I put it in my report this morning."

Singh nodded. "I saw. Ten o'clock. White van. It's Mr. Dow's. He already told us he drove up there looking for Chloe." He went on: "All right. Lawrence? What's the news from the school? What about MacArthur?"

"Well, we re-interviewed him."

"And?"

"I think his interest in Chloe was unprofessional. He's showing a lot of strain. But I don't think he did anything, let alone killed her. Anyway, it turns out he has an alibi. He did say something interesting, though."

"What?"

"We've been asking the kids if Chloe had changed in any way recently. Most of them haven't a clue. I get the impression they'd pretty much stopped paying attention to what she told them about her modeling contracts and celebrity parties and so on. But MacArthur said something. Wait, I've got it here." He flipped through his notebook. "He'd been 'teasing' her—his own word—about her glittering future, and she said, 'I don't want to talk about it.'"

He closed the notebook. "It stuck in his mind. He couldn't remember Chloe ever passing up an opportunity to talk about herself. Maybe she was just tired or in a bad mood. But all her life she can't stop talking about what she's going to do, then suddenly she won't talk about it at all?"

Singh got up and walked to the window and looked out. "Chloe's turning out to be a girl with a secret," he said quietly. "I don't like it. Was she just making herself look older on Thursday? Or was she putting on a disguise? And what was she doing on Friday afternoon before she went for her run?" He turned and looked fiercely at the operational chart behind him, still blank for Friday afternoon. He thought for a moment and came back to his desk. "Anything else? What about that janitor? Does his alibi stand up?"

Mal Nolan nodded. "I interviewed him. He was drinking with a friend in a pub called the Jolly Boatman down by the canal. It checks out. But there's something that doesn't. I went back through his file and his past employment records are missing. The school's chasing them up. Again, it's probably nothing. But I agree with Lawrence. He's an oddball. Unstable, somehow."

"Get Archives to double-check the records on the database."

She nodded again.

"And I'll talk to Bob about the Porsche. He's moving too slowly."

After they left Singh sat at his desk, immobile, staring at the opposite wall.

Chloe Dow, a girl with a secret.

He went out of his office and spoke to his assistant. There were seventeen demands for statements from various news outlets, ten requests for interviews, and three messages from the chief.

Singh sighed. "I'll call him now. Did the pathologist ring? I left him a couple of messages about the new autopsy report."

"No."

"Keep trying to get hold of him. It's important I speak to him. Anytime for the rest of the day. This evening if necessary."

"Yes, sir."

Then he went back into his room and prepared to call the chief.

21

Garvie Smith was in trouble. He'd been in trouble half his life, in fact, and gradually he'd grown used to it, even come to like it in a funny sort of way. But this time the trouble was more serious: He'd just been put through a three-way conversation with his mother and Queen Bitch on the speakerphone in the teacher's office.

It was hard to know why adults were so uptight, why they endlessly nagged about unimportant details, why they couldn't see the futility of their self-defeating cycles of threats. It was so boring. The school would start to obsess about something, they'd get heavy with him, he'd make the promises they wanted to hear, the school would back off, huffing and puffing a bit, and everything would return to normal until the next time, when it would start up all over again.

What was the point? Really, it would have been beneath his notice if this time they hadn't gotten his mother involved.

He thought briefly, uneasily, of his mother.

There was that job offer of hers from Barbados. He was used to her planning changes that never happened, but this felt different.

She'd mentioned it again on the phone, and the tone of her voice made him think she had news to tell him.

Then there was the other thing, the usual thing. He didn't actually want to piss her off. Yes, he could argue with her. Yes, she was unfair, dictatorial, unforgiving, endlessly on his case. But piss her off? She'd had enough of being pissed off in her life. Now she'd scheduled a "serious talk" with him before they went out to have dinner with Uncle Len and Aunt Maxie—and he knew what that meant.

It was the *interrogations* he didn't need.

So he walked up Bulwarks Lane, thinking. He'd gotten as far as the shops when his phone rang. He looked at it and sighed before he spoke.

"Jess."

"Hey, bad boy. Want to come over?"

"Nothing would please me more. But I have an appointment with a firing squad."

"What, like the army?"

"No, Jess. Like my mother."

"You're funny, Garv."

"Yes, I'm hilarious. Though in approximately fifteen minutes I'm also going to be dead."

"Don't you want to come over instead?"

"Jess. We seem to be stuck in a time loop. Nothing would please me more, but, et cetera, et cetera."

"Got something to tell you."

There was a silence.

"Garv?"

"Go on, then. I'm waiting. Tell me."

"Tell you when you get here, bad boy."

"Tell me tomorrow, Jess. Or next week. Or can it keep till this time next year?"

"It's about Chloe."

Garvie stopped walking. He sat down on the bench outside Jamal's. "What about Chloe?"

"Something you don't know, Sherlock."

Garvie thought about this. He looked at his watch. "I bet I do."

"Not this. No one knows this." She lowered her voice to a whisper so hissy Garvie could almost feel wetness on his phone. "Not even Mr. Police Turban."

"You're lying."

She giggled. "I wouldn't lie to you, Garv. I'm not a bad girl. I'm not *always* a bad girl."

Garvie looked at his watch, considered the situation. "I'll be there in ten," he said, and hung up.

Jessica Walker's house was in one of the narrow streets at the edge of East Field, a brick house in a row of brick connected houses behind worn patches of earth and spasmodic hedges. All the parked cars were builders' vans or taxis.

It was right next to the school. Garvie considered this while he waited at the door.

Jessica let him in. "Mum's not back yet," she said. "So we're all alone," she added. "Hope you're not scared."

"I am, a bit," Garvie said. "And I really haven't got much time."

He followed her into a front room decorated entirely in purple. Purple shag carpet, two-tone purple wallpaper, dark purple woodwork. The sofa was purple, the lampshades were purple, and the furniture was off-purple. Jessica's gray cat, Barbecue, was almost the only non-purple thing in the room; he lay fatly on the warm ledge in the bay window where the afternoon sun shone strongest.

"Want a drink?" Jessica said. "Get you a beer if you want one."

"You haven't got anything to shield my eyes from all this purple, have you?"

She just stared at him. She'd changed out of her uniform into a tight T-shirt and denim shorts. All she had on her feet was nail polish (purple), very bright and badly scuffed.

"Thanks, but no beer," he said. "No time. You said you knew something about Chloe."

"Something you don't know." She patted the purple sofa. "Come over here and I'll tell you."

As soon as he sat down she swung her legs across his lap. Garvie removed them.

"Look, Jess. I haven't got time. And I really doubt you know any-thing about Chloe that I don't."

"Do too."

Garvie stared at her for a moment. Then he said, "If you're going to tell me that Mr. Police Turban's been here interviewing you, don't bother, I already knew that."

Jessica said defensively, "It was a special interview, 'cause I knew her so well."

Garvie went on. "And if you're going to tell me you told him Alex was stalking Chloe, don't bother—I already know that too."

Jessica flushed. "I never," she said. "Not like that. I just—"

"And don't bother telling me that Singh asked if you stole Chloe's running shoes, because I know he did. And don't tell me you said you didn't, because I know that too. Though, by the way, we both know you stole a lot of her other stuff."

"Oh . . . ," Jessica said, and fell silent.

"Well?" Garvie said. "Can I go now?"

Jessica found her voice. "No. There's something else."

Garvie looked at her for several seconds. "Is it about Naylor?" he asked suddenly.

"Who?"

"The janitor at school."

Jessica flushed again, across her throat this time, and down her chest above the neckline of her T-shirt. "Well, no. But . . ."

"But what?"

"Now you mention it, there *was* something odd about him and Chloe. He was always staring at her."

"Everyone stared at Chloe. You know that."

"No, but . . . she liked it."

Garvie considered this. "She liked *him?*"

"I don't know. I don't think so. But she . . . liked him looking. You know what she was like. Always flaunting herself. I thought it was wrong. And he's a bit, you know, strange."

"Yeah. I'd noticed that. A bit psycho. One minute he's a jumble of nerves, the next he looks as if he's working out how to kill you." He looked at his watch. "Sorry, but I've really got to go, Jess. You don't understand. If I'm late . . ."

He removed her legs once more, got up, and went across the room. But he hadn't gotten as far as the door when he heard her say, in a small voice, "There *is* something else. Serious, Garv."

He sighed and turned back. "You sure, Jess? 'Cause if I'm honest I don't think you'd know what serious was if it reared up and bit you in the back of the leg."

She looked up at him the way she always did, with big, melting eyes. "I was the last person to see her alive," she said in a hoarse whisper. And then she burst into tears.

He sat on the sofa with his arm round her.

"Better now?"

She stopped sniffling and he took his arm away and she put it back again.

"Okay, then. But now you have to tell me. When did you see her?"

She wiped her nose on Garvie's shirtsleeve and took a deep breath. "Friday afternoon."

"What time?"

"Two."

"Where? School?"

She shook her head. "Here."

"How come you were home?"

"I wasn't feeling great. Besides, I was going out later, so I thought I'd have a little nap. You know."

"Yeah, I know, get your beauty sleep. Who else have you told?"

"No one."

"Not even Mr. Police Turban?"

"I've been too scared. It was scary, Garv. I just keep thinking of it. Me, the last person to see her alive. I mean, except for the man . . . the man who . . ."

Garvie waited until she had stopped crying again.

"All right now," he said. "Take your time and tell me exactly what happened."

Chloe had turned up, Jess said, lugging her sports bag with her, looking like a refugee from hell. It was a double shock. They hadn't spoken to each other since arguing earlier in the week when they'd been studying for a math test together at Chloe's house. More shocking was the way she looked, standing there on the doorstep. Her hair was all over the place, her eyes were small and creased, and her mouth looked bruised, as if she'd been biting her bottom lip. It gave her such a strange expression that although Jess had been about to ask her what she was doing there, with her kit bag and everything, the first thing she said was, "What's happened?"

Chloe just shook her head and went past Jessica into the front room, where she stood by the window looking out.

Jessica asked her if she wanted anything, and after a moment Chloe shook her head again, distractedly.

"It was like she was in some sort of trance," Jessica said.

"Then what?"

Chloe had relaxed enough to ask for a glass of water and they talked a bit, about trivial things. But even while they talked, Chloe never sat down; she kept moving around the room, carrying that bag of hers, glancing out the window. A few minutes later she abruptly said she had to go. And, without saying good-bye, she marched back down the hall, Jessica scurrying behind her, and out the door and across the bare earth of the front garden as far as the corner of the hedge, where she paused, looking back at Jessica, and gave her a lopsided smile. Then she turned away and was gone.

"Gone," Jessica said mournfully. "Just gone. Gone for good, Garv."

Garvie sat on the purple sofa gazing at the purple carpet. "What time did she leave?"

"About half past."

He sat there thinking in silence, and Jess sat next to him, gazing at his face.

He said, "Why did she come here?"

"I dunno. That was the weird thing. She never said."

"Tell me what she did say."

"Nothing. Boring stuff. You know. About the weekend and that."

He looked at her sternly. "I need you to remember everything, Jess. Did she ask you for money?"

"No. I told you before."

"Did she say anything about a new man?"

She shook her head.

"Anyone call her while she was here?"

"No one."

"Did she say anything about a Porsche?"

"Give it a rest, Garv. Everyone knows that was bollocks."

"Anything about the Imperium?"

"What, the casino? No, nothing."

"Think, Jess. Please. There must have been something. Something unusual, something odd, something that didn't make sense."

She shook her head.

"*Think*, Jess."

She put her little fists against the sides of her head and screwed up her face until her eyes bulged, and fell back against Garvie with a defeated sigh.

Garvie frowned, and there was a long silence in the purple room.

"Wait . . . ," she said in a slow, faraway voice. "There was something."

"What?"

"Not exactly odd. Rude, really."

"What, Jess?"

She looked at him, and her eyelids fluttered coyly. "Can't you guess, Sherlock?"

He stared back for two, three long seconds, and a look came over his face. "Yes," he said. "Yes, I can."

"Really?" She looked put out.

"She said, 'What big feet you've got.' Didn't she, Jess?"

She gave a little frump of a sigh. "Lucky guesser. She said, 'You're all right, Jess—it's just your feet are too big.' And then she did this stupid little laugh. I thought, *Cheeky cow*. Typical Chloe. Garv? What you doing, Garv?"

He'd jumped up and was looking down at her, his face pale.

"What were you wearing? Was it your Nikes? Your mauve-and-white Nikes?"

"Yeah, that's right. Never knew you'd noticed my Nikes, Garv. You been watching me?"

He said, half to himself, "They would have been perfect."

"Garv?"

"I know why she came here. She needed a pair of running shoes. And yours were a perfect match, Jess. But you're, what, size eight?"

"Eight and a half."

"And she took a six."

"I still don't get it. Why did she need them?"

He looked at her for a long moment. "Because her life depended on it."

The way he said it made her eyes flood suddenly with tears. "What? I don't . . . I didn't . . ." She shook her head in distress.

"Doesn't matter. Not your fault." He paused. "At least I know now about the money."

"What money? *Garv!* I don't understand."

He was silent and calm again. Stepping forward, he bent down and put his lips to the top of Jessica's head. "Thanks, Jess. You did good."

Wet-eyed and bewildered, she looked up at him, smiling. "Do you want to stay a bit longer, Garv? I can get you that beer."

"A bit longer?" He looked at his watch and clapped a hand to his forehead.

"You don't have to go, do you, Garv?" Jessica said. "If you stay, I'll . . ."

But he'd already gone. She heard the door slam and the receding sound of running steps across the earth and into the street.

22

Location: notoriously claustrophobic interview room (steamed-up window, hanging laundry, ironing board); interviewer and interviewee sitting facing each other across the kitchen table (empty except for sauce bottle, glass of milk, documents typed on official Marsh Academy notepaper under general heading Attendance).

Aspect of interviewer: intimidating; bug-eyed; vengeful.

Aspect of interviewee: disheveled; cute; wary.

GARVIE'S MOTHER [*picking up sample page of document*]: Do you want to go through them one by one?

GARVIE SMITH: Do we have time?

GARVIE'S MOTHER: Okay, then. I'll just pick a few. This morning, period three, further math.

GARVIE SMITH: I told you. I was in school. Even Perkins admits that. I just . . . forgot about the lesson.

GARVIE'S MOTHER: Ah, yes. Boy with famous memory forgets lesson. All right now. Yesterday, period four, double chemistry.

GARVIE SMITH: Same thing. It slipped my mind.

GARVIE'S MOTHER: Ah right, that famous mind again. Or did you think the lesson had been relocated to Limekilns? Where Detective Inspector Raminder Singh encountered you at half past two in the afternoon.

GARVIE SMITH: Oh, *that* double chemistry? Well, I—

GARVIE'S MOTHER: Okay. Monday now. Period four, geography. Period five, English. Period six, history. Clean sweep of absences, three in a row.

GARVIE SMITH: I'm pretty sure I went to at least one of them.

GARVIE'S MOTHER: Says here [*reading*], "Garvie Smith and Liam Fricker absent all afternoon. Liam Fricker later picked up on the roof of Spinks newsagent's."

GARVIE SMITH: I definitely don't remember going up on Spinks's roof.

GARVIE'S MOTHER: I'm not going to beat around the bush with you, Garvie. You're missing all kinds of school. How do you think you're going to pass any exams?

GARVIE SMITH: Academic qualifications aren't everything—you told me that.

GARVIE'S MOTHER: I'm making an exception for you. For you they're a matter of life or death. We've been through this. You know what I'm about. Look at this here, Garvie. So-called "Felix" Fricker burglarizing the newsagent. Alex Robinson selling that stuff out at Limekilns. Ask yourself! What sort of friends you hanging around with?

GARVIE SMITH: They're all right. Alex is just in a bad space right now. And Felix is . . . Felix doesn't often get caught, to be fair.

GARVIE'S MOTHER: And you? You're getting caught quite often, aren't you? By the police now. Tell me this. How much are you smoking? If I walk into your room now, how much of that stuff am I going to find?

GARVIE SMITH: I really hope none of it.

GARVIE'S MOTHER: You're getting into trouble. Trouble with your teachers. Trouble with the police. More and more trouble. [*Silence*] Look me in the eye now and tell me it's nothing to do with that poor girl.

GARVIE SMITH: What poor girl?

GARVIE'S MOTHER: Don't give me "what poor girl." This morning I've had Detective Inspector Raminder Singh on the phone telling me you're going straight to a correctional facility if you interfere with his investigation again.

GARVIE SMITH: He's just a hothead, Mum.

GARVIE'S MOTHER: And Mrs. Dow telephoning me to thank me for the flowers I sent.

GARVIE SMITH: Yeah, well. She's a bit nutty at the moment.

GARVIE'S MOTHER: Not as nutty as I feel.

GARVIE SMITH: Hey. [*Putting out a hand*] You're not that nutty.

GARVIE'S MOTHER: Don't try to sweet-talk me now, Garvie. I know you. You think I won't do anything, won't get around to it. Well, time for that's past. It's time to be serious. You can admit it or you can hide it from yourself, but things are not good here. And now I have the chance to make a new start in Barbados. A new start for you.

GARVIE SMITH: I don't want a new start.

GARVIE'S MOTHER: I'm not asking what you want. I'm done with that. I'm your mother. I have to decide. And I've made up my mind now, to go back.

GARVIE SMITH: No.

GARVIE'S MOTHER: It feels right to me.

GARVIE SMITH: I won't go. I'll crash here with friends.

GARVIE'S MOTHER: In that squat at Limekilns? Okay. I can't manhandle you onto the plane, that's for sure. I'm telling you what *I'm* going to do. Take the job, sell this place, take that good opportunity in Bridgetown. My mind's made up, Garvie. I'm sorry. I gave you a chance to show me it was the wrong move, and all you done makes me think it's absolutely the right one. Look at me, Garvie. I'm serious.

GARVIE SMITH [*reflective pause*]: I know.

GARVIE'S MOTHER: All right, then. Enough now. [*Standing up*] Let's go to Uncle Len's.

GARVIE SMITH: Mum?

GARVIE'S MOTHER: What?

GARVIE SMITH: I'll do a deal with you.

GARVIE'S MOTHER: Deal? What deal?

GARVIE SMITH: Wait until the results.

GARVIE'S MOTHER [*sitting down, considering this in silence*]: Hmm. And?

GARVIE SMITH: If they're bad I'll come to Barbados with you, no arguments. I promise. But if they're good we stay here.

GARVIE'S MOTHER: What makes you think the hospital will wait till your exam results come through?

GARVIE SMITH: At least ask them. I can do it, I know I can. I'll put in the work, I promise.

GARVIE'S MOTHER: And all the other nonsense?

GARVIE SMITH: No more nonsense.

GARVIE'S MOTHER: How serious are you? Let me look at you.

GARVIE SMITH: Serious, Mum. Straight up.

GARVIE'S MOTHER [*silence*]: Hmm. All right, then, I'll ask them. I'll tell you if they say no. But the deal starts now. Show me your knuckles.

GARVIE SMITH: [*puts out knuckles*]

GARVIE'S MOTHER [*puts out knuckles*]: Okay, then. Now we'll see. Get your schoolbooks—you can take them to Uncle Len's.

When Garvie and his mother arrived, Uncle Len was up in his study with a work colleague. Downstairs in the living room Aunt Maxie got Garvie's mother an apricot fizz, and Garvie a Dr. Pepper, and they all settled on the old, comfortable chairs in the living room.

"Garvie's brought some studying to do after dinner," his mother said.

"Good for you, Garvie," Aunt Maxie said.

Garvie didn't say anything. He was staring at the coffee table.

"Lost in thought," Aunt Maxie said. "Garvie?"

They looked at him sitting there in a trance, and Aunt Maxie giggled. "What can he be thinking about so hard?"

"Best not to know," his mother said. She tsked. "One day that boy'll go too far."

"Something serious. Look at him. He can't even hear us talking about him. What can it be?"

"Complex numbers," Garvie said, without taking his eyes off the table.

"Oh."

With a suspicious glance at her son, Garvie's mother asked Aunt Maxie about the new local convenience store, and they settled into a conversation about the scandalous rising prices of food.

Garvie carried on thinking.

$a+bi$, where i has the property $i2=-1$. The product of a real number and an *imaginary* number. You don't compute complex numbers, you *rotate* them. You move them into an imaginary dimension and the answer is an unexpected jolt from the blue.

"Garvie? *Garvie?*"

He looked up at his aunt. "Alex is lying," he said.

His aunt fixed him with a bright, uncomprehending smile. "Excuse me?"

"Where else would she go?"

His mother asked sharply, "Where else would *who* go?"

He glanced at her sideways, focused, and looked shifty. "No one in particular," he said, draining his Dr. Pepper and getting to his feet.

"Where are you going?"

"To see Bojo. Is that okay?"

"It's okay," Aunt Maxie said. "But don't wake him if he's asleep."

Garvie went up the stairs and along the landing, and was just going past the study, where his uncle was working late, when he heard a voice from inside.

It wasn't just any voice. It was the voice of Detective Inspector Raminder Singh.

It was also a surprise. Very naturally Garvie stopped. Briefly, he glanced back in the direction of his mother, and—momentarily—the thought of his recent promise not to interfere in "all that nonsense" came into his mind. But inside his uncle's study he heard Singh say the words "Chloe Dow," and the moment was quickly gone. Besides, if anyone was interfering here it was surely Singh. He was interfering with Garvie's uncle's dinnertime. Certainly it wasn't Garvie's fault if he happened to overhear what was being said in his own uncle's study. Although, in fact, he couldn't quite make it out. So, very naturally, he tiptoed forward and put his ear to the crack of the door.

"No traces at all?" Singh was saying.

"None," his uncle replied.

"Alcohol?"

"No."

Singh made an exasperated noise.

There was a pause. Garvie heard his uncle say, "Raminder, are you okay? You look . . . tired. I know what it's like, you know. The stress. Don't let it destroy you."

Singh said something in a low voice and Uncle Len sighed.

"What about this here?" Singh asked, brisk again.

"Ah, that." His uncle began to explain something, and Garvie pressed his ear closer to the crack.

They were now talking in low voices about technical matters. Then there was another pause. His uncle said, "So what's all this about a breakthrough, Raminder?"

Garvie pushed his ear very hard against the door crack. That was his mistake. The door suddenly swung open and he staggered forward into the room.

23

His momentum carried him almost to the edge of the desk, where he fell and lay in a crumpled heap looking up at his uncle and Inspector Singh, their faces cartoonish with surprise.

"Have you found her old running shoes, then?" Garvie said from his position on the floor.

Uncle Len recovered sufficiently to frown at his nephew. "I apologize," he said to Singh.

Singh said nothing.

Getting to his feet, Garvie said, "Maybe you haven't. Alex doesn't have them. You can close that line of inquiry."

Still Singh said nothing. His face was expressionless.

"Jess Walker doesn't have them, either."

Singh just looked at him.

"Shall I tell you who does? Or is it more fun if I let you work it out for yourself?"

Uncle Len stepped forward. "Garvie!" He apologized again to Singh, who stood there silent and unmoving.

"I suppose," Garvie went on thoughtfully, "that you're pursuing other lines of inquiry. Now you know what Chloe looked like on

Thursday night you'll have been rerunning all the CCTV footage from Market Square."

Now Singh's eyes widened just a little. Enough.

"I mean," Garvie went on, "all that black hair, that makeup, those proper grown-up clothes. You're looking for a different woman now, right?"

There was a pause then as the two men looked at him.

Uncle Len spoke. "How do you know all this, Garvie? What have you been doing?"

Garvie shrugged. "None of that's as important as the Porsche. Eh, Inspector? Assuming, of course, you got that far."

This was too much for Uncle Len. "Garvie! Go downstairs. I'll be down in two minutes and we'll talk about this then."

Garvie said, "But—"

"Go on, *now.*"

At last he turned to go and Singh spoke for the first time. "Wait."

They all stopped where they were.

"What makes you think the Porsche exists? No one else thinks there's a Porsche involved. Any more than all the other luxury cars she fantasized about."

Garvie grinned. "It's obvious. You've heard what she used to say. 'It's so comfy riding in a Porsche. It's so quiet. Everything matches.' *Everything matches.* That's not the sort of thing Chloe would make up. That's the sort of thing she'd *notice.*"

Singh looked at him thoughtfully.

"She was a girl who liked everything to match," Garvie said. "Like her running shoes and running kit. Anyway," he added, "I assume you've found the car by now. I mean, you have the methodology, you have the men, what's to stop you?"

Singh said nothing.

"Besides, it's right under your nose. Big, big man. Big, big money."

Uncle Len frowned at him again. Singh's face was a blank but a muscle twitched in his cheek.

He said, "You're referring to Mr. Winder, the proprietor of the Imperium casino, where I saw you two nights ago."

Uncle Len let out a grunt of astonishment and Garvie avoided looking at him.

"That line of investigation is closed," Singh said. .

"You really need to reopen it."

"I'm not in the habit of wasting police time. In a case like this there is no time to waste."

Garvie said passionately, "All you have to do is check the decor, man. It's not hard. See if the upholstery matches the trim, the trim matches the dash. You can do that, can't you?"

Now Uncle Len, who had been listening to the conversation with increasing bewilderment, stepped forward and said angrily to Garvie, "That's it now. This is getting out of hand."

"Isn't it? And time's short, as the inspector says."

Uncle Len had opened his mouth but Singh put his hand on his arm and the pathologist fell silent. Regarding Garvie with a long, cold look, Singh took a card out of his pocket and handed it to the boy.

"There comes a point," he said at last, "when you have to cease to concern yourself with all this. That point is now. I think your uncle will agree with me."

Uncle Len agreed with him.

"You're a minor," Singh went on. "I have a responsibility to ensure your safety and it's clear to me that you've been putting yourself at risk." He indicated the card in Garvie's hand. "Details of our helpline. From now on I don't want to find you involving yourself ever again. Is that understood?"

Garvie glanced at the card.

> City Police Child Helpline
> 01632 960951
> Police Child Protection Program
> City Squad Police Center
> Service House
> 30 Cornwallis Way

He handed it back.

Singh looked at him. "I gave it to you because you might need it."

"I've memorized it. Anyway, it's not me who needs help. I'd give you *my* card, only I don't have any."

His uncle said, "Go now, Garvie. Don't make it worse. The inspector's right."

He went—as far as the door. Then he turned.

"One word before I go. Buttons!"

Singh's eyes narrowed. Garvie avoided his uncle's furious look.

"You know what I'm talking about, don't you? You clocked Alex. Fair enough. But, seriously, did you think a girl like Chloe had just one stalker? Famous Stars and Straps. You got the wrong end of the sandwich, man. It came from a different sleeve. There were two men in her garden that night!"

Then he was gone.

Dinnertime at Uncle Len's and Aunt Maxie's that evening was uncomfortable. They'd agreed not to talk about it anymore but the unspoken issue of Garvie's behavior hung heavily over them all. After the meal was finished he sat alone at the dining table with his books, studying in silence, frowned at periodically by his mother.

It was also uncomfortable for Inspector Singh, driving across the city back to the station. He took barely any notice of his surroundings. He drove, tight-faced and unblinking, down Pollard Way, past the car showrooms and furniture outlets on the highway, on to The Wicker past Fiesta and the Imperium, round the one-way system at Market Square, past downtown civic buildings now closed and darkened, all the way to the underground parking lot below the police station in Cornwallis Way—twenty-five minutes in all—in a state of rigid, unproductive mental concentration, his notebook open on the seat beside him, with two words scrawled in large, untidy writing across the page: *Second stalker?!*

24

It was foggy on the Marsh Fields that Friday afternoon. Rain clouds hung low over the trees. Putting their hoods up against the damp breeze, they went slowly across the tufted grass, keeping their voices down. It had been raining and the ground was wet.

"It's as bad here as up at Pike Pond," Garvie said.

Alex grunted. "I know it."

They labored on. After a while Garvie said, "Thought you hadn't been up there for weeks."

Alex stopped and bit his lip. "Yeah, well. I know what it gets like."

In the quietness they listened to the muffled noises in the fogbound trees—the call of a bird, the wind in the leaves—then went on again.

"By the way," Garvie said, "do you know if Chloe was doing any modeling those last few weeks?"

Alex shrugged.

"Come on, you were stalking her."

"Maybe she was. But I never saw it." He shook his head. "What sort of modeling?"

"Nothing in particular. Doesn't matter."

They clambered across a ditch, pushed their way through a holly hedge, and at last reached the edge of a garden, where they stood half hidden in the shadow of a clump of hawthorns, peering around.

"Looks like a dump to me," Alex said.

"You should talk. You live in a squat."

"Not my squat, though."

"Not his house, either. It's the school's."

"Yeah. But it's his mess."

The janitor's bungalow stood in a fenced-off area of grass in a corner of the school grounds abutting the Marsh Fields. It was a square brown-brick building with matching brown roof and small, oblong windows with municipal-green frames, like the buildings in parks for changing rooms and toilets. On the grass all round lay piles of building materials, abandoned appliances, and general garbage. There were things under tarpaulin and half-opened boxes of stuff and rusty equipment lying everywhere.

"Not exactly house-proud, is he?" Garvie said.

As he spoke a shadow appeared behind a small pebble-glass window and slid away.

"He's in there. Better keep our voices down."

Alex grimaced. "All right. But you got to tell me what we're *doing* here. First I got the police coming down on me with their questions, now you got me doing all this stuff. It's confusing me. I'm getting busted up just thinking about it."

It was true. He looked jittery. All afternoon he'd been asking the same questions over and over.

"Just tell me," he said again. "Is this the man?"

"Let's not jump to conclusions. All we know for certain is he's an oddball."

"Oddball?"

"He has a shoe fetish, for one thing."

Alex didn't smile. He caught hold of Garvie's arm. "Can't you tell me something straight for once?" His grip was hard but trembling, his voice harsh.

Garvie gently removed his hand. "It's not straight, man. None of it. Specially that Friday night. And if it's not straight there's no point in looking at it straight. So we have to look at it crooked."

Alex looked more confused than ever.

"Listen. Take the simplest thing. She was out for a run, right?"

"Right."

"Suppose she wasn't."

Alex stared at him. "What do you mean?"

"Suppose she was running for her life. There's a difference."

Alex struggled to get his head round this. "But . . ."

"Suppose she was scared, Alex. Terrified. Had no one to turn to. No friends. No one she could trust."

Alex muttered to himself: "No one to turn to." Then he looked at Garvie. "Why scared?"

"That's what we're trying to find out. So keep it together, man. And keep your voice down, yeah? Or we're only going to get into trouble."

"Trouble!" Alex turned from him. "I got trouble already."

They split up, each working his way round the fence in the oppo-site direction, getting a feel for the place, trying to identify some of the stuff heaped up in the bungalow's garden.

For some reason it seemed foggier once Garvie was alone. He crept through nettles and cow parsley heavy with wet, between the fence and the edge of the wood, peering at the bungalow and occa-sionally pausing to look the other way into the whitened darkness of the trees. Twice he checked his watch. He'd told his mother he was spending all evening studying differential calculus at Smudge's and had promised to be back by ten. It was only five fifteen now. But he reflected for a moment that Alex wasn't the only one already in trouble. He shook off the thought and went on again.

Round the other side he met up with Alex again. The layout of the bungalow was easily guessable. Living room and kitchen at the front, two bedrooms and bathroom at the back. In the garden at the front of the house a path ran from the door to a gate, Alex said. Beyond that the school asphalt drive receded alongside the running track across the school playing fields to Bottom Gate and Marsh Lane.

"There's another path," Garvie said.

"Where?"

"At the back. Behind that piled-up brushwood there."

In the fog a gap in the fence was just visible, and the beginning of a muddy path disappearing into the woods.

"Well-trodden too," he added. "What do you think he's been doing in the woods? Shall we take a look?"

But Alex suddenly grabbed his arm and pulled him down into a crouch. He pointed.

Round the side of the bungalow Naylor had appeared. He was wearing a red-and-yellow varsity jacket and carrying a blue motorcycle helmet. As the boys watched, he went over to a tarpaulin and threw it back from the moped underneath. He began to put on his helmet.

"I need to know where that path goes," Garvie whispered to Alex. "Can you do it for me?"

"All right. But where are you going?"

He gestured toward Naylor. "Don't know yet."

"Careful, Garv. You said it. He's an oddball. Psycho, man."

"Yeah. But harmless. I hope. I just want to know where he's going."

They touched knuckles, then Garvie was gone, slipping like a shadow along the fence and sprinting round the edge of the misty playing fields toward Bottom Gate.

The city was a vast pattern of light and shade. Once the neighborhoods were left behind, it grew bigger and closed in. No parks or gardens here, just concrete, steel, glass, and asphalt. Buildings grew taller, roads wider and busier. Even this early the lights were on in the windows of showrooms and shops and offices. Evening shadows deepened under flyovers and bridges, loomed overhead in the shapes of tower blocks. It was a maze, huge and complicated.

You can hide in a city. Hide a secret. But if you lose something in it, how can you hope to find it again?

Garvie sat in the back of the cab catching his breath. He'd been lucky to find Abdul free at the stand. He'd only just climbed into his cab—to Abdul's mingled confusion and delight—when Naylor came whining past on his moped.

"Garvie man, you go somewhere?"

"Same place as that guy there," he'd said. "Stick to him, Abdul, don't lose sight of him."

Abdul had looked at him nervously in his rearview mirror but said nothing as he pulled away after the moped.

They followed Naylor down Pollard Way to the highway and into the rush of commuter traffic. Twice Garvie thought they'd lost him, but each time the moped came weaving back into view.

"There he is, Abdul!"

"I see! He go quick quick."

"That's right. Like he's late for something," Garvie said.

Naylor exited at the Market Square turnoff with Abdul right behind, and they moved slowly together round the crowded one-way system. Garvie kept low in his seat. It was unlikely Naylor would spot him but the man was a watchful type. Watchful and calculating. All week Garvie had been keeping an eye on him and he was sure Naylor knew it; he had the furtive, sullen expression of a man who feels himself observed. A man with a secret.

Looking out the cab window, Garvie thought again that the city was the perfect place to bury a secret in.

"Garvie man?"

"Yes, Abdul."

"I go police like you say."

"Good. Were they grateful?"

Abdul shook his head in puzzlement. "They people *très très* confuse," he said at last.

"You got that right."

The moped turned sharply onto Littlegate, and Abdul concentrated on keeping up with it. Garvie sat thinking in the back. Occasionally he leaned forward and peered out the window to check his bearings. The dome on top of the theater. The clock tower of St. Leonard's Cathedral. The neon sign of Maximilian's. They rattled past the last of the diners and wine bars of Market Square, turned into Well Street, back down Park, and headed toward the business district, Naylor just ahead of them. Here, suddenly, it was quieter. The streets darkened as they drove between the tower blocks. It was nearly six o'clock and most of the people who worked in the offices, institutes, and civic buildings had already left for the day. At night the whole area was a dead zone: empty tower blocks, vacant car lots, construction sites of waste ground and the occasional old building, usually decrepit, left over from an earlier era. Traffic was light, the sidewalks almost deserted. A hush hung in the streets.

Abdul gestured through the window and looked puzzled. "Is all shutting," he said. "Men go home. Is strange this man come."

Garvie nodded. "He's a strange man."

The moped turned into a side street and turned again into a small parking lot.

"Here," Garvie said. "Just after the corner."

Abdul turned to him. "I wait?"

"No, man, it's okay. I don't know how long I'm going to be."

Abdul frowned. "You okay?"

"It's cool. Catch you later."

For a few moments after Abdul pulled away Garvie stood round the corner of a high-rise watching Naylor lock up his moped. He'd parked it in front of an old building, once perhaps a library or town hall, grand on a small scale, with a colonnade of columns at the front, a sweep of steps to the front door, and big square windows. Now it looked shabby and functional, lost among the glass-and-steel tower blocks that dwarfed it. But unlike them it was still lit.

As he finished securing his moped, Naylor glanced up and Garvie ducked behind the wall. When he peered round again, the man was already hurrying up the steps of the building and a second later had disappeared through the door.

Garvie glanced at his watch. Just before six. He ran across the parking lot and up the steps of the building. A sign by the entrance read: CENTER FOR PUBLIC SERVICE PARTNERSHIPS. Peering through the glass panel, Garvie watched Naylor talking to a receptionist behind a desk. The receptionist looked at her watch and said something sharp. She held up an appointments book, pointing to something in it, and Naylor looked away, scowling. Then a man in a navy-blue uniform appeared and escorted him through a security door at the far side of reception.

Garvie considered his options.

He could wait. He could go home. Or . . .

He violently rubbed his hair and burst in through the door with a crash.

"Sorry I'm late!" he said, panting. "Even later than Naylor! What room are we in this evening?"

Leaning against the receptionist's desk, he squinted down at the appointments book in front of her.

The receptionist narrowed her eyes. Garvie flashed her a smile and she shut the book.

"Who are you?"

"Friend of Naylor."

"Who's Naylor?"

Her voice was like ice.

A flicker of a frown passed across Garvie's face but he carried on: "Came in a second ago. I saw him. Just tell me what room and I'll catch him up."

For a second the receptionist was silent. She was a gray-haired lady with a big old-fashioned jaw and a hard look.

"I don't know who you are," she said at last. "And I don't know what game you're playing. But you better leave. Now."

She picked up the phone and held it threateningly in her fist, and Garvie wasn't quite sure if she was going to call security or smack him on the head with it.

"All right, Conan," he said. "Keep your hair on."

He turned away. Behind him she let out an exasperated sigh, and Garvie heard her mutter, bitterly, under her breath, "Why can't they just leave them alone!"

It was cold outside. A wind was blowing in the steep channels between the high-rises. Garvie walked all round the Center for Public Service Partnerships, thinking, before settling finally in a shadowy doorway in a side street with a clear view of the entrance. He looked at his watch again. Six thirty. A vague prickle of anxiety went through him: He didn't want to be late home. He really didn't want to be interrogated by his mother again. But there would be time to think about that later. Now he had other things to think about.

Like why the receptionist hadn't recognized Naylor's name.

Like why she'd echoed what Naylor had said before about leaving him alone.

Blowing on his hands, he stuffed them into his pockets and settled back to wait, an anxious look on his face.

25

At seven o'clock in the evening Detective Inspector Raminder Singh stood in his office, facing the corner of the wall. He was just about to perform the rehras. But the phone rang and he returned to his desk and sat down.

"Singh."

Most members of staff had already left the building and there was a hush throughout the fifth floor. In this empty silence Singh sat there listening to the voice on the other end of the phone.

"Yes," he said after a while. "Yes, I understand." His voice was quiet, tense.

"No," he said. "I take responsibility. But it's my belief that the Porsche will prove to be—"

He was silent, and the silence of the building closed around him again.

"Yes, sir," he said, and a muscle jumped in his cheek.

"Yes," he said. "They arrived yesterday . . . There have been some technical hitches. We're hoping this is the breakthrough we've—No, sir . . . Yes, I do. Tonight. Tomorrow at the latest."

He swallowed.

"I understand my position. Yes . . . No, I'm—"

He held the silent phone for a moment before replacing it, and glanced at his watch. Then he opened the dossier in front of him and flicked again through the transcripts of all the interviews they'd conducted, which he'd finished rereading a few minutes earlier.

He reread the interview with MacArthur, then the interview with Alex Robinson, then sat there thinking.

After a while he picked up the phone and called Mal Nolan.

"Mal?"

"What's up?"

"I have a question about the janitor at the Academy. Naylor."

"Yes?"

"Could he have been stalking Chloe?"

There was a silence while she thought. "It's possible. But I don't remember any of the kids saying Chloe talked about him."

"No. There's no reference to him in any of the school interviews. None. Chloe claimed lots of men were stalking her, but never Naylor. Perhaps that's what makes me think of him." He paused. "Did you trace his past employment records?"

"Still waiting for them to come through. It's odd. First they go missing from the school system; now Archives can't find them, either. But they did find a couple of things. I was just going to call you about them."

"What things?"

"He's been pulled in as a material witness a couple of times recently. One was for breaking and entering. Never charged. Lack of evidence."

"Was the school informed?"

"No. You know what the regulations are. But the second thing's more interesting. Last year Customs interviewed him in connection with a drug bust. Again, not charged. Apparently he knew one of the guys who went down but that was about it."

"So?"

"There was a note in the file about a previous incident. Seems Naylor has a temper. There's reference to a fight he got into. I followed it up, tracked down the guy."

"And?"

There was a pause.

"He's still in a harness. Eighteen months later. Naylor nearly wrenched his head off."

Singh was silent.

"Did the man bring charges?"

"No. Too terrified. Naylor's violent. Very."

Singh thought.

"Do we have anything linking Naylor to Pike Pond?"

"No."

"Let's go back to those Froggett Woods residents who gave identifications before. Get a photo from the school. See if they remember ever seeing Naylor."

"Will do."

After Singh had put down the phone he sat quietly gazing at the desk, gathering his thoughts. But almost immediately the phone rang again.

"Yes?"

It was Lawrence Shan with the calls team. As he listened, Singh's face suddenly contracted. "What? Who did?" He listened intently. "Friday what time?" His knuckles were white round the receiver. "What witnesses? Are they sure?" He got to his feet. "Yes, immediately," he said. "I'm setting off now. Put a backup team in place when you get there and wait for me. Yes, armed. And Lawrence? I don't want anything going wrong. We bring him in safe and sound. You know what the press will make of it if he's harmed."

26

It was eight forty-five, completely dark, and Garvie was numb with cold by the time his wait came to an end. For some time he'd been wondering anxiously about getting home before his curfew and he was on the point of calling it a day when he heard voices, and a few moments later half a dozen men appeared round the back of the building, walking together on the other side of the road. They must have been let out of the rear exit. It was too late now to move so he pushed himself farther into the shadow of his doorway and hoped they'd go past without noticing him.

They came closer along the sidewalk opposite. Naylor was at the back of the group on his own carrying his blue motorcycle helmet. Like the others, he walked with his shoulders up and his head down against the wind, smoking. From his doorway Garvie watched as they came up the road together, their silhouettes sliding along the dark wall behind them. They drew closer, heads still down, until they were directly opposite him, then began to move beyond him, and they were almost all past him when Naylor suddenly glanced across the street and met his eye.

At first Garvie thought he hadn't recognized him. Naylor gave no sign of it, just carried on walking along the side of the building and round the front to the parking lot. Leaving the others, he spent some time unlocking his moped, pulling on his gloves and helmet. Then, just as Garvie thought he was going to mount up and drive away, he turned sharply and looked directly toward the doorway where Garvie was hiding.

Garvie slipped into the street and walked in the shadow of the wall in the opposite direction. It was instinct. There wasn't a conversation, however awkward, he couldn't talk his way out of, but something in that small movement of the man's head when he turned to look in Garvie's direction gave off the wrong sort of vibe. He felt what he'd felt before: The man was hot and cold. An obsessive. The sort of man who hid inside himself, watching, until he'd worked out what to do, and then did it, however savagely, until he couldn't do it anymore. Alex had been right: He was a psychopath. How long had he been watching Chloe and what had he done?

In any case, he was the wrong sort of man to have a disagreement with.

As he walked Garvie heard the moped start up behind him. The engine ticked over, revved up once, twice, and settled into a whine as it set off. Garvie walked on without looking back, listening to it. In a second it would either fade away as Naylor drove off in the other direction or get louder as he came after him.

It got louder. Much louder, very quickly. All at once the engine roared, and Garvie turned to see the moped's headlight hurtling out of the darkness of the street directly toward him.

He considered the situation. Beside the sidewalk next to him was a low wire-mesh fence bordering three sides of a vacant lot standing between two tower blocks, and he hopped over it and headed diagonally across the waste ground through weeds and broken bricks toward the far corner, where he could see a glimpse of road. A few seconds later he heard Naylor reach the fence behind him and turned to see what he would do—drive past, or turn back and head for home. He did neither. He screeched to a halt and sat there in his helmet, twenty meters away, staring at Garvie over the wire. He didn't say anything, just stared. But his fury was unmistakable. There was something else about him too, a purposefulness. As Garvie watched, he silently reached behind him and took something out of a box on the back of his moped. Something thick and heavy-looking, glinting silver in the streetlight. A wrench. Attaching it to his wrist with a loop, he looked along the fence both ways, as if considering his options, then kicked his moped into action, up the sidewalk toward a footpath that ran round two sides of the fence to the other side of the lot where the road was. He was going to try to head Garvie off.

Garvie was a rational thinker, precise and unsentimental, and therefore he took a moment to think, rationally, precisely, and unsentimentally. Then he ran.

In a sprint he went across the broken ground toward the road at the far side, occasionally glancing across to check Naylor's progress round the perimeter. By now the man had maneuvered his moped onto the path and was whining noisily along the fence to the far edge of the lot. He was going much faster than Garvie had expected.

Garvie picked up speed. He leaped a pile of rusty wire which appeared suddenly at his feet and got to the far side of the lot just as Naylor was rounding the near corner of the fence.

Running down a shallow embankment, he reached the road. BANK AVENUE, the sign read. It was a wide road, well-lit and completely deserted, and Garvie had no knowledge of it. He looked both ways, then ran across it, sprinted along the front of an empty office block, and turned smartly into a side street, Clavell Way.

Hearing the moped whining behind him, he knew Naylor had already left the footpath, and a second later the roar of the engine told him the bike had crossed the embankment. Garvie ran thirty meters down Clavell Way before throwing himself into a doorway. He was just in time. A second later Naylor came into view along Bank Avenue. The man slowed to a standstill and sat motionless on the idling bike, looking down the street, scanning it from side to side intently. For a moment he seemed to look straight at Garvie lying in the shadow of the doorway. Then he turned, kicked the moped forward, and accelerated away, out of sight. Garvie picked himself up and looked at his watch. He had a couple of minutes, maybe less, before Naylor realized his mistake and came back for him. He set off again, checking his bearings as he went.

Thirty seconds later he heard the moped in the distance slow down, come to a stop, and then, unmistakably, start back again.

Now he ran hard, looking from side to side for options, but Clavell Way was a long straight road without side streets, parked cars, or any other distractions. There weren't even any doorways for him to hide in, only plate-glass windows and smooth, high walls of the office blocks. The far end of the street was more than two hundred meters away.

Behind him the moped sounded suddenly nearer and, glancing back, he saw a headlight turn onto the street. He ran on, hearing the mounting whine of the engine as Naylor came after him.

He had no choice now but to keep running. He ran in full view down the middle of the road, looking left and right as he went.

He thought to himself: *What I could really do with now is a calming cigarette.*

He ran harder. The moped behind him got louder.

Still he ran, looking from side to side all the time for an escape route that didn't exist. No exits in the long, tall-sided street. No barrier to duck under, no fence to hop over, no alleyway to dodge into. No break at all in the smooth, high walls . . . except, suddenly, a small gap of shadow that appeared out of nothing and could have been anything, just up ahead, on the right.

The moped roared in his ears. Lit up in its headlight's beam, he saw his own running shadow appear waveringly on the road in front of him and knew he was out of time. Swerving sideways, he leaped across the sidewalk and threw himself full-length into the gap at the side of the road.

He fell.

He went tumbling down a concrete flight of pedestrian stairs and landed on the walkway below. Above him the moped gave a scream, then there was silence.

Lying there on the ground, dazed and coughing, he looked back up to the street. At the top of the steps Naylor slowly appeared astride his moped, a black silhouette staring down at him. Garvie scrambled to his feet and stood there, looking up. Neither of them moved or spoke. Garvie could almost see Naylor working out if he could leave his moped and catch him on foot. But Garvie had a head start, and luckily Naylor didn't look much of a runner. After a long moment Naylor slowly backed off the sidewalk, swung his moped round, and drove away at speed, back toward Bank Avenue, the sound of the engine narrowing into the distance.

Garvie felt himself all over and cursed. His pack of Benson & Hedges must have fallen out.

He stood there listening. In the distance the sound of the moped faded, came back, stopped, started up again, all the time moving away. Where was Naylor going now? Was he going back to wait for him in Bank Avenue? Or was he trying to head him off again? Garvie looked along the walkway to where it disappeared between railings into the shadows of the surrounding tower blocks. Perhaps Naylor knew where it came out. Garvie didn't. Standing there, he admitted to himself he had no idea where he was at all.

27

If the city is a maze, the business district is an unlit maze.

Big blank buildings dark and empty. Sheer walls of reflective glass and shiny black stone. Deserted plazas surrounded by arcades full of nothing but shadow.

Not a maze. A trap.

The first thing he did was call Abdul.

"My Garvie, how is?"

"Is a bit weird, Abdul. Are you up at the shops?"

"*Non, non,* I go big job. At the airport."

"Oh. Is that where you are now?"

"*Oui,* is where."

"Doesn't matter, then."

"Is okay, Garvie man?"

"It's fine, Abdul. Yeah. Catch you later."

He hung up and looked around. Sighed.

For three quarters of an hour he made his way along walkways, across plazas, down steep-sided streets and alleys, staying in the shadows of the tower blocks, listening all the time for the sound of a moped. Several times he heard it whining in the distance. It came and went, sometimes nearer, sometimes farther off, as if Naylor was circling round, waiting for him to reappear.

He met no one. All the cafés he passed were shut up for the night. Everywhere was deserted.

As he went he checked place names. Exchange Street. Fulton Plaza. City Gate. Corporation Tower. One by one he put them in his mind. He made a map in his head, interlocking and precise. For half a mile, a mile, he walked backward and forward until he had worked out exactly where he was.

Eventually he came to a junction of two roads and an unlit alleyway, and without hesitation turned into the alley and made his way in the fetid darkness past industrial bins and Dumpsters until he came, as he knew he must, to a main road that ran toward Market Square. It was a wide road, well-lit and deserted. If he wasn't wrong, it was Bank Avenue again. He checked the road sign. He wasn't wrong. He calculated he was about quarter of a mile east of where he'd last left it. Looking along it, he could see the clock tower of St. Leonard's that stood on Bridgewater Street at the corner of Market Square. All he had to do now was walk down the road to get to it and hide himself among the crowds of friendly people. Nothing simpler.

He didn't move. He stayed exactly where he was, in the shadow of the alley corner, listening. There was no sound of Naylor's moped anymore. A solitary car went past, and after two or three minutes another came by the other way. Otherwise everything was silent. Still he made no move to step out into the open road. Another minute passed. And another. He checked his watch. Quarter to ten. He cursed as he remembered his promise to his mother. It was time to go. And at that moment he heard a moped start up loudly not fifty meters away, and as he watched from his hiding place Naylor turned onto the road out of a nearby side street and cruised along it, looking around. He drove past the alley without seeing Garvie in the shadows and went on toward Market Square, his moped whining. Garvie waited for a minute longer, then turned and quietly went back the way he'd come.

First he phoned Alex. No answer. Then Felix. No answer. Smudge's voicemail message told him "The Smudgster's not available right now. So get lost." He looked at his watch. Nearly ten o'clock. Finally he called home, but his mother didn't answer, either. If he was in luck she was already at work. If not, he was in trouble.

For a long time he went among the streets, moving stealthily from shadow to shadow. He walked so far he left the business district altogether and came to the side of a canal, a place of derelict warehouses and lockups, old cobbled streets collapsed into the ground, weed-choked courtyards behind tumbledown brick walls. There were no streetlights here. But there were people; he saw them standing around blazing oil drums and squatting on tires, their tents and lean-tos standing among the rubbish. Dogs scavenged here and there. He watched them for a while, then turned and went back among the tower blocks.

It had been some time since he heard the distant whine of a moped circling round. But he wasn't going to take any chances. He made his way to Fulton Plaza, an oblong space of smooth granite, accessible only via pedestrian walkways from lower levels except for a single narrow street hidden between high concrete walls. There were arcades on opposite sides of the plaza, dark, quiet, hidden places with stone benches for resting on.

In the darkest shadow of one of these arcades he settled himself on a bench and prepared to outlast Naylor. It was a safe place sheltered from the chilly night breeze. If the worse came to the worst he could stay there until morning. He listened. Everything was quiet now, as if the whole city were asleep. It was half past ten.

He called Alex again and there was still no reply. It was strange for him not to answer and Garvie wondered uneasily why he wasn't picking up. He called his mother on her cell phone, and this time got her voicemail.

"Hey, Mum," he said in a bright, false voice. "Smudge and I got a bit carried away with our calculus and I didn't realize what time it was. Best if I stay over, Smudge says. Just wanted to let you know. See you tomorrow."

His voice echoed briefly under the arcade, then everything was quiet again. He switched off his phone. Drawing up his knees, he stared across the plaza and gave himself up to thought.

He thought of a running girl. A girl on the run. Running from a stalker. Running into town to meet a stranger. Running for help to a friend who hated her. Running all the way to Pike Pond, to end up with nothing left, not even her own running shoes. The technical description of them ran in his head, clear and precise, like a strip of ticker tape.

Item: Ladies running shoe, left foot. Color lime green with orange pattern and laces. Size 6. Asics "Lady GEL-Torana 4 Trail Running Shoes"; synthetic materials. New. No visible damage.

Item: Ladies running shoe, right foot. Color lime green with orange pattern and laces. Size 6. Asics "Lady GEL-Torana 4 Trail Running Shoes"; synthetic materials. New. No visible damage.

He knew where the old shoes had gone. But where did these new ones come from? A girl like Chloe would never buy a pair of shoes like that. So who did?

He checked his watch. Quarter to eleven. Everything was peaceful and quiet. Still he sat without moving, gazing across the plaza at the arcade on the other side as he sorted through the questions in his mind one by one. Another five minutes passed. He squinted and frowned. Something about the shadows in the arcade opposite bothered him. He focused. In the shadow was a deeper shadow. Just a shadow. Nothing extraordinary about it. But he couldn't make it out. The longer he stared at it, the more it became the irritating sort of shadow that the imagination seizes on, that makes no sense, that seems somehow to shift, changing into things it isn't. A cart? A kiosk? A man sitting on a moped? Garvie looked away and back again. The shadow was still there. He closed his eyes, but when he opened them again it hadn't moved. Another five minutes passed, slowly. At last he couldn't bear it any longer and got up to go across the plaza, to see what the shadow really was and put his doubts to rest.

He walked halfway across the plaza and stopped. In the middle of the shadow a headlight came on suddenly, blinding him, and as he put his hands up to shield his eyes he heard the moped being kicked into life and the engine roar as the bike came rushing out of the arcade toward him.

Turning, he sprinted down the narrow street, the moped so close behind he could hear the tires skidding on the ground at his heels. For a second it came alongside him, and out of the corner of his eye he saw Naylor twist his body round, and he ducked as the wrench swung over his head with a *whop* of air. Veering sideways, he pulled a bin over behind him and heard the moped scream as Naylor swerved to avoid it. Then he was in Exchange Street (he knew without look-ing), up on the sidewalk, dodging between parked cars, crossing the road and crossing it again, doing whatever he could to put space between himself and his pursuer.

Leaving Exchange Street, he ran into Fulkes Passage, took a sharp turn into Besom Road, and set off westward, Naylor still close behind. While he had energy he could dodge the moped. But he'd soon tire. Worse, as he turned into Cornwallis Road he realized he'd already run off the edge of his mental map. He was in unknown territory now.

Cornwallis Road was clear and well-lit. All the buildings were tower blocks. There were no parked cars or any other obstacles. Like all the other streets around here it was deserted. Hesitating, Garvie looked both ways. Northward the road bent out of sight behind a high-rise. Southward it ran straight for ten blocks or more before disappearing under a flyover. A hundred meters up on the left was a side street.

A half thought went through Garvie's mind, like a small, faint pulse of electricity. *Where there's a Cornwallis Road maybe there's a Cornwallis Way.*

He had no chance to think anything else. The moped came screaming round the corner, accelerating toward him, and he turned south and ran.

He ran hard out in the open, no longer trying to dodge, keeping his eye fixed on the entrance of the side street ahead. Slowly the street sign came into view and he felt a surge of hope. He made as if to run past; then, as the moped drew alongside him on the right, swerved left.

His heart sank. Beyond the midsize buildings that lined both sides of the short street was the high blank brick wall of an old warehouse. Cornwallis Way was a dead end.

Still he hoped. He staked everything on his one idea. He ran, looking out for the numbers on the entrances of the office blocks. Number 20 appeared on his left, and he took a deep breath and picked up speed as he heard the moped circle back and come down Cornwallis Way after him.

He ran past 24.

Past 26.

The moped was almost upon him. He ran full-pelt toward the dead end of the road, not knowing if he could make it, just running.

As he passed number 28 the moped caught up with him and clipped his legs, and he stumble-danced sideways, found his feet again, and ran on. He ran without thinking. Ran without breathing. Ran without glancing round, even when the moped crowded him again, screaming and shoving.

And as he ran a figure suddenly stepped out of the doorway of number 30, ten meters in front of him, and stopped under the fluorescent blue sign CITY SQUAD POLICE CENTER, mouth open.

There was confusion. Furious shouting, a glancing crack on Garvie's shoulder that smacked him forward into a spin, the scream of the moped veering abruptly away, and the astonished face of Detective Inspector Raminder Singh as Garvie took off into the air. There was nothing he could do now except briefly admire the way Singh stepped aside at the last second as he hurtled past, head over heels, and hit the ground some way beyond him.

Then there was silence and a vague whiteness in the dark street.

When he focused again, he felt oddly calm. Looking around, he found to his surprise and delight that his pack of Benson & Hedges wasn't lost after all but lying, conveniently open, on the sidewalk next to him. He took out a bent cigarette and put it in his mouth. Propping himself up on one elbow, he found his Swan Vestas in a pocket, struck a match on the gritty sidewalk, and lit up. He took a deep, deep drag and blew out a long, slow, satisfying, clear-blue puff of smoke upward in the direction of Inspector Singh, who stood over him in a fixed attitude of incredulity.

"I was just passing," Garvie said at last, "and I remembered your office was down here. So I thought I'd pay you a visit."

Singh's face became as quiet and cold as ever. "And I've been trying to get through to your mother all evening," he replied, "to ask you to come down to the station."

"Pleasant of you," Garvie said (with a sinking feeling). "Why?"

"We've just arrested your friend Alex Robinson on suspicion of killing Chloe Dow."

28

Garvie went with a young constable down two flights of stairs and along a corridor to a security door, and the constable swiped them through and they went on again, their footfalls quiet on the plastic floor.

"I know who you are," the constable said after a while.

His short black hair stood up from his head in a layer of fine bristles; when he smiled his teeth were large and pleasantly crooked. He didn't look much older than Garvie himself.

"Oh yeah? You been looking at the wanted posters?"

"You're Leonard Johnson's nephew."

"You know Uncle Len?"

"Everyone knows Len."

The young policeman smiled pleasantly. They went through another door and along another corridor, functional and windowless, overbright with old fluorescent strip lights.

"You okay?" the young policeman asked. "You've cut your face."

"I'm fine. It's this guy in here I'm worried about."

They came at last to a door with a small grille in it, and the policeman peered through before swiping it open.

"Nice meeting you," he said. "When you're ready, knock on the door and I'll let you out."

They shook hands and Garvie went into the room and heard the door shut behind him.

Alex was sitting on the floor of the cell, knees up to his chest, back of his head resting against the wall. His face showed no expression as Garvie went in. No expression was possible on a face so puffed and bruised, one eye closed already, the other closing fast, and an upper lip like smashed fruit.

The panel lights overhead lit him up like a magazine shoot.

"Hey, man."

Alex inclined his head and winced.

"Resisting arrest is what they told me. Refusal to cooperate. Won't talk to anyone except G. Smith."

Alex cleared his throat. "Hard talking at all, Garv." His voice was like underwater gravel, gritty and wet.

"There's a couple of coppers not talking much, either, according to Singh."

Alex's one visible eye glittered briefly. Lifting a hand, he indicated the side of his head, and Garvie put his own hand up and winced.

"I know. Got a bashed shoulder too. Remember harmless Naylor? Well, he isn't."

He went forward and sat down on the cell bench, and they looked at each other for a moment in uneasy silence.

"Singh tells me they've got something serious on you. He didn't tell me what. He also says you're refusing to give an alibi."

Alex groaned deep in his chest. He whispered, "I didn't kill her, Garv."

"You better say what you did do. Or the police might muck things up and stick a charge on you."

"Not talking to the pigs. Never."

"Talk to me, then."

Alex thought about that. "Almost as bad."

Garvie looked around the cell. "Perfect place for an interrogation."

"No, man, no. Not again." He rested the back of his head against the wall and for a long time was quiet and stony-faced.

"I'll just start you off," Garvie said, "and you can take it from there. Let it all out." He sighed. "Thing is, Alex, you've been lying to me. You said you hadn't been up at Pike Pond for weeks."

The boy groaned.

"Friday evening?"

He groaned again.

"Someone must have seen you. One of those old biddies in the big houses, I bet."

"Garv, I was there for, like, five minutes. 'Bout nine thirty. I made the deal and left. Didn't see anyone else. No one."

"I believe you. But Singh's got other stuff on you too, hasn't he?"

Alex said nothing.

"Come on, man. Spill. I know it's nothing to do with Blinkie's Porsche."

"That troll. I only got close to Blinkie 'cause I thought he was the one Chloe was going with. It threw me, all that talk about a Porsche."

"Right. It's something to do with those kids at your place, I'm guessing."

"All right, you freak. They saw the piece. They were pushing me for stuff and I wouldn't give it them and they shopped me. Police found it when they came for me."

"That's bad."

"Something else too before you get all guessy. The police got records of the calls I made."

"To Chloe? That's bad too."

"Sometimes I was pretty mad at her. I said stuff."

"Very, very bad. Anything else the police know?"

Alex shook his head slowly, painfully. "That's it."

"What about what they don't know?"

"What do you mean?"

"Stuff you haven't told them. Stuff you haven't told me."

"I told you everything now. What I didn't tell you guessed anyway."

"Friday afternoon, Alex."

The boy was silent.

"Don't make me guess this too. You were up at Pike Pond at nine thirty, but you weren't there at three in the afternoon, were you?"

Alex stared at the plastic cell floor.

"At three you were home in your lovely squat."

Alex breathed hard, twice.

"And you had a visitor. Didn't you, Alex?"

Nothing broke the silence in the cell except for Alex's ragged breathing.

"Come on, Alex, help me out." Garvie sighed. "She left Jess's about two thirty. Fled, more like. She needed help. And who would she go to, Alex? Who was the only person she could trust with her life?"

With a long groan of pain Alex broke down, and Garvie let him weep.

"All right, dude. Tell me how it happened."

Chloe had turned up at Limekilns at just gone three. It was a shock. Big time. For months she'd avoided him, refused to see him, refused to talk to him, pretended he didn't exist; then suddenly she was standing there on that broken-down, filth-puddled doorstep. And he hadn't had a clue what to say to her or even what to think.

"Can I come in, then?" she said at last. And went past him up the stairs.

For a moment he wondered if she was coming back to him. But she looked strange—beautiful as usual, but pale and blurred around the eyes—and he was confused, and went up the stairs after her without any idea what was going to happen next.

What happened next wasn't his fault. She told him she was in trouble but not how or why. She wouldn't. He guessed, of course. It was that new man of hers, the guy she saw in secret, but though she all but admitted it, she wouldn't say anything about him. Nothing. It made Alex mad. She ignored all his questions, just kept saying she needed to go somewhere for a while, but by then he wasn't listening. She started to cry but wouldn't let him hold her. Soon it all got out of hand. He was shouting, she was crying, and there was no sense to any of it anymore, just noise and temper.

"And what happened then?"

"Nothing. Nothing, Garv. I swear."

"Of course, you told her you were going to find him anyway, this man of hers, and sort him out."

"Well. Yeah."

"And did you tell her you were going to sort *her* out too?"

The boy didn't reply.

"Did you, Alex?"

After a long pause, he said quietly, "I didn't mean it."

"But you were that mad you wanted to show her you did. And how did you do that?"

"Don't, Garv. Please!"

"Getting out that 'protection' of yours and waving it under her nose?"

"Garv, I never would've—"

"Chasing her down the rotting steps with it?"

"Yeah, but—"

"Driving her away when all she'd done was come to you for help?"

"Stop it, Garv! *Stop!*"

He broke down again and wept in spasms, his back scraping like sandpaper against the cell wall, and Garvie went across and put his hand, softly, on Alex's shoulder, and Alex reached up and took hold of it, and they stayed like that for a minute or more.

"I did all that," he said at last. "But I didn't kill her."

"I know. But it doesn't look great, does it? What with the identification up at Pike Pond and the police finding the piece and all those abusive calls. So now you got to do what you really don't want to."

"What?"

"Talk to the pigs."

"Oh *man*."

"Least it's not hard. Really, all you got to do is give them your alibi."

"Alibi!"

"I know you've got one—there's no point pretending you haven't. What time did Chloe leave you Friday? Three thirty?"

He nodded.

"What time did you show up in her garden that night? Ten thirty?"

He nodded again.

"So all you have to do is say what you were doing for those seven hours. How incriminating can it be? You were up at Pike Pond doing a deal at nine thirty. That's awkward, but at least it's an alibi. What were you doing the rest of the time?"

Alex snuffed.

"Come on, Alex."

"I was at home having my dinner," he said quietly. "I was that sad."

Garvie didn't smile. "You big buffoon. I knew you hadn't forgotten your mum's stews. So all you got to fess up to is being safely home at dinnertime. Doesn't do your image much good, but at least it means you won't get sent down."

He sat again on the cell bench and rested his chin on his hand. "All right. Now I've got to think."

There was a long silence in the bright white room. Alex briefly fell asleep and when he woke Garvie was sitting exactly as before, thinking, sphinx-faced and immobile against the cell's white wall.

"Course," he said, as if continuing a conversation, "you're the easy part of all this. The hard bit's the boyfriend."

Alex grunted and shifted painfully against the wall.

"Didn't she tell you anything about him?"

"No."

"What kind of car he drove?"

"No."

"Where he lived?"

"No, Garv. Nothing. She just said he was trouble."

"Did she? What sort of trouble? Violent?"

Alex thought. "She was scared, man. Like he was—what's the word?—unpredictable."

"A man with a temper."

"Right."

"Someone she couldn't get away from. Someone living round here. In Five Mile. Working at school, maybe?"

"I don't know. I mean, she didn't say anything definite. Besides"— he hesitated—"I wasn't really listening."

"She must have let something slip."

Alex shook his head.

Garvie pondered. "How about this? Did she say anything odd?"

"Odd?"

"Something that didn't add up."

"I don't . . . I don't think so."

"Try to remember. Something unusual. Something that stood out."

For some time the boy was silent. Then he said, "You got something, Garv. Yeah. I'd forgotten. In the middle of all that row she said . . . what was it? I don't remember. But, like you say, it was something that didn't add up."

"What was it?"

He frowned and shook his head. "I can't get at it. There was so much shouting and stuff. But it was funny. Something catchy. You know, like one of those slogans. *It's getting better all the time.*"

"It's getting better all the time?"

Alex shook his head. "But something like it. You know what I mean? Like a jingle." He scowled hard. "*It's all in the mind.* That's not it, either. It's no good, I can't remember, Garv."

He began to cry again. "Garv," he said in a gasp. "She came to me for help, Garv."

Garvie hesitated. "Yes, Alex. She did."

"I know it now. You were right, she was running scared. And I just gave her more trouble. I let her down." He shook his head, moaning. "I let her go. That's the worst. She came to me and I turned her away. And I know where she was going too."

Garvie said sharply, "Where?"

"To meet him. Her man."

"You don't know that, Alex."

"I know!"

"How do you know?"

"'Cause after she left me I knew what I'd done. I knew, Garv. And I called her."

"Did you? When? What time?"

"Ten past four. I looked at my watch 'cause I was wondering where she was. I called her and she picked up. She wouldn't talk to me but I could hear her listening. And I could hear something else too before she hung up. Someone in the background. She was with someone, Garv. I could hear him."

Garvie got to his feet and looked at the ceiling, and when he looked back at Alex his eyes were glittering. He went over and banged against the cell door with the heel of his hand.

"I'm going to talk to Singh, get you out of here, man. Back home. Or back to your lovely squat, if you prefer. All you have to do is tell them what you told me."

The door opened and the young constable smiled at Garvie with his friendly lopsided teeth. "Finished?"

Hesitating on the threshold, Garvie looked back. "One last thing, Alex."

"What?"

"After she hung up, did you call her straight back?"

The boy looked puzzled. "No. But why—"

"Doesn't matter. Get some rest. Catch you later."

As the boy leaned his head back against the wall and gave himself up to fresh despair, Garvie left the cell with the friendly young constable and made his way upstairs to the fifth floor.

It was just midnight.

29

Location: Detective Inspector Singh's office: DI Singh sitting behind his desk; Garvie Smith sitting on a swivel chair in front of the desk; operational chart, half empty; three blank walls; small smeary window; digital desk clock showing 00:09; overflowing in-tray topped by a copy of a newspaper with its headline circled in black pen: POLICE LOSE PLOT IN BEAUTY AND BEAST STORY.

Aspect of interviewer: uptight; exhausted; deliberately expressionless.

Aspect of interviewee: bruised; cute; deliberately casual.

DI SINGH [*long pause*]: It's time—

GARVIE SMITH: Nice chair. [*Swivels*] Nice office too. Bit boring.

DI SINGH: I spoke to your mother.

GARVIE SMITH [*stops swiveling*]: Oh. Did you have to?

DI SINGH: In fact she contacted us, half an hour ago. To report you missing. When she found out you weren't at your friend's house she was anxious. Understandably. She's reassured now, and—

GARVIE SMITH: Probably wild with rage.

DI SINGH: As soon as we've talked, one of the night staff will drive you home so you can explain.

GARVIE SMITH: Oh. Good. I love explaining.

DI SINGH: Then you can explain to me what was going on outside the station with the man on the moped.

GARVIE SMITH: What about Alex?

DI SINGH: Alex has been very stupid. The gun, the visit to Pike Pond, the constant phone harassment. [*Pause*] Enough about Alex. I want you to tell me about this evening.

GARVIE SMITH: Does he get compensation? For wrongful arrest?

DI SINGH: We're not discussing Alex now. We're discussing you. I'll ask the questions and you'll do your best to answer them.

GARVIE SMITH: By the way, have you checked out that Porsche yet?

DI SINGH: Please. It's time for you to stop interfering and start cooperating.

GARVIE SMITH: How about I show you where her old running shoes are?

DI SINGH [*pause*]: One thing at a time. Who was the man on the moped?

GARVIE SMITH: Here's a better question. Where did she get her new shoes?

DI SINGH: Don't play games with me.

GARVIE SMITH: Or this one. Who was driving the Porsche?

DI SINGH: I said *no games*.

GARVIE SMITH: Why did she go up to Pike Pond? Why did she smile at Jess? What did she say to Alex? What did she need the money for?

DI SINGH: [*silence, exasperated*]

GARVIE SMITH [*suddenly pointing*]: Look at your chart, man. It's half empty. Thursday night? Blank. Friday afternoon? Blank. Friday evening? Blank. You're asking the wrong questions, dude.

DI SINGH [*angrily*]: And I suppose you think you can fill in all those blanks for me.

GARVIE SMITH [*pointing*]: Thursday night she was at Imperium. Think what you like, but being dropped off by Abdul near Market Square at six thirty doesn't mean she stayed there all evening.

[*Silence*]

GARVIE SMITH: Friday afternoon, two o'clock till two thirty she was at Jessica Walker's trying to borrow running shoes.

DI SINGH: You don't know that. [*Hesitation*] *How* do you know that?

GARVIE SMITH: Then she took a bus out to Limekilns. Number twenty-seven. Check it out. Got to Alex's at three.

DI SINGH: *What?*

GARVIE SMITH: Ask him. He'll tell you now. They argued. She said something to him. And she left at three thirty. [*Pause*] There you go [*pointing*], you can fill it in a bit more now.

DI SINGH [*long silence, looking first at Garvie, then at chart*]

GARVIE SMITH: I can fill it in for you if you've got a marker pen.

DI SINGH [*quietly but angrily*]: Listen to *me* now. Even if you're right about where she was at those times—and you've just given yourself a lot of questions to answer—you still don't understand. This *is not a game*. We're not *playing* at being policemen. A girl has been killed. There is a point to what we do, and that point is to find out what happened, not here [*hitting chart*], not here [*hitting chart*], not here [*hitting chart*], but here [*hitting chart hard*] on Friday evening, when she was killed. Do you understand? That's what I'm focused on. You tell me she left Alex Robinson's at three thirty. But I want to know what happened next, here, between four and nine, when she was murdered. And you can't tell me that, can you?

[*Silence*]

DI SINGH [*breathing heavily*]: You can't tell me where she went or who she met.

GARVIE SMITH [*quietly*]: Yes, I can even tell you that.

DI SINGH: And you can't tell me that because . . . [*Falling silent*] What did you say?

GARVIE SMITH: I can tell you exactly where she went after leaving Alex's. And I can tell you who she was with at four o'clock.

DI SINGH [*long pause*]: Who?

GARVIE SMITH: Me.

The silence in the office was the silence of shock—like the stunned silence that greets public announcements of disasters, or the hand-to-the-mouth silence of women finding lipstick on their husbands' collars, or the small frightened silence of the medical consultant's private room—and in this silence Garvie took out a Benson & Hedges and lit up, and said, "Next thing is, you'll be asking me what happened."

Still nonplussed, Singh looked vaguely at the smoke, up at the smoke detector in the ceiling, back at Garvie. He opened his mouth.

"Relax," Garvie said. "They hardly ever go off. And I'm just about to tell you something useful. I said before, I'm only trying to help." He scrutinized the end of his cigarette for a moment. "Course," he went on, "you'd've known all this already if you'd bothered to interview me like everyone else." He took a drag, exhaled, and focused. "Four o'clock," he said at last, "not long after final bell, I was up on Top Pitch. Trying to unwind after a hard day in the classroom."

Singh came to life and felt around his desk for his notebook. "Alone?"

"Till Chloe arrived. I was unwinding nicely. Then she comes up the slope from Bottom Pitch, looking . . . strange."

"Strange how?"

"I'll come to that. It was a surprise to see her at all, to be honest. We weren't talking that much. Nothing heavy. I just wasn't expecting her."

He drew deeply on his cigarette, tilted his head, and blew smoke at the ceiling. Stared at it for a moment or two. He said, "Looking strange 'cause she wasn't looking like Chloe. Not just that she'd lost her mascara and her hair was all over the shop and her face looked like putty. Because she didn't seem to care or even to notice. That was the weird thing. You know? As if she'd forgotten how to *be* Chloe."

"What did she want?"

"I would have thought that was obvious by now. Money."

"*Money?*"

Garvie shrugged and blew smoke.

Frowning, Singh said: "Money for what? She was in trouble? Is that why she was panicking? How much money did she need? A lot?" His pen hovered above his notebook.

"She didn't say. Easy enough to work it out, though. Don't you think?"

Singh didn't look as if he was finding anything easy. The muscle in his cheek twitched, twice.

"Forty-nine ninety-nine," Garvie said.

Singh's face looked as if it was starting to come apart.

"The price of a pair of new running shoes," Garvie added.

A few days earlier a more self-confident Singh would have exploded. Now he looked as if he no longer knew how to explode. His eyes fled all around the room as if looking for an exit, and found themselves, panting slightly, back with Garvie.

"New running shoes?" he repeated hesitantly as if testing the words to see if they would bear his weight.

Garvie said nothing. He smoked.

"New running shoes," Singh murmured again. He was still looking at Garvie, but he wasn't talking to him anymore. His face was turned inward, as if hunched over a problem, and Garvie watched him, letting him talk.

"Why did she want to buy a pair of running shoes?" Singh asked himself. "Because," he answered himself, "her old ones had been stolen. But why did she need to buy a new pair straightaway? Because she was going up to Pike Pond. Yes, but why was she going up to Pike Pond?"

His knuckles clenched around the pen.

"Because," he said, "she had to. Because she'd *already arranged* to. Because she was going to meet someone up there and couldn't be late."

He focused on Garvie. With a new sense of purpose he opened his notebook and leaned forward. "This is important," he said. "Tell me everything she said to you. Everything. Try to remember."

Garvie let out a long, slow breath of smoke and watched it drift above him, blue tissuey rags against the fluorescent glare of the panel lights in the ceiling.

"Remember?" he murmured. "Oh, man. All I do is remember."

Her eyes were washed out, tiny lights wobbling in them as she looked down at him, and he knew she'd been crying. That was unusual. But it wasn't the strangest thing. The strangest thing was the faint beige shadow on her throat. It told him something far more interesting. It told him that she hadn't looked in a mirror since taking off her makeup the night before.

"Hey," she said. She dumped her bag and sat down next to him.

"Hey."

"Thought you might be up here. Self-medicating."

"Want a smoke?"

"No thanks."

She looked in need of a cigarette, but he didn't tell her that. He waited for the silence to slow her down before asking, casually, "What's up?"

She just shook her head.

"Let me put it another way. What do you need?"

"Money." She gave a little laugh.

"I wish I had some to give you. Anything else?"

"Yeah. A bit of luck."

She chewed her nails and looked around, peering down toward C Block, squinting into the hawthorns behind them. The blue polish on the nail of her left-hand index finger was scuffed.

"Men, eh?" Garvie said.

She made a small, contemptuous coughing noise.

"Welcome to your life," Garvie said.

"It's different this time."

"It's always different. I remember how different it was."

She ignored him. She carried on looking about her, checking the school, checking the trees. He carried on smoking and she got to her feet.

"Got to get going."

"If you find any of that money, let me know where it is."

She looked down at him thoughtfully, eyes weirdly bright, and he looked up at her, waiting.

"What?"

"Garv, do you ever wonder if we—" She bit her lip.

"If we what?"

She shook her head. Made a little snorting noise. "Nothing."

He flicked the glowing butt of the cigarette into the long grass. "Don't make it sound so pathetic, Chlo. Nothing's the only thing I'm any good at."

She laughed then, once, a short, sharp bark. "Least you always made me smile." And when she turned from him, her hair swung round in that perfect blonde curve, the way it always did, an arc of light against the dark shadow of the trees; a moment to lift the heart. Then she was gone.

Singh was impatiently tapping his notebook. "Come on. You must be able to remember something."

Garvie looked at him with pity. "Here's one thing. Something she said as she left."

"What?"

"*Cheer up, it might never happen.*"

Singh's pen hesitated above his open notebook.

"Stuck in my mind," Garvie said. "Thing is, I was cheerful already. You see, she wasn't talking to me. She was talking to herself. *It might never happen.* But I think she already knew it would."

"You think . . . she knew she was going to die?"

Garvie didn't answer. Slowly he took out another Benson & Hedges, and Singh sat watching him, waiting, tense.

"Who called her at four eleven?" Garvie asked abruptly.

Singh blinked with surprise. "What?"

"I gather you've finally got the calls record. Alex called her at ten past. And someone else called exactly one minute later."

Singh collected himself and stared at Garvie. His face seemed different, not so bottled up, not so coldly Singh-like. As if slowly coming to a decision, without taking his eyes off the boy, he reached out and pulled a dossier toward him across the desk and rested his hand on it. "Yes, we got the calls record. It arrived, finally, last night, just before I visited your uncle. No recordings, of course, just the times and durations of the calls. But I know without looking which caller you're talking about."

"Traceable?"

"No. It's a stolen phone."

"But it's him, isn't it?"

Singh said carefully, "Whoever it is, he called Chloe thirty-seven times between one fifteen Thursday night and eight on Friday evening. That's more even than Alex." For the first time he was looking at Garvie as if, despite all that had happened, he no longer wanted to scare him into submission or pack him off to a correctional facility. "Tell me what you know, Garvie. You saw her take the call? What did she say?"

"It wasn't what she said. She didn't say anything."

"What was it, then?"

Lighting up, Garvie blew out smoke and sighed. "Oh, man. It was the way her face changed."

He sat very still, watching the smoke uncurl from the cigarette in his fingers, and Singh watched it too. At last Garvie said quietly, "Like watching someone realize their time's almost run out."

30

Something had changed between them and they both knew it.

The clock on Singh's desk said 00:43. There was a part of Garvie that was bone tired; there was another part of him that was already asleep. Most of him ached. He looked at Singh, pale-faced and long-nosed, no longer so uptight—or upright—and thought he must be tired too. It was as if, in their tiredness together, they had found a sort of understanding.

"You're a very unusual boy," Singh said quietly.

"You're pretty unusual yourself. Though you can be a bit snippy, to be honest."

Singh didn't appear to hear him. He said, "Tell me now about the man on the moped."

Garvie sat there thinking for a long time while Singh waited patiently.

"What man?" he said at last.

Singh started. He shook his head. "Oh no," he said. "Don't do this. Not now."

"What moped?"

"Don't, Garvie. No more of that nonsense."

"All right, I tell you what, I'll do a deal with you."

"A deal? What deal?"

"I'll tell you what was going on outside with Mr. Muffin the Moped Man if you let me see something."

"What thing?"

"Can't you guess?"

Singh did not at that moment look like a man who liked guessing. "Her shoes?" he said.

"No, not her shoes. I know all about her shoes. The note."

"Note?"

"The note she left when she went running."

"It's classified. I can't show you the note."

"You don't have to show it me for long: I've got this photographic memory."

Singh collapsed back into his chair and a shiver went through his previously immobile face. For a moment it wasn't clear if he was going to ask Garvie to leave or break down and weep. Garvie thought probably the latter. Instead, he did something totally unexpected. He smiled. A crooked, bewildered, surrendering smile.

Garvie had never seen him smile before, and it was a shock. "Don't see what's so funny," he said. "I keep saying, I'm only trying to help."

Singh shook his head. "If you can't find what you're looking for it's because you're looking in the wrong way."

"Really?"

"Police manual."

"It would be."

"The truth is everywhere and eternal, even in the saying of a child."

"That's the police manual?"

"No. The teaching of Guru Granth Sahib."

"Yeah, well. Less of the 'child,' if you don't mind."

Singh nodded briskly. He sat upright again. "All right. Perhaps I'm now insane, but, against all the rules, I'll show you the note. For one minute only. Then you tell me everything about the man on the moped. That's the deal."

Garvie shrugged. "Okay. Deal."

He put out his knuckles, and Singh raised his eyebrows and put out his own knuckles and they touched them together.

Garvie stood behind him while Singh brought up the PDF of the note on his screen.

"What about the back of the sheet?" Garvie said. "Is that here too?"

Singh scrolled down to show him. "See? Nothing on the back actually. Completely blank. But I'll give you an extra minute to look at it when you've finished looking at the front."

"I've finished looking already," Garvie said, walking away.

Singh stared after him. "Don't play games. I'm not giving you any more time."

"I don't need any more time."

Singh snorted.

Garvie stood at the window, staring out. He said, "Single sheet of white medium-lined letter notepaper torn from a student refill pad, hole-punched for ring-bound filing. Recto. In other words, from the right-hand side of an open pad. The holes are in the left-hand margin. Yeah?"

Singh glanced at the screen. "Yes. Though it's unimportant. What's important is the message."

"The message, then. In Chloe's handwriting in the center of the page, in black felt-tip pen, circled. It says, *Gone for a run Back 7:30 p.m.*"

"Yes. That's it. Well remembered. It's not lengthy, however."

"Full stop missing after *run*."

Singh frowned and leaned toward his screen. "Yes. As it happens."

"Various doodles and notes above and below the circled message," Garvie went on, still looking out the window.

"Yes, yes," Singh said. "But no need to fill up your photographic memory with irrelevant details. Sit down now. Let's talk about what was happening outside the station."

"Doodles," Garvie repeated, remaining where he was, "which appear in the same black felt-tip, in the same handwriting. In the top left-hand quarter of the sheet, fifteen words in a list, in ten lines: *plain choc, milk, white, butter, pecans, plain flour, baking powder, eggs, vanilla essence, castor sugar.* In that order. *Caster* spelled wrong."

Singh scrutinized the screen. "A list of ingredients, obviously." He paused. "Impressive. But still unimportant."

Garvie went on, "Bottom right-hand quarter, in the same handwriting, in the same black felt-tip, numbers in the form of an equation— *one over x plus two in brackets plus one over three equals minus one.*"

Singh examined the screen again. "Yes. A math problem. Homework of some sort."

"Standard-grade probability question. X equals minus eleven over four, by the way. But Chloe wasn't to know that. Probability wasn't her thing. Though I hear her chocolate brownies were top notch."

Singh said nothing.

"Finally," Garvie said, "in the bottom left-hand quarter of the sheet, in the same handwriting, same black felt-tip, a single word: *jacket*."

"Yes," Singh said. "Okay. I'm impressed. But the basic message is—"

"Though I ought to mention as well," Garvie went on, "that the sheet is a bit creased, from left to right. And that there's a vague doodly scribble underneath the probability equation. And a smear of something yellow across the words *eggs* and *vanilla*. And the left-hand edge of the sheet is jagged and slightly torn an inch from the top."

At last he fell silent.

"Did I miss anything out?" he asked.

"On the contrary, you remembered too much. Obviously Chloe ripped the page out of her pad to write her message on. All these other things—homework, recipe, and so on—are just what were already on the pad."

"Yeah, I know. Interesting."

"Why is it interesting?"

"I don't know yet."

Singh frowned. "Okay, then," he said.

There was a moment of contemplative silence. Singh raised his eyebrows. Garvie nodded briefly.

Singh said, "Good. Now it's time for your side of the bargain. Finally. What was going on outside the station?"

Finally Garvie told him.

"So, in your opinion, Naylor is her second stalker?"

"Obviously. On Thursday night he stole her running shoes out of her locker with his pass key. Which meant, of course, she didn't have them for Friday evening. Probably he nicked other stuff of hers too. He was always watching Chloe at school, she told Jess. He used to hide in her garden to spy on her. If you check his varsity jacket you'll find a button missing on the left sleeve. And it turns out he's a bit psycho."

Singh nodded. "He has a history of violence, we just discovered."

"Me too. There's a lot against him, seems to me. If I were you I'd bring him in."

"You don't need to tell me what to do. But I doubt he's Chloe's killer. His alibi checks out. He was drinking with a friend in a pub that evening. Besides, there isn't as much against him as you think."

"What about all the stuff I just told you?"

"Hearsay. Conjecture. Not even circumstantial. You didn't see him steal the shoes. You didn't see him watching Chloe. You didn't see him in Chloe's garden. What we need is direct evidence."

"Well, I've got pretty direct evidence of his violence against me. You should see my shoulder."

Singh looked at him. "I don't think you realize. It's not as easy as that."

"He attacked me. You saw him!"

"I saw a man on a moped wearing a varsity jacket and a blue helmet. I never saw his face. I didn't have time to check his license plate. I doubt a court would accept my evidence as corroboration of Naylor's identity. And what about your own evidence? It's not as strong as you think."

"Come on, man! *I* definitely saw him!"

"Could you identify him for a court of law?"

"Course."

"After he reappeared in Fulton Plaza, did he ever take off his helmet so you could see his face?"

"No, but—"

"Did you have a chance to get a clear view of his license plate again after he came out from under the arcade?"

"Course not, I was too busy running."

"A court of law requires proof beyond reasonable doubt. If Naylor's smart he'll go home, dispose of his varsity jacket, and get himself another helmet."

Garvie was quiet. "I'd at least get him in," he said. "He knows something. He was watching. If he's not the killer, he might know who the killer is."

Singh took his time; he put his hands together and rested his chin on his knuckles.

"I'll do a deal with you," he said at last.

"A *deal*?"

"I thought you liked deals. I'll question Naylor again. I'll even do my best to bring charges against him for assault on you. So long as you promise me now not to involve yourself in any of this ever again. Not ever."

Garvie scowled.

"Listen to me," Singh said. "Don't you see? You've done exactly what I hoped you wouldn't do. Got yourself into trouble. Dangerous trouble. And when you get into trouble *I* get into trouble."

Garvie folded his arms. "And if I don't agree? You going to put one of those tags on me and send me off to a correction facility?"

"I don't think that will be necessary. I told you, I talked to your mother on the phone earlier. She told me about her new job opportunity in Barbados. I think all I'd have to do is have a word with her."

Garvie scowled again, more deeply.

"Is it a deal?"

In the silence the clock on the desk clicked: 01:30. Garvie's shoulders slumped. Suddenly he felt tireder than he'd ever felt before. He looked at Singh holding out his knuckles, and with a sigh he reached out and reluctantly touched them with his own.

He took a scrap of paper out of his pocket and scribbled on it and passed it to Singh.

The policeman frowned. "What's this?"

"My direct line. When you get stuck you might need help."

Singh controlled himself. "Go along the corridor to the end office. A constable's waiting for you there. He'll drive you home. And remember!"

Garvie turned in the doorway.

"You need to watch your step. I didn't want anyone developing a grudge against you—least of all a man with psychopathic tendencies. He's violent and he's done a bit of breaking and entering. I don't think it would be hard for him to find out where you live." He hesitated, glancing at Garvie with sudden feeling. "I don't want you coming to harm."

Garvie looked back at him. "Yeah, well. I don't want you coming to harm, either, man. Anyway, it's not Naylor I've got to worry about."

Singh raised his eyebrows.

"I promised my mum I'd be back at ten and you've gone and made me late."

Before Singh could react, the phone on his desk rang, and as he answered it Garvie left his office and went down the corridor to where the young policeman was waiting for him. The last thing he heard Singh say was, "Yes, Chief. I didn't know you were still in the building. No, no, I'm on my own. I'll come up now."

31

In the early hours of Saturday morning the highway was finally quiet. Five Mile slept peacefully under a cloud-heavy night sky, still and dark. In Eastwick Gardens the only light showing was the wall light above the lobby door. Everyone was asleep.

Not quite everyone. There was a slight noise in the stairwell. A soft noise, creeping and purposeful. It slid, like a shadow slides, up the stairs, through a door, and along the lightless hallway of the top floor. Something metal gave a quiet chink and a shape formed in the shadow of a doorway. For some time there was no other sound, but the silence seemed to thicken with a sort of tension, with some invisible effort of strength. There was a sharp click and a hiss of breath suddenly released. Then the door of Flat 12 soundlessly opened and closed, leaving the hallway empty again.

Inside the still flat there was a shadowy hint of movement in the dark living room where there had been none before. A new sound, very low, like the breath of someone keeping quiet, blurring the silence. Soft footsteps of someone feeling his way forward. A shadow moving toward a room where a boy slept.

The living-room lights came on suddenly like a whiteout of sheet lightning, revealing Garvie's mother standing in the doorway of her bedroom and Garvie frozen in a creeping position halfway to his room. Both looked at their watches at exactly the same time.

"Let's talk about this," Garvie's mother said. "Right now."

Location: kitchen at 12 Eastwick Gardens; Formica-topped table covered with real estate agents' brochures; wipe-clean chairs; sugar bowl; sauce bottle; empty coffee mug.

Aspect of interviewer: thunder-faced; dressing-gown-wrapped; dangerous.

Aspect of interviewee: exhausted; cute; badly bruised.

GARVIE'S MOTHER: Ten o'clock I telephoned your friend. Called Smudge. Not a clue what I was talking about. Half past ten I get a pure nonsense message from you saying you're still at Smudge's. So then I call your other so-called friends, the burglar Felix Fricker, the drug dealer Alex Robinson. Nothing. No trace of Garvie Smith. At eleven o'clock I phone the police. Missing persons hotline. Put through at last to a policeman already familiar with the name of Garvie Smith. Half an hour later he calls me back. Garvie Smith has turned up at the police station. There's been a, quote, slight disturbance, unquote. No need to worry. Look at me. Am I worried?

GARVIE SMITH: Yes, Mum.

GARVIE'S MOTHER: Have you ever seen me so angry?

GARVIE SMITH: No, Mum.

GARVIE'S MOTHER: You haven't seen nothing yet.

GARVIE SMITH: Mum, I'm very tired. Can we talk about this in the morning?

GARVIE'S MOTHER: You think you're going to live to see the morning? Let's have your explanation.

[*Silence*]

GARVIE'S MOTHER: You can do better than that.

GARVIE SMITH: All right. I wasn't at Smudge's. I wasn't studying differential calculus.

GARVIE'S MOTHER: I'd worked that out already. What were you doing?

GARVIE SMITH: I was out.

GARVIE'S MOTHER: Out where? Out with who?

GARVIE SMITH: You're not going to like this.

GARVIE'S MOTHER: That's the first thing you said I'm agreeing with. Out with who?

GARVIE SMITH: With Alex.

GARVIE'S MOTHER: You were right. I don't like it. If you're out with Alex Robinson I know what you were doing. And I don't like that, either.

GARVIE SMITH: I know. I'm trying to stop. It's just, it's hard to resist, Mum. But I am trying, I promise. I don't want it to affect my performance in my exams.

[*Silence*]

GARVIE SMITH: Sorry, Mum. Sorry for worrying you.

[*Silence*]

GARVIE SMITH: Well, thanks for listening. I'm really tired, so I think I'll just—

GARVIE'S MOTHER: Sit down. You haven't told me yet how you got that dirty great bruise on your head.

GARVIE SMITH: Oh. That. It's funny, I can't really remember. Doesn't actually hurt. Much.

GARVIE'S MOTHER: Or how you ended up at the police station. The last place you'd go near if you were smoking puff.

GARVIE SMITH: Well, it was Alex, really. Stop and search, you know. But I went in to keep him company.

GARVIE'S MOTHER: Or about the, quote, slight disturbance, unquote.

GARVIE SMITH: Well, that, I didn't have anything to do with. Alex got a bit testy and the coppers didn't like it. Handbags, really. Very slight, quote, unquote.

[*Long silence*]

GARVIE'S MOTHER: This isn't anything to do with Chloe Dow, is it?

GARVIE SMITH [*shocked*]: No, course not.

GARVIE'S MOTHER: Interfering, like that inspector said? Getting into trouble?

GARVIE SMITH: No, no. Nothing like that.

GARVIE'S MOTHER: We have a deal. Remember?

GARVIE SMITH: You won't take that job unless I do badly in my exams.

GARVIE'S MOTHER: Well, the deal's off.

GARVIE SMITH: *What?*

GARVIE'S MOTHER: I was formally offered the job yesterday.

GARVIE SMITH: But Mum!

GARVIE'S MOTHER: No need to congratulate me. I've got four weeks to accept it. No longer. Which means you've got four weeks to impress me. Look here. What do you see?

GARVIE SMITH: Brochures.

GARVIE'S MOTHER: Real estate agent left them today. I'm all ready to put this place on the market. Step out of line once more— just once—and that FOR SALE sign goes up, but straightaway. You hear me?

GARVIE SMITH: Yes, Mum.

GARVIE'S MOTHER: Whatever you've been doing, it's over now. Understand?

GARVIE SMITH: Yes, Mum.

GARVIE'S MOTHER: Go to bed now. You'll be up bright and early. To study.

32

Garvie was waiting at Bottom Gate when Smudge arrived for school on Monday morning. Hands jammed in his trouser pockets, hood up, shoulders hunched, he leaned against the railings, thinking. He was thinking how comfortable it would be to have a memory lapse now and then. Unfortunately, he remembered everything.

Her pale face blurred by crying, for instance, the damp-breath sound of her voice as it trailed into silence. That disconcerting beige smear on her throat. Worst of all, the wet gleam sliding in her eyes. Once again, in his memory, she looked at him silently for something he could never give her. What was it? Money? Help? Or something they'd lost a year ago and couldn't forget?

Singh might or might not have the right idea about her having arranged to meet someone up at Pike Pond. But he hadn't seen what Garvie had. The point wasn't just that she intended to go up to Pike Pond. The point was that she seemed desperate to get there.

Something had gone wrong for Chloe. Garvie didn't know what but he knew when: on Thursday night. And he knew where to look for it: at Imperium.

Thinking of the casino brought another memory into his mind, another girl's face—shockingly pretty, with humorously cool gray eyes and a smiling mouth and dimples like punch lines in a joke he'd never heard before.

A voice reached him.

"My man Sherlock! Bit early for you, innit? Here, what you done to your face?"

Garvie ignored him. "Got any smokes, Smudge?"

"Run out?"

"Mine are all a bit bent."

He threw the cigarette into the corner of his mouth with his old ease and lit up.

"Had your mum on the blower on Friday," Smudge said.

Garvie glanced at him. "Oh yeah? What about?"

"No idea, mate. Made no sense to me. Something about couscous, sounded like. Bizarre."

"*Couscous*, Smudge?"

"Yeah."

"Couldn't have been *calculus*, could it? Differential calculus."

Smudge shook his head. "Nah, wasn't that. I don't even know what that is." He scratched. "Eat that stuff over your place, do you? Couscous."

"Well, Smudge, we don't exactly eat it."

"No?"

"No. We smoke it."

"Really?" Smudge looked impressed. "What's it like?"

But he never found out because a call came from down the lane, and they both turned to see Jessica Walker stalking toward them in regulation school uniform and non-regulation strappy wedge sandals. They watched her approach.

"Looking good, our Jess," Smudge said to Garvie out of the corner of his mouth. "Know what I mean?"

"Yeah. You mean you wouldn't mind giving her one."

"Not stepping on your toes, is it?"

"No, no, Smudge, go right ahead."

"Hey, Garv."

"Hey, Jess."

"Got to talk to you, Garv."

"What about?"

"Important stuff."

"Hey, Jess, girl," Smudge said. "Looking good."

"Whatever. It's about, you know."

"Hey, Jess, I'm liking those shoes. Liking those legs too, girl."

"Shove it, fat boy. Listen, Garv, can we go somewhere?"

But before Garvie could answer, a familiar voice broke in from the other side of the school gate.

"Smith. Howell."

The temperature seemed to drop a couple of degrees as they turned to face Miss Perkins. Prim and small, she hardly reached to the top of the gate, but her voice seemed to cut laserlike through it.

"I see you've mislaid the school regulations about smoking."

Smudge mislaid his cigarette and did a shifty impression of innocence.

Garvie snuffed his and put it carefully in his top pocket for later. "Technically, Miss Perkins," he said politely, "we're off school property."

Perkins pinned him with one of her notorious stares. "Come with me, Smith. Or I'll technically have you deported."

"Deported, miss?"

"As of ten minutes ago, I have an understanding with your mother. I call her, you leave the country in four weeks' time. Got it?"

"Got it, miss."

Jess hovered near him, whispering, "Garv? You won't forget? See you after."

"Walker," Miss Perkins said. "Return home and change out of your pole-dancer sandals into regulation footwear. Then report to my office for detention for late arrival."

Smudge raised his eyebrows and Garvie raised his eyebrows back and turned to follow Miss Perkins up the drive. As he went he heard Smudge say to Jess, "Don't know if you need any help changing out of those sandals, Jess, but . . ."

"Keep up, Smith," Perkins said over her shoulder.

They walked past Naylor's bungalow. The area around it was as untidy as ever: scattered junk, piled-up brushwood, gap in fence opening to muddy path through the woods. The moped was back under its tarpaulin. There was no sign of the janitor himself.

Round the corner of the drive they passed the principal, Mr. Winthrop, coming the other way, escorting Detective Inspector Singh toward Naylor's bungalow.

Singh and Garvie exchanged glances and went on in opposite directions.

After a moment Garvie took out his phone.

"Alex, mate. You home yet?"

"Smith?"

"Hang on, mate. Yes, Miss Perkins?"

"What are you doing?"

"Phoning a friend, miss."

"Phoning a friend?"

"About a path, miss."

"Well, stop it."

With a sigh, he pocketed his phone and followed the teacher into C Block.

33

Singh walked with Mr. Winthrop down the drive, the principal still complaining about the inconvenience caused by the long series of police interviews, only just completed, with pupils and staff.

"So disruptive," he said. "And so time-consuming."

Singh made no reply. He wasn't listening. Seeing Garvie again had reminded him unpleasantly of the middle-of-the-night conversation he'd had, after the boy left on Friday, with the chief constable. It hadn't been much of a conversation in the formal sense; the chief wasn't a talkative man. Like Singh himself, he was a starer, but quieter and colder. He made brief statements that were not to be contradicted or explained away or even answered, and let his silence amplify them. He had shown Singh a photograph of Alex Robinson pinned to the road by two burly policemen, which had already been obtained by a national newspaper proposing to print it under the headline INNOCENT VICTIM OF POLICE BRUTALITY: WHO ARE THE BEASTS NOW? He had reminded Singh how many days had passed without any charges being brought or indeed any real suspects being investigated. He had calculated the number of hours lost, and the cost of those hours, on looking for a Porsche that did not exist. He had reminded Singh that results matter and that a detective inspector without results is a reasonable definition of a constable on traffic duty in a small, dirty town far away. His comments made Singh suspicious that someone in his team was giving the chief his private opinions. With more time, there might have been ways to shift Bob Dowell or Darren Collier into other areas of the investigation. But he didn't have any time. The chief had given him a week to sort it out or give it up. And giving it up, he had made clear, meant giving up not just the case but all his career prospects too.

Mr. Winthrop opened the gate to Naylor's small garden and ushered Singh through, tutting.

"Such a neat man around the school, and look at all this!"

He knocked on the bungalow door and when Naylor answered he introduced Singh to the janitor, then made his excuses and left them together.

It was the first time Singh had met the janitor face-to-face. He was oddly good-looking, he thought. Wiry, with dark cropped hair and strong features. What a girl might call a "bit of rough." But his nervousness was immediately apparent. Standing awkwardly in front of Singh, he kept chewing his bottom lip, his eyes flicking from side to side.

"I understand you own a moped," Singh said.

"So?"

"Can I see it?"

Scowling, the man led him across the litter-strewn grass to a small paved area, and lifted off the sheet of tarpaulin.

Singh nodded. It might have been the one he saw in Cornwallis Way or it might not.

"What's in the pannier?"

"Nothing."

"Show me."

Naylor opened the box on the back of the moped. It was empty. Singh nodded again, and they went back into the bungalow.

Inside the house it was as messy as the area outside. The walls were streaked with rusty water stains from an old leak and there was a smell of grease. Singh stepped onto a dirty strip of loose linoleum and walked down the narrow hall. Hanging on a coat peg was a red motorcycle helmet.

"This your helmet?"

"Yes."

"Do you have any others?"

"No."

They went on into the small living room and sat opposite each other on junk-shop chairs across a low table piled with unwashed crockery. Through a doorway Singh could see into a small kitchen, the sink filled with pots and pans and tools of some sort. There was no need to ask whether the man lived alone.

"I been interviewed already," Naylor said. "I don't know what this is about. It's not right. I answered all the questions before." He glanced away, biting his lip.

"Well, I want to ask you them again," Singh said calmly. He took a file out of his briefcase. "About the night of the thirteenth."

Naylor repeated his alibi. It had been a half day for him, and from around four o'clock he'd been with a friend in a pub called the Jolly Boatman. His friend had already verified it. As he talked, Singh watched him. The man couldn't stay still; he kept wiping his hand across the stubble of his face and chewing his thumbnails, and whenever Singh met his gaze he looked away, scowling.

"Do you know Pike Pond?"

"Never been there in my life."

"What about Fox Walk?"

"Where?"

He answered all questions with the same surly unhelpfulness. "I done all this already," he said again and again.

Singh considered him. "Tell me more about Chloe Dow."

Naylor looked at him furiously. "I told you. I don't know nothing about her. I never even spoken to her."

"Did you like the look of her?"

Naylor shot him a furious glance. "I told you. I wouldn't even remember her if her picture wasn't in the papers every bloody day."

"People say you used to watch her."

"Well, people's wrong 'cause I never."

"They say you used to watch her running at the track."

"Didn't even know she went running."

Singh paused. Keeping his eyes fixed on Naylor, he said, "Chloe had several things stolen from her locker over the last few weeks of her life. Did you steal them?"

Naylor trembled violently but didn't look away. "No, I bloody didn't." He stared at Singh. "Search the place if you want; you won't find nothing."

In the silence that followed he kept his eyes on Singh's the whole time, and at last Singh dropped his to make a note in his book.

As he wrote he said, "By the way, where did you work before here?"

"Didn't have a job."

"You're what? Twenty-nine? This is your first job?"

"Did bits and pieces. Building sites mainly."

"Where?"

"Here and there." He sniffed. "I never was on welfare. Wouldn't do it."

Singh nodded and fell silent for a moment. He said, "You were out last Friday in town. Is that right?"

At once Naylor's expression changed. He opened his mouth and shut it again.

Singh said sharply, "Is that right?"

Naylor nodded.

"You went out on your moped?"

"So? What's this got to do with anything?"

"Where did you go?"

For almost a minute Naylor said nothing, just sat biting his lip and rubbing his face with his hands. Singh leaned forward.

"Meeting," Naylor said at last.

"What meeting?"

"Private meeting."

"What private meeting?"

There was a long silence.

"Mr. Naylor," Singh said at last, "I want to avoid any misunderstandings. So I advise you to answer the question."

Naylor shook his head.

"I put it to you that you went to a meeting at the Center for Public Service Partnerships on Deal Street. What was the meeting?"

"I was told it was confidential," Naylor said angrily.

"This interview is confidential. Nothing you say to me will be repeated to anyone at the Academy, if that's what you're worried about."

Naylor looked as if he were about to burst into tears. After a moment's agitated silence, he said in a rush, "I got issues, right? Anxiety is what. They said it was all confidential, and now look. They know how I get. Panic attacks, and now look." He groaned and briefly closed his eyes.

Singh said calmly, "I see. Was the meeting with the health service?"

"Mental health," Naylor said. "Group counseling for anxiety. They said it wouldn't go on my records. Only bloody reason I went. I didn't have to go." He bit his knuckles. "Why can't people leave me alone?"

Singh said, "There's no shame in seeking help for a problem, Mr. Naylor. We all have problems. And I agree, you should have the space to work things out for yourself. It's just that I needed to know."

He made a note, closed his file, and looked up. Between his hands Naylor was peering at him fiercely; there was a flash of something in his expression, then it was gone.

Singh frowned and paused. He said, "That Friday night I saw a man on a moped chase down a boy in Cornwallis Way. Was that man you?"

"No, it bloody wasn't."

"A man in a varsity jacket wearing a blue helmet."

"My helmet's red and I haven't even got a varsity jacket."

"At about eleven o'clock."

"The meeting ended at nine and I came back here. At eleven o'clock I was probably bloody asleep."

Singh nodded. He got to his feet and turned away down the hall toward the front door. As he went he glanced again at the red motorcycle helmet hanging on its peg and noticed it was new.

Behind him, Naylor had subsided into weeping and, without saying anything, Singh let himself out of the bungalow and slowly walked back toward the school.

Up the drive Singh came almost immediately to the running track. It was no more than fifty meters from the house, in full view. Naylor had never even noticed Chloe running there? Walking slowly round the track's perimeter, he reviewed the conversation he'd just had, thinking over the things Naylor had said.

"Search the place if you want; you won't find nothing." Singh believed him. But what if he had somewhere else where he could stash stuff? He glanced back at the house and across to the woods beyond.

From his car he phoned the station for Mal, but she wasn't there and neither was Lawrence Shan. At last he was put through to Darren Collier.

"Darren. I've just been speaking to Naylor. The school janitor."

"I remember. Yeah?" Singh thought he detected a new coolness in his voice.

"Has Mal anything to report from Froggett Woods? She was going to show his photo round."

"No idea."

There was a silence. Singh went on: "Another thing. I want his alibi checked again."

"Been done. Twice. He was drinking with a friend, right? The Jolly Boatman. Bob went back and talked to the landlord."

"Did he talk to the bar staff too? Does anyone else remember him being there that night? I want someone to go back to the pub and check."

There was silence.

Singh continued, "And I want his previous employment records located. Mal told me they'd gone missing. Archives have been looking but there's no trace of them there, either."

"If Archives haven't got them, no one has."

Singh thought. "I want you to call up his criminal record. He was pulled in and interviewed a while back. Find out who talked to him. No, wait. Get hold of the people at the Center for Public Service

Partnerships. Start with them. Naylor was at a meeting there last Friday evening. Anxiety issues. Mental health department. Got that?"

"I got it all right."

"Well, then."

There was a vague noise of discontent at the other end of the phone, but before Singh could say anything else Collier had rung off, and Singh sat silently in the car, staring out the window at the running track.

Suddenly he was exhausted. His energy drained away and with it his self-belief. No wonder his colleagues had lost faith in him. The chief constable was openly critical. Singh's hunches had been wrong. Dowell's team was still searching in vain for a Porsche. He'd made a mistake in arresting Alex Robinson. Now Naylor was proving to be more difficult and perhaps more dangerous than they'd thought.

Beyond the running track he could see the edge of Marsh Woods. Beyond that was the highway and the path out to Pike Pond. Even at this time in the morning the sky above it was gloomy. It was a gloomy place, isolated and bleak. A thought came to him. If Chloe had arranged to meet someone up there, in the ruin of Four Winds Farm, was that person Naylor?

He didn't know. Frustrated, he felt that if only he could look at the questions in a new light, turn them round somehow, he would find the answers. But he couldn't turn them. Slapping the steering wheel to shake himself out of his lethargy, he turned the key in the ignition, and with a grim, pale face drove out through the school gates. He was a policeman and a Sikh. He wouldn't give up. He had an iron will. He would never quit.

34

"Thing is," Garvie said, "I'm thinking of quitting."

"Quitting, Smith?"

"It's a bad habit, miss."

"Quitting smoking, you mean?"

"Smoking tobacco. Yeah."

Miss Perkins looked at him hard and Garvie looked back. She had ginger eyebrows; they made her eyes look colder. Glancing around her office, a model of functional, soulless efficiency, he sighed. Through the soundproof glass office door he could see other students going erratically but silently along the corridor to their lessons.

"By the way," he said, "I think I'm meant to be in citizenship. Or maybe physics. So, if that's all, I'll just—"

"Stay where you are, Smith. I promised your mother I'd have a word with you. There are one or two things that need to be made clear to you."

"I wish," he said. He was thinking of things connected with Chloe Dow. But remembering what his mother had said to him the night before—and the real estate agents' brochures she'd shown him—he put the thought out of his mind. It really looked as if he'd have to get down to his schoolwork. Some of it, at least.

Miss Perkins opened a file on her desk and flipped through a few pages. "You're not the stupidest boy at this school," she said.

"Thank you, miss. Smudge'll be relieved."

"Smudge?"

"Ryan Howell, miss. He prizes his position as stupidest boy."

She stared at him narrowly. "Don't talk, Smith. Just listen." She looked down at her file. "It says here that you have the highest IQ of any Academy pupil in its entire history."

He nodded politely.

"But you have the worst grades. Quite possibly the worst grades ever recorded."

He shook his head in what he hoped was a sad and defeated manner.

Perkins frowned. She closed the file. "I've seen it before. Not quite so spectacularly. But similar enough. Lack of motivation. Disaffection. Bad habits."

Garvie nodded, even more sadly. He turned his head away, as if reluctant to face the full horror of what he'd become, and through the glass door saw Jessica Walker in the corridor making gestures at him. She was pointing at her watch and mouthing something. When he shook his head, she pouted and gestured toward the cafeteria with her thumb. He shook his head again. He put his index finger to his temple and pulled the trigger.

"Smith?"

"Yes, miss?"

"What are you doing?"

She came round her desk toward the door and Jessica skittered away down the corridor. Turning to Garvie, Miss Perkins said, "Leave her alone, Smith."

"But I wasn't—"

"Certainly you weren't. You wouldn't know how to."

"Miss?"

She stood small and straight and stern in front of her desk, looking at him. "You see, Smith, you have no idea. How could you? You have no understanding of female psychology. None. You might have heard rumors that it exists, but for you it remains *terra incognita*." She continued to look at him. "*Terra incognita* is a Latin phrase."

"Does it have something to do with terror?"

"It means *unknown lands*."

"Very handy, miss. I'll remember to use it in my conversations with girls."

He glanced sideways at Jessica, who had reappeared in front of the glass door, making her weird gestures again. As soon as Miss Perkins followed his gaze, the girl continued on her way down the corridor.

Perkins clicked her tongue. "At least leave her until after your exams. Listen to me now, Smith. Bad habits are your own business, but bad grades bring down a school. And no one is going to bring down this school." She stood in front of him. "Your mother asked me to ensure you took all your exams, but I did better than that; I promised her that you would achieve grades commensurate with your intelligence. Do you think that was rash?"

"Yeah. A bit."

"But I'm not a rash person, am I, Smith?"

"No, miss."

"What sort of person am I?"

"Utterly ruthless, miss."

"That's correct. I'm very glad we understand each other. You see, Smith, all you need to do is a little work. And you have four whole weeks to do it in." She brought her face closer to Garvie's. "And I know that's what you're going to do. How do I know that's what you're going to do?"

"'Cause otherwise you won't hesitate to have me deported."

"That's correct."

She returned to the other side of her desk with an air of having achieved her objective, and sat down again.

"From now on you're being monitored. Miss a lesson and your mother gets a call. Miss a second lesson and I'll pull you from all your exams. I won't risk substandard grades, and of course if you have no chance to get any sort of grades things will be greatly simplified for your mother. From what she told me I think you'll be in Bridgetown by the end of the month. Any questions?"

Garvie thought for a moment.

"If you were young, blonde, and attractive, miss, what would you do if you found yourself entangled with the wrong sort of man? Thinking of the psychology-*terra-incognita* angle."

Miss Perkins sat rigid, glaring at him. At first it seemed she was about to call security, or perhaps just turn him to stone with the appalling power of her stare, but after a moment she said, in a frozen voice, "I would not put myself in that position in the first place, Smith."

"That's exactly what I thought you'd say," Garvie said. "Perhaps I'm getting the hang of that psychology thing after all. At least with utterly ruthless women."

And, nodding affably, he got to his feet and exited the room before Miss Perkins could come out of her trance of fury.

He got as far as the so-called IT Suite before he was ambushed by Jessica.

"She likes you, bad boy. I can tell, the way she was looking at you."

"No, Jess. She doesn't like me. She doesn't understand me. To her I'm *terra incognita.*"

"In-cog-what?"

"Doesn't matter. I'm due in citizenship, and I really have to be there. Sorry."

"Wait. Got something to tell you."

He shook his head. "No time, Jess."

"About *her.* Chloe."

Turning away, he began to walk briskly along the corridor, and Jessica caught him up and scampered alongside him.

"I know what it is. You can't stop thinking about her, can't get her out of your head. And I know why. You still love her, don't you? Even though she dumped you. Even though she's gone."

Rolling his eyes, saying nothing, Garvie walked on. He pushed his way through the fire door and set off across the yard in a drizzle that had stained the streaky asphalt to wet-dog gray.

"I know how it feels," Jessica went on. "Can we stop for a bit, by the way? My feet hurt."

Garvie went round the corner of A Block saying nothing, and crossed to the entrance to Humanities and Arts.

"I can't walk in these flat shoes," Jessica wailed.

He went up the staircase two steps at a time.

"She wasn't who you think she was, Garv!" Her voice echoed below him in the stairwell.

He climbed as far as Music, then through fire doors into another corridor, striding past classroom doors, lockers, and vending machines toward Modern Languages, Jessica gamely stumbling after him.

"She never loved you!" she called. "She never even loved Alex."

Garvie pulled away from her and she faltered, limping and pouting.

"She only liked her new man 'cause of what he promised he'd do for her!" she cried, and finally came to a halt, gingerly holding an ankle, watching despairingly as Garvie disappeared round the corner of the corridor.

A second later he reappeared.

"What?"

She languished against the scuffed and peeling wall, a bird with a broken wing. "It hurts, Garv."

He came back down the corridor toward her, and she languished a bit more.

"You didn't tell me anything about the new man before, Jess."

"I only just remembered."

"What did he promise to do for her?"

"I don't know. She never said. But I know it was something she really wanted."

"Who was he?"

Jessica shook her head. "All I know is, he was someone she really, really shouldn't have got involved with."

"Go on."

She winced. "Thing is, my ankle's still hurting. It needs a little rub, Garv."

He turned away and Jessica said, "No, wait. I'll tell you. She said if anyone found out about them, all hell'd break loose. As bad for him as for her, she said. Worse."

"Why?"

"She didn't say."

"Why would all hell break loose? Because he had a job here?"

"I don't know."

"Or because of what he was going to do for her?"

"She just said one day everyone would know everything, but by then it'd be too late. There. That's it. I've told you it all. Will you give my foot a rub now, Garv? Just for a minute?"

He looked at her, then at his watch, then at her foot, and then his phone rang.

He took it out of his pocket and frowned at it before holding it to his ear. "Yeah?"

His face changed. It changed so dramatically that Jessica put a hand out as if to steady him.

"Garv? What is it, Garv?"

He stood there with a hand in his hair, listening, his face fierce with concentration.

"Yeah, I got a question," he said at last. "Why are you calling me?"

For a while he listened again.

"I wouldn't do that if I was you," he said.

He was silent a moment.

"How about because I'm telling you not to?"

He went on, "You're not making much sense. How can I trust you? Really? After what you did that night?"

For a long time he was silent, eyes glittering. Then he said, "All right. I'll meet you. Where? Yeah, I know it. Late. I've got somewhere to go to first. No, later. Eleven. All right."

There was a pause, then he said, "You want to know what I think? I don't think we should do this. But I know we're going to do it anyway. Yeah, and you."

He stood there distracted, holding the phone between his fingers like a card he didn't know whether to throw away or play.

"Garv? Who was that? What are you up to, Garv?"

Jessica limped away from the wall but he was already halfway down the corridor.

"Sorry, Jess. Got to go. It's going to be a long day."

"But Garv!"

"Try the school nurse!"

And then he was out of sight and she heard only his steady footsteps receding into the distance.

35

All the way back to headquarters Singh felt tired and dispirited. But he couldn't afford to rest, and as soon as he got into his office he called Collier, who appeared with a file ten minutes later.

"Did you find the meeting Naylor was at?"

Collier put the file on the desk in front of him. "There were eight meetings that evening, in different rooms. It's a busy place."

"So which one was Naylor's?"

"None of them."

Singh frowned and opened the file. "Here," he said, pointing. "This must be it. SAD. Social Anxiety Disorder. Group therapy. Six thirty to eight thirty."

"He didn't go."

"Didn't turn up?"

"He's never turned up. He's never been to a SAD meeting. He's not even registered. Look there. Check the list of attendees." Again Singh detected a trace of hostility and exasperation in Collier's voice. "He's never been to any meeting at the Center at all. I checked back five months. There are the lists for all the meetings. Took me an hour. No Naylor. Not him. He wasn't there."

"But he was seen going in."

"By who?"

Singh hesitated. "Doesn't matter. I'll check it myself."

After Collier had gone Singh sat disoriented for a while. He believed Garvie when he said that Naylor had gone to the Center, so why was there no record of him there?

He read through the list of meetings on Friday evening. There were eight, as Collier had said.

5:30–8:30: Group Therapy (SOTP)

6:30–8:30: Cognitive-Behavioral Group Therapy (SAD)

7:30–8:30: Class on Budgeting for Non-Financial Managers (CE)

7:30–8:30: Dealing with Domestic Crisis course (FID)

8:00–9:00: Positive Behavior Support classes (ILD)

8:00–9:00: Female Self-Defense Class (CDA)

8:00–9:00: Group Session (GA)

8:30–9:30: Coping with Cocaine Addiction group session (GDC)

It was all familiar and ordinary: sessions giving help for the usual mix of problems and addictions. ILD was the Institute for Learning

Difficulties, GA Gamblers Anonymous, FID Families in Distress. The only acronym he didn't recognize straightaway was SOTP. He looked it up.

And sat there looking at it.

Sex Offenders Treatment Program.

He looked through the list of attendees for the program obtained by Collier. There was no Naylor on it. For five minutes he stood by his window looking out at nothing. Then he made three phone calls.

The first was to Probation Services, the group responsible for SOTP, who told him that disclosure of further information, even to police services, would involve formal legal intervention taking a minimum of two weeks.

The second was to the Sex Offender Register, who half an hour later sent through a report of all the Naylors on their records, none of whom matched *his* Naylor.

The third was to Archives.

"Bill? Raminder Singh here. City Squad."

"What's up, Raminder?"

"Remember we asked you to find records for a school janitor?"

"That's right, somebody Naylor. We drew a blank. Incomplete record."

"I think we were looking for the wrong man."

"Wrong man?"

"Right man, wrong name."

There was a silence at the other end of the phone.

Singh said, "I'll come over and explain. If I'm right, we've got more searching to do."

It was lunchtime, but Singh ignored his hunger. On his way past his assistant she said, "The chief called."

He hesitated, and walked on, saying, "I'll be over at Archives. Maybe all afternoon. But if Mal calls I want to know straightaway."

Then he was gone.

Bill Archer was a young guy with wiry orange hair and an Australian accent. He met Singh in reception and took him up to the open-plan offices above. As they walked between the pods of the data archivists and researchers (a few of them glancing curiously at Singh in his turban as he went by), Singh explained what he wanted, and by the time they reached the glass-fronted office at the far end Archer was ready to get to work.

He accessed the database. "Here's the data hole. See?"

Singh peered over his shoulder.

The system held all the usual information for Naylor—date and place of birth, current medical records, social security data, financial and insurance details, police record and current employment details— but no record of his upbringing, schooling, or any previous employment. Even if he'd been unemployed before, there should have been something in the records—at least his application to Marsh Academy, or his references, or his previous address. There was nothing. A whole part of his life had disappeared.

"So where's it gone?" Singh asked.

Archer shrugged. "My first thought was it had just gone astray. It happens."

It wasn't uncommon for data simply to go missing. It had happened on a big scale when Archives migrated to the new system a couple of years earlier. It still happened from time to time, for instance when data was transferred from one region to another.

Archer went on: "But you say he's changed his name? That's a different problem. What's missing here isn't a chunk of Naylor's past. It's the link to the records of whoever he was before." He looked up at Singh. "Who was he?"

Singh handed him a copy of the list of attendees from the SOTP meeting and Archer raised his eyebrows.

"He's one of these guys?"

"If he's a convicted sex offender the chances are he changed his identity after his release. He'd be Naylor to everyone now except the SOTP. His real name would be one of these."

"But without the link in Naylor's file you don't know which." He looked down the list. "Nineteen of them—that's not too bad. But first initials are notoriously unstable; you'll have to scan the whole surname groups. And you've got some of the commonest here. Miller, Johnson, Williams. With a population this big, that's a lot of slow work. I mean, really."

Singh winced. "Is it quicker to pull out photographic records from the Sex Offender Register instead?"

Archer shook his head. "Only half those records have photo-graphs. Besides"—he smiled wryly—"the systems don't talk to each other."

"Then there's no alternative."

Archer nodded. "I'll set you up. But I've got to warn you: It could take a very long time."

Singh took off his jacket, rolled up his sleeves, and began. It was half past two. Beginning with the less common names, he plugged in Naylor's age, ethnic profile, and the years he was likely to have worked, and ran the searches. He selected the closest matches and drilled down until they were ruled out, and ran the searches again. Archer had been right. It was slow work.

Time passed. Three thirty, four thirty. A broad bar of sunlight swept slowly across the desk and carpet, and disappeared into the corner of the room. Outside the building, colors cooled and leaked from things. Soon it would be evening and twilight. Five o'clock, six. The offices and pods around Singh emptied. Noises of footsteps and voices ebbed to nothing, and then there was silence.

Alone, Singh worked on, slowly, methodically. The time for his rehras came and went, but he stayed at the terminal, plugging in his data and running his searches, as night fell around him.

36

Garvie Smith arrived home from school on time, took his high-tops off at the door, made his mother a cup of tea, went into his room, and settled down at his quite astonishingly tidy table to begin his evening's schoolwork.

"Citizenship," he said, "from four till five. Biology, five till six. Geography after dinner."

His mother examined him carefully from his bedroom doorway.

"All right," she said at last. "I don't know if it's going to stick, but at least you're doing something. I recognize it."

"Told you. These exams are all I'm thinking about now."

"Is that right?" She looked at him skeptically. "What's your first? Tell me that."

"Math, higher tier, calculator paper."

"And you know what you've got to do?"

"Answer all questions in the spaces provided. You must not write on the formulae page. Mark allocations are shown in parentheses. If your calculator does not have a pi button, take the value of—"

"All right, Garvie. When *is* the exam?"

"Monday, May the twenty-eighth, two thirty."

She looked skeptical again. "Doesn't give you long to do a whole year's work from scratch."

He glanced at his watch. "Twenty-eight days. Six hundred and seventy-two hours."

"Hmm."

"Forty thousand three hundred and twenty minutes."

"*All right*, Garvie."

"Two million four hundred and nineteen thousand . . ."

But his mother had already moved away and was standing in the kitchen looking out the window.

At five o'clock Garvie dutifully began his biology homework.

At six o'clock he had his dinner.

At seven o'clock he began his geography, finished it, and pushed on with physics.

And at eight o'clock, as arranged, the telephone rang. He didn't look up. He didn't even look as if he was listening as his mother went across the living room to answer the phone.

"Hello."

She caught the name of Felix and frowned. "He's studying," she said shortly.

After that there was a long silence from Mrs. Smith in which she did a lot more frowning, then a low murmured conversation that was difficult for someone in another room to make out.

Eventually she reappeared in the doorway of Garvie's room, where he was apparently engrossed in his *Physics Study Guide*. She was already changed into her hospital uniform.

"That was Felix, your burglar friend. Says he's studying math."

"Felix? Studying? Are you sure?"

"Must be taking an evening off from robbery. Says he's stuck. He wanted me to ask you if by any chance you could go round and maybe help him with his probability. On account of you being a mathematical genius." She looked at him suspiciously.

Garvie said, "Can't it wait till tomorrow?"

"He says he has to do it now. His study schedule must be packed."

"Well." Garvie checked his watch. "I suppose I have put in four hours already on top of a full timetable at school. But, look, I won't go if you don't want me to. No way. I'll stay here and do another couple of hours."

His mother gazed at him for what seemed like a long time.

"All right, then," she said at last. "Maybe you need a break. And even burglars benefit from an education. I'm due on in half an hour, so I won't be here when you get back. But don't be later than ten. I don't want any more distractions for you now till after the exams are over."

He met Felix at the Old Ditch Road playground, as arranged, and they sat on the merry-go-round and swapped bags. In Garvie's rucksack were several math textbooks. In Felix's were the familiar single-cuff Jil Sander shirt, black Acne jacket, Ralph Lauren stretch chinos, and black brogues, all courtesy of Felix's older brother, who knew nothing of the transaction, being currently on a job out of town.

"You investigating again or just gambling this time?"

Garvie ignored him. "Got the card?"

Felix handed it over. "Goes without saying that if you lose it or get any of his kit damaged we're both dead."

"That's fine, Felix. I'm pretty sure I'm immortal. And you, my friend, have been dead for years. Did you get the money too?"

Felix took the note out of his pocket and passed it over. "It's a lot of dosh, man. There's going to be plenty of glum faces if it doesn't come back."

"It'll come back."

"Don't know why you wanted it all in a single note, either."

"Basic subterfuge, Felix. Looks better. I'm an out-of-luck rich boy down to his last C-note."

Tucking it into his top pocket, he stepped off the merry-go-round and posed in front of the climbing frame. "Do I look the part?"

"You look like a tosser."

"Perfect."

Felix handed him his bike. "You going to tell me what's happening in the great investigation? While you've been out and about, Plod's been into school on a daily basis. We've all had to give our alibis and stuff. Smudge is convinced they think he did it. I'm seriously worried he's going to break down and confess."

"Smudge is a natural-born killer. But you know, Felix, the police get too hung up on alibis. I think it's best not to pay too much attention to them."

"Oh yeah?"

"Yeah. They're like complex numbers."

"Oh yeah?"

"Yeah. The numbers are real but they exist in an imaginary dimension."

"Yeah, yeah, very true, Garv. Just take care of the stuff, all right? Oh, and don't get caught by the bad guys."

It was a twenty-minute cycle ride to the casino. Relations with his mother being so delicate, Garvie didn't want to risk using Abdul and word getting back to her.

He went up Bulwarks Lane to the track along the bypass and rode south through the surf-noise of traffic toward the sewage plant, past the back ends of tenement streets and fenced-off waste ground, until he came to the old railway path, and turned down it into darkness and sudden quietness. Under old brick bridges and overhanging haw-thorns he went, along asphalt walkways split by weeds and crusted with garbage as far as the canal, then along the towpath until he reached the Southside retail park. Here he left his bike. He cut across the vast near-empty parking lot, walked over the pedestrian bridge, and came at last to The Wicker and the full-on blare of big-city enter-tainment. Even on a Monday night the place was busy.

As before, he crossed the forecourt of the bowling alley next to the casino, went down the pathway between the properties into the shadows, and hopped over the wall into Imperium's parking lot.

First thing he saw was a Porsche. It was red. He went past it, circled round the parking lot twice, seeing no other cars in any way resembling Porsches, and returned to the shadows by the wall, where he smoked two Benson & Hedges, frowning, thinking partly about

Porsches and partly about a girl in a toga with shoulder-length brown hair.

In the pocket of Felix's brother's Ralph Lauren chinos he found a coin, and he flipped it up and caught it and showed it on the back of his hand. Heads. He grinned, dropped his cigarette butt, and ground it out. Stepping out of the shadows, he joined a group of people leaving their cars and made his way to the front of the casino.

37

The familiar soft noise washed over him as he went through the sunken lobby and on, through chatter and laughter and lyre music, into the gaming rooms. She wasn't in the poker room or by the roulette and blackjack tables, she wasn't in the coffee lounge or bar, and at last he came to rest by the end of the slot machines, in a space away from the crowds, to think.

A blonde girl in a toga came up with a tray of drinks—Livia, according to her name tag—and he took a glass of bubbly.

"Hypatia around tonight?"

She gave him a look. "You a fan?"

"No, I'm her twin brother."

She looked him over, smiling. "Aren't you a little young?"

"It's a medical condition."

She rested her fingers briefly on his arm. "Is it catching? I hope so."

"If you see her, will you tell her Garvie's looking for her?"

"I might." She moved away with a long backward glance. "Or I might just keep the information to myself. Garvie."

To pass the time he sipped his bubbly and watched blackjack, a game he knew nothing about. Six players sitting round a curved green baize table and an unsmiling girl labeled "Messalina" dealing them hands from a long plastic box. It was an easy game to pick up: Each gambler played against the house, and the highest hand closest to twenty-one won. There were some other rules and conventions to learn, a few hand gestures, but two things really caught Garvie's interest: All the cards were played face up and the dealer never shuffled the deck after the first time.

A new session began. Messalina unwrapped four new decks, shuffled them together, stacked them in one of the boxes, and began to deal.

Garvie concentrated.

After twenty minutes exactly three-quarters of the cards had been played. Five of the players got up, leaving a woman sitting alone. She was wearing a long emerald dress and the southward slope of her bare shoulders showed what sort of luck she was having. Garvie went over.

"Hi."

The woman looked up at him with big confused eyes. "Don't sit anywhere near me, hon. I'm bad luck."

"You look good to me."

She was about thirty, with a glass of champagne, a cute mouth, and a bob of bottle-black hair disheveled by so much bad luck. She laughed once and began to run her hands through it again. "Oh, the flattery." She looked him over, raised an eyebrow, and involuntarily smoothed down her dress.

He handed Messalina the C-note, got a brief look of surprise and a pile of chips, and they began to play.

"You a big blackjack player, hon?"

"Never played before in my life." He put down a white chip, got a seven of hearts and a nine of clubs, and refused another card. Bad Luck got a six and eight of spades, hit for another, got a ten of diamonds and bust. Messalina showed the house hand of a nine of clubs and eight of hearts, and Garvie's chip disappeared along with Bad Luck's.

She sipped her drink and pouted. "That's a shame. You deserve a bit of beginner's luck."

"Best hand I could have got," Garvie said. "Same as you."

She smiled and sipped again. "I don't think you've got the hang of this yet, hon."

Garvie smiled too, and went back to watching the cards. In the box forty-five remained.

They played two more hands and the house won both.

"Told you," she said. "Bad Luck. That's me. In a minute my boyfriend's going to come over here and find out I've lost all his money."

Sipping from her glass, she moved her hair around and kept an eye on her last few white chips.

There were twenty-seven cards left in the box. They played one more hand, the house won again, and now there were nineteen.

Garvie had now lost four hands in a row. "I can't believe how well this is going," he said. "It's time to step up the betting." He slid a few big chips across the table.

Bad Luck frowned at him. "I wouldn't do that if I were you, hon. You're getting things backward. This is a losing streak for both of us."

He shrugged. "If I were you I wouldn't do it, either." He leaned in toward her and whispered, "But I would if someone told me there were three aces, one king, two queens, one jack, and two tens left in that box."

She looked at him pityingly. "Okay, Mr. X-Ray Eyes."

He was dealt two nines, and he split and pushed over another pile of chips, got a jack and a ten, and beat the house hand of seventeen, twice.

She blinked and said, "Oh."

"That's right," he said. "Beginner's luck kicking in."

He was gathering his chips when there was a new voice at his shoulder.

"I heard you were looking for me, Garvie Smith."

He turned in his seat and she was standing there with a tray of champagne flutes, one hand on her hip, looking at him with those large, amused gray eyes, and for a moment his words stuck in his throat like a catch of the breath. She was taller than he remembered, and even prettier, and there was a dimple in one cheek and not the other, which seemed so beautifully improbable he felt a goofy smile start up on his face. Straightening out the smile as fast as he could, he said, with all the cool originality he could muster, "Hey."

Another dimple appeared, and he took this as sign to help himself to a drink.

She gave him a look. "I'm not supposed to serve drinks to minors. Even lucky ones."

"I need to talk to you."

"Now?"

"In a minute. I have to win my money back first."

Without comment she walked away toward the one-armed bandits, and Garvie said to Bad Luck, "Sorry, but I have to finish this off."

He pushed forward half of all his chips, and she gave him a wry look. "Okay. At least it looks as if it's going to be quick."

He nodded at Messalina and got two queens. He looked at Bad Luck.

"Split? I wouldn't," she said.

He split, and looked at her again.

"Bet big? I really wouldn't," she said. "I really, really . . ."

He pushed across all his remaining chips and she shook her head sadly. "That's everything you've got. I can't believe it. You had one little bit of luck and you just kicked it in the nuts."

She hid her face behind her tilted champagne flute, and Messalina put the ace of hearts on one of Garvie's queens, and Bad Luck took an accidental gulp of wine.

Then Messalina put down the ace of spades on his other queen, and Bad Luck sprayed the wine across the green baize.

Messalina said, "House pays three to two," and pushed a substantial pile of high-value chips across to Garvie, and Garvie helpfully banged Bad Luck on her back until she stopped coughing.

"Didn't mean to shock you. It's just that I have to go."

She stared at him. She looked as if she wanted to prod him to see if he was real. "Did that really just happen? Double blackjack?"

He shrugged. "Call it basic mathematical probability."

She nodded uncomprehendingly. "I guess I'm just not probable enough, mathematically." And as he stood, her expression changed from dizzy to distraught, and she tossed her last white chip onto the green baize and dropped her empty hands into her emerald lap.

She smiled at him overbrightly. "Go," she said. "You made it so much nicer. I'll be fine."

Garvie didn't say anything to that. He put his hand briefly on her shoulder before moving away through people toward the one-armed bandits.

"You're a gambler now?"

"I can gamble."

"Does your mother know?"

"My mother knows everything."

"And you?"

"I know nearly everything. Only one thing worth knowing I don't know, in fact."

She raised her eyebrows. "And that would be?"

"That would be your name."

She laughed then, her head tilted back so her shining hair fell around her shoulders, and his heart did dance steps.

"Poor Garvie Smith. The one thing I can't tell you. And now you've run out of questions to ask me. Luckily I can think of something to ask you." She was staring at him curiously.

"What?"

"Did you just drop all your gambling chips into that woman's bag?"

He frowned and turned and looked back at the woman in the emerald dress, still sitting dejected at the blackjack table, her open bag hanging on the back of her chair.

"No." He looked into her gray eyes. "I kept this." He held up a black chip. "It's not mine. I have to give it back."

She rewarded him with dimples. "You're a very unusual boy, Garvie Smith."

"You're not so usual yourself, oh nameless one. Got another question for you."

"All right."

"About Imperium."

"What about it?"

They looked across the rooms together. While a new crowd of players settled round the blackjack table, the emerald lady sat alone, quietly weeping. The big man, Winder, appeared from the poker den and pushed his way through the bar with a face like slapped steak, the smaller man Garvie had seen before going after him, like a dog on a leash, glaring from side to side. Garvie tilted his head and listened. The bright rattle of the roulette balls was the sound of someone losing money, the soft noise of laughter that came from the bar was the laughter of bravado, forced and shrill, and whenever it failed there was an agitated hush, like a frightened man holding his breath.

"Seems like a lovely place," he said at last.

"It's hell."

He looked at her sharply. "Hell?"

"You wouldn't believe. There was something the other week—" She stopped and wiped a hand across her face. "Sorry. Usually I'm tougher than this. I've not been well. Well, you saw me faint the other day. That's not like me, either. Anyway, what was your question?"

"What's a girl like you doing working here?"

"Reasons of poverty." She smiled. "But I've got a plan to escape. A couple of months, that's it, I'll be off. Gone. Out of here. Up, up, and away."

"Nice. You're going to be a balloonist."

"Travel rep, actually."

"Where?"

"India."

"Can I come?"

"Girls only. My friend and me. We're going to rep together. She's out there now."

"What's *her* name?"

She smiled at him. "She doesn't give out her real name, either. Calls herself the Tick Hill Travel Bug. That's because she's been everywhere. And according to her, India's the place to be."

"Why?"

"Well, Garvie, just try to think of somewhere that's the complete opposite of this place, somewhere warm and full of light and color, and exotic, and romantic. That place is India. Put it this way. My friend tells me that when she writes her autobiography she's going to call it *From Trailer Park to Taj Mahal*. See? India's just . . . lovelier than here."

Garvie thought about this. "Don't suppose I can persuade you to come to Barbados instead?"

Another waitress came past them then, gave Garvie a look, and said to Hypatia out of the corner of her mouth, "Better get a move on. He's got his eye on you."

From the other side of the blackjack room they saw the small man glowering at them.

"Time to go."

"Wait. Who is he? Guy with the pig-crazy eyes. He was staring at me last time."

"The manager. Looks after the place when Scumbag's not here. He's a creep. Well, Garvie Smith . . . our time ran out." She smiled at him, and for a second he thought she was leaning in toward him, but she swayed away and went toward the Staff Only door.

"Wait, about that *something* the other week . . ."

But she'd gone.

He looked at his watch and sighed. Down by the blackjack table Bad Luck had been joined by a man in a tuxedo, who paced to and fro in front of her while she shook her head, and Garvie went past them on his way out.

"All of it?" the man was saying. "Just like that? Are you sure? Have you checked your purse? Have you checked your bag?"

Garvie sauntered past the bar and coffee lounge, on through the sunken circular lobby and out of the main door onto the walkway outside, where he was accosted by the man with the pig-crazy eyes waiting for him with a bad expression on his face washed blue by the casino's wall lights.

"Leaving?"

"Sharp. You must be with Special Branch."

"Don't bother coming back."

"It's okay, I've got to be somewhere else, anyway."

"I mean, ever."

Garvie glanced up at the billboard above the entrance. "Last year's model," he said. "Like your customer relations."

The man did an odd thing. He didn't go for Garvie or yell at him. He gulped like a pantomime villain and, turning sharply, stumbled back inside the building.

Thoughtfully Garvie gazed after him, stroking his nose with a forefinger. Then he glanced at his watch, saw it was already half past ten, and ran down The Wicker toward his bike.

38

Singh sat exhausted but upright at his terminal, a lonely and exposed figure in the white glare of the glass-walled office. The afternoon had passed, evening had arrived, and night had fallen while he worked. People had come and gone, and now he was alone in the building except for the security guard downstairs in reception.

The number of data hits he'd already investigated was enormous. Most searches had required further searches, sometimes extensive. There had been a Rolfe, J., matching Naylor's profile exactly, who'd worked as a janitor in a primary school up north during the right years, but his archive had lacked a photo so it had taken a full half hour of follow-up searches in related databases before Singh learned that Rolfe, J., had retired on disability benefits two years earlier after an accident that had lost him a leg. It was seven o'clock by the time the last of the Williamses had been completed and the final name group, "Johnson," was ready to be trawled. Singh was tired but he forced himself on.

There were 172 Johnsons matching Naylor's profile who'd been employed in various capacities at schools over the right years. Further searches showed thirty-seven of them working in what was described as "Facilities"—caretakers, janitors, and groundsmen. He went through them methodically, dismissing five in short order, investigating three more only to eventually dismiss them too, and running even more detailed but ultimately fruitless searches on eighteen others before finally reaching "Johnson, Paul," groundsman at a nearby school called Maltby. There he stopped.

Maltby was only twenty miles away but it came under the jurisdiction of another regional educational authority. Paul Johnson's profile matched Naylor's in every way and his years of employment fit perfectly, but what really caught Singh's eye were two details. Johnson's employment at the school had lasted only four months, as if its termination had been sudden and unplanned. And his disciplinary record contained an allegation made against him by another member of staff—of assault.

A little jolt went through Singh. Suddenly he was alert again.

It was seven thirty.

There was no photo of Paul Johnson in the records. He spent thirty minutes searching a variety of databases for contact details for the principal, finding her number at last on a free public directory. But when he called her she was unavailable, and all he could do was leave a message.

He was tired again, but still he wouldn't give up. He accessed the school's website, and there found a section of photographs called "Golden Years at Maltby," a large but disorganized collection of hundreds of random images of school life. Without a moment's rest he began to search through them, one by one.

Official portraits of staff, both individual and grouped.

Formal portraits of tennis teams and soccer squads.

Prize-giving ceremonies, theatrical productions, and celebrity visits.

Private photos posted by ex-students showing groups of friends talking and laughing in the cafeteria or walking through the yard or capering together on the grass.

By eight thirty he'd found nothing at all and his tiredness was like a belt tightening around his chest. His eyes ached. Getting up suddenly, he went and stood, eyes closed, by the window, where, almost automatically, he began to recite the rehras. But after a minute he broke off abruptly and went back to his seat. Wiping his hand across his face and blinking, he concentrated on the screen again—and immediately found what he'd been looking for.

In the photo two girls wearing navy-blue uniforms stood in front of a shed on the school grounds, smiling toward the camera, making comic gestures. They were tagged, Singh noticed, *Jazz* and *Ellie*. But he didn't look at them. He looked at the shed in the background. Leaning against it, wearing green overalls and rubber boots, with one hand on the handle of a wheelbarrow and the other in his pocket, was the younger but still unmistakable figure of Naylor, watching the girls.

At that moment his phone rang.

"Singh."

It was the principal at Maltby calling him back. Before he could explain why he'd called her she interrupted him.

"I assume it's about the reason for his leaving."

Singh hesitated. "Why did he leave?"

"He went to prison. But you must have known that."

Singh hesitated again. "I don't have that information. Was it connected with the alleged assault against one of the teachers?"

"No. That was never proved."

"Then what was he convicted of?"

"Rape."

They were both silent for a moment. The whole building was silent around Singh.

"Rape?"

"Yes. A girl here at the school. But it must be in his records."

"His records have gone missing," Singh said after a moment.

There was another long pause. Then the principal said, "Does this mean that something's happened?" And when Singh didn't reply, she added, "What's he done now?"

As he left Archives he was already putting through calls to the others. By the time he was back at Cornwallis Way, Lawrence Shan and Darren Collier were waiting for him in his office with copies of the SOTP profile of Paul Johnson, aka Ben Naylor.

He went over to his desk, sat down, and began to read.

It was a brief institutional record of a deprived childhood and violent youth culminating in a four-year prison term served for the rape of sixteen-year-old schoolgirl Livvy Warren, Johnson's last recorded public act. On the Sex Offender Register he remained Paul Johnson, but for all other purposes he'd become Ben Naylor, free to start a new life after his release, conditional on his continuing participation in a variety of counseling programs and with the knowledge that any future employer would automatically be shown his SOTP record.

"But the link to Johnson's records was lost," Singh said aloud. "So Marsh Academy never knew who they were employing."

"What now?" Shan asked. "We don't want to rush in like last time. The press had a field day."

"Where's Mal?"

"Still up at Froggett Woods."

"And Bob's rechecking Naylor's alibi?"

"Yes."

Singh said, "Naylor's record changes everything. I want to make the arrest as soon as possible. Darren?"

Collier looked sour. "I was wrong about the man," he said. "I admit it. And we all know the re-offending stats for rapists. But there's still the issue of his alibi."

"That's why we're waiting for Bob," Singh said.

They waited.

Dowell arrived ten minutes later. He came into the room without looking at any of them and threw himself into a chair.

"How's his alibi?" Singh asked.

"He doesn't have one."

There was a sharp jolt in the atmosphere of the room.

"*What?* You checked it before. Twice. You went back and talked to the landlord."

Half angrily, half apologetically, Dowell explained. Firstly, the man who'd originally corroborated Naylor's story—that he was in the Jolly Boatman all Friday evening—had gone missing. Then the landlord who'd seen Naylor at last orders had admitted that for most of the evening he hadn't been in the pub at all; he'd been taking care of business elsewhere. Then the bombshell: The bar staff had confessed that there'd been a power cut earlier on, the result of some japester behind the bar knocking out the fuse box with a fire extinguisher. They hadn't dared tell the landlord, just patched it up by the time he got back. But while the power was out there was no one in the pub at all.

"What time was the power out?"

Dowell swallowed. "Five till nine."

"The exact window of the time of death."

"That's what I said," Dowell said, avoiding Singh's eyes. "He's got no alibi."

"So if Naylor wasn't in the Jolly Boatman, where was he?"

At that moment Singh's phone rang.

"Mal? What's the news?"

Without preliminaries she said, "I've got a positive ID for the thirteenth. He was up here at Pike Pond."

A muscle jumped in Singh's cheek. "What sort of ID? Will it stand up?"

"Solid. One of the residents has just come back from holiday. She recognized his picture at once. He was at the side of the path tinkering with his moped at about four, and when she asked him what he was doing there he told her to get lost. It was definitely him."

Singh said, "We're going round to get him now."

"Just remember," she said.

"Remember what?"

"He can be violent."

Singh put down the phone and looked at his watch. Ten o'clock. He said to Shan, "Come with me, Lawrence."

To Dowell he said: "You run things here. I want backup at the school in half an hour. I'll call if we need anything else."

As he went out of his office an alarm bell went off faintly in his mind. Naylor had a head start on them. Since Singh's visit in the morning the man had known the police suspected him, and he knew also who had led them back to him. He was an emotional man prone to violent obsessions. What might he do to an interfering boy who had made himself such an easy target for revenge? But there was no time to think about this now, and he went at speed across the open-plan room toward the elevator, Shan close behind.

39

As they pulled out of the underground parking lot in Cornwallis Way they clamped on the siren and accelerated loud and bright down Cornwallis Road, out toward the bypass. Shan drove, glancing occasionally at Singh sitting next to him in the passenger seat, agitated and brooding. His face was clenched. His turban was crooked. Every few minutes he looked at his watch.

After a while he muttered, "Go faster."

Then: "What if he's not there?"

Shan stepped on it and said nothing.

"We've given him enough warnings," Singh said, half to himself. "He knew this morning we were onto him."

"If he's gone," Shan said, "we'll find him."

"There's a boy," Singh began, and hesitated.

"What boy?"

Singh shook his head. "Doesn't matter." He sat staring ahead. "I've been stupid," he added after a moment.

Shan said nothing to that, and they went the rest of the way in the screaming car without comment.

At the school gates they were met by backup and the vehicles went together, lights and sirens off, down the long drive through the grounds to Naylor's bungalow. From a quarter of a mile away they could see it lit up against the darkness of the woods behind, every window in the building blazing.

"Looks like he's home," Shan murmured to Singh.

Moving quickly across the light-striped shadows of the untidy lawn, the men took up positions and Singh went forward and rapped on the door.

There was no answer and he rapped again.

"Police!" he called.

Still no answer. He gave a nod, and a man on either side of the door kicked it down and they ran in together, weapons up, down the narrow hall, sliding on the loose linoleum, into the front room and beyond, kicking open doors, shoving over furniture and shouting.

It took them no more than thirty seconds to realize there was no one there.

In the middle of the chaos Singh stood staring around the tiny living room. The mess was even worse than before, and there was a smell, sweet and somehow dirty, like burned sugar. Crockery had been knocked off the little table and trodden into pieces; clothes were strewn across the floor. On a chair was a plate with a cigarette lighter on it and an empty cola can lying on its side.

Singh picked up the can and turned it over. The bottom was blackened; round the side were several small puncture marks. He lifted it to his nose and sniffed.

Shan, standing next to him, raised his eyebrows.

Singh said, "Cocaine."

Before Shan could react, one of the men shouted urgently from the bedroom: "Sir!"

When they went in, the policeman gestured at the bed. "Thought you should see this, sir."

A laptop lay carelessly on the duvet.

"It wasn't powered down properly," the man said. "I just restarted it, and . . ." He turned it to face Singh and there was silence in the room.

Singh blinked once, as if in pain. On the computer screen was a photo of Chloe Dow.

"It's a slideshow," the man said after a moment.

He pressed a button and new photos appeared. Chloe standing with a small group of girls in front of C Block. Chloe pushing open the fire door in B Block. Chloe sitting on the grass of Top Pitch with two boys, one of whom—Singh saw—was Garvie Smith.

The policeman leaned over to pause it, and Singh stopped him.

"Keep it playing," he said.

One by one, more photos appeared. Chloe in the playground. Chloe in a corridor. Chloe by the school gates. There were dozens of them, perhaps hundreds. Many were blurry, scrappy, as if taken surreptitiously, but others were clear and close-up. In some Chloe was looking directly at the camera, her expression hard to read.

"She knew," Singh said quietly. "She knew he was photographing her."

They watched for another minute, mesmerized by the apparently limitless number of pictures, until Singh said, "Wait! Stop there."

On the screen was a long-distance shot of Chloe. She was wearing a deep-pink tank top and pink shorts, and she was running, head up and springy-legged, in open countryside between fields of yellow rapeseed.

Shan sucked in his breath.

"Pike Pond," Singh said.

Shan swore. "He's our man. He was up there waiting for her."

Singh nodded, tight-faced. "But where is he now?"

They left the room issuing orders, Shan radioing in to Central to get an emergency broadcast put out, Singh talking on the phone to Dowell, asking for more backup and lighting equipment.

"It's him, then?" Dowell asked.

"Looks that way."

Dowell swore.

"Wait a minute," Singh said. Still holding the phone, he ran out of the house onto the litter-strewn grass and went here and there among the rubbish until he found a sheet of tarpaulin lying loosely on the wet grass.

"His moped's gone," he said into his phone. "Get the registration and put out an alert. He won't be far: I don't think he's been gone long. I want every officer in the county watching out."

Then he ran back into the house, where Shan was waiting for him with a strange look on his face, holding out his phone to him.

"The chief," he said.

Singh took the phone and stood listening, suddenly isolated in his own zone of quietness while his men busied themselves noisily around him.

"I hear you know who killed Chloe Dow," he heard the chief say.

Singh began to respond, but the chief went on: "I also hear you've let him go."

Singh grimaced. "We'll find him," he said. He began to explain the situation but realized after a few moments that he was talking to no one, and with a heavy feeling handed the phone back to Shan and resumed giving instructions to the men. They went out together, leaving three men to secure the house and await the Crime Detection Unit, which was already on its way.

The Unit was slow in arriving. Singh stood upright by his car, pale and silent, and after a few minutes Shan gave up trying to talk to him. As soon as he was on his own Singh took out his notebook and withdrew from it a scrap of paper with a number scrawled on it. Taking out his phone, he made the call and waited anxiously, listening first to the ringing tone, then to the voicemail message. The boy's voice was oddly unrecognizable. But what he said was completely typical: "Really can't be bothered to answer the phone right now. Catch me later."

Singh clenched his jaw. He checked his watch and called another number, and waited impatiently while it rang. He was about to give up when it was finally answered, and he said in a rush, "Mrs. Smith, it's Detective Inspector Singh. I'm sorry it's so late. Can I talk to your son?"

He heard a snort. "There's a whole queue of folks waiting to talk to that boy. And I'm in front of you."

"He's not there? Where is he?"

"Soon as I get to talk to him I'll ask him."

"He didn't tell you where he was going?"

"Detective Inspector, I'm guessing you don't have children of your own. I just came home between shifts at work to find a note on the kitchen table telling me he's had to go out. Bit of an emergency, he says. Exclamation mark. I'll exclamation mark him."

"Does he say who he went to meet?"

"I'm only a mother, Detective Inspector. Confidential information like that doesn't often come my way."

"And he doesn't say where?"

He heard her sigh. "Wait. Let me get the note."

There was a silence.

"All right. I have it here. *Sorry, Mum, had to go out. Bit of an emergency.* Exclamation mark. I told you that. Ah. On the back of the note he's written something else."

"What?"

"*Badger Lane.*"

"Badger Lane?"

"Don't know it. Maybe it's where a friend of his lives."

Singh said nothing. In the silence, Mrs. Smith said, "Speaking of confidential information, are you going to tell me why you want to talk to him? Because if he's been getting into trouble again I'd like to know."

Singh hesitated. "He's not in trouble, with us."

And before she could ask what he meant he hung up.

Shan was looking at him strangely. "What's the matter, Raminder? Who's this boy? You mentioned him before. And what's that about trouble?"

Before Singh could answer, his phone rang and he answered it at once and stood listening in silence.

"Yes?" he said. "Good. Very good. Where are you?"

The answer seemed to terrify him. He flinched, almost dropped the phone, and when he spoke again his voice was a strange hoarse whisper.

"Pull everyone in. I want everyone there now. *Everyone!*"

"What's up?" Shan asked.

Singh's face was white. "They've found Naylor's moped."

"Fast work. Where?"

For a moment Singh didn't seem able to speak, and Shan stared at him in astonishment.

"Where, Raminder?" he repeated.

Singh found his voice at last. "At the end of Badger Lane," he said. "Where the boy is."

40

Badger Lane was an old country road, broken and unlit, full of mud and dead leaves. Used by joggers by day and the occasional trash dumper and dealer at night, it ran from the back of the new houses in Fox Walk past boggy grass fields and scrubland to peter out eventually at the edge of the Marsh Woods.

Lit up in the beams of a stationary police car, Naylor's moped lay on its side in rough gravel under ash trees where the road gave way to a footpath. Singh went forward and opened the pannier and saw there was nothing in it.

Oblivious to the men waiting by the cars, he took out his phone and dialed, and listened once more to the voicemail recording: "Really can't be bothered to answer the phone right now . . ." before turning at last, his face drawn and anxious, to address the others.

"Listen to me," he said.

They gathered around—Shan and his men, Bob Dowell and the backup team, the men and women of the Dog Support Unit, and the patrolmen who had found the bike—and when he finished speaking they fetched their lights and their animals and walked into the woods together. No one said anything. They went with slow, awkward steps, peering about them, crouching and bending through the tangled darkness made more confusing by the swooping beams of their lights. They went behind their straining dogs along the path, and spread out between briars and bushes in a rough line, stumbling in and out of hollows and splashing through streams, their breath fogging the night air around them. Long ago the wood had been community garden plots, and from time to time they found themselves clambering over tumbledown brick walls, and stepping on the jagged remains of greenhouse panes glinting underfoot, and stooping under archways of gigantically overgrown privet. No one knew the place and their progress was slow and uncertain.

Singh had told them that Naylor was dangerous, probably still under the influence of drugs. He'd also told them that he might have lured a boy into the woods.

For half an hour they forced their way, grim-faced and uncomfortable, through trees and undergrowth, doing their best to stay together, finding nothing except refuse, the charred remains of old campfires and rusty junk, but going on with the same unspeaking, crunching determination. Singh walked in the middle of them with Shan and a woman from the Dog Support Unit, saying nothing to either, though twice he took out his phone and called the same number as before, listening helpless and white-faced to its voicemail message.

"Really can't be bothered . . ."

It was now a quarter past eleven. A cold rain set in.

Suddenly there was a shout.

"Sir!"

Lights swept wildly in all directions.

"There, sir!"

Momentarily the outline of a figure stood out in the darkness of a slope ahead, and at once disappeared.

Cries went up from several policemen. One ran forward and fell heavily, and Singh's voice could be heard shouting for calm over the uproar, during which they all caught another brief glimpse of the figure ahead dodging silently between trees.

At last Singh found his whistle. "Quiet! Stay where you are! Get your lights on him!"

The slope in front of them lit up in the beams of two dozen high-powered flash lamps: a deserted patch of dense holly and young beech trees, their slender trunks pale against the darkness of the thicket behind. The rain was coming down harder now, crackling in the leaves and flickering like pinpricks of metal in the artificial light, and everything was dripping wet.

Singh called out, "Naylor?"

For a long moment there was nothing in front of them but black holly and pale beech trunks darkening with rain; then the figure appeared again, the police lights following him as he dodged from shadow to shadow, a figure in a red-and-yellow varsity jacket with a hood pulled low over his face.

"Stay where you are, Naylor!" Singh called. "This is an armed unit!" There was the chinking noise around him of weapons being brought to bear.

Still the figure took no notice, and they saw now that he was coming closer. As they hesitated he floated through the last of the trees and out into full view, slowing down as he approached them, walking—to their astonishment—almost lazily down the rough slope toward Singh until he stood right in front of him and threw his hood back from his face and said, "Dude, do you want to keep the noise down a bit?"

Singh's eyes bulged. "Smith!" he said at last.

"Good to see you too, man. But you're way too noisy. Naylor'll hear you."

"Naylor? Where is Naylor? And why are you wearing his jacket? And what the *hell* are you doing here?"

"Calm down, man, you sound like my mother. I'm here 'cause this is where Naylor stashes his stuff. And this isn't Naylor's jacket. I thought you would've known that. The button's missing off the wrong sleeve, see? It's Alex's. You just missed him, by the way. He sends his apologies. I hate to say this, but he just didn't want to see you again."

Singh couldn't control himself anymore: He caught hold of Garvie by the arm and dragged him to one side. "What are you playing at?" he hissed.

Garvie regarded him coldly. "Listen, if you don't want my help you only have to say so. You don't need to start pulling me around by my friend's jacket sleeve. You could have had the other button off."

"Your *help*! You promised *not* to help." Singh looked around. "I'll get a man to take you back to the cars."

Garvie finished straightening his jacket and looked up. "You really want to blunder around in the woods all night? Or do you want me to take you to Naylor?"

There was a path nearby, and they followed the boy along it, keeping their lights to a minimum and their animals quiet.

"It leads all the way back to Naylor's house," Garvie said to Singh. "There's an opening in the fence he's hidden with brush."

"And where does it go to?"

"You'll see. But you have to be quiet."

For a quarter of a mile or more they went slowly in single file between trees, past an old quarry strewn with moss-covered boulders, a fallen cavern in a steep slope of alders, and weed-choked ponds, black and gleaming, deeper into Marsh Woods.

"If this is a wild-goose chase . . . ," Singh said at last.

"Shh."

Garvie pointed, and Singh saw within the trees ahead a denser shape among the bushes.

Garvie whispered, "Naylor's hut. Alex found it yesterday and gave me a call this morning. It sounded odd to me, and Alex was . . . Well, Alex was odd too. I won't tell you what he was planning to do but it was scary stuff. Look!"

Now Singh saw the weak and narrow gleam of a light through a window. "He's in there?"

"Last time I looked."

Singh nodded and put his hand on Garvie's shoulder. "Now it's time for you to leave."

"What, and miss Singh of the Yard getting his man?"

Ignoring him, Singh moved away to talk to Shan and Dowell, and when he returned after a few minutes he brought a man with him who took hold of Garvie's arm.

"Hey!"

Singh put his finger to his lips. "You have to go back," he said quietly. "You know why as well as I do." To the policeman he said, "Take him." And without another look at Garvie, he turned to Shan and Dowell and began to talk.

A few minutes later the policemen moved forward, one by one, quietly creeping off the path round the side of the hut until they were all in position.

The rain had stopped, but the moon was obscured by cloud and everything was dark except for the one crack of light in the window of the hut. There was no sound from inside. Nothing. From his position near the door Singh looked around carefully one last time to check everyone was in place—and flinched to find Garvie standing next to him. When he opened his mouth, Garvie just put his finger to his lips, and grinned. It was too late for him to do anything about the boy now, and with a face of fury he turned again to the hut and called out with sudden loudness:

"Naylor! Police! Come out!"

His voice echoed briefly and fell away into the quietness of the dark wood. There was still no sound from inside the hut.

"Police!" he called out again, even louder, with the same result.

Everything was peaceful and still, far too still, and out of nowhere a thought struck him so hard it made him wince.

"Naylor?" he cried questioningly, and this time his voice was anxious. But before he could act Garvie had stepped forward alone to the hut door and pulled it open, and it was too late to do anything but run after him, with Shan, Dowell, and the others close behind, crowding into the hut, all shouting, weapons raised as per training, only to come to a sudden stop in the small room, let their arms fall to their sides, and stand in silent shock around the body of Naylor, aka Paul Johnson, hanging from the roof.

41

It was long past midnight. Garvie sat silently in the police car as Singh drove slowly down the potholed Badger Lane away from Marsh Woods, and the rain came down again in steady gusts out of the low cloudy sky.

"I called your mother," Singh said, "to let her know you're on your way home."

Garvie said nothing. He hadn't said anything since the discovery of Naylor's body in the hut. He slouched against the car door, gazing vacantly out the window, his black hair wet against his forehead.

They bumped down Badger Lane. Singh was beyond tired, empty but alert, as if he would never need sleep again—just as well, since he knew he wouldn't get to bed that night. Later he would return to Marsh Woods to meet the chief pathologist and the forensics team. One reason for taking Garvie home immediately was to prevent his uncle meeting the boy at the crime scene. But at least, he thought to himself, in a few days it would be over. All that remained now was the summing up—the filling in of the last few gaps in the reconstruction, the media liaison, the ordering of the files—then the legal processes would take over and he could leave the Dow case behind and give in to his exhaustion.

He glanced over at the boy sitting silently next to him gazing out the window at the wet gray-black sky as if there were nothing in the world capable of sustaining his interest. A dissatisfied boy, Singh thought. Difficult, selfish. He was clever, of course, but strange. Singh didn't know whether to dislike him or pity him.

"You saw they found her running shoes?" he said. "A lot of her clothing too. He must have been taking things for a long time. Out of her locker with his pass key, as you said."

Garvie didn't reply, didn't even turn in his seat, and Singh had a brief intuition of what it must be like to be Garvie's mother.

Frowning, he drove on, staring ahead through the windshield wipers into the rain-flickering darkness. After a while he began to talk again. Though he didn't understand the boy, he wanted to bring things properly to an end, to make sure Garvie knew that the case was finally closed. He told him about the photographs of Chloe Dow they'd found on Naylor's laptop, and how they'd discovered that he was a sex offender, and about the link to Naylor's records going missing in Archives after his identity change. He explained that Naylor's alibi had been bogus, that he'd actually been seen up at Pike Pond on Friday afternoon. They knew now that he'd been up there before, perhaps many times, taking pictures of Chloe running.

"And I think we'll find the stolen phone he was calling Chloe on," Singh said. "That's the final piece of the jigsaw. Except for explaining that number in the call records there's really nothing else to prove."

Garvie said nothing to any of this. Singh couldn't even tell if he was listening.

Leaving Badger Lane, they accelerated into the lights of Bulwarks Lane and went across Pollard Way into the Five Mile estate.

"I can understand if you're upset," Singh said.

Still Garvie ignored him.

"You're shocked. But you'll be okay. It's over now; you can stop thinking about it. You have to. It's time to move on."

Clearing his throat, Singh went on, "In my report I'll acknowledge the . . . assistance you gave us. I can call it assistance, I think. I'll make it clear to your mother too, and to your school. But"—he glanced sideways—"there's something I have to say, something I've said before." He was never able to rid himself of his habitual stiffness, even at delicate moments, and he was aware of his own dry manner and clipped voice. He cleared his throat again as he reached for phrases remembered from the police handbook on codes of conduct. "You really shouldn't have got involved. You didn't realize the danger you were putting yourself in. I hope you see that now. Listen, the police have a duty of responsibility to young people. There've been times, many times, when I couldn't even guarantee your basic safety. Like tonight, back there," he added, remembering how Garvie had stepped up alone to the door of Naylor's hut.

Finally he reached the end of Eastwick Road and parked across the entrance to the flats.

"I'm sure you understand all this," he said, in what he hoped was a quieter, friendlier tone. "Think of your mother, if nobody else."

After he turned off the engine they sat there together in silence for a few moments. It was twenty to one; Five Mile lay sleeping around them.

At last Garvie stirred, as if coming out of a trance, and looked at Singh for the first time since leaving the woods.

"So Naylor, Johnson, whatever his name was. He was a sex offender?"

Singh looked at him curiously. There were times when the boy seemed oddly dim. "Yes. I told you."

"On the Sex Offender Register?"

Singh frowned as he nodded. "As I just told you."

"Then," Garvie said sadly, "he's almost certainly not your killer."

And without saying anything else he let himself out of the car and went through the gate to Eastwick Gardens, where his mother sat waiting for him.

42

They sat facing each other under bright lights across the kitchen table.

"Talk," she said, and sat staring at him, oddly.

She was wearing her old blue flannel dressing gown and broken-soled slippers, and her strange expression made her face look out of place, as if it wasn't really her own.

"Talk to me," she said. "While you still can."

"I thought you were at work," he said uneasily. "I didn't think you'd worry."

"I came back between shifts and found your note. While I was here the inspector called. I knew then there was trouble. I been here ever since, waiting."

He was too tired to be charming and his mother's odd expression was too disturbing, so he said as humbly as he could that he'd gotten into trouble again, with the police.

"What trouble now?"

He noticed that his mother's voice was strange too—so strange he almost decided to tell her the truth. But not quite. Truth was a slippery sort of thing. Besides, he didn't know if he could trust himself to speak or even think about Naylor just yet.

"Same as before," he said cautiously.

"Meaning?"

"Got caught with a bottle in the Old Ditch Road playground."

He was expecting her to lay into him, to deliver a few home truths in her usual high-volume, maximum-impact style. But she said nothing, just stared at him in her new strange way.

"Smoking that stuff too?" she said at last.

"No, Mum."

"No?"

"I've finished with all that."

"Finished with it, have you?"

He nodded.

After a moment she reached into her dressing-gown pocket and took out a small plastic bag and placed it on the table between them.

It was a ten-spot from Alex.

"Found it in your room," his mother said.

He didn't say anything to that.

"But you tell me you didn't have any with you tonight in the Old Ditch Road playground?"

"I didn't. I swear."

"Don't worry, I know you didn't. Because you weren't in the Old Ditch Road playground, were you?"

Garvie sat silent.

"I know where you've been," she said. "And I know what you've been doing."

He saw her lip tremble and her eyes well up, and with a sense of horror he realized what her strangeness was. She wasn't going to lay into him. She couldn't. All her loudness and certainty had gone, and with them her authority, and he realized immediately that this was far worse.

He started to get up, but she shook her head and began to speak in that strange voice, quieter and harsher at the same time.

"You see it now, eh? What it means, to be a mother. Means sitting here at midnight wondering where you are. Means asking what's happened to you. Means telling myself that whatever trouble you get yourself into it's my fault. My fault you're out all night, my fault you're smoking puff and running with those thieves and dealers, my fault you're wasting all the talents you were born with. Mine, Garvie, not yours. I can lose you, but you can never lose yourself. You understand me?"

Tears ran down her face. Her cheeks puckered and glistened.

"I'll tell you what else it means. It means knowing what Mrs. Dow is thinking now. That nutty woman you like to laugh at. Knowing what she's thinking at night when she can't get to sleep no matter how many pills she takes. Her daughter's dead, but she's alive to tell herself every night of the rest of her life that she's lost her, and it was her own fault and nobody else's."

Her chin was wet, her nose was running.

"And you now. Playing your games like it was a bit of fun, like it was a puzzle you can drop in the trash when you've solved it. Like it . . ."

She said no more.

She sat with her hand across her mouth as she wept. Cheeks wet, eyes swollen, weeping angrily without noise, almost unrecognizable, almost a stranger, as if his mother were disappearing in front of his eyes.

He got to his feet so fast he knocked over the chair, but she put up a hand to stop him hugging her and, glaring at him wetly, rose from the table and went away, still weeping, across the living-room floor into her room and shut the door behind her, leaving him standing alone at the kitchen table.

She'd always said that one day he would go too far. But he'd never known what that really meant. He did now. He didn't have to be a genius to know that his bad day had just gotten much worse.

43

As the dawn came up murky green in Cornwallis Way, Detective Inspector Singh sat alone at his desk with the list of the meetings at the Center for Public Service Partnerships in front of him. His tunic was dirty and torn, his turban soaked, his drawn face gray. But his posture was still upright, still unbending. He had never hidden things from himself. Without excuse or qualification he recognized that this was, by far, the worst day of his short, almost certainly doomed, career.

In his mind he went through recent events. He thought about the mistakes he had made. He thought, with a feeling of fury, about Garvie Smith, remembering the way the boy had turned to him in the car just a few hours earlier to tell him that Naylor was not the murderer of Chloe Dow. He remembered how he'd felt. Exasperated. Furious, even. Afterward he'd driven back to Naylor's hut as planned, to meet the pathologist, determined not to think any more about what Garvie had said. But despite himself he began to be doubtful, and the longer he worked at the hut in the dripping woods with the forensics team, the longer they failed to find the phone that Naylor must have used when he called Chloe, the more his doubts nagged at him. He kept going over the evidence in his mind. It was strongly against Naylor. The groundsman was a man of violent tendencies exacerbated by his addiction to cocaine. He'd raped before. He'd been obsessed with Chloe, stealing her things, photographing her, stalking her at school, spying on her at home, pursuing her as far as Pike Pond, where he'd even been seen the Friday afternoon of her murder. He'd lied about his alibi, which had turned out to be bogus. It was beyond all reasonable doubt: In the old clichéd terms, he had the means, the motive, and the opportunity.

And yet (damn that boy) Singh's doubts nagged and would not stop. It wasn't until he was driving home at four o'clock in the morning that he finally realized what Smith must have meant, and at once turned his car round and drove at speed to Cornwallis Way, where he surprised the night staff by striding past them without a word, then running up the stairs and across the empty open-plan area into his office, and pulling open the filing cabinet drawers to hunt for the list of the meetings at the Center for Public Service Partnerships.

Then he sat at his desk staring at it while the murky green dawn came up. Staring at one entry in particular:

5:30–8:30: *Group Therapy (SOTP)*

It was so obvious he'd forgotten it. Naylor had been enrolled on the compulsory SOTP program. Every Friday he attended the weekly group sessions. *Every* Friday, taking into account his travel time, he was occupied from five o'clock till nine o'clock—exactly the window of the time of Chloe's death. It was his alibi for the thirteenth. He'd lied to them about it not because he was guilty of Chloe's murder but to hide the fact that he was a sex offender.

A call to the night staff at Probation Services duly confirmed it: Paul Johnson had been at the Center on the evening of Chloe's murder.

So Singh sat alone in his office, his morning prayers completely forgotten, watching the dawn come up.

He was still sitting there, haggard and filthy, when colleagues who had heard the news came into his office to congratulate him on the closure of the case. In their faces he saw how he must look, with his wet turban and bloodshot eyes, and he saw their puzzlement when they failed to get a response from him other than a disgusted stare. Occasionally he heard them whispering questions to his assistant outside. Some time later he heard Dowell and Collier at the water cooler outside his office addressing a group of younger officers about the investigation, Dowell saying, "It took longer than it should have but we got there in the end."

Then all conversations died away, and he looked up to see the chief constable come into his office and carefully close the door behind him. They looked at each other. There was no trace of congratulation on the chief's gaunt face as he told Singh that he was relieved the Dow case was finally closed.

Singh couldn't wait any longer, and, rising to his feet, said, "We got the wrong man."

The chief looked at him with the same dead expression. His eyes seemed lidless.

"He was her stalker," Singh said, "but not her killer."

Still the chief said nothing. His eyes were locked on Singh's. Singh began to explain about Johnson's SOTP program, but his voice failed and there was silence in his office.

"To think," the chief said slowly, "that I promoted you."

He left the thought hanging in the air for a moment, standing silently watching Singh as if he expected the man to shrivel, implode, and turn to dust. In fact, that was what Singh felt was happening to him.

"To think," the chief said again, quietly, "of the mistakes. Of the blunders. Of the stupidities."

Singh was unable to speak. No speaking on his part was required, however.

"To think of the suicide of an innocent man," the chief went on. He rested his cold eyes on Singh. "Of the wrongful arrest of Alex Robinson. Of the hours and hours, stupidly, moronically, spent looking for a nonexistent Porsche."

Even when he was quiet it seemed to Singh that the chief's face continued to glow slightly, alien and phosphorescent, with the force of his contempt.

"There's a press conference in twenty minutes," he added, and at that moment the phone rang.

Singh stood looking at it stupidly.

"Answer it," the chief said.

Singh picked up the phone, and heard Shan's voice say, "I know it's meant to be all over, but something's come up. Can you come in?"

Singh glanced at the chief. "I'm busy," he said to Shan.

"It's something I don't understand. Something that doesn't fit. You better come and see it."

Despite himself, Singh felt a little jolt of curiosity. "What is it?"

"Footage from CCTV at Bootham Street. Near Market Square."

Singh didn't reply but slowly replaced the receiver, frowning. For the first time that morning he felt something other than despair. Despite everything, he felt the wild, improbable sense of a last chance.

"At the press conference—" the chief constable began again, but Singh took a breath and said, "Please. Wait a moment. There's something you have to see."

The chief stared at him. Singh managed to hold his gaze.

"*Wait* a moment? What *is* this?" the chief said in a whisper.

Singh took a breath. "A nonexistent black Porsche, I think."

The angle of the CCTV camera was all wrong and the footage muddy-colored and granular, but the picture was clear enough to show the distinctive contour of Bootham Street with its church and bank, the early evening traffic heavy in both directions, and blurry, speeded-up lines of people knotting and unknotting as they made their way along the sidewalk to the bars and clubs in Market Square.

After a moment Shan slowed the tape and pointed to the figure of a dark-haired woman wearing a dark dress and pale jacket waiting by the curb.

"Chloe Dow," he said. "The reason we didn't spot her sooner is we were looking at Market Square. She was just south, in Bootham Street. I'm sure it's her, though. See the clothes and the hair. And the way she's looking out for someone. Now watch."

He speeded up the tape again, and they saw a low-slung car with the familiar Porsche profile approach from the Market Square end of the street, turn out of the jerky flow of traffic, and pull up alongside the curb. It was black. The passenger door was pushed open from inside, Chloe stepped down off the sidewalk and got in, and the car at once edged back into the traffic and flowed away in the direction of the highway.

"It's not possible to work out the license plate at this distance," Shan said. "But there's analysis to be done on the car. And the driver. Probably a man. Could be a woman. No one else in the car, so far as we can tell."

The chief constable shifted his gaze from the screen to Singh and raised one eyebrow.

Singh took a breath. "Chloe Dow was scared. She was being harassed by her ex-boyfriend. She was being stalked by Naylor. But the person who really scared her is in that car. That Thursday night she got dressed up and went out with him and something happened."

There was a silence while the chief contemplated this.

"What?" he said at last.

"I don't know."

Another silence.

"If she was so scared, why did she get into his car?"

Singh took another breath. "I don't know."

The chief continued to stare at him. "Who is the man in the car?"

"I don't know that, either. But if we find out what happened after she got into that car on Thursday evening we'll find out what happened the next day at Pike Pond, I know it. I can guarantee it. I was right," he added stubbornly, "about the black Porsche. No one believed me except . . ."

"Except who?" the chief said sharply.

Singh put the thought of Garvie Smith out of his mind. "Except the stepfather. He saw it when Chloe came home that night."

He ran out of things to say, and stood, almost to attention, facing the chief.

For a full minute the chief eyeballed Singh and Singh returned his gaze. At last the chief took a step toward him, and brought his face up close to Singh's, and said in a low, compressed voice, "Go to the press conference. Tell them what you've done."

He turned away.

Singh said, "Does that mean . . . ? Can I ask if . . . ?" He cleared his throat. "Do I remain in charge of this investigation?"

"I haven't decided yet," the chief said, not troubling to turn round, and continued out of the office.

44

There was nothing anyone could say or do to cheer him up. Not Smudge or Felix, for all their jokes and smokes at the Old Ditch Road playground. Not Jess with her pretty bare feet and slinky ways. Not even Abdul, who greeted him with characteristic eagerness every morning as Garvie trudged past his stand at the Bulwarks Lane shops.

"My Garvie man, how is, how is?"

But all he'd get was a shake of the head and a few muttered words: "Is bad, Abdul, *très* bad."

He didn't shun people, but he didn't talk much. When he smoked, he smoked as if he were alone, lost in the swirl of his thoughts as in the swirl of the smoke around his face.

The only person pleased by this change in him was Miss Perkins: His spirit was so broken that for three days running he attended all his timetabled lessons—including lunchtime and after-school classes. His mother should have been pleased too. But she was still barely speaking to him.

From time to time a memory would come unbidden into his mind: his mother weeping in her dressing gown. Like all his memories it was sharp and real, and as well as giving him pain it raised painful issues. She was right. He'd been playing a game. He'd treated Chloe's murder like a puzzle, a formal problem with interesting features, to be solved at his leisure and promptly forgotten, careless of the consequences. Almost as bad as the memory of his mother weeping was the image of Naylor hanging from the roof of his hut.

And now the fact that Chloe's death remained unsolved was terrible in a way it hadn't been before. The thought of it sat in his mind like a guilty secret.

Worst of all, he had to attend all these stupid after-school classes. And so he plodded in and out of school, hardly talking.

Friday lunchtime it was sunny, and Smudge and Felix went up to Top Pitch for a smoke, and Garvie sat with them, staring across the playing fields toward the city center.

"Seems to me," Smudge said, "anyone could've worked out it wasn't Naylor that done it."

Felix blew out smoke. "How's that?"

"Well. It was just too obvious. It's all right for books. But it's never like that in real life."

"What do you know about real life, Smudge?"

They smoked in silence.

After a few minutes Smudge nodded in the direction of the school and said, "Here's a bit of real life I'd like to know more about."

Jessica Walker was climbing the grassy slope toward them, pausing every so often to adjust the straps of her wedge sandals. She'd taken off her cardigan and tied it around her shoulders, and she was wearing sunglasses, very dark against her pale face.

"Jess, girl, looks like you just come off set."

Ignoring him, she walked over to Garvie. "Hey, Garv. Got a cig for me?"

Without looking he tossed over his pack and carried on gazing across the field, and she slipped off her shoes and settled down next to him and lit up.

"Did you get my texts?"

He didn't say anything.

"Come on, Garv. You can't brood forever."

He raised an eyebrow slightly.

"You got to let it go." She blew out smoke. "You can't bring her back. Even if you had . . . you know. Feelings for her."

Garvie sighed wearily.

She said softly, "If you need help, you've only got to ask." Her lips parted slightly and she blew a little noose of smoke toward him. "You know what I mean."

Smudge called over, "You're wasting your breath, girl. He's got some sort of disease means he can't talk no more. He's not said nothing for, like, three days. We can still talk over here, though, Felix and me. Though Felix is a bit boring, to be honest."

She gave him the finger and lowered her voice further. "Come on, Garv. I'll make you forget her."

He glanced at her; for a moment it seemed he was finally going to speak, but instead he sighed again and lowered his head into his hands with a groan.

"I keep trying to tell you, Garv. All you got to do to win is play. Know what I mean? We could be so good together, you and me."

Garvie didn't move or lift his head out of his hands, and she pouted and struggled to her feet.

"But I'm not going to wait forever," she said.

Smudge looked interested.

"Now we're talking, Jess!"

"Leave it out, pie boy."

She put her sandals back on and turned away, and without lifting his head Garvie said into his hands, "What did you say?"

Jess hesitated. "I said, 'Leave it out, pie boy.' But I was only talking to Smudge. I wasn't—"

"Before that."

She glanced uneasily at Smudge and Felix, who sat looking at her with interested expressions. "I said that about not waiting. You know, forever."

Garvie looked up. "You said, 'All you got to do to win is play.'"

"Yeah. Well." She fiddled with her ear, embarrassed. "Clear enough, innit? No need to broadcast it."

She would have said more, but she was silenced by the sight of Garvie leaping to his feet with his phone already clamped to his ear, and she watched him, astonished, as he began to pace up and down on the sunlit turf.

He paused briefly and looked at them all. "I am a moron," he said in a slow, deliberate voice. "A *moron*."

Now even Smudge looked embarrassed. "No worries, mate. We can't all have brains."

Garvie stopped pacing and spoke urgently into his phone. "Alex, mate. Don't think, just react. *All you got to do to win is play.*"

Hard-eyed, tense-faced, he stood listening.

"You sure? Definite? Safe. Doesn't matter what it means. Yeah. It is. Very important. Catch you later, man."

As if Jess wasn't surprised enough already, Garvie took her in his arms and kissed her on the cheek. "Jessica Walker," he said. "You're a bit of a star."

Smudge said, "Here, Sherlock, do you want to tell us what this shit storm's all about?"

Garvie looked back from the top of the slope. "Don't you remember, Smudge? You asked what gambling's got to do with anything."

"Yeah. So?"

"Chloe could have told you."

"Told me what?"

"Play to win. Give it a shot. Take a chance. Stake it all. Lose your shirt. Don't you think that sounds a bit like Chloe?"

"Yeah, but . . . Yeah. But . . ." He stood silent.

"Friday afternoon she was at Alex's and they had this blow-up row. She said something to him he thought was odd but he couldn't remember what it was. Well, he just remembered. *All you got to do to win is play.* Muttered it to herself. Bitter. It happens to be the Imperium slogan."

Momentarily forgetting Jessica's presence, Smudge scratched, deep and hard. "I still don't get it, though," he said at last. "I mean, what was her game?"

"Good question. That's what I'm going to have to find out."

Then he was gone.

45

There was another way of looking at it: All you got to do to *lose* is play. But Chloe would have scorned thinking like that. She was the brass girl, tough and durable. She didn't do slow and safe: She wasn't made that way. She took risks, seized the day. But why did he think suddenly of Chloe's mother, puffy-faced and lost-eyed in her dressing gown? Why did he remember the photographs of Chloe as a child along the mantelpiece in her room, the teddy bears on her bed? He wiped a hand across his face and sighed. Then he went over the Imperium parking lot wall in the usual way and made his way through the cars and shadows.

The first thing he saw was a black Porsche sitting by the casino's back entrance. Strolling over to it, he walked around it once. It was short and low-slung, so black it was almost blue. He peered in through the windows, gave a low whistle, and strolled away again into the shadows on the far side of the parking lot, where he lit up and smoked for a while, telling himself he was trying to decide what to do next, though he already knew, as he always seemed to.

Inside, he resumed his stroll with a complimentary glass of champagne, seeing no one he knew—partly a bad thing, partly a very good thing—and thinking about Chloe. Why had she come here? To win, obviously.

But—as Smudge had asked—what game was she playing?

Keeping an eye out for the manager, he strolled methodically through the baccarat and poker rooms, past the roulette and blackjack tables, past the slot machines and one-armed bandits, across the coffee lounge and bar. And as soon as he had refreshed his sense of the layout of the place, he strolled through a door marked STAFF ONLY and disappeared from view.

On the other side of the door it was suddenly quiet. There was no Roman theme. It was plain and functional. Garvie looked both ways down the corridor and turned left. Soon he came to the foot of a staircase carpeted in black shag with a gold chain hung across the entrance, and he looked up the stairwell for a moment, then continued along the bare corridor. From time to time he passed a door on the right-hand side, always locked. He turned left and left again, noting how the corridor turned to follow the perimeter of the public rooms of the casino. Soon, he calculated, he'd reach the restaurant and cocktail bar. A minute later he heard voices ahead and, turning left again, found himself in a small lounge area filled with sofas and low tables half obscured by overlarge potted plants of an exotic nature. It was deserted. But on the opposite side were three doors, one of them open, and through it came the sound of an angry voice.

"What the hell's wrong with you?"

A male voice. A voice harsh with cheap authority. And something else, Garvie thought. Anxiety. Or fear.

That was interesting.

Garvie sat down on one of the sofas and lit up. Half hidden under the broad leaves of what looked like a palm tree, he sat back to listen.

"I got no time for this," the voice said. "What are we running here, a charity?"

"No, sir. It's just this headache—"

"You think I give a shit about your headache? You think the players out there want to know about your headache?"

"No, but—"

"You got a face on like Grumpy the dwarf. All right, you're short. But you can smile, can't you?"

"Yes, sir."

A girl in a toga came through the door, wiping her face. She was short. Also unsmiling. She went between the sofas without seeing Garvie, and out a door on the other side. As it opened there was the brief hum of voices and the clank of slot machines, then quiet again as it closed.

The voice in the room said, "What's her name, anyway?"

Another deeper, slower voice, said, "Messalina."

"I mean, what's her real name?"

"Madonna."

There was a short pause suggesting astonishment.

"You're shitting me. Madonna? Listen, my old man sees so-called Madonna pulling that long face out there, he's going to first of all rip her head off, which I don't care about, and second of all rip *my* head off. Which bothers me. If he looks like he's getting pissed off, I want to know. All right?"

There was a pause. Then the same voice said, "Christ, I hate it when he's here on a Friday."

There was another pause.

"Listen."

Now his voice was cautious.

"He had another visit this morning. Some rag-head DI."

"What's he after?"

"Nothing. I don't know. What are they ever after? What I want to know is: We run a pretty tight ship, don't we?"

"Yeah."

"No rats."

"No rats."

"What about the tarts? That's my only worry. See? What about this Madonna? What about that new one? Hannah, isn't it?"

"Yeah. Hannah."

"Thinks she's such an independent spirit. What about her? She going to shoot her mouth off?"

There was another, longer pause, as if dedicated to hard thinking.

"See what I mean?"

"Yeah."

"I just want to make sure no one's saying the wrong things."

"Don't worry about it. I'll have a word."

"All right. Good."

A moment later two men came out of the room. The first was big and bald, dressed like the doormen in an overtight dinner jacket and black bow tie. He went across the lounge with massive shunting movements and exited into the casino. The other man was the manager. Garvie noticed again how young he was. Twenty, twenty-one. He had a raw, moist face and a twitchy expression. And pig-crazy eyes. He followed the big man, stopped suddenly, sniffed, looked all around without seeing anything, swore, and went on into the casino too.

After a while Garvie finished his Benson & Hedges, dropped the butt in the palm-tree pot, and followed them.

46

It was a risk. But then, like Chloe, he liked risks. With one eye he kept tabs on the whereabouts of Pig Crazy, and with the other he went searching through the crowds for a girl in a toga. A girl with shoulder-length brown hair, amused gray eyes, and winking dimples. He couldn't find her. She wasn't in the bar or coffee lounge, or around the blackjack or roulette tables, or in the poker or baccarat rooms. In the end he waited by the one-armed bandits, and that's where she found him.

"Taking a risk, Garvie Smith. You're strictly verboten. The manager told us to report it if we see you."

"Yeah, well. Risk's my middle name." He wasn't sure he'd ever said anything so corny.

"Is it? How funny. Now I know three of yours and you still don't know any of mine."

"I could know yours."

"I don't think so."

"I'm a very good guesser."

"Really?"

"As it happens, guessing is my specialty."

"And you think you can guess my name?"

Looking at her, he thought he might just drown in her gray eyes instead, and he pulled away his gaze and said, "Best if I warm up on someone else." He gestured around the blackjack room. "Go ahead, test me. Pick someone. Anyone."

"All right, Sherlock. Guess her name."

"Who, the dealer?"

"Her."

"All right." He winced. "I have to concentrate for this. Might need a glass of champagne."

"Guess first."

He sighed deeply, pinched the bridge of his nose with his fingertips, and fixed his attention on the unsmiling girl with the blackjack decks.

"A girl with problems, clearly," he said after a moment. "Headaches, I'd say."

Hypatia's eyebrows went up. "Go on."

"Unhappy too. Been crying recently. See how stiff her hair is at the front where she's been wiping her face? My guess is, the manager doesn't like her. Most probably he's been bawling her out."

Hypatia looked at him curiously, a half smile on her face.

"But in fact," he went on, "she doesn't really like herself."

"Really? And why's that?"

"Wishes she was taller."

Hypatia stared at him. "Okay. Interesting. But what's her name? You still haven't told me that."

"Coming to it. Her name's . . . one of the things that makes her unhappy."

"Why?"

"Doesn't suit her. She feels weighed down by it. She doesn't look like the sort of person to have such a name."

"Very interesting. But what is it?"

He sighed. "I'm just going to have to take a wild guess."

He was silent.

"Go on, then," she said.

He beckoned her closer, and leaned in toward her, and whispered, "Madonna."

For a second she stared at him in wonderment. Then she began to laugh. It was the prettiest laugh he'd ever heard. And when she stopped laughing she punched him on the arm. It was a good punch too.

"Er. Ow?"

"All right, so you must have overheard her name. You get three more minutes of my time. Apart from my name, which is still a secret, what do you want to know?"

"That man there. Mr. Pig Crazy."

She followed his eyes to the manager, who appeared briefly on the other side of the blackjack table and went away through the coffee lounge.

"Yes?"

"Do I detect a family resemblance to the owner?"

"Another clever guess. Yes, Darren's his son."

"And what was it you saw Darren doing?"

Her face went very still, her large eyes even larger.

"Three weeks ago yesterday," Garvie said. "Something happened here to a friend of mine. And my third good guess of the evening is that Mr. Pig Crazy was involved. He's a bit highly strung, and he's frightened of something, and I can't help thinking that he might have—"

She put her hand on his arm and he fell silent. Following her eyes, he turned round slowly and found himself squashed against the tightly jacketed belly of a man he recognized as the manager's meaty sidekick.

"Manager wants a word," the man said impassively.

"Kind of him," Garvie said, "though to be honest I'm a bit rushed at the minute. I wonder if—"

But the man took hold of his arm and they went together, a little awkwardly, round the blackjack table and through another Staff Only door to the manager's office.

It smelled of aftershave. It was a smart room, plush even, but abused. The exotic plant in the corner had died, there was litter heaped up around the brass wastepaper bin, and the dimpled leather sofa was covered with debris: cardboard boxes, bits of equipment, rolled-up promotional posters. The large walnut desk was dusty and stained with water rings.

Behind the desk sat Winder junior, the source of the aftershave smell. His face glistened.

"Member's card," he said, holding out his hand. His hand trembled slightly.

"Not really worth it, to be honest. It's a fake."

Garvie glanced around the room. Meathead was standing behind him, by the door. The cardboard boxes on the sofa were all the same, small and oblong and unmarked. Underneath them, a tripod and photographer's umbrella were visible. A corner of an unrolled poster showed the words *All you got to*. Through the window above the sofa he could see a snippet of black Porsche.

"Nice car," he said.

"Shut up."

"Bet everything matches inside."

"Shut up, I said."

"Does your dad let you drive it sometimes?"

Winder's eyes bulged. When he spoke, his voice seemed to bulge too. "Think you're a big man, do you?"

Garvie looked at him sweating behind his desk. "Yeah. Enormous. As you can see."

Winder tore at his thumbnail with his teeth. He seemed to be trying to chew it down to the knuckle. "Think you got the smarts on me, do you?"

Garvie said nothing to that. No answer was required. Instead he wondered why Winder was so uptight. Generally people are uptight when they're scared. Scared of something, or someone. Or scared of what they've done.

"You won't be so smart when I have you prosecuted, you fucking schoolboy."

Garvie gazed at him sweating and twitching behind his desk. It was interesting how angry he was. Angry people make stupid mistakes. They get themselves into situations and lose their heads.

"Hey? You won't be so cool about it when I call the police."

"You're not going to call the police," Garvie said.

"You think I won't call the police?"

He made no move toward the phone. He ran his hands through his thinning hair and grimaced.

"You're fucking right I won't call the police. I wouldn't waste my time. I couldn't care less if you're not prosecuted. What I care about is keeping overcurious brats like you out of my business. You're leaving." He glanced at Meathead. "Now."

Meathead shunted forward and took hold of Garvie's arm.

"Oh, one last over-curious question before we part company," Garvie said. "How often did Chloe come here?"

Winder jerked in his seat as if he'd been flicked with a whip, and alarm flashed in his white face. For a moment there was a pause, made ragged by his openmouthed breathing, then he said to Meathead in a croak, "Get him out quick before I break his face open."

There was a back entrance with a stiff fire door. The big man used Garvie's head to open the door, and parts of his shins and knees to check the three concrete steps for tension cracks, before pushing him along, like an inconvenient bit of furniture destined for the dump, into the parking lot.

"Mind the nice car," Garvie said, muffled, from his doubled-up position close to the ground. "You wouldn't want to scrape it with my face."

Meathead launched him safely beyond the Porsche, and Garvie plunged onto the concrete with a bone-hard crack and lay there huddled, waiting for the pain in his knees and elbows to subside.

When at last he rolled over and focused again, he found Meathead still standing there, like an actor waiting to deliver his big line.

"And *don't come back*," the man said with slow but impressive diction and, turning, went away across the parking lot with that thickened, shunting motion of his, and hauled himself back up the concrete steps.

"Thank you, then," Garvie called after him. "Don't call us, we'll call you. Find your own way home, can you?"

The man slammed the fire door.

47

The media frenzy triggered by news of Naylor's suicide had led, as predicted, to a full-scale public outcry, and for a long, difficult week Detective Inspector Raminder Singh had cut a forlorn figure in television interviews attempting to answer questions—all of which, in their different ways, asked why levels of police competence had sunk so abysmally low. General opinion was that the mystery of Beauty's murder would never be solved while the current investigation team was in charge. In a separate development, attorneys representing the family of Paul Johnson had announced their intention to bring legal proceedings against the City Squad on the grounds that their harassment had directly contributed to the suicide of a "troubled young man." There had even been demands for the resignation of the chief constable, a man whose qualities had never been questioned before.

By the following Monday there was the unmistakable sense within the service that they had only a few days in which to make progress with the case before public pressure forced major changes. Singh was aware of this as he parked his car that morning in the underground parking lot at Cornwallis Way and walked across the dim concrete concourse toward the exit staircase. Though his uprightness remained, he was haggard with lack of sleep. The last person he wanted to encounter was the chief constable, approaching the staircase from the other direction.

The chief looked at him lidlessly, and with no other acknowledgment they ascended the steps side by side. The chief said nothing, the silence stretched on, and by the time they reached street level the twitch had returned to Singh's left cheek.

Together they went through the main entrance. Together, in the same awkward silence, they went through security and along the corridor, and up in the elevator to the fifth floor, and across the open-plan area toward Singh's office. Where they walked people stopped to look at them, the chief going ahead, silent and grim, Singh lagging slightly behind, pale and taut. The chief's reputation for brutality with those who disappointed him was legendary. Demotion was invariably accompanied by public disgrace. So the staff in the open-plan area watched with horrified fascination as the two men went toward Singh's office. Bob Dowell came to a halt by the photocopier, Mal Nolan turned round from the water cooler, Collier looked up from his coffee and followed them with his eyes. When the two men finally reached Singh's door, the chief stopped and Singh stopped too, exposed to all the watching people, waiting, like them, to be told what was to be done to him. But after a moment, without a word, the chief continued on his way, leaving Singh standing there alone, facing all those still watching him in silence across the long open space. He hardly saw them. Numbly he stood until he felt sweat come into his eyes, then turned unsteadily. His assistant had come round her desk and was attempting to talk to him, or perhaps offer him medical assistance—"Sir? Sir?" she said. "You ought to know . . . There's a . . ."— but he went past her, hardly hearing what she said, and retreated at last into the safety of his office.

Where he found Garvie Smith sitting in his chair with his feet on his desk.

GARVIE SMITH: Come in, Inspector Singh. Glad you could make it. Take a seat. I won't keep you long.

DI SINGH: [*stationary, blinking, looking at Garvie, looking at his office door, looking back at Garvie*]

GARVIE SMITH: You left your window open.

DI SINGH: [*looking bewildered at the window*]

GARVIE SMITH: Don't be soft. We're on the fifth floor. Michael brought me up. He's a nice lad, Michael. Knows my uncle. Very friendly and willing to please. I like that in a policeman. Anyway—

DI SINGH: [*coming to his senses at last, hastily shutting his office door, striding forward, taking hold of Garvie and pulling him out of his chair*]

"All right, all right, don't lose your blob."

In a hiss not to be overheard by his assistant outside, Singh said, "What do you think you're doing? I told you never to come here again."

"Yeah, well. There's new stuff."

"Stuff?"

"You know. Shocking discoveries, vital clues. Listen, do you have to keep grabbing my arm like this? I find it off-putting."

Singh let go of his arm. "We had an agreement, remember?"

"No. My memory's not so great. Did I sign something?"

"I made it clear that it was over."

"Tell that to the papers. They think it's never going to end."

For a moment Singh glared at Garvie so fiercely it seemed he was about to push him up against his office wall and clap him in handcuffs. Then he let out a long, exasperated sigh. "I'm not going to argue with you." He went stiffly back to his desk and sat down. Adjusted his turban. "Tell me what you want, quickly now. Then you have to leave. The nice young policeman will take you back down."

"I've been trying to tell you. There's a car you might be interested in. Porsche. Black, as it happens."

Singh looked at him for a long moment, deciding what to do. "Yes, I know," he said at last, with a glance over his shoulder at his shut office door.

Garvie raised an eyebrow. "That's a bit more definite than last time. Do you have something new to go on?"

Singh hesitated.

"Come on, man, you can trust me. Besides, I can help you. What's it look like, this black Porsche of yours? Eighteen-inch sport techno wheels? Carrera rear spoiler? Single oval-tube tail pipes, one each side?"

Singh said at last, "It's possible. The footage isn't as clear as we'd like."

"Where did the CCTV catch it?"

"Bootham Street on Thursday evening. She was picked up by someone driving a Porsche that may match that description just before seven o'clock."

"And drove off in what direction?"

"The highway."

"Toward Imperium."

Singh nodded.

"You've been back there. You've seen it, seen the upholstery, all those clubs and diamonds and hearts and spades. Remember what Chloe said? Everything matches inside."

For a while Singh was silent. Then he sighed. "Yes, I went back to talk to Winder. And yes, it could be his car in the footage. But he's absolutely and definitively ruled out."

"Why?"

"He was in Monaco all week. The car was locked up in his garage."

"What about his son?"

Singh breathed heavily through his nose. "Please don't make this mistake."

"Any sightings of it up at Pike Pond Friday night?"

"None. Now listen to me—"

"She was there, you know. At Imperium. I told you before. If I were you, I'd find out what went on at the casino Thursday night. My informants tell me something happened."

Singh stared at him. "What?"

"I don't actually know."

"What informants?"

"I can't divulge that. It's classified."

The policeman clicked with exasperation. "Then why are you telling me all this?"

"Why? Because I like you, man. You're cool, and funny, and you're always up for a—"

"I'm serious. Why?"

"Oh." Garvie thought. "I don't know. I guess I just like to interfere. Why are you listening to me?"

Singh made no answer. He sat in silence, frowning. "I don't know, either," he said at last. "But I'll admit this. You have a knack for finding things out. As well as for irritating me. All right, then. Listen, I have less than a week to turn this investigation round. If I don't I will be a failure; there will be no place for me here. Just by talking to you I'm breaking my code of conduct. You mustn't come here again. Ever. After this we speak only on the phone. I already have your number."

He pulled out his card and scribbled on it and handed it to Garvie, who glanced at it and handed it back to Singh. Without smiling or showing any sort of emotion, the policeman put it in his pocket.

"All right. This is what I suggest. You call me if anything crops up. I'll call you to let you know what we're doing. But only," he added, "if you promise me something."

"I know. Keep off the grass."

"You mustn't come back here. More important, you mustn't ever go back to Imperium. You don't know what the Winders are like. We do. Over the years we've seen far too much of them."

"They're not just gamblers?"

"The same old story: Nothing has ever been proved. But a lot of people have got hurt. I'll keep you informed if you keep away from them. Is it a deal?"

He put out his knuckles and after a moment Garvie shrugged and put out his own.

"Is it a deal?" Singh repeated.

"Yes, it's a deal."

"You won't go back to Imperium?"

Garvie shook his head.

"You promise?"

"Crikey, don't you trust me?"

"Do you promise? Say it out loud."

"I promise. I promise, I promise, I promise."

48

In the daylight, Imperium Restaurant and Casino looked shabbier, like an unwell face, Garvie thought, with the makeup scrubbed off. The stone walls were discolored, the smoked glass was smeary, and there were cigarette butts in the orange-tree pots.

At seven o'clock it was still closed. Only reception was open, taking bookings for parties. There were no bouncers on the door, no managers loitering in the corridors, and Garvie went inside unchallenged, and down the silent slot-machine-lined hallway to the sunken lobby. A middle-aged lady sitting at a desk next to the unlit fish tank looked up from her laptop. She had a predatory face full of glints and bony outcrops.

"Hi," Garvie said winningly.

The lady said nothing. Her eyes contracted slightly.

"Message for Hypatia," Garvie said, holding out an envelope. "Any chance you could pass it on?"

The woman looked at the envelope as if working out how to make it disappear. Then she returned her stare to Garvie and tried to do the same thing to him.

"Who's it from?" she said eventually. Her voice was as cold as a drip on a concrete floor.

"An admirer."

She looked at him for a long time. "No Hypatia here," she said at last.

"Are you sure? A waitress. Croupier. Shoulder-length chestnut hair. Gray eyes. Dazzlingly pretty. Although," he added politely, "seems to me you're all dazzlingly pretty."

The woman thought about this. "Doesn't work here anymore," she said.

"She left?"

Now the woman smiled, a ghastly sight. She picked up a phone. "Why don't you talk to the manager?" Her finger hovered over the key pad. "Who shall I say it is?"

Garvie didn't reply. But he had a sudden sick feeling.

At one o'clock in the morning Imperium was back to its best, all dressed up, the dinner-jacketed doormen in place, the orange-tree pots swept out, the soft light from the blue globes washing the walls clean.

Garvie watched the entrance from his position in the front yard of the bowling alley next door. Luckily his mother was still working late shifts. Frowning, he pushed the thought of his mother out of his mind, and focused on the casino entrance. He was tired, but that wasn't so bad. Much worse was his fear. He thought of a loose-limbed girl with shoulder-length chestnut hair and gray eyes. A girl who'd seen something, who'd been seen talking to an over-curious brat. A girl who'd disappeared. Maybe she'd gone to India already. He didn't think so. He remembered what Singh had told him about the Winders. So he waited, watching.

An hour passed. Bored, he took out his phone and punched in a number.

It was answered immediately. There was a sharp crack, as if the phone had been flung against a wall, then an overloud voice making an urgent unintelligible noise.

"Chill, dude, it's only me. What's up?"

After a longish pause Singh said, "Garvie?"

"The same. I was just wondering if you had anything you wanted to share."

"Garvie. It's two o'clock in the morning."

"Is it? You weren't asleep, were you? I didn't think you slept. I thought Singh of the Yard was ever vigilant."

"There's no news," Singh said. "If that's why you're calling."

"So what have you been up to?"

He heard Singh sigh. "We've interviewed Winder senior again. Nothing. We've been interviewing staff. Nothing there, either. No confirmation of Chloe at the casino on Thursday night."

"Well. Keep at it."

Singh made a noise. "I hope I don't need to remind you to stay clear of Imperium."

"No need at all. All right, then, catch you later."

And he hung up and went back to watching the casino.

By quarter past two the gamblers had all gone home, and the doormen closed the doors and went inside. At half past the waitresses and croupiers came out, strangely un-Roman in jeans and T-shirts. He ticked them off in his mind. Agrippina, Sabina, Flavia, Livia . . . But not the person he was waiting for.

He waited another half hour to make sure, then walked slowly back to his bike in the superstore parking lot and cycled home. The sleeping city spread out around him, vast and empty. Little creatures came out to scavenge and kill one another; he heard them scuffling in the scrub. Nearing home, he saw a muntjac deer cross the deserted bypass, trotting unperturbed across the asphalt toward the cash-and-carry wholesaler, and he stopped and waited a moment next to a litter-filled privet hedge, watching.

He thought of Chloe riding in a black Porsche.

Everything matched. If only it did. He put a number of things in his mind one by one. A photographer's umbrella discarded on a sofa in the back office of a casino. The pseudo-gorgeous carpet of the staircase. The son left in charge. The dressed-up girl. He added a pair of ugly lime-green and orange running shoes. A note scribbled on a torn sheet of letter notepaper. They all matched, he knew they did. But how?

He thought of a girl without a name, dazzlingly pretty.

And when he focused again, the deer had gone, disappearing like a conjuring trick into the shadow of the roadside. But no trick of the mind could alter his feeling of growing dread.

The next night, as he waited by the bowling alley he had a surprise. A call from Detective Inspector Singh. It was still early: eleven o'clock.

"Yeah?"

"Singh here. I know it's late. Can you talk?"

"Yeah, I can talk. I open my mouth and words come out. I've been doing it since I was small."

He could almost hear Singh frown. "I'm keeping my side of the deal. Half an hour ago we got a call from Mrs. Dow. She's found something in Chloe's room she can't explain."

"What?"

"An Imperium gambling chip."

"Where'd she find it?"

"In a white jacket of Chloe's."

"The one she was wearing on Thursday night. Which pocket?"

"Outside, right-hand side."

"I don't like it."

Singh hesitated. "But it confirms what you suspected."

"That's why."

Now he could hear Singh being puzzled.

"You told me once that hard evidence is the only thing," Garvie said. "What we need's a witness statement. Someone who saw Chloe there."

"We're interviewing everyone."

"Staff?"

"Staff, of course."

"Ex-staff?"

Again he could hear Singh's puzzlement. "Why do you say ex-staff?"

Glancing up as he listened, Garvie saw a figure come out of Imperium's parking lot. A small figure. Unsmiling.

"Got to go," he said.

He could hear Singh listening to the change in his tone.

"Where are you, by the way?"

"Where am I? It's late, man. It's eleven o'clock. Where do you think I am?"

"Good. Stay there. You're safe at home. That's the other reason I called you. We've had the Winders in again, and their legal team. They're showing signs of strain. Keep away from the Imperium. I don't want you annoying them."

The short, unsmiling girl had crossed the street and was heading toward a bus idling at the stop on the other side of the road, and Garvie, still talking, moved after her.

"Listen, man, don't you go annoying the Winders, either. I don't want them taking it out on any of their staff. Or ex-staff."

"Why—"

"Got to go," Garvie said, picking up speed. He added, "If I don't get back to sleep now I'll be awake for hours. Laters."

Then he was running out of the bowling alley parking lot and across the street.

* * *

As the late-night bus rolled along The Wicker he made his way down the aisle, trying to get his breathing back in order. He went between the seats, most of them unoccupied, until he came to one where a short, unsmiling girl sat.

"Mind if I sit here?"

She took out her earphones, glanced briefly at the empty seats around her, and shrugged.

He settled down in his usual slouch.

After a few minutes she took out her earphones again and turned to him. "What's your problem?"

He continued to look at her with a friendly, if not outright tender, expression. "Sorry. Didn't realize I was staring. It's just that I recognize you. You're one of the glam croupiers at Imperium, aren't you?"

She looked at him suspiciously. "Maybe."

"Definitely. I don't forget a face like yours. I even remember your name. Wait a minute, it'll come to me. Messalina. Not your real name, of course."

She didn't smile.

"Don't you remember me? Playing blackjack the other day. Big winner."

She looked him over and colored slightly. "Maybe. We get lots of players in."

He glanced at his watch. "It's a bit early to be going home, isn't it? Shouldn't you be dealing out cards?"

"Headache," she said shortly.

"Oh. Sorry."

While the bus waited at a light he was silent, but when it juddered off again he went on.

"When I was in I got chatting to one of your friends there. Hypatia. Not her real name, either."

"I know her," the girl said. She looked at him watchfully. "She's all right," she added.

"Hypatia," Garvie repeated, with a smile. "Or should I say *Madonna*?"

"What?"

"Her real name's Madonna, right?"

Frowning, the girl opened her mouth, and Garvie said, "Wait, I'm getting it mixed up. Sorry. She's Messalina, *you're* Hypatia. Right?"

She opened her mouth again, and Garvie said quickly, "Or you're Madonna and she's . . . Messalina. Real name Hypatia?"

The girl shook her head impatiently. "You've got it all mixed up. She's Hypatia, real name Hannah. I'm Messalina . . ." She hesitated.

"Real name Madonna?"

She nodded reluctantly.

"Okay. I got it finally. Madonna." He gazed at her. "Not everyone could carry it, I know. But for the right person . . . Wow!"

He raised an eyebrow appreciatively, and finally she blushed and smiled.

"Madonna," he said. "And she's Hannah. Wait. Not Hannah Briggs whose brother got sent down last year for that business with the detergents scam?"

She frowned. "Clark's her name. Anyway, she doesn't work at Imperium anymore."

"Really? What happened?"

Her face closed down. "I don't know. Nothing. She just doesn't work there."

Garvie nodded. "Well, Madonna. Lovely talking to you. Here's my stop. Save a smile for me at the blackjack table."

He wondered if he might get a smile straightaway, but Madonna was looking at him suspiciously again, and he turned and went down the bus toward the doors, and all the charm fell like a mask from his face and left him pale and staring.

49

The city is a maze—the city at night is a trap.

Abdul kept glancing at him nervously in the rearview mirror as they drove through the evening darkness to the Strawberry Hill estate.

"Garvie man. You have trouble?"

Garvie shook his head. "Not me, Abdul. Someone else."

"This *personne*, he hiding good, eh? We looking here, we looking there."

"I don't know if she's hiding at all. I hope she is. We'll find out soon enough. When we get there."

And he looked again out the window across nearby rooftops to Strawberry Hill's tower block as Abdul changed gear and turned toward it.

It was ten o'clock, Wednesday, cool under an overcast sky now dark with fat rags of navy-blue cloud. Nearly twenty-four hours had gone by since he'd learned Hannah's name, a name he'd instantly recognized from a conversation overheard earlier.

What about that new one? Hannah, isn't it? Thinks she's such an independent spirit. She going to shoot her mouth off?

The words had been in his head all day. They made him feel sick but he couldn't seem to stop listening to them. Or stop thinking of a girl with chestnut-brown shoulder-length hair, gray eyes, and a smile like a sudden splash of sunlight. All day at school he'd gone from class to class without speaking, and at home in the afternoon he'd sat staring unfocused at a book, apparently incapable of movement, until his mother left for her shift at the hospital, when he instantly jumped up, grabbed his jacket, and ran to meet Abdul at the stand.

The city phone book had listed twenty-three Clarks with H as an initial. The calls he'd made earlier in the day had eliminated all but five. With Abdul as his driver he'd visited four of the addresses so far, none of them Hannahs; now there was only one left: Apt 138, Hornbeam Tower, Strawberry Hill.

Abdul pulled up at the side of the road and turned in his seat. "She live here?"

"Maybe."

Together they looked up at the tower.

Abdul said, "You want I wait?"

"It's okay, man. I know you've got an airport job."

Abdul made tsking noises and waved his hands.

"No need to fret. I owe you several already."

Abdul gave a half smile. Half pleased, half fretful.

Garvie got out and Abdul leaned out the window.

"Be safe, Garvie man."

For a moment Garvie stood watching the cab recede down the road, then he crossed to Hornbeam Tower. There was a wide sidewalk in front of an arcade of shops, mostly shut, and a plaque on the wall reading HORNB A TOWER. A group of kids sat on their bikes staring at him as he went past and through a heavy steel door into the entrance hall. He didn't know any of them. Inside, the hall was pale gray and empty, brightly lit by florescent tubes high in the ceiling above. Across the washed gray concrete floor was an empty office with a wooden door labeled STAFF ONLY and a window obscured by a gray blind. Opposite was a pair of metal elevator doors.

He waited, and a man wearing army fatigues came in and waited with him.

The elevator came, and they got in and stood together silently in the bright light, going up slowly. On the eighth floor the man got out, and Garvie went on alone to the twenty-third.

There was an alcove, and he stepped through it onto an exterior walkway and stood in a slight breeze gazing through the gap between metal railings and concrete ceiling at the evening sky curdling over the sewage plant and car works. Turning, he went along the walkway, past pairs of doors with glass fronts, some of which had been replaced with metal grilles, until he came to numbers 137 and 138.

The glass panel of number 138 had been smashed and someone had fixed a strip of cardboard over it.

He pressed the bell and heard it ring faintly inside the apartment, a sound as lonely as a telephone ringing after hours in an empty office. After a while he rang it again. A few minutes passed. He banged on the door frame with the side of his fist.

"Hannah!" he shouted suddenly. "Hannah!"

A few inches to his left the door of number 137 opened a crack, and an elderly woman in a pink dressing gown peered out. She had a long loose face and gray hair in curlers, and she held the edges of her dressing gown together under her chin.

"No point in banging," she said. "She's gone."

"You mean Hannah?"

She looked at Garvie with tired, bitter eyes and sucked in her face. "Went off. Four or five hours ago. Who are you?"

"A friend."

"That's what they all say, to start with."

"Do you know where she's gone?"

The old woman thought about this for a long time, chewing her loose lip. "I don't want any trouble," she said in quiet disgust, and started to close the door.

Garvie jammed the toe of his shoe in it and she recoiled. The door flapped, and he had a brief glimpse of a small room with a loud carpet of chocolate and caramel swirls.

"I don't want any trouble," she cried again. "Whatever she's done."

"What do you mean, trouble?" He looked at her fiercely. "What do you mean, *done*?"

He jammed his foot farther into the door, and the woman said in a nervous rush, "Anyway, she'd gone by the time they came for her."

"Came for her?" He felt sick.

"That's right."

"Who?"

"Three of them. And a dog. But she'd gone. Took herself off. And the baby."

"*Baby?*"

"Scared something might happen to it, I should think."

It was too much. He removed himself from her door, stepped away, and sat down suddenly against the railings. Confused, the woman peered at him curiously for several long seconds.

"Are you all right?"

"No."

Nodding sourly, she began to close the door again.

"Wait," Garvie said. "You have to help me. Where did she go?"

"How would I know?"

"Please. It's important." Even as he said it, he saw it wasn't important to the woman. "She must have said something," he added.

The woman shook her head. "If she's done something you should call the police."

He leaped to his feet and she withdrew in alarm, shutting the door behind her with a snap, and though his momentum carried him across the walkway, he let his hand fall to his side. Banging on doors makes nothing happen. He looked at his watch. Ten thirty. Lighting a Benson & Hedges, he paced down the walkway to the corner of the building and stood at the railings looking out. The sky was the color of wet ash. Almost half the city lay below him. Around the tower block, the low-rise apartments and maisonettes of the Strawberry Hill estate, haphazardly arranged in blocks and lines. To the east, the dense rows of Five Mile and the gray mass of Limekilns. Northward was Tick Hill and City Central Hospital, pale against the dark hills beyond. In the south he could see the bright lights of clubs and casinos, and far away to the west, the blank skyscrapers of the business district, flat and blocky against the paler night sky. Everything was meshed together, like puzzle shapes of an enormous maze.

He smoked quietly, thinking. Somewhere in that maze a girl was running for her life. A girl with a baby.

Where would she run to?

As he smoked he remembered her. He saw her in his mind, the way she'd looked in Imperium in her short white toga. He saw the shape her mouth made when she spoke and he listened again to what she'd said, about getting out of the casino, about traveling, about India, with its sun and its colors and its—

He jerked out of his trance and stood there wide-eyed. Looking at his watch, he saw it was ten forty. Cursing, he flung his cigarette, still glowing, out into the night air, and, turning, ran as fast as he could back along the walkway.

50

The boys on their bikes jeered as he ran past them. He crossed the road and ran down the opposite sidewalk in the direction of the bypass. He ran across a bridge over railway tracks, down a darkened street of maisonettes and flats, onto Cobham Road, the main drag of the Strawberry Hill estate, and ran on, hard, past offices and shops that were shut up for the night behind metal grilles. Panting heavily, holding his side, he took out his phone as he ran and dialed.

"*Oui?*"

"Abdul? Garvie."

"Garvie man, what is? You hurt?"

"No. I'm fine. Where are you?"

"Soon it will be airport. Five, six minute."

He cursed.

"Garvie man. What happen? It sound like you swim the sea."

"Nothing happen. I'm just jogging. But I need information."

"Information? What is?"

"Is Tick Hill. Do you know it?"

"*Mais oui.*" Abdul sounded pleased with himself. "I go Tick Hill many many time."

"That's good."

"But you have trouble. I hear it."

"No, man. That's just my lungs bleeding. Otherwise I'm absolutely fine."

"You want me come?"

"No. Listen. I don't have long. I've just got a question about Tick Hill."

"For you, Garvie man, is *plaisir.* Ask it."

Tick Hill was six or seven miles away, on the northern edge of the city. That was a long way at night when the buses were infrequent. After ten minutes of running the pain in Garvie's side had spread round his back to join another, different pain at the base of his spine. Without slowing down, he turned off Cobham Road onto a street of small brick tenement houses and hobble-ran down the narrow sidewalk past wheelie bins and bikes, peering about him, until he found a bike chained up with a combination lock.

Standing there, panting, he gave silent thanks to Felix. There was no noise from any of the houses and, after listening for a moment, he bent to his task.

He set the four numbers of the combination lock to *zero* and gave the lock a short, sharp sideways tug. No give. He moved the first number to *one,* and tugged again, and kept going until he felt a slight gap open up momentarily between the keys. Then he moved on to the next number and began the process again.

In less than a minute the bike was free. It wasn't a great bike but it would do. On a strip torn off his cigarette packet he wrote: *Bit of an emergency. Back soon,* and wrapped it around the lock, which he left coiled on the doorstep. Inside the house a dog barked once, but by then he was already at the end of the street, cycling briskly onto Cobham Road.

It was midnight by the time he reached Tick Hill. There was space here, and air. Disheveled, sweating freely, he pedaled doggedly along wide quiet roads past connected houses behind grass strips half reverting to their natural state. He could feel a breeze off the reservoir somewhere ahead of him in the darkness. If Abdul was right, there was a country road nearby and, at the end of that, a trailer park.

In his mind he saw Hannah in the Imperium and heard her talking to him: "Calls herself the Tick Hill Travel Bug . . . When she writes her autobiography she's going to call it *From Trailer Park to Taj Mahal.*" Yes, the Tick Hill trailer park, a place where a travel bug might live, dreaming of the Taj Mahal. A friend's place, empty now. A place where a frightened girl with her baby might run to if she had nowhere else to go.

He looked at his watch and pedaled harder.

His phone rang.

Without slowing down he fished it out and looked at the caller's number. "Yeah?"

There was a pause at the other end. "What are you doing?"

"Spot of exercise. Didn't you know I'm a fitness fanatic?"

Singh let this go. "I'm sorry to call so late. But there's been another development. A big one. You need to be aware of it."

"I'm listening."

"A sighting of the Porsche, up at Pike Pond."

"For the Friday night?"

"Yes. One of the Froggett Wood residents returned from Botswana today. Turns out he's a jogger. He ran past Pike Pond at five on the Friday afternoon and saw the car parked there. He ran right past it."

"Close enough to get a look at the upholstery, then."

"It's very distinctive, as you said. There's no doubt it's Winder's car."

"Pig Crazy."

Startled, Singh paused. "Well, I was only—"

"Winder junior. I'm assuming he was in the car."

"Yes, that's right. Sitting waiting."

"For Chloe?"

"Not that he's admitting."

"Have you arrested him?"

"Yes. He's just now been released on bail. That's the reason I'm calling you. The Winders are really worked up now."

"Don't worry about me," Garvie said. "I wouldn't dream of getting involved." He pedaled out of a long well-lit street toward a narrow road marked GOOSE LANE, and clattered into the darkness of the countryside. As he went over a hidden pothole the bike's front light fell off into the road, and he cursed.

Singh said in a puzzled voice, "What are you doing, exactly?"

"Just breathing. Go on. You're about to tell me what you think happened."

Speaking slowly, Singh said, "I think you're right that Chloe went to the casino on Thursday night. And when she was there, something happened to upset her. I don't know what."

Garvie was silent for a moment, pedaling in the darkness. Then he said, "Are you familiar with a redhead in tassels who's just won a fortune on the roulette wheel?"

There was a pause. "A gambler?"

"Imperium's pinup girl. You've seen her, over the entrance at the casino. *All you got to do to win is play.*"

"So?"

"Looks like last year's model to me. I think Darren brought Chloe there to take pictures of her. I think she was going to be Imperium's new poster girl. Or that's what he told her. She wasn't dressed up like that just to get in. She wanted to look as old as possible so when she was three meters high on that concrete wall, people wouldn't rumble her as a fifteen-year-old schoolgirl."

"I see. And what do you think happened?"

"Your guess is as good as mine. Actually it's probably not, but you know what I mean. How well do you know Mr. Pig Crazy?"

"Darren? Not at all. But the psychological profile in his records makes interesting reading. He underwent a compulsory course of counseling after an incident when he was seventeen."

"What incident?"

"Exposing himself in public. He's a mass of compulsions. Who wouldn't be with a father like that? There's a history of suspected beatings at home. Social services were called in three times when he was at school. At the same time he had a record for bullying. It's classic."

"Right. So you can imagine. Dad away abroad. Weirdo with uncontrollable urges and a camera. Girl in low-cut dress. Things got out of hand, I expect. I'm thinking of that private suite at the top of the staircase covered in black shag carpet."

"Whatever it was, it upset her."

"Course."

"Then, on Friday, things got worse for her. My belief is that all the calls she received from that untraceable number were from Darren Winder."

"Yeah. He was sweating about whatever he'd done the night before."

"Yes."

"Probably he'd found out she was only fifteen. His dad wouldn't have liked that."

"He must have been terrified. I think he was trying to get her to meet him."

"Yeah. Put some pressure on her. Show her who's boss. Make clear what his dad'll do to her if she tells anyone what went on the night before."

Taking his bearings from the pale line of hedge at the roadside, Garvie sped into the darkness, looking around. Somewhere nearby there was the quietly gurgling noise of a stream. He glided on between tall hedgerows, past five-bar gates and, as he went round a corner, saw faint lights up ahead and pushed himself on, panting.

Singh said uncertainly, "Are you jogging?"

"No. Thinking. You still have to explain how she ended up at Pike Pond."

"I don't know. Perhaps he told her to meet him there."

"Or she told him. Are you familiar with the term *terra incognita?*"

"Of course, but—"

"And you realize Chloe was a blonde?"

"Yes, but—"

"Blonde, attractive, and utterly ruthless. It's a type of *terra incognita* psychology, man. She might have been scared but she was tough too. She was at risk of getting entangled with the wrong sort of man so, naturally, she decided to dump him, blow him off. Pike Pond's perfect from her point of view. She doesn't want a scene outside her house. She doesn't want anyone wondering what she's up to. She can jog up there like she's done loads of times before and no one will question why."

In the darkness ahead of Garvie the glow of lights slowly grew brighter and he pedaled harder.

"There was a problem, though," he said reflectively.

"What problem?"

"The running shoes, of course. Naylor'd nicked them the night before. That's why she went round to Jess's on Friday afternoon, to borrow some. But Jess's feet are really big. So she had to buy a new pair pronto. No time to be fussy. Any sort would do, even orange and lime green. Soon as she got them she set off. I've always thought it odd no one noticed her running up there at seven. I mean, she was really noticeable. If she ran up at five, that would explain why."

Up ahead in the shadows the hedge gave way to a high brick wall, and Garvie accelerated, panting as he went.

Singh said thoughtfully, "Yes. Yes. It could have happened like that. But we need proof. We need a sighting of Chloe at the casino on Thursday."

"Exactly," Garvie said, crouching forward over the handlebars. As he shot toward the trailer park entrance, he could see, over the top of the wall, the steady glow of an arc light, and he was just daring to think he'd made it in time when the quiet of the rural night was shattered by the explosive noise of a car engine starting up somewhere nearby. A second later headlights came out of the trailer park entrance a hundred meters ahead and swung away in the opposite direction. The engine roared and the taillights disappeared down the lane at speed.

"Oh no!" he said savagely under his breath. "Not that." He pedaled furiously.

Singh said, "Garvie?"

"I'm out of time, man. Listen. As you say, we need that sighting of Chloe at the casino Thursday night. Is there no one talking?"

"No. The staff are too frightened of the Winders to say anything."

"Course. But what about the ex-staff?"

"You said that before. We've talked to several, nearly all of them."

"Just one to go?"

There was a pause. When Singh spoke there was a new note of suspicion in his voice.

"How do you know that?"

"Girl called Hannah Clark?"

"Garvie? We haven't found her yet."

"You're not the only ones looking for her," Garvie said through gritted teeth. "Thing is, she's the one who saw something."

"Garvie?" There was alarm in Singh's voice. "What are you up to? *Where are you?*"

Garvie said nothing. With every last ounce of his strength he pedaled. Glancing up, he saw there was a new light at the top of the wall, a flickering soft light glowing pale orange, and he frowned.

"Nearly there," he panted into the phone.

"Nearly where?"

"Nearly at the place where Hannah Clark's hiding out with her baby. Here we go now. Pray that I'm not too late."

He swept round the end of the brick wall into the trailer park, and his face was suddenly lit up by a red glow.

"Oh God!" he yelled.

Ten miles away, in his office, Singh shouted too. "What are you doing? Where are you?"

He heard Garvie begin to say something; then there was a wild engulfing noise like an explosion in a bucket, and the phone went dead.

51

The trailer park was exactly as Abdul had described it. Near derelict. A construction company's billboard at the entrance gave out information that the site was being redeveloped. Many of the mobile homes had already been removed: Regular dark patches of earth indicated where they had stood. The ones that remained, in three short rows at the back of the lot, showed all the usual signs of abandonment—smashed windows, graffiti, litter—except for the one at the end of the nearest row. And that was on fire.

Garvie took in all this in an instant before crashing the bike into a pile of builder's sand, and scrabbled up again, spitting grit, to run toward the flaming caravan, yelling.

"Hannah! *Hannah!*"

There was no reply from inside. It stood slightly separate from the others in the row, once white, now mildewed, with an aluminum door and three black windows set flush with the walls. Flames rose from the back of it, writhing into the air, dirty red against the blackness of a copse of trees behind.

"Hannah!" Garvie yelled again, and cursed himself for wasting breath.

The door was locked.

He ran round the back, shielding his face from the heat, and saw fire coming out of a gash high up in the metal of the caravan wall. He ran back round to the front and thumped the windowpanes again.

Still no reply.

As he stood there, panting, there was a second small explosion at the back—another gas canister perhaps, or an electrical appliance. He tried the door again, a thin metal panel warm to the touch and locked fast. He tugged violently at the handle, and let it go, and stood there, panting uselessly.

"Think!" he said out loud.

And then: "Don't just think!"

He ran back to where the bike lay at the edge of the pile of sand, and took a deep breath and charged forward. He ran hard over fifteen meters, accelerating all the time, and at the last second took off into the air, leaping feetfirst into the door, which buckled and burst with a hideous noise of metal on metal, and flung him backward onto the ground.

He lay there in agony. The pain shot up his legs into his pelvis and farther into his chest. He put a hand to his face and it came away bloody. When he tried to stand, his ankle gave way, and he yelled once before forcing himself forward, crawling over the threshold into the caravan. At last he hauled himself to his feet and stood, looking.

At the far end flames were consuming what had once been the kitchen area. Curtains and furnishings roared. A cloud of black smoke rolled toward him, as solid as surf.

He wrapped his hands in his sleeves and thrust himself forward into the smoke, choking and blind, feeling about him. Everything was already scalding hot to the touch, the ragged bits of carpet on the floor smoking and shriveling. Kicking his way past toppled furniture and other debris, he groped in the swirling incendiary murk and felt a narrow bed against the caravan side. There was no one in it. He turned round, lost his bearings, and tripped over something lying on the floor. At the same moment he heard a noise, a tiny cry. He fell to his knees and found the girl lying huddled with the baby wrapped in a blanket pressed against her chest. She didn't respond when he shook her. In desperation he tried to lift them both together, but they were too heavy and awkward. Snatching up the baby, he stumbled away from the leaping flames, lurching in pain and confusion back along the caravan to the door, and fell through it onto the ground outside.

As he placed the baby on the hot grass, there was a third explosion from inside.

He knew then that he'd failed. Nevertheless he turned back, bleeding and filthy, and forced himself into the caravan again. Flames were everywhere now, spreading with incredible rapidity. Groping blindly, he went forward until he found Hannah lying on the smoking floor in exactly the same position. Her feet were on fire. He ripped off her shoes with his burning hands and, taking hold of her ankles, began to drag her toward the door. Something cracked overhead and a sharp hail of glass raked his face and he staggered sideways, eyes shut. Fire was all round him now, and he blundered among the flames. He was sure he was on fire too, but it didn't seem important. More important was the fact that he no longer knew which direction the door was. He stopped moving. He reeled slowly round on himself. In the flames there were noises. The noises themselves seemed to burn his ears. For the last time he opened his mouth, but there was no air left, only fire; his tongue seemed to burst into flames and he reeled again and staggered, and the last thing he heard was the shouting of his own voice in an oddly tangled uproar like the roar of many other voices, all of which were inside his own head.

Then he toppled forward into blackness and was lost.

52

This is what he became. A silence in the noise. A rag of smoke floating, softly torn to shreds in the tops of the trees, a spreading drift of final thoughts. He was glad he'd left his body behind. Watching it dance and crackle, he felt nothing but a bystander's mild curiosity. Other figures now rose out of the noise to keep him company: a hanged man who slipped his noose of flaming curtain and swam gravely out of the smoke, a redhead in tassels lit up like candles, a girl with chestnut-brown hair and gray eyes who opened her mouth and laughed a jet of orange light, bright as a blowtorch flare. A huge sheet of lined notepaper turned into a flying carpet of smoke, and he lay on it remembering things he'd never seen. Darren Winder breaking open Abdul's face with a photographer's tripod. Detective Inspector Raminder Singh sitting naked and cross-legged in a temple. His mother dancing heavily on her own in a tiny room of plain white walls. They were all indices in the same equation, numbers rotating like smoke through the air to lead him to the perfect solution, and he rotated with them, slowly, among the treetops, following the trail of a smoke-filled girl dressed immaculately in heliotrope-colored running shoes. But something was wrong. This wasn't what dying should be.

For a moment he swam on effortlessly with the others. Then he faltered. He grew heavier. The silence swelled, slowly at first, then faster. He rose with it and fell, leaped and plunged like a fish in water, like a little kid on a roller coaster, holding on grimly, feeling sicker and sicker, swooping and lurching heavily in and out of the flaming treetops until he reached the end of the ride and fell suddenly downward, and rolled over on the hard sandy soil, and threw up.

"Is better," a voice said quietly. "My Garvie man."

Then blackness again.

When he woke, minutes or hours or days later, he was in pain, writhing on the ground while people bothered him with things and noises and flashing blue lights until finally it came clear, and he opened his eyes and looked up at Detective Inspector Singh.

"Don't talk," the policeman said.

Others were talking. They gave each other low, urgent instructions obscured by the noise of vehicles arriving and leaving. Blue lights swirled over everything. There was pain in his hands and legs, and his face was numb.

"I'm not dead anymore," he said to Singh woodenly. The pain flared up and he began to think again. "Where are they? Hannah? The baby?"

"Don't talk. It's bad for you."

"Tell me!"

"The baby's okay. On its way to hospital now. It's going to be fine, they think."

"Hannah?" he croaked.

Singh frowned and looked away. "They're doing everything they can."

Garvie tried to lift himself and Singh held him back. "You're going to hospital yourself. They're just coming with the stretcher. There's nothing you can do now. You've done enough. More than enough."

Garvie lay there thinking. "I couldn't make them work out," he said sadly.

Singh looked at him, puzzled.

"The numbers."

"You're delirious," Singh said.

Garvie blinked painfully and thought about that. "I mean, I couldn't get *them* out. Hannah and her baby."

Singh shook his head and frowned. "You got them out. When we got here the three of you were lying on the grass."

Garvie lay there trying to remember. A man in a green paramedic uniform came up and loosened his burned shirtsleeve to give him an injection.

"Rest now," Singh said.

Garvie frowned. "But I didn't tell you where I was."

"No." Singh was grim and pale. "We didn't know until we got a call from one of the residents at Tick Hill. Out late walking his dog and saw the flames."

Garvie lay there. "What resident?" he said at last.

"Wouldn't give his name. Foreign, we think. Nervous type. Please, rest now."

Garvie lay there, smiling with his numb face. Then he stopped. He felt very sleepy. "Singh?"

"What?"

"I don't think my mum's going to be very pleased."

"I don't think so, either. Here she is now."

There was the sound of a car drawing up, and a door slammed.

Singh said, "She knows everything. I told her. It's all over now, Garvie."

He heard running footsteps. Then his mother's face appeared, full of pain and tears.

"Oh *Garvie!*"

Everything was slipping away again. "I'm sorry, Mum," he mumbled as he fell asleep. "I'm sorry for everything."

53

It was all over. From the window of his ward on the twelfth floor of City Central Hospital Garvie watched spring give way to summer. The rain showers dried up at last, blue skies opened out behind the tower blocks in the business district, the sun shone, and the city sparkled below him like a handful of glass beads. He sat in a chair next to his bed staring at it hour after hour. His body healed quickly. After a few days they took him off the antibiotic drip and stopped giving him daily injections. They removed the dressings from his burned hands and gave him gauze bandage-gloves to wear. His blistered nose peeled, his cracked lips flaked, and the raw rims of his ears crusted over. The swelling in his ankle went down, and soon he could get around on an aluminum crutch.

At the end of his first week Felix and Smudge came to visit, and slipped him a pack of multifilter Kings hidden in a sock, which was immediately found and confiscated by his mother, who came up to see him every hour from the ward below where she was working, and every hour from home when she wasn't. Abdul came to see him too, standing shyly at the end of the bed. By now everyone knew his part in the drama, and he was embarrassed to find himself briefly the center of attention. They didn't say much to each other, but after a few minutes Garvie put his hand to his heart in a gesture both tender and daft, and Abdul went away with shining eyes.

Every day he asked for a newspaper and they refused to bring him one. Radios and televisions were switched off throughout the ward. Whenever he complained, the nurses just smiled sympathetically and told him they had their instructions from the police and the Child Protection Agency, and he would limp back to his chair and sit in silence, staring out over the city again.

In the middle of the second week Singh visited him. He came early in the morning on his way to a meeting with the prosecution services, and against hospital regulations put a bunch of tulips in Garvie's plastic water jug.

"They're going to let me go home soon," Garvie said.

"Good. You can do no more damage. The case is closed at last."

Both Winders, father and son, remained in custody after being refused bail. Darren had been charged with the murder of Chloe Dow. From a warehouse out on the highway police had retrieved computers containing photographic images datable to Thursday the twelfth of Chloe standing in the private suite at the top of the shag carpeted stairs wearing a white jacket and blue dress and holding a hand of playing cards. There were emails too from Darren inviting Chloe to trial as Imperium's new *All you got to do to win is play* poster girl. But in several of the pictures Chloe was semi-naked and weeping. Something had gone wrong. This was corroborated by witness evidence from the Thursday night and by texts from Friday found on Darren's phone—a barrage of threats interrupted by a single reply from Chloe: *Meet me at Pike Pond at 5.* In a drawer of the desk in Darren's office they had found duplicate keys for both the Porsche and the garage where it was kept while his father was abroad.

"He's not the brightest," Singh said.

Winder senior had been charged with aiding, abetting, procuring, and counseling the assault on Hannah Clark and her baby. The car that Garvie had seen driving away from the Tick Hill trailer park had been traced. Three men from Riga had been charged with assault, arson, and attempted murder—but their original instruction had come from Winder senior.

"He had a lot to hide. Gambling isn't all that goes on at the casino. He knew if we went in on the back of the Dow case we'd start to find things. When he heard what his son had done he went berserk. Darren's got a broken arm. There's no doubt they're both going down."

Garvie had listened all the time in silence. Now he said, quietly, "Witness evidence? *Attempted* murder?"

Singh nodded.

"So she's alive. Hannah Clark."

Singh nodded, more slowly.

Garvie looked at him. "All this time I've not known."

"For your own good. It's been touch and go, in fact. But she's pulled through. She's going to need surgery, quite a lot of it, but she'll recover."

"I want to see her."

"I know. But you can't. She's part of the witness protection program." He made an empty gesture with his hands. "I couldn't help you even if I wanted to. I've no idea where she is. But she's safe. And her baby too."

Garvie thought. "What did she see?"

"A lot more than Darren knew. It was Hannah told us about the photographs and where they might be found. She'd seen the end of the so-called modeling session, after things had got out of hand. And she'd seen Darren manhandling Chloe before she broke away."

Garvie was silent. "I put her in danger."

"No."

"If I hadn't gone to Imperium, if Winder hadn't seen me talking to her—"

"You're not responsible for what he did. You're responsible for getting her out of the caravan."

"Actually, I couldn't even do that on my own."

"Abdul's a hero. But she wouldn't have got out without you, either. You know it. Enough. No more."

Garvie stared at him and nodded at last. "I wanted to see the papers but I'm not interested anymore."

"It's been frenzied. As you can imagine. My only worry is that the coverage they've given the Winders will delay the trial." He looked at Garvie. "There's been a lot of speculation about Hannah and her baby. What happened to them couldn't be kept out of the press. But I'm glad to say you hardly feature at all. Abdul, I'm afraid, is having to learn to deal with fame."

Singh stood and prepared to leave. "They're letting you out soon, you say?"

"Couple of days."

Singh nodded back. "I'm glad. I've been talking to your mother. If I remember correctly, you'll just be in time to take your exams. Life goes on, Garvie." He paused. "For some of us."

54

After two weeks away, Flat 12 Eastwick Gardens seemed different. Smaller, stranger, full of things he hadn't noticed much before, like the not-quite-blue and white stripes of the upholstery on the kitchen chairs which, he saw now, matched the curtains, or the smell of Bajan cooking, so oddly personal after the anti-smell of the hospital.

He stood on the threshold gazing around. His mother went through to the kitchen and began to carry things about, clearing space at the table. She seemed different too. That was because she'd actually changed. She'd lost weight. Her broad face had a new hollow look and her mouth was pinched. She was quiet now, as if no longer physically capable of her former loudness. Like someone who had suffered and expected to suffer again, her eyes were watchful. Most of the time they watched him.

She went to and fro across the kitchen as he stood there looking at her. At first she was clear and distinct, a middle-aged woman in a not-very-smart coat, then she was blurred and intermittent, and finally she was a shape without an outline drowning in a melting kitchen.

He dropped his crutches with a clatter to the floor, and she turned and saw him lift his arms to her, and there was a moment when nothing in the room seemed itself but irrelevant shadows before she went in a rush across the room toward him.

"I know now," he whispered, his mouth squashed against her wet shoulder. "I know what it means to be a mother. I know what it means for everything to be your fault."

It was Garvie who first raised the subject of his exams. It was two days after he came out of hospital, Friday evening.

"Got the first one Monday. Math."

"Is that right?"

She continued to clear the table of their dinner things.

"Higher tier, calculator paper. One hour forty-five minutes. Calculators may be used."

His mother said nothing, looking at him warily in silence.

"Think I'll go and brush up on probability," he said.

Still she said nothing.

"Put in a bit of effort," he added.

She just looked at him.

"Course," he said, "you might not believe me. That'd be normal."

They looked at each other for a long time in silence; then he went into his room and worked for an hour on sines and cosines and quadratic equations—from a mathematical point of view a totally unnecessary exercise.

Numbers worked again; they fell into the old patterns. But he didn't do the equations in order to see them perform their usual gymnastic tricks, their feats of completion; he did them to stop himself from thinking of other things. He was so unhappy he had to keep reminding himself that the Winders were in custody awaiting trial, that what he'd done had not been without purpose, that Chloe's murder would not go unpunished. But over and again his thoughts went to a girl in a white toga, a girl with laughing eyes, a girl so unselfconsciously pretty she seemed more herself than other people were, and each time he thought of her it was as if he saw the toga burst into flames and could feel her burning feet in his burning hands.

His appetite failed, he slept badly all night, and the next day was just as miserable and empty.

At some point on Saturday afternoon, despite his best intentions, his concentration flagged. There was birdsong in the tree outside, and he went to stand at the window, looking down into the communal garden. Garden, so-called. Matted grass full of thistles, flower beds choked with brambles and bindweed.

Chloe's garden in Fox Walk came into his mind, so neat and precise. Except, of course, for the fence broken where Alex had leaped over. *Probably mended by now,* he thought.

Life goes on, for some. Not for Chloe. Some things can't be mended.

Other memories came to him before he could stop them. In life, unlike math, there was nearly always something left over. A feeling not accounted for. A memory which doesn't add up. Like that brief moment when he'd stood with Felix in Chloe's room wearing her wet-look gray jeggings and pink T-shirt and short white jacket smelling very clean. Posing, hands in her jacket pockets, turning this way and that, asking Felix if it all matched. He remembered it exactly: the jeggings, the jacket, the T-shirt, the look on Felix's face. He remembered with absolute clarity that there'd been nothing in the jacket pockets.

Just one of those things: something that didn't fit, something left over.

In the room next door his mother turned on the taps at the sink and began to wash up, and he put all thoughts of Chloe firmly out of his mind and sat again at his table. Opening his book, he worked in semi-engaged fashion through half a dozen standard-grade probability questions, trying to keep his mind under control. But his memory went its own way: He couldn't stop himself remembering the probability question that Chloe had attempted on the sheet of paper she'd used for her running note.

$$1/(x+2) + 1/3 = -1$$

And now, despite himself, he felt a familiar mental itch.

He couldn't help it. He sat, puzzled, at his table.

For a while he considered the equation. It was so simple it was dull: $x = -11/4$. Somehow that wasn't the point. The point was elsewhere, tantalizingly out of reach.

What was it?

Trying to rid himself of the itch, he got up and went to the window again, and stood there restlessly and went back to the table. The itch remained, itching furiously like the itch on a phantom limb, impossible to scratch because it didn't exist. Like an imaginary number, which existed only in the imagination.

Everyone knows what you have to do with imaginary numbers.

He started to tremble.

He glanced at his bedroom door. Then he ripped a sheet of lined paper from a pad and looked at it for a few seconds, and carefully tore it on the left-hand edge about an inch below the top. Taking a black felt-tip pen, he wrote without hesitating fifteen words in a list ten lines long in the top left-hand quarter of the sheet:

plain choc
milk
white
butter
pecans
plain flour
baking powder
eggs
vanilla essence
castor sugar

When he'd finished, in the bottom right-hand quarter he wrote:

$$1/(x+2)+\frac{1}{3}=-1$$

And in the bottom left-hand quarter: *jacket.*

And finally, in the center of the page: *Gone for a run Back 7:30 p.m.*, which he circled in a thick black line.

Even as he wrote it he didn't like it. But he forced himself to look at it. After a while he added a vague doodley scribble underneath the probability equation and got some spit on the tip of his finger and smeared it across the words *eggs* and *vanilla*.

He didn't like it any better than before. The itch hadn't gone away, either.

He stood at the window with his knuckles between his teeth.

"There was nothing in the pocket," he said out loud. "No casino chip, nothing. It doesn't matter. It doesn't mean anything. It doesn't—"

He froze midsentence, his head cocked to one side as if listening to the sound of three very precise memories rotating into a different dimension.

He went back to the desk, took up the paper, folded it in half, crumpled it, threw it in his wastepaper basket, fished it out again, smoothed it and put it back on the table. And stared at it for five seconds.

"Shit," he said.

First he called Felix.

"Got a memory test for you, man. Remember Chloe bringing chocolate brownies in to school?"

"Yeah. Sort of."

"What day was that?"

Felix heaved a sigh. "Don't know, Garv. Not long before she got bumped. Sometime that week."

"I need to know the exact day. You said it was MacAttack's birthday."

"Yeah, but it's not like his birthday's in my diary."

"Come on, Felix. Think. You said he was doing the roll call."

"Oh yeah. Must have been . . . Must have been the Wednesday, then. He has meetings or something the other days, and this temp does it."

"You sure?"

"Definitely. Wednesday. Do I get something for remembering so well?"

"No."

Next he phoned Jess.

There was a small noise, something between a gulp and a sob, at the other end of the phone.

"Jess? That you? I need some information."

There was a long silence. "Can't your new girlfriend tell you?"

"Don't pull that, Jess. This is important."

He heard her snort.

"Only you can help me. I need your perfect memory. Listen. When you told me about Chloe turning up that Friday, you said you hadn't spoken to her since studying with her for a math test."

"So?"

"Test on probability, right?"

"What's that?"

389

"Outcomes. Lots of fractions. One over x plus two plus one over three equals minus one. That sort of thing."

"Yeah. I s'pose."

"You were studying at Chloe's."

"That's right. But, Garv, I—"

"What day?"

There was a long silence. "I dunno."

"That same week?"

"Yeah."

"All right. What days do you have math?"

There was another long silence. "Monday. Wednesday. And Friday."

"Okay. So the test wasn't Monday, 'cause you'd have studied for it the week before."

"I s'pose."

"Was the test Friday? Had you just had it that morning?"

"No."

"So it must have been on Wednesday. So you'd have been studying Monday or Tuesday night."

"Yeah, that's right. I remember now. It was Monday. The test was on Wednesday. We didn't do much, to be honest. And anyway, she went off for a run after a bit."

"Okay, Jess, that's perfect. Thanks."

She was about to say something else but he hung up fast. He had one more call to make.

He looked up the number and dialed.

"Bolloms' dry cleaning." A harsh voice, all pins and starching.

"Hi. I wonder if you can help me. It's about a jacket left for cleaning a few weeks ago."

"Name?"

"Dow. Chloe Dow."

The phone went dead. Several minutes passed, then the voice said, "Dow?"

"That's right."

"Jacket, white, cotton."

"That's the one."

"Picked up already. Long time since, I think."

"Really?"

"Yeah, really."

"Can you tell me when?"

A silence followed, broken only by snippets of harsh breathing and the tapping of a keyboard. Garvie was holding the phone so tight his knuckles almost popped.

"Yeah," the voice said at last. "Got it right here."

"What day?"

"The eleventh. Wednesday."

He sat there shivering.

Ingredients for chocolate brownies taken in to school on Wednesday.

Studying math for a test on Wednesday.

Reminder to pick up a jacket on Wednesday.

He'd been right. Everything matched. Grabbing his coat, he went fast out of his room and was halfway to the front door before he remembered his mother in the kitchen. When he turned, she was looking at him with those watchful eyes and he muttered, "It's okay, it can wait," and went back into his room.

He called Alex.

"Man, I need a favor. Yeah, right now. Listen, you know the sports shop in the Center? Yeah. I want you to go there and ask some questions. You got a pen? Write this down. *Asics Lady GEL-Torana 4 Trail Running Shoes. Size 6. Lime green with orange pattern and laces.* Got that? Okay. Here's the question. Somebody bought a pair of those shoes from that place the Friday Chloe got killed. Late afternoon. That's right. I want you to find out who that person was. No, it wasn't Chloe. Yes, it's important. It's the most important thing you've ever done in your life. Yeah, well, ask. Get hold of whoever who was serving. Those shoes are evil ugly. There's a chance they'll remember. Give me a ding soon as you know."

When he got the call an hour later he was lying on his bed, hands behind his head, staring up at the ceiling. His mother had been in twice but he hadn't responded to her, hadn't even moved. But when his phone rang he leaped like a salmon to grab it.

"Alex? What's the news?"

And he stood there in the middle of his room, listening in horror.

55

On Monday morning he finished breakfast, his mother wished him luck, and he went down the stairs with his bag containing everything he needed for his exam and out through the lobby into the morning sunshine. Halfway down the street he turned to look back and saw her still watching him, arms folded at the window, and forced himself to walk on, slowly, all the way to the end and round the corner.

Just out of sight he stood there, considering. In one direction was school and exams and pleasing his mother. In the other was doubt and pain and the desperate pursuit of something like the truth. He glanced down the street toward school. Then hurried across the street and caught a bus going in the opposite direction.

At ten o'clock Fox Walk was deserted: Most of the people who lived there had gone to work or to school. The cul-de-sac lay empty and gleaming in the sun. Red and yellow tulips were out in the front gardens, and purple pansies in hanging baskets, and a few early roses, white and pink, in plastic tubs. The council had trimmed the strips and the grass was the fresh green of summer. Garvie ignored all this. He walked past the end of Fox Walk to the wicket gate leading to the

Marsh Fields and turned onto the path that ran along the backs of the houses. As he'd thought, the fence behind Honeymead had been repaired but it wasn't difficult to climb, and inside a minute he was standing on the patio next to one of those modern vinyl doors beloved by Felix.

Garvie's information was that Mrs. Dow had returned to work and the house would be empty, but he stood for a moment listening. Except for a blackbird in the shrubbery everything was quiet. He unrolled the oilcloth Felix had lent him and took out a tension wrench and the half-diamond pick. Putting the short end of the wrench into the plug of the door-handle lock and holding it firm with the thumb of his left hand, he slipped the end of the half diamond in with his right and prodded around for the shift of the pins until they fell into line, then swung the tension wrench counterclockwise until the handle moved freely. He repeated the trick with the deadlock above. Again he waited for a moment, listening. Then he opened the door and went quietly into the Dows' conservatory.

"Never stay longer than an hour. Always secure more than one exit." Remembering Felix's advice, he crossed the living room to the hall and unlocked the front door. In the hallway he paused, listening once more before padding silently up the stairs. The heavy silence of emptiness filled the house, but he took no chances, going along the landing as quietly as possible, ducking below the level of the window. Chloe's room was still sealed, a drooping piece of police tape strung across the door. But it wasn't Chloe's room he was interested in. He went past it to the spare room at the far end of the landing. He'd seen inside it once, in that brief period when he was going out with Chloe, and he remembered what was in it: a desk and a chair and lots of shelves. It would be where Mr. Dow did his paperwork. Garvie opened the door and slipped inside.

He sat at the desk and tried the drawers. The first was filled with stationery—neatly bound bundles of pens and pencils, boxes of paper clips and drawing pins. The second contained cables, plugs, and chargers, again all neatly bundled together and secured with plastic ties. The third was packed with files—records of jobs and copies of invoices. It was only when Garvie took them out that he found something more interesting at the back of the drawer. A ten-spot and a packet of cigarette papers. Mr. Dow had a secret little habit. Garvie thought about that while he put the papers back and looked around the rest of the office.

The files he wanted were on the top shelf, all neatly labeled: *House, Car, Garden, Holidays, Misc, Bank, Tax*. He took down the file labeled *Misc* and began to look through it. Twenty minutes went by in slow quiet stages. He put *Misc* back on the shelf and took down *House*. More minutes passed as he flicked steadily through correspondence about the conservatory extension and receipts for bamboo-cane furniture, then he put *House* back and took down *Garden*.

He marveled at the obsessive orderliness of Mr. Dow's files. He himself had no use for neatness whatsoever; to him it seemed a form of private stupidity. In fact he was hoping to prove it.

He put *Garden* back, took down *Holidays* and went through it slowly, glancing at brochures of hotels in Spain and printouts of booking confirmations, then put it back and took down *Tax* and went through it more rapidly, and put that back too. Looking at his watch, he saw he'd been there for nearly an hour, and sighed and got to his feet. And that was when he saw the other file, lying open on the floor.

Everything in *Leisure* was arranged in chronological order, and he flipped straight to the place for Friday the thirteenth, and there, neatly logged in a little plastic jacket, he found the thing that should never have been filed at all, that really ought to have been thrown away; the thing that proved neatness a fatal stupidity.

His hands were shaking so much he could hardly make the call.

"Singh."

"Get here now. Honeymead, Fox Walk."

"Garvie? Is that you?"

"Now. Immediately. Straightaway."

"What are you talking about? Why are you whispering?"

"Just get here, fast. I've found something new. It changes everything."

"Oh no. Not again. Don't do this, Garvie, I beg you." Singh's voice was brisk, but there was no disguising his anger. "Listen to me, Garvie. If you have anything to say about any detail of the Dow case, you can ask your mother to arrange a meeting at your house, and I'll—"

"It's the running shoes."

There was a brief silence at Singh's end.

"What about the running shoes?"

"I know what happened. I can prove it. I've got the proof right here, in my hand. *Come on*, Singh. Trust me."

Something in the tone of his voice must have been convincing. He could almost see Singh's face change at the other end of the phone. "I'm on my way," the policeman said, and hung up.

Leaning against the desk, Garvie closed his eyes and allowed himself to relax for a moment. Then there was a click, very near, and he opened them to find Mrs. Dow standing a couple of meters away in the doorway wearing a plump pink dressing gown and pink felt slippers, looking at him openmouthed in astonishment.

"Mrs. Dow," Garvie said politely.

She said nothing, staring at him blearily, her face crumpled with sleep. Confusion made her slow. She glanced behind her toward her bedroom and back at Garvie. "I'm not well," she faltered. Then, anxiously: "I heard voices, Garvie." She peered past him, as if to find someone else there.

He nodded. "I can explain."

"Explain . . . why you're here?"

"Explain . . . about Chloe. But why don't we go downstairs and talk in the kitchen? If you're not feeling great I could make you a cup of tea."

"Explain what about Chloe?" she said, not moving, looking at him with the unpredictable blankness of a hysteric.

"Well, it's a bit difficult."

"I want you to tell me about Chloe."

"Okay." He spoke soothingly, as he might to a child. "I know how hard this has been for you, Mrs. Dow. I know how much you've suffered. Every time the police say they've got it sussed it turns out they've made a mistake. But now I know what really happened."

Lulled, she nodded her head. "Good," she murmured. "Tell me."

He only hoped he wouldn't get to the end before Singh arrived. Speaking in the same soothing voice, he said, "Do you remember the note?"

"Note?"

"The note Chloe left on the living-room table, telling you she'd gone for a run? It said: *Gone for a run Back 7:30 p.m.* You remember that."

She nodded.

"Well, there was other stuff written on the paper too: jottings and doodles. A list of ingredients for making chocolate brownies. Some math homework. A reminder to pick up her white jacket from the cleaner's."

A sad smile appeared very briefly on Mrs. Dow's face. "I bought that jacket for her. For her fifteenth birthday."

He nodded sympathetically. Keeping his voice as low as possible, he went on.

"Well, she picked the jacket up on the Wednesday of that week. Wednesday was the day she took those brownies in to school too, and it was Wednesday she had the math test she was studying for. So, you see, all those doodlings and jottings on the piece of notepaper must have been written *before* Wednesday. Which is interesting."

"Why?" Mrs. Dow was listening more closely now, her head cocked to one side, her eyes smaller and harder. Garvie began to wonder how long it would take for Singh to arrive.

"Because," he went on, "it made me think, *What if the bit about the run was written before Wednesday too?* Everything was written in the same black felt-tip pen; it could easily have been written all at the same time. And, in fact, it turns out that everything in the note was written on . . . Monday."

"I don't understand."

"Chloe left the note when she went out for a run on Monday night. And when she got back she threw the note away, in the living-room wastepaper basket probably."

She gazed at him for a long time, and he began to think she could see it all. But she couldn't.

"I still don't understand," she said. "It was on the living-room table when Mick and I got back from the Center on Friday."

Garvie took a deep breath. By now he was listening out all the time for the sound of Singh's car.

"I can explain that too. Unless you'd like a cup of tea first."

"No," she said. "I want you to explain it."

Very carefully, Garvie went on. "On Friday Chloe had a problem. There were two—no, three—men bothering her. You already know about the janitor at school and Darren Winder at the casino. Friday afternoon Chloe was trying to sort things out. She was scared. She didn't know what to do. After lunch she left school and went to see Jess. You know Jess."

"Yes, she's a little cow."

"Well, it didn't do Chloe any good seeing her, so she left and went to see Alex."

"I know him too. He's no good."

"That didn't work, either, so . . . she came to see me, at school."

Mrs. Dow smiled. "She always liked you, Garvie. I liked you too. Before all this."

He said, very carefully, "But I didn't know what Chloe's trouble was, so seeing me didn't do her any good, either." He paused. "I'm sorry about that."

"Don't worry," Mrs. Dow said automatically. "We can't know everything, can we?"

Garvie went on, slowly. "She came home then. About half past four. She'd decided what she was going to do. She was going to pick up her bank card, which she'd left here, and go out to the shops to buy some new running shoes. But while she was here, before she could go out, she met him."

"Who?"

"The other man." He paused and looked at her sadly. He swallowed. "The man who killed her. He should have been at work," he said. "But he was here."

She remained staring at him, her head cocked to one side, her eyes so small he could hardly see them, and before she could say anything else he went on, in the same quiet voice.

"After he'd killed her he didn't know what to do. I mean, here he was, in the house, in the middle of a Friday afternoon, with a dead girl and no excuse. But he saw the note that Chloe had thrown away on Monday lying in the bin and he had an idea. He smoothed it out as best he could and left it on the living-room table, to make it look like Chloe was out for a run. Then he went upstairs and got Chloe's running kit and put it on her. But there was a problem."

Mrs. Dow was looking at him now as if he were a person in a dream. The street outside was completely quiet and he cursed Singh's slowness.

"What problem?" she asked.

"The running shoes. She didn't have any. He could have panicked then. But he didn't. He hid Chloe's body—in the garage is my guess—and went out to buy some new shoes from the sports shop in the center. And later in the evening, when the coast was clear, he put the shoes on Chloe's feet and drove her body out to Pike Pond and dumped her in the water."

She was so still, standing there staring at him, he couldn't tell if she was breathing or not. She said, very quietly, "What are you telling me?"

"That when you got home on Friday and thought Chloe was out for a run, she wasn't. She was here, in the house. Already dead."

"Already dead?"

"Yes."

"But . . . who killed her?"

He swallowed. "The other man. The man who'd been . . . bothering Chloe."

"Who's that?" Mrs. Dow whispered.

Garvie couldn't delay any longer. He said, "Your husband. Mr. Dow. I'm sorry."

She was perfectly calm. He watched her put the thought in her mind and test it out.

"But he *was* at work," she said after a moment.

Garvie shook his head.

She continued to think, calmly, quietly, and there was a moment when he thought it was going to be okay. But only a moment. He'd never seen anyone have hysterics before. Her head began to shake from side to side. She made wild, dithering movements with her arms and moaned like a beast.

Garvie tried to calm her but she shook him off.

"Liar!" she screamed. "Liar!"

She staggered backward onto the landing, screaming, and Garvie followed at a distance, pleading with her to be quiet. As he went he glanced at his watch, and again cursed Singh for taking so long. Mrs. Dow threw her arms from side to side and rolled her eyes. She kicked off her slippers, and her dressing gown came undone and showed her nightdress, large and rucked, swinging around her.

"I'm sorry," Garvie cried. "But it's true. I can prove it. Look, Mrs. Dow! This is the receipt for the running shoes he bought at the Center. He filed it away, just as you said he always did."

She snatched the receipt from him and waved it in the air without looking at it. She screamed once, fell silent, and advanced on him, her face distorted with fury. And at that moment a car drew up on the driveway outside and they both stopped, listening.

With a sigh of relief Garvie said, "That's Inspector Singh, Mrs. Dow. He can explain it to you."

"Inspector Singh?"

"I phoned him. He can explain everything." He smiled at her reassuringly, and called down, "Singh! Door's open! We're up here!"

There was the sound of the front door opening and closing and footsteps on the stairs.

She was quiet now, waiting.

"It's going to be okay," Garvie said to her softly. "You'll see. I'm so sorry about what happened. But the inspector will explain. Here he is. *At last.*"

And they turned together to look toward the top of the stairs. The sound of footsteps came closer, and after a moment, round the corner of the banisters came Mr. Dow. He stood at the end of the landing in his paint-spattered overalls and tool belt, looking back at them silently.

56

"Mick!" Mrs. Dow cried in ecstasy. "*Mick!*" Without hurrying, he came along the landing and she collapsed into his arms, and he held her up, looking at Garvie evenly over the top of her head.

"It's okay, love," he said to his wife. "Hush now."

"But Mick, you don't understand, Mick."

"Don't try to talk. You're not well, you know you're not. I came back to see how you were. I'm just on my way to another job."

She pushed her face against the bib of his overalls and made soft weeping noises.

"She's not herself," he said to Garvie.

"Mick," she said once more, and held him tightly.

"Well," Garvie said, "I'll leave you two lovebirds in peace. Thing is, I've got this math exam, so I'll just—"

Mr. Dow stepped across him and blocked his way. "I don't know why you're here," he said in his slow, flat voice.

Before Garvie could speak Mrs. Dow reared up out of her husband's arms and said, "Lies! He's been telling me lies."

Mr. Dow tried to calm her, keeping his eyes on Garvie. "Shush," he said. "Don't be silly now."

"Lies about you," she insisted.

He held her again, smoothing her disordered hair with one hand, and at last said, in the same flat, slow voice: "What lies?"

Confusedly she talked—about Chloe, about the jacket she'd taken to the dry cleaner's, and the note in the wastepaper basket, and the running shoes bought that evening at the Center. "He said there were three men," she said, gulping hard. "*Three,* Mick! *Bothering* her—and I know what that means!"

He pressed her facedown to his chest again and tried to quiet her. "Shush," he said. "What are you talking about?"

"Lies about the running shoes!" she shouted, rearing up again. She waved her hand holding a bit of paper in his face. "Lies about where you filed the receipt!"

"Hush, love," he said again. "Please. You'll only make yourself worse. It's all nonsense, you know it is." He held her tightly, murmuring quietly to her, trying to calm her down, keeping his eyes all the time on Garvie—until, after a minute or more, in the middle of her confused talking, he made a sudden angry movement, as if he couldn't bear her hysteria anymore, and Mrs. Dow fell forward onto the carpet and lay at their feet.

He put the claw hammer neatly back in his tool belt, and stood looking at Garvie.

Garvie looked down at Mrs. Dow and saw blood on the carpet by the back of her head. "You shouldn't have done that," he said quietly, carefully keeping the horror out of his voice. "That's going to be a really hard stain to get out," he added. But the horror remained.

Mr. Dow said nothing. He began to breathe heavily, the only sound in the hush of the house and the quietness of the deserted cul-de-sac around them. There was no way past him downstairs. In the silence there was a small intrusive noise, and Garvie took out his phone and just had time to see a text from Singh reading *Stuck in traffic* before Mr. Dow stepped forward with unexpected speed and knocked it violently out of his hand.

"Careful now," Garvie said, taking a step backward. "You wouldn't want to break it, would you?"

Mr. Dow looked down at the phone on the carpet and stamped on it heavily in his workman's boots, and there was the smothered crunch of smashed plastic.

"I see," Garvie said.

He backed away again, and Mr. Dow took another step forward, still staring at him in silence.

"Well," Garvie said conversationally, "I know this is a cliché, but in fact the police are on their way. The house will be surrounded. You can't escape. You shouldn't do anything rash. I needn't go on." He paused. "Need I?"

Mr. Dow stepped forward again and Garvie took another step back.

"Though I should probably try to keep you talking at this point. If you could ramble on about how you killed her it would help."

Saying nothing, Mr. Dow advanced heavily, and Garvie went slowly farther backward.

"Actually, I've got a question. About that job you were doing Friday. You must have left the property straight after the carpenter and electrician went at four, with the painting still half done. But it was all finished by start of work Monday morning. So did you go back at the weekend to—"

The man caught him midsentence by the throat and heaved him wriggling against the wall and hung him there, choking. He drew his arm so far back Garvie couldn't see it anymore, and punched him suddenly in the eyes with a loud crunch. Falling sideways out of his grip, Garvie staggered down the narrow hallway, blind and gasping, as far as the Dows' bedroom, where he stopped and turned, just as Mr. Dow lunged at him again. He ducked to the side of the blow and caught the man off-balance with a hack to the leg, and scrambled through the bedroom door and slammed it behind him. Bracing himself, he gulped for air. He couldn't see out of one eye. Wiping blood from the other, he blinked and flinched with pain.

The bedroom door, which had no lock, burst open almost immediately, flinging him forward, and Mr. Dow came into the room behind him, breathing hard. There was no doubting the man's brute strength. Garvie retreated limping round the far side of the bed, watching out of his one good eye as Mr. Dow came after him again, methodically. Even now, as if in useless self-mockery, his brain registered the fine detail of the room. It was all pink and cream, very neat. There were built-in ivory-colored wardrobes and a double bed with an ivory-colored duvet, and bedside chairs upholstered in pink velvet. On a dressing table stood a jewelry box, hairbrush set, and two large china vases, both hideous. Mr. Dow took the claw hammer out of his tool belt. Garvie saw that in detail too. The sticky end of it was bristly with hairs.

Garvie spat blood. "This is your last chance," he said in a gargle, "to give yourself up quietly."

As Dow came after him, hammer raised, he leaped up onto the bed and staggered bouncing across it, but Dow was quicker than he thought and caught him meatily on the point of his shoulder with another blow of his hammer, sending him crashing face first into the wooden paneling of the headboard. He fell over the side of the bed, flailing. Dow appeared above him, and he flung a pair of pajama bottoms which he found in his hand upward into the man's face, and scrambled into the bathroom, where he slammed the door and turned the key.

His legs gave way then, and he fell against the tiled wall, panting. His shoulder glowed fiercely with a burning pain and his right arm hung down numb and useless. There was no fight left in him, he knew. The flimsy door shook as he looked, one-eyed, around the tiny bathroom. There was nothing in it to save him; nothing of use in the washbasin, toilet, shower cubicle, freestanding rack of toiletries. Not even a monkey could have escaped through the scrap of frosted glass in the window.

For a moment there was complete silence except for the small wet gasps of his own breathing.

With a noise like a gunshot, the hammer crashed through the flimsy paneling.

Garvie tried to pull himself together. "Toilet's occupied," he called out. "You'll have to wait a minute."

The hammer crashed through the door a second time and a jagged piece of paneling fell out, revealing Mr. Dow on the other side lifting the hammer again.

"Think of the mess," Garvie croaked. "Not to mention the expense."

With his left hand he squirted shower gel through the gap in the door, and Mr. Dow wiped his face and lunged forward with his hammer a third time.

There was nothing left now for Garvie to do. He stood up with the sinking feeling that all his gambles had failed, and quietly faced the door. The hammer crashed through it a final time, the last of the paneling flew apart, and Mr. Dow stood there in front of him.

Garvie looked at him through his one eye. *This is how he must have looked to Chloe in the end,* he thought. *A big, silent man with empty eyes and violent hands.*

He spoke up to say one final thing. "Your biggest mistake was not to understand your wife."

The incomprehension in the man's face was replaced by a spasm of hatred, and at last he broke his silence.

"That bitch," he said with a twisted leer, and lifted the hammer.

There was a blur of movement behind him, and a noise like a dropped bottle. He fell forward heavily, and Mrs. Dow appeared behind him, ragged and ghastly, with the remains of one of the hideous dressing-table china vases in her hands.

She stood over him, bleeding. "You killed my daughter," she said thickly. "You bastard."

And as Garvie tottered through the shattered door to take the shard of vase from her, there was the sound outside of cars drawing up at speed and car doors slamming.

They looked at each other.

"Typical, isn't it?" Garvie said thickly. "They never arrive until you don't need them anymore."

57

June arrived wet and cool. Rain fell onto the city out of numb gray skies; it dripped from trees, gurgled down drains, and stood everywhere in puddles as dull as the sky overhead. On Bulwarks Lane the gutters overflowed, flooding the road outside Jamal's. A smell of rot hung in the streets, and people's houses filled with soaked shoes, dripping umbrellas, and steaming coats.

One rainy evening at about nine o'clock Detective Inspector Raminder Singh drove into Five Mile. It was the first time he'd been into the estate since his dash to Fox Walk a week earlier. He went past the turn to the Dows' house, along Old Ditch Road past the kiddies' playground, onto Pilkington Driftway, and drew up at last outside Eastwick Gardens. The first thing he saw was the For Sale sign for Flat 12 and he let out a small sigh. He couldn't blame Mrs. Smith, but he knew what Garvie thought about a move to Barbados.

Carrying his briefcase, he left his car and walked with his usual self-possession through the downpour to the flats' entrance, and a few minutes later followed Mrs. Smith into her flat. Voices met him: Leonard Johnson and his wife finishing dinner in the kitchen. Looking around, he saw Garvie brooding in the corner and nodded briefly, but the boy gave him no more than a blank stare before returning his attention to the floor.

In his briefcase were documents relating to Garvie's absence at his exams: They confirmed what the police referred to as "unavoidable involvement in police business." Garvie's mother took the envelope from the inspector and went to find her glasses, and Leonard Johnson came over and shook hands with Singh and congratulated him on the outcome of the Dow investigation.

"I can't think of it with satisfaction," Singh said. "There were too many mistakes."

"You can say that again," Garvie said, still staring at the floor.

Uncle Len frowned. "You might as well enjoy it, Raminder. They kick you when you're down and ignore you when you're up."

He was referring to the media. All week the headlines had been about the "Beauty and the Beast" case. Most attention had gone as usual to the killer, the "Beast," a familiar journalistic farrago of astonished outrage and righteous fury. The police had received little more than a grudging acknowledgment that in the end they hadn't entirely failed to rise above their initial incompetence.

"What's the chief's view?"

"His homicidal urge has subsided. I am allowed to remain in position."

"I'm glad."

"The law-abiding world will be glad," Garvie said to the floor. "Criminals everywhere will shake in terror."

His uncle rounded on him. "I don't see what you've got to complain about. You've been remarkably fortunate. You shouldn't have got involved, you were told not to get involved, and you got involved anyway. It was only by some fluke you managed to avoid serious danger. Look at you."

They looked at him. He still wore an eye patch, his face was swollen, and there was a black scrawl of stitches across his lower lip. He wore a sling round his right arm. When he shifted his position under their gaze, he winced.

"It's not me I'm thinking of," he said quietly.

"Well, your mother's thinking of you," Uncle Len said. "You don't know what she's been through."

"I know," Garvie said.

In fact it was Uncle Len who didn't know; he hadn't been told the exact nature of Garvie's involvement—it was thought it might unbalance him.

"You've been lucky," his uncle persisted. "You even get a mention in the press."

It was true. Although details had not been released by the police, it was known that a boy—unidentified for legal reasons—had been in the Dows' house when the police arrived to apprehend Chloe's killer. It was speculated that he had been present during the violent altercation between the spouses in which Mr. Dow had eventually been overcome. As yet no journalist had connected this boy with boys mentioned at various points earlier: in reports of the conflagration at the

413

Tick Hill trailer park which had led to the arrest of the Winders, the events surrounding the suicide of Paul Johnson, aka Ben Naylor, in the woods at the end of Badger Lane, and the unfortunate arrest and detention of Alex Robinson, whose family was currently suing the police for mistreatment.

Uncle Len returned to Singh. "There are several things I don't understand, Raminder. It was announced early on that this man, Dow, had an alibi. He was at a house finishing a paint job."

Singh nodded. "He said he stayed at the property where he was working till quarter to six and a neighbor corroborated it. He heard Dow working all afternoon and saw him drive off to meet his wife at the Center."

"So what really happened?"

"It turns out Dow has a marijuana habit. When his workmates left, he got the idea of sneaking home for a quick smoke. To give the impression he was still at work, he left the radio on and his van parked outside the house and rode back to Fox Walk on a bicycle he found at the property. It's only ten minutes away. He was in his back garden when Chloe came home earlier than expected. Usually at that time she was on the track. It seems he acted at once. But when he tried to force himself on her, she fought back, and it got out of hand. He's a powerful man. It was probably all over in a few minutes."

There was silence.

"What about the paint job he was meant to be finishing?"

"He went back on Sunday to finish it while Mrs. Dow was sedated with sleeping tablets." He paused. "He was a good liar: He stuck close to the truth. He explained the marks on his face by a fall from his ladder which had been witnessed by his workmates. He guessed that someone might have spotted his van up at Pike Pond while he was dumping Chloe's body so he told us straightaway he'd driven there that evening looking for her. It fitted."

Aunt Maxie said, "How could he think so clearly? How could he think at all after what he'd done?"

"He thought fast too. He didn't have much time. The idea with the note, for instance. And when he couldn't find her running shoes, he didn't panic. He just left the body in the garage and went out to buy a new pair."

"Right under the nose of his wife," Aunt Maxie said.

Uncle Len nodded. "And dumping the body in the pond, that was smart. Water destroys so much forensic evidence. It made people think she'd been attacked up there."

"He remembered to throw her phone in too," Singh said. "Some of the calls he'd made to her over the previous weeks were probably threatening. We know now that he'd been pestering her for some time. Mrs. Dow reported arguments between him and Chloe: She thought they were motivated by Chloe's jealousy. The truth is, he's a sexual predator who was waiting only for the right moment. I think he knew that Chloe was being intimidated by other men. He knew about Alex, he'd seen the Porsche once before, perhaps he even guessed what was going on at school with the janitor. That afternoon he must have sensed she was particularly vulnerable. He was a decisive man, and ruthless, and he didn't make mistakes."

"He made three mistakes," Garvie said, and they all turned to look at him. "Three obvious mistakes a child of six could have spotted."

There was an uncomfortable silence.

"Those shoes," Garvie said. "Orange and lime green. Basically, Chloe wouldn't have been seen alive in them."

"All right. What was his second mistake?"

"Filing the receipt. That's colossal. Being neat makes you stupid. Everyone should remember that. But his third mistake was the worst."

"What was that?"

"The gambling chip. He must have been worrying about how stupid the police were being. That's understandable. He'd already supplied them with the clue about Winder's Porsche but they didn't follow it up as he hoped. So he took a risk to make the connection stronger, and slipped an Imperium chip into her jacket pocket. Dense. I'd tried on that jacket at the Dows' a couple of days after her death and there was nothing in the pocket."

They all looked at him.

His mother said, "You tried on her jacket?"

"Yeah." He looked at them all looking at him. "It went pretty well with her gray jeggings and pink T-shirt. Felix thought so."

There was a disapproving silence.

Aunt Maxie said, "It's strange to think about Chloe now. Don't you think? We didn't know her. She had so many secrets. There were so many people trying to use her, and nobody knew."

Garvie's mother said, "If only she'd told somebody. If only there'd been someone she could tell."

"She was too young," Uncle Len said. "Fifteen's no age. You can imagine. She didn't know what to do, the poor girl."

There was a sharp crack of furniture as Garvie abruptly got to his feet and made for the door.

His mother frowned. "Where are you going?"

"Out."

"Out?"

"Felix's."

"You've still got your exams to do, you know that. Next month."

"Said I'd pick up those math books from him."

Their eyes met.

"Okay," she said quietly. "Be careful."

He nodded.

Singh caught Garvie's eye and they looked at each other for a moment. "I have to go now," the inspector said. "I can give him a lift."

They drove slowly out of Eastwick Gardens and down Pilkington Driftway, Singh peering through windshield wipers, Garvie slouched in the passenger seat, staring out the streaming window at the blurred haze of rain lit up in ragged patches of streetlamps that were just coming on, his face a mask of inscrutability.

Singh glanced over at him and cleared his throat. "Finally," he said, "it *is* the end."

Garvie made no reply and Singh went on, "Don't take it the wrong way if I say I hope there won't be much opportunity for us to see each other again."

A snort implied that this was not high up on Garvie's list of griefs. Singh clicked in exasperation, and they drove on in awkward silence to the end of the Driftway and into Old Ditch Road.

Garvie tapped on the side window. "This'll do."

"Here?" Singh pulled up. "This is where your friend lives?" Looking through the rain, he saw that they were parked alongside the Old Ditch Road play area. In the blurry darkness he could see the outlines of figures sitting on the merry-go-round and swings.

"Near enough," Garvie said.

Singh watched him haul his bag out from under his feet with his one good hand. "What's in the bag?" he asked.

"Half-finished bottle of Glen's, some tobacco, cigarette papers, and a five-spot from Alex."

"Really?"

"No. I'm just messing with you."

He sat there staring back at Singh, who shifted stiffly in his seat, and there was a pause between them that went on and on.

"I know you don't want to talk about Chloe . . . ," Singh began.

Garvie said, "I heard it all back there, man. Poor Chloe Dow. Poor pretty little fifteen-year-old Chloe Dow. If only she hadn't got mixed up with the wrong people, if only she'd hadn't had so many secrets, if only she'd *told* someone. Yeah, well, you know what? I'm not going to think of her like that. Maybe I didn't like her. Four weeks going out with her was enough for me. But I respected her, right. Why else do you think I let her give everyone the impression she'd dumped me? She was the brass girl. She was a gambler, she played the

418

cards she'd been dealt. Girls like that"—he shook his head fiercely—"they get hit on, they get harassed, and they have babies and have to work for some scumbag in a casino somewhere, and they tough it out. They're not perfect, but they're not victims. They live their lives. It's not because they're victims they get the fuzzy end of a bad deal."

He came to an end then, panting slightly, and Singh bit his lip.

"I know you think about Hannah too," he said quietly.

For a while they sat listening to the small rain crackle softly on the car roof. Then Singh said, "I've got something for you."

"Oh yeah? A summons?"

The policeman took a package out of his jacket pocket and handed it to Garvie, who stared at it suspiciously.

"I haven't got anything to give you back."

"That's okay."

Inside the package was a plain steel bracelet, grooved at the edges.

"A *kara*," Singh said. "One of the five kakars, symbols of the Sikh faith."

"I wasn't thinking of converting."

"Non-Sikhs are encouraged to wear the *kara*. It symbolizes the need for righteousness." He hesitated. "Also it can be used as a knuckle-duster in *loh mushti*, iron-fist fighting. Though naturally I do not recommend that," he said stiffly. "It will remind you," he added. "If you can bear to be reminded."

Garvie shifted uncomfortably.

"It's an odd thing to say," Singh continued, "but perhaps it will remind you of this country when you've gone."

"Gone? Gone where?"

"To Barbados. I know you don't want to. But I'm sure your mother knows what's best for you."

Garvie shook his head and pushed open the car door. "Just so you know, man. We're not going to Barbados. I don't know what gave you that idea. Mum got a promotion at City Central. We're moving to be near my aunt and uncle."

"Oh. Then you must be glad. At least, a little."

Garvie said nothing. He didn't look as if he ever expected to be glad again. He pushed himself away from the car, pulled up his hood, and there was a clink of bottle glass inside his bag as he swung it up onto his good shoulder. Through the rain-streaked window of his car Singh watched him cross the road toward the playground, a boy in slouch skinny jeans and baggy hoodie, so alone and slender his figure seemed to waver in the vertical drizzle as he disappeared into the gloom beyond the streetlamps, to be swallowed up in the quiet and darkness of the playground, and, faintly, Singh heard a boy's voice call out, "Hey, Sherlock! Got a mystery for you."

He heard nothing else. He put his car in gear and drove away.

Acknowledgments

The writing of a book is a collaborative effort. Warm and comradely thanks to David Fickling and Bella Pearson, whose characteristically expert advice made this book a better thing, and to Hannah Featherstone, Matilda Johnson, and Hannah Leigh for their acute reading and invaluable comments. More thanks to Sophie Nelson for her judicious copyediting and to my friend Ted Walker for his review of the math. Special thanks to my agent of twenty-five years, Anthony Goff, whose belief in this book will remain a talking point between us for years to come. Ultimate thanks, though, to Eleri and Gwilym, who told me why I was getting it wrong, and to Eluned, who told me I would get it right in the end.